Peace + Hope!
Carlene Thiss

CALLED FROM SILENCE:

THE FATHER SANDERS NOVEL

BY CARLENE A. THISSEN

iUniverse, Inc.
New York Bloomington

Called from Silence
The Father Sanders Novel

iUniverse books may be ordered through booksellers or by contacting:

iUniverse
1663 Liberty Drive
Bloomington, IN 47403
www.iuniverse.com
1-800-Authors (1-800-288-4677)

Because of the dynamic nature of the Internet, any Web addresses or links contained in this book may have changed since publication and may no longer be valid. The views expressed in this work are solely those of the author and do not necessarily reflect the views of the publisher, and the publisher hereby disclaims any responsibility for them.

ISBN: 978-1-4401-1877-7 (pbk)
ISBN: 978-1-4401-1878-4 (ebk)

Printed in the United States of America

iUniverse rev. date: 02/25/09

DEDICATED TO THEIR MEMORIES

"Dick lived in an awareness of God, the way St. Paul described it:
'Him in whom we live and move and have our being.'
It was like he didn't exactly carry God around, he floated *in* God.
That is the great reality that we're all floating in.
Most of us aren't in touch with it, but he was.
He knew how to stay there somehow."

Joan Sanders

"I feel Father Sanders in the old church at St. Peter's sometimes.
Air blows as if someone just walked by,
and I hear him whisper, 'Martin.'"

Martin Hernandez

TABLE OF CONTENTS

V –NONE (1978 – 1981)

VI – VESPERS (1981 – 1984)

VII – COMPLINE (1985)

INTRODUCTION

I never met Father Richard Sanders, but learned of him when researching my previous book, *Immokalee's Fields of Hope*. His story wasn't earthshaking, and he wasn't a saint, at least not in the traditional sense. Or was he? Not long after I started this research, a close friend was diagnosed with cancer. As soon as I heard, I felt compelled to send tiny pieces of weed and dirt from his grave. Within a few months, her tumors disappeared.

Here's what I used as a model for his story. Several years ago, a street painter created a depiction of my own father who died in 1993. Initially, he argued with me. "I can't paint your father," said Charlie Ward, "because I didn't know him. I can only paint people I know." There must be a way, I persisted, and he finally agreed to consider it: "Bring me pictures and tell me stories." When I spotted the completed painting from a far corner of Jackson Square, I started to cry. It was not a perfect likeness. My father's nose was too thick, his jaw too large and his guitar too big and flat. But Charlie Ward had captured his spirit.

That is what I have tried to do with *Called from Silence*. Over a four-year period, people who knew and loved Father Sanders showed me pictures and told me stories. They brought him to life.

This is not a typical biography. Few written documents exist, so I relied heavily on people's memories. It is written in a genre that seeks to provide novel-like reading ease yet adheres as closely as possible to truth.

"It breathes life into the characters, especially the rich and complex person of Father Sanders," said Sister Eileen Eppig, who worked closely with Father Sanders in Immokalee.

I took liberties in creating and interpreting dialogue, introduced a few fictitious scenes to help readers visualize reality and, in some cases, combined multiple characters into one. I changed the names of people I could not locate for final approval and some who asked to remain anonymous. Other than that, I remained faithful to the stories I was told and the sources I read. Some of the writings I have that were actually his are included in the text: letters to his mother from Mepkin Abbey, holiday letters to friends, the Mass for Terry Lundy's First Communion, the eulogy Father Sanders wrote for himself and his 1984 Christmas Eve sermon.

The section headings are the names of "prayer hours" recited at fixed times of the monastic day and night, called Divine Office or Liturgy of the Hours. They correspond well to the sections of his life.

Father Sanders was a humble man who would not have wanted a book written about him, but he would have approved the message. In the end, I only hope I have captured his spirit.

Carlene Thissen

PROLOGUE

Grief hung over the town like a dark shadow. His body was laid out inside the church that was open day and night as hundreds of mourners came to say goodbye. Women in white kept a constant vigil at the head and foot of the coffin, and the church bell tolled for twenty-four hours.

"What a mournful sound," Sister Eileen Eppig would say later. "I feel as if I will hear it forever, in my bones."

Over a thousand people attended the funeral, held outside because so many would not fit inside the church. Mexican, Haitian, Guatemalan, U.S.-born white and black mourners came from all walks of life and all economic and educational backgrounds, from Immokalee, Naples, Miami, South Carolina, New York, Illinois and Texas. Three bishops and over forty priests took part in the funeral celebration in English, Spanish, and Haitian Creole. Each nationality served part of the Mass. The Haitians brought the gifts, dancing and swaying sadly to the beat of steel drums. Our Lady of Guadalupe smiled lovingly down from the tree where her image was fastened.

The funeral procession lasted for hours as they carried his coffin around the church grounds and into the street, replacing each other with a tap on the shoulder like men cutting in on a dance – everyone wanted to carry him. The people followed, filling the grounds with flowers, as a Mariachi band played mournfully.

> *Te Vas Angel Mio...*
> My angel you are departing,
> You leave my soul wounded and my heart to suffer

The Anglos, Mexicans and Guatemalans cried, and the Haitians wailed in grief. Even those from central Mexico, usually stoic about death, felt as if they would fall to the ground sobbing and kicking their feet. "I didn't want to cry," remembered Miguel Flores, "but my tears kept coming out."

Suddenly, some of the altar boys started to laugh. "I don't know what happened," said José Dimas, then just fourteen years old. "We knew he was dead, and what that meant, but we were so joyous! We knew he was in heaven because that is where he told us we would all be someday. That's why we were so happy."

They lowered his body to rest near the church he loved, opposite the grotto of Our Lady of Guadalupe. His headstone reads:

RICHARD SANDERS
PRIEST
JULY 29, 1937   MARCH 18, 1985

LOVE ONE ANOTHER, AS I HAVE
LOVED YOU   JOHN 13:34

I

VIGILS

1955 - 1957

CHAPTER ONE – THE FUTURE MONK – 1955

Richard "Dick" Sanders was a quiet yet regular guy who smoked, drank and partied with friends – that's why nobody took him seriously about his plans. With high school graduation only a few months away, however, people had started questioning. It began one afternoon when Betty Sanders and Eliza Trompeter sat chatting with Dick and his friends at the Trompeter's home. When one of the boys brought up the monastery, Betty, who had seemed fine with the idea, suddenly wasn't.

"You need to tell Dick how you feel," said Eliza. As the boys watched, surprised, tears began to fall slowly down Betty's cheeks.

"Alright I'll tell you," she said, embarrassed, as she turned and stared intently at her son. "Before you were even born, your sister died. As soon as your brother graduated high school, he went off to the Jesuits. Then your father died, and now you're going into a monastery. I had three children and a husband, and now I have no one. I'll be all alone. And I never get to have grandchildren. Why are you doing this?"

Dick was shocked at the outburst but felt sad for his mother and for the first time, a little guilty. Had he been selfishly focused only on his own happiness? With that much grief in her life, what could he possibly say that would comfort her about the fact that he was leaving forever? He couldn't articulate his innermost feelings, couldn't tell her about the soft calling that drew him.

It turned out that his buddies, Art Trompeter, Joe Story and Duke Micheli, were as confused as Betty Sanders was. Dick had talked about the Trappists for a long time, but the boys had never thought he would actually do it. With graduation coming up, Dick's dream of the monastery was becoming a reality and they weren't sure he knew what he was doing. Trappist monks, the common name for the Order of Cistercians of the Strict Observance, entered their monasteries and never left, ever. They lived their lives in silence, focused on prayer, sacred readings and manual labor. That was about all the other boys knew.

After Betty left, Joe started the questions. He was Dick's closest friend, with sandy blonde hair that he wore in a flat-top similar to Dick's, but shorter. "Is it really true that you can't come home, even for weddings or funerals? Ever?"

Dick nodded and the other boys frowned.

"What kind of labor do they do?" asked Art. A little shorter than his friends, he had a round face, round glasses and straight, straw-colored hair.

"Different abbeys do different things," Dick explained, sounding casual yet in the back of his mind, worrying about his mother. "At Gethsemani they make and sell fruitcakes, cheese and fudge, plus they grow their own food. They're also doing a lot of construction now. There are so many monks entering that they need more space."

"Have you been accepted yet?"

Dick lit up a cigarette and shook his head. Per instructions from the vocation director at Our Lady of Gethsemani, he had sent a letter explaining his spiritual history, along with recommendations from his pastor and a couple of monks at St. Bede Academy. In two weeks he would go to Gethsemani for an interview. He prayed they would take him, but there were no guarantees.

The boys talked about possible influences on Dick's vocation, beginning with Thomas Merton's books, especially *The Seven Storey Mountain: An Autobiography of Faith*. Published in 1948 when Dick was just eleven, it was Merton's story of conversion and his journey to the Trappists at Gethsemani Abbey. Dick loved the end where Merton, frustrated at delays in being admitted, prayed to St. Therese the Little Flower: "If I get into the monastery, I will be your monk. Now show me what to do." Although he was in New York, at the end of this prayer, Merton heard the bells of Gethsemani Abbey in Kentucky. His faith gripped him so powerfully that he hastily gave away all his things and made an intense journey on trains, buses and automobiles, to get there.

Dick had never had quite that breathtaking of an experience. His calling was more of a gentle desire. He wanted nothing more than to pray, in an effort to grow closer to his heavenly Father. Certainly, though, Thomas Merton had had an influence. In the era in which Dick and his friends grew up, Thomas Merton was the leader of a movement toward spirituality.

Then Joe had another thought. "Are you sure this isn't just a competition with your brother, him being the Jesuit and all?"

"I don't know," replied Dick pensively, although the question had merit. Eight years older than Dick, Jim Sanders was handsome, athletic, smart, popular and confident. He was a local hero, especially with Dick's friends. Jim excelled at baseball and football, won the school's Golden Gloves boxing tournament and was named Athlete of the Year.

Dick, on the other hand, did not excel at anything. Standing about 5'11", he had average looks with reddish-brown hair that he wore in a high wavy flat-top. His green eyes always seemed to be squinting and his nose was a little odd. His most attractive feature was his warm, engaging smile. Scholastically he was on the low side of average and was athletically limited, too. When he watched Jim, Dick could not imagine having the breath or the energy. The only exercise he enjoyed was swimming, but never competitively. Dick wasn't even very coordinated. He thought back to years before when Jim had tried to teach him to play catch. It ended with Jim walking away shaking his head, wondering what kind of a kid couldn't even catch a ball.

It never bothered Dick, though. He was comfortable with who he was and enjoyed quieter activities like building things or figuring out how mechanical devices worked. As a child he had loved Lincoln Logs and as a teenager, moved on to bigger projects like the tree house he and Joe Story built in the Sanders' back yard.

Dick was proud of Jim and enjoyed talking about his brother the Jesuit, a member of the Society of Jesus, an elite order that served popes, renowned for intellectual pursuits as they became teachers, scholars and scientists. To Dick and his friends, however, it was more than that – Jesuits were cool. In quieter moments, the idea of besting his brother did have some appeal as he thought with a slight smile, "Jesuits are cool, but Trappists are cooler."

Duke, tall and thin with black hair, pressed on with the questions, stretching out his long legs. "You know, becoming a priest is one thing, but a monk is a whole different story, especially a Trappist! Are you sure you want to do that?"

This wasn't what Dick he needed from his friends right now. He deflected with his own question back at the three of them. "Let's talk about what you're all gonna do with your lives."

Put on the spot, they hesitated, and then Joe spoke up.

"I'm gonna go to college and become a pharmacist," he smiled, as if already happy with his future. "Then I'll come back here and work at Kunkel's Drug Store. I can see myself coming home to my beautiful wife and children. We're gonna have lots of grandkids, too."

The other boys were not about to get sidetracked from the subject of the monastery just yet, however.

"You know what I never thought of?" asked Art. "You don't have a single priest or nun in your whole family. Why would there be two from yours?"

"I don't know. It is kind of weird." Dick wondered if this discussion would ever end.

"Are you sure you want to do this?"

"Yeah, I want to do it," replied Dick, getting more annoyed by the minute.

"What about the cigarettes?" asked Art, who had always lectured Dick about smoking. "How the hell will you give that up? Um... excuse me, 'Brother.' How the heck will you quit the weeds?"

"What, are you writing a book?" asked Dick, showing his irritation now. "I've been cutting back. Quitting shouldn't be too hard."

Joe realized they had gone too far. "We didn't mean to rattle your cage, man. It's your life."

"Forget it," said Dick, zipping up his jacket. "I'll see you later."

As he walked, Dick noted traces of snow that still lay between the sidewalks and red brick streets. Chirping birds signaled that lawns in front of the modest houses would soon turn green, and pear, peach, plum and apple trees would bloom. The crisp air felt clean in his lungs.

Peru, Illinois, in the center of a farming area in the Illinois Valley, was settled in the 1830s. With its "sister town," LaSalle, it had a combined population of some 25,000 people, a community of children and grandchildren of immigrants who came because of a demand for their labor.

Located at the end point of the Illinois and Michigan Canal that ran between Chicago and the Illinois River, Peru was one of the main reasons Chicago had become a transportation hub between the East Coast and the Midwest. German and Irish immigrants came first, to dig the canal. Later, when coal was discovered, Italians, Poles and other ethnic groups moved in. Since the late 19th century, LaSalle-Peru had also been the home of the Westclox Company, makers of Big Ben and Baby Ben clocks, a factory that drew additional immigrants. Catholic parishes were identified by their ethnicity, as each group built its own church and brought in its own priest: German, Irish, Polish, Italian and Slovenian.

About halfway home, Dick stopped in front St. Mary's, still focused on the origin of his priestly and monastic intentions. Thinking about never coming back here made him focus more than usual on details. It was just beginning to sink in that, once he entered the abbey, he would never see his hometown again.

He had gone with his family to Mass at St. Mary's all his life and almost every religious experience he ever had, happened there. His father had even insisted that they go to Mass on the Fourth of July – he was of German heritage, but patriotic, grateful and proud to be American.

Dick stood at the corner of the church complex and pondered the years he had spent there. Though their family was German, they lived in what was originally an Irish parish and still had an Irish pastor, Father Gildea, who spoke with a heavy brogue. Dick walked slowly around the complex on the sidewalk, noting the rectory and elementary school, both built of red brick to match the church. The parish center and sisters' convent were large white wooden houses. The complex also included a baseball field and large playground.

He thought about the school bells that called them to class. The first bell meant stop playing; the second, get in line; third bell, stop talking and stand up straight. Most mornings the priest would walk down the lines as if inspecting troops, as each line chorused, "Good morning, Father." Good morning, Father. Good morning, Father.

Father Gildea also gave out report cards personally, a difficult ritual for Dick. The priest would call each child to the front of the room and study the grades. Then, before handing the card to the student, he would make comments that the whole class could hear. He spoke more softly when it came to Richard Sanders, but usually shook his head and sighed. Sheepishly, Dick would retrieve the embarrassing document and return quickly to his seat. School had been hard for him. Formal study, writing reports and taking tests just bored him and he didn't always pay attention. Maybe it's all related to how much I like something, he used to think to himself. Religion, for example, was one of his favorite subjects and he usually did well in it.

Like their counterparts all over the United States, the teachers at St. Mary's used the *Baltimore Catechism* to teach the children about the Holy Catholic Church. The Sisters read the questions and the children recited the answers in unison.

Who made us?
God made us.
Who is God?
God is the Supreme Being who made all things.
Why did God make us?
God made us to know Him, love Him and serve Him in this world, and be happy with Him in the next.

He remembered the catechism and its many diagrams, particularly the one featuring steps that explained the hierarchy of the Church. Christ, at the right hand of God, the invisible head of the Church, sat on the top step inside a cloud. On the next step down was the pope, the "visible head of the church, the successor of St. Peter." Under the pope were bishops who were

7

successors of the Apostles and under them were priests who were pastors of churches. Beneath the priests was the laity. Religious brothers and sisters were on the top of that step and below them all other Catholics, men above the women and at the very bottom, children. As a child, Dick had understood the diagram better than the words, but he questioned the distance between Christ and the children. The Gospel of Matthew said, "Let the little children be, and do not hinder them from coming to me, for of such is the kingdom of heaven." Why, then, would Christ be so far away from them? It was a paradox in the pecking order that he still did not understand.

Walking around to the front of the school, he peered in through the first-floor window at the large, single room where he had attended first and second grade. He could almost see the Sisters of St. Francis, in their long habits and veils. One sister per floor was responsible for two grades at the same time, teaching the children on one side of the room while the others did assigned work.

He thought back to preparation for his first confession and First Holy Communion that began in that room when he was six years old, where Dick and his classmates learned about their faith so they could take part in sacraments. There were seven sacraments in all, rituals designed to give God's grace to Catholics and keep them from harm. The only sacrament he had never understood was baptism. He still didn't get it. Celebrated soon after a baby's birth, baptism took away original sin. He just didn't believe that innocent babies were born with sin in their tiny souls. A related point of confusion was that un-baptized babies who died were sent to a place called limbo, a pleasant place, the sisters had taught, but the babies would never see the face of God and never meet Christ. This had always struck Dick as illogical and even cruel, especially because Jesus loved the children so much. It wasn't the babies' fault that they weren't baptized.

He had also learned to distinguish between different types of sins, mortal and venial. Dick smiled at his reflection in the schoolhouse window, remembering how he used to mentally dissect the difference, trying to determine the severity and potential punishments of some of the things he did. Mortal sins were the worst; if not confessed before death and without at least an Act of Contrition, they led to a punishment of everlasting hell. The punishment seemed extreme to Dick, but he accepted it and vowed to never risk failing to confess mortal sins. Venial sins were less serious but even so, would lead to time in purgatory, a place like hell but from which one could eventually rise into heaven. Souls who still had the blemish of sin would stay in purgatory until they were purified. Most souls would spend time there, according to his teachers, because everyone had faults. People on earth could pray for souls that were in purgatory. Dick's mother and father had always reminded him to pray for Jane, the sister he never knew, and he did, believing that each prayer helped her rise into heaven. He often wondered how long it might take her to get out of there, and about the ratio between sins and the length of time spent in purgatory. Hopefully Jane was out already. How many sins could a ten-year-old girl have committed?

Dick walked over to the front steps of St. Mary's Church, went inside, blessed himself with holy water and then sat in the back, staring at the altar he had known his whole life. Confessions would be heard soon, but no one was there yet. He thought back to his first confession when he was seven years old. Like his friends, he had anticipated it with trepidation, but confession was required in order to take part in Holy Communion with Christ. After they confessed, if they were truly contrite and agreed to say their assigned penances, the priest granted them absolution or forgiveness of their sins. The sisters told them that Christ had given the ability to the apostles who passed it down to the priests: "…whose sins you shall forgive, they are forgiven them; and whose sins you shall retain, they are retained." He wondered how much value the power of absolution would have at the abbey, but then reminded himself of how little he really knew about monastic life. Who knew what kinds of sins monks held in their hearts?

Dick's experience as an altar boy also had an impact on his vocation, of course. He loved being on the priest's side of the altar rail, truly taking part in the Mass, dressed in white robes and a cloth belt that matched Father Gildea's vestments. He hoped that he would be chosen for the incense at every "High Mass," lighting and swinging the gold censer around and above the altar and out toward the people. Incense was used in ancient times to purify animal sacrifices, but now it was burned symbolically to signify that the sacrifice of Christ would ascend to God with an odor of sweetness and that the prayers of the people would rise to God's throne in a pleasing manner. For Dick, however, incense was more than that. Its unique, pungent scent, coupled with the priest praying in Latin, transported him to an ancient world of peace in which he could lose himself and the limitations of his physical body. He thought for the first time that the desire to remain in that holy place might have been the start of his monastic leanings.

Getting lost in the incense also seemed to be the only time he was free of the urges that tormented him. He cringed, thinking of warnings against "self abuse," a sin the boys understood to be punishable by an eternity in hell.

Dick left the church and his steps took him down the bluffs of the Illinois River, over the tracks of the Rock Island Railroad and along Water Street past the lumberyard, warehouses and taverns. The river was about two football fields across, with strong currents that carried oil and lumber barges. On its opposite side, the low-lying plain was flooded as it was almost every spring. Dick remembered fishing there with his father, helping him catch bait minnows with a fine net.

The sun was out, shining brightly now. Sitting on an old overturned rowboat, he lit up a cigarette and got back to the question at hand, thinking about a book Jim had sent him years ago: *The Man Who Got Even With God*, by Reverend M. Raymond, O.C.S.O – a Trappist monk. It was a fascinating story of "a violent, vindictive cowboy who became a Trappist brother." The main character, John Green Hanning, left his family and their frontier home after burning down the barn because he was angry with his father. He lived for years on the range as a tough cowboy that most men feared, until a conversion led him back home and eventually to Gethsemani Abbey where he became Brother Mary Joachim.

Dick remembered a chapter in that book that explained why men became Trappists. What was the term they used? *Matatonia? Metania? Metanoia* – that was it –a Greek word that referred to a complete change in attitude, a transformation, a change in the way a man viewed the world, in the way a man viewed God.

As he walked back to their home, he took in the scenes around him and tried to hold them in his mind, focused on the fact that he would soon leave and never return. He thought about his mother who had sounded so sad that morning. She had a point about grandchildren. Dick had no interest in marriage or a family, but he thought Jim might have. Jim had a nice girlfriend before he went into the Jesuits. If priests could be married, she and Jim could have had grandchildren for Betty. Then Dick wouldn't have to feel guilty.

He was so lost in thought that he was surprised when he reached home. Opening the porch door, he remembered happy evenings when the family sat there together. Their house was typical of the neighborhood: the porch, two bedrooms, one bath, a living room, dining room, kitchen and basement. Dick thought about evenings when his father and mother used to sit side by side in chairs in the living room. His father read the paper and one classic novel after the other, making a constant effort to become better educated. Bill's father had died in a coal mining accident when he was only fourteen years old and he had to quit school to support his mother and two younger sisters. Still, he finished high school at night. Dick gained an appreciation of the value of education by observing his father's constant efforts to improve himself. Betty would sit in the chair next to her husband, sewing and reading women's magazines. Dick's father took pride in being able to support his family and never wanted his wife to work, so she focused on being a first-rate homemaker.

Dick, Bill, Betty and Jim Sanders, 1947

While their parents read, Jim and Dick did their homework, Jim at the small desk in the corner of the dining room and Dick on the couch. Dick was always amazed at how hard and long Jim studied. He actually seemed to like it.

On Saturday and Sunday nights, the family listened to radio shows with Jack Benny, and George Burns and Gracie Allen. Later, they bought a black and white television and watched Bishop Fulton J. Sheehan with his flowing robes and inspirational sermons. Dick paid close attention when the bishop preached about the evils of Communism and asked for prayers for the conversion of Russia. Dick and his schoolmates said prayers for the end of Communism in school, too. Its biggest danger was that it was focused on eliminating the concept of God and churches. Dick actually liked some of the other Communist concepts such as equality for all people and the elimination of poverty, but understood the difference between theorizing and turning theory into reality.

On Friday nights, Dick's parents drank beer and played Pinochle with aunts and uncles. Those were happy times. The only uncle who ever got drunk, his father used to joke, was the one who was not German! There was some bias toward other ethnic groups, especially the Irish, but nothing hateful, and it did not affect the family practically. Jim and Dick both had Irish friends, and Jim's best friend was Irish.

Dick walked into the kitchen where his mother was rolling dough for a pie. Watching her, he wondered whom she would bake for when he was gone. When she brought up the morning's conversation, saying simply, "I'll be fine," Dick breathed a sigh of relief. She said she was still trying to figure out what it would be like to live alone for the first time in her life. Part of it scared her, but another part was exciting. She would be able to do whatever she wanted, whenever she wanted to do it. If Dick wanted to be a Trappist, she would support him.

When he nodded strongly, his mother smiled and turned back to her pie dough. Relieved, he walked back toward the front door to his room next to his parents' room... his mother's room. He had never really gotten used to the fact that his father was gone.

When Bill Sanders' high blood pressure first became a problem, he was sent to St. Mary's Hospital in nearby LaSalle. Everyone thought he would get well, but he died on April 12, 1952, of a stroke followed by uremic poisoning, when Dick was just fourteen years old. Jim, allowed home from the Jesuits because of his father's grave illness and Betty's need for her eldest son, was there when their father died. Jim seemed almost happy as he tried to reassure his mother. "Dad had time to prepare, Mom. He made his last confession, had last rites and is in God's arms."

The look their mother gave Jim made it clear that she was not mollified. When the funeral was over, Jim would return to the Jesuits, but Betty and Dick would return to a house that would be dark with grief for a long time. At the cemetery, Dick stared questioningly at the family headstone where Jane lay alone, now to be joined by their father, and wondered for the first time where he would be buried.

Later at the house, Jim explained how much their mother would need Dick's help and support. Also, at her request, Jim started to explain the "birds and the bees." Too embarrassed to have the conversation, Dick quickly informed his older brother that he already knew. Later, however, he wished he had not dismissed his brother's offer so quickly. What he really wanted to know was how Jim dealt with the urges. What did priests do with those feelings?

The third anniversary of his father's death was coming up and it still depressed him, but he shook the memories out of his head. He had homework to do and a few classes to pass in order to graduate. He wanted decent grades so the Trappists would let him be a choir monk and study for the priesthood. The alternative was to become one of the lay brothers who spent most of their time at manual labor. There were times when Dick got so frustrated with Latin that he considered becoming a lay brother just so he wouldn't have to study, but his desire to say Mass kept him focused.

His room was still much like it was when he shared it with his brother, though Jim had been gone since Dick was eleven years old. The Jesuits had not allowed Jim to bring anything with him, so most of his things were still there. Even Jim's model airplanes still hung from the ceiling. Dick wondered what the Trappists would let him bring.

He looked at the picture of Mary that hung over his bed, Mary as a young girl, blessed and beautiful with a halo and a sweet smile, she had watched over him throughout his childhood. He tried to study but could not focus so he threw the Latin book onto Jim's bed. He found *The Man Who Got Even with God* and the reference to *Metanoia* he had been trying to remember earlier that day.

> *Metanoia* is the gateway to real life. Passing through it, one gets new standards – the standards of God. The mind is made hungry for truth, but for the truths of eternity... Thus is the whole man changed, and to keep that change permanent, the wise man cloisters himself. Not to lock himself in but to lock the world out.

Late that evening, he lay down to sleep and imagined himself at Our Lady of Gethsemani with his brothers in Christ.

CHAPTER TWO –
OUR LADY OF GETHSEMANI – 1955

Dick headed to Gethsemani in mid-April for a retreat that would include his interview. It was a beautiful spring day and he drove with the windows open, listening to the radio. He had been to Gethsemani twice before, and those two short weekends had solidified every desire of his being into one goal. To make it even better, the novice master was none other than Thomas Merton himself, the famous monk/author. Merton's religious name was Brother Mary Louis, as all Trappists took the first name of Mary to honor the Blessed Virgin.

Dick was still wondering how to express his vocation, assuming it would be one of Father Louis' first questions, but relaxed with the thought that, once he was within the walls of Gethsemani, the answer would come. As he neared the Abbey he noted the rolling hills, cleared fields and grazing cattle tended by a monk in a brown habit. He watched impatiently for the tall white spire of the church and his heart beat faster when it appeared above the trees. When the enclosed complex came into view he thought, as he had last time, how much it resembled an ancient medieval stone fortification.

In this abbey, however, lived the holiest of men, men who gave up everything to seek God every waking moment, as they lived, worked and prayed together. He walked confidently and reverently to the gatehouse, stopping to pray at the white statue of the Virgin Mary that looked gently down on him from over the main gate. Under her feet were the words, *"Pax Intrantibus."* Peace to all who enter here. The gatehouse brother handed him the schedule for Laymen's Week-end Retreats and sent him to the guesthouse. Once inside the gate, Dick looked fondly at another statue of the Virgin Mary that stood in the center of the sculpted gardens surrounded by a white decorative fence with the words, *Salve Maria*. Hail Mary. In his room, Dick knelt and prayed again, looking out the window over the plowed fields and tree-covered hills behind them. He wished only that he held a real monastic schedule in his hands, one that he would follow for the rest of his life.

At suppertime, he joined the other retreatants in the guest dining area. The thick vegetable soup, homemade bread and fresh milk satisfied his hunger as he listened carefully to one of Gethsemani's monks read the day's inspirational reading. It was from *Lives of the Saints*, writings of St. Bernard of Clairvaux. Like all Cistercians, Bernard was devoted to the Queen of Heaven.

> Remember, O most gracious Virgin Mary, that never was it
> known that anyone who fled to thy protection, implored thy
> help, and sought thy intercession, was left unaided. Inspired with
> this confidence, I fly unto thee O Virgin of virgins, my Mother,
> to thee I come, before thee I stand sinful and sorrowful.

After supper he made his way to the church, marveling as he had before at its beauty, especially the huge nave with its gothic arches. He sat in the pews behind the lay brothers with the other retreatants and watched as choir monks processed into their stalls, faced each other and then turned toward the altar. When they began to chant the psalms of Compline, Dick's heart soared.

> *Extollilte manus vesttras in sanctta et benedictite Domino*
> Lift up your hands in the holy place and bless the Lord

After the Angelus the monks processed out to their dormitory, which laymen never saw, and Dick, wishing he could follow them, walked instead back to the guesthouse. Not long afterwards at "lights out" for retreatants, he lay down on a lumpy mattress but had trouble falling asleep, as he normally did not go to bed until after midnight. He lay still in the darkness, listening, as the monks did, for the voice of God.

At 3:15 a.m. the bells of the monastery rang, signaling Vigils. Dick had planned to join them, but when he looked out the window at the pitch darkness he decided against it, and anyway, people on retreats did not need to rise until 5:00. He rolled over, thinking to sleep for just a few more minutes but did not awaken until he heard the bells of Prime. Looking at his watch in horror, he saw it was 7:15. He hastily put on his clothes, washed up and walked quickly to the church. He had missed the early morning prayers.

The rest of the day, however, he followed the schedule, looking forward to his meeting with the novice master that afternoon. Everywhere he looked he saw men dressed in monastic habits, and he was consumed with a desire to call them brothers.

That afternoon, just after the prayer hour called "None," he went as instructed to the novice master's office. Father Louis looked up, smiled, said hello and asked him to sit down. He had round, warm, face and a dimpled smile.

"So, why do you want to become a Trappist?"

Dick took a deep breath, wondering why it was so difficult for him to articulate his desire. After a moment of trying to find the perfect answer, he responded, "It's the most I can give to God."

Father Louis smiled as if intrigued and then added, "And the most you can get." Dick smiled shyly.

The novice master explained that Dick was younger than the men they usually accepted. He commented on the smell of cigarettes on Dick's clothes and Dick assured him the he would quit soon, remembering from *the Seven Storey Mountain* that Thomas Merton had smoked before he entered. Father Louis asked a few more general questions about Dick's upbringing, family and religious history and then, abruptly, handed him a psychological evaluation. He explained that some men were not capable of adjusting to monastic life, so they had developed this test to try and determine that, before they caused themselves and the community emotional or psychological harm. Then he changed the subject again and asked Dick to sing a scale. "Choir monks sing."

Singing was not one of the items on Dick's short list of skills, but he did his best, which apparently was good enough. Then he went to the classroom next door, filled out the test and left it on the desk, per the novice master's instructions. They would send a letter with their decision. Father Louis warned that it might take a while because there were so many men wanting to join.

Dick went to the church and knelt for a long time in prayer as professed monks came and went in silence. Then he sat back in the pew and thought about the life he felt called to enter. Now that it was truly becoming a reality, he wanted to be absolutely sure he could handle it. The silence might be more challenging than he had anticipated. With few exceptions for studying or work, the only time he would ever hear his or any other voice would be in the psalms he chanted along with his monastic brothers. Another odd thing was that he would not get to know these men in the traditional sense. The rule of silence kept them from sharing stories about their lives, their histories or even their real names. Dick liked people and enjoyed his friends, and might miss that kind of interaction. The strict diet also gave him room for pause. The monks ate plain vegetarian food and during Advent and Lent, they fasted. Then there were the hours and the structure of the days. Getting up at 3:00 a.m. every day and going to bed at 8:00 at night would take some getting used to. Most of all, though, he worried about the monotony of it, the same prayer, study and work hours, day after day, week after week, year after year, in an environment where almost nothing changed. It occurred to him that it might drive most normal people crazy. But then, Trappists were anything but normal.

After about an hour of praying for a confirmation of his vocation, he decided that the austere and silent lifestyle was conducive to what he wanted most: to focus on God with all his being, all the time, in an atmosphere designed for that purpose. He loved prayer and contemplation and here he would get to do it for the rest of his life. The benefits were so great that he knew it would be worth whatever he had to sacrifice.

Later that Saturday afternoon he walked the grounds and came across the cemetery, row upon row of simple crosses marked with dead monks' Trappist names. He prayed to Mary to help him live, die and be buried at Gethsemani.

He spent that night and part of Sunday viewing the life of the Trappists from the back of the church, the guesthouse dining area and the guesthouse sleeping quarters. Late Sunday morning he drove blissfully back to Peru to await his acceptance letter.

CHAPTER THREE – WAITING TO ENTER – 1955, 1956

Two months later, on a hot day in late June, Dick and his best friend Joe Story were out driving around in Betty's Kaiser. Joe rode shotgun as they sang along with the music, windows down, elbows resting on the car doors. The radio played a new song, *Rock Around the Clock* by Bill Haley and His Comets, one of their favorites.

With some effort, Dick had graduated from St. Bede Academy and was still waiting for his acceptance to Gethsemani Abbey. He checked the mail every day, but still had heard nothing.

Joe interrupted his thoughts. "We better have a going-away party for you, huh? State Park?"

"Sure," said Dick, easing into a broad smile. It wasn't like they needed an excuse.

"Do you think you'll miss Peru?"

"Yeah, probably. People, too." He spent a lot of time with friends who worked at the Recreation Department. "Jim, Duke, Art, Francis, Judy, Lucia, Barbara, Ken, Don, Celeste, even you!"

"Thanks a lot, man. Hey, how come you never dated any of those girls?"

Dick shrugged. "I don't know. I always found girls attractive, but I'm too shy. Maybe I always knew I was gonna be a monk."

"Well, we've always been just a gang of friends hanging out together, anyway, right?"

Dick nodded.

"Hey," said Joe. "Who's going to drive us home now after the parties?"

Dick usually drove because he was the most sober and he had access to a car. And what a car it was. One of the first Kaisers made, in 1947, it had a flat-head six, one hundred horses under the hood and one of the new automatic transmissions. Dick grinned and lit a cigarette, feeling guilty because of his commitment to Father Louis to quit, but then decided it was OK; he really was cutting back.

Changing the subject, Joe had another question. "I know you're not exactly in tune with some of the Church's rules. Doesn't the Abbey require 'strict obedience?' Doesn't that include agreeing with everything? And, if I'm not mistaken, questioning some of the Church's teachings is a sin, isn't it? I'm remembering words like *de fide definita* – 'must be believed.'"

"I don't know. There's a lot that maybe I just don't understand. I'll be studying at the Abbey. Hopefully that will clear things up for me."

Joe probably knew Dick better than anyone. He spent a lot of time at the Sanders' house, often sleeping over, and went with the family to visit Jim at the Jesuit facility in Indiana. Joe had helped Dick build the two-story tree house in the Sanders' back yard, and, in one of their less brilliant moments, they heated it with a kerosene heater that started it on fire. Dick's mother had to call the fire department to put it out.

Then Joe asked one last time about Dick's vocation. Rather than getting frustrated, Dick tried to explain the passion that drove him. Joe was religious himself, and Dick thought he might understand.

"OK, this is gonna sound weird, but I'll explain it to you the best I can. It's like you get 'called,' they say, like you get this real strong urge."

Joe raised his eyebrows and looked sideways at his friend.

"OK that's not the right word," said Dick, "but it's the best I can come up with. And then you start praying, and then things happen."

"Enlighten me, Brother Dick."

The future monk smiled sheepishly and continued, stringing more words together at one time than he usually said in an hour.

"It's like this feeling I got a couple of times when I prayed. You know, like, really prayed, for a long time, like in church when no one was there. It happened really strongly at Gethsemani. It was so quiet, such a holy place, that I could feel God."

Joe frowned. Was his friend losing his mind?

"OK, not exactly 'feel,' but it was like a glimpse, or a whisper. Then, in a split second, it was gone. But I felt it."

Now his friend was listening intently. Dick hesitated, then repeated the phrase with more emotion.

"Joe, I could feel God. Can you imagine what that could be like? The first thing they say to guys who want to become monks is, 'Listen.' Monks listen for God all the time. That's why they live in silence, except for singing at prayers. They're listening. I want to spend all my time listening for the voice of God, because I've known the smallest touch of it and I want it forever because it was the most incredible thing I've ever felt." His voice grew louder and more passionate as he continued. "This kind of 'connection' came over me, like, the world was huge and beautiful yet at the same time it was small and safe, completely and lovingly warm. And it was, like, all mixed up together with this intensity – you wouldn't believe how intense it was, and at the same time, I felt perfect peace, just for that instant."

He was now embarrassed that he'd shared so much of his intimate feelings, but after a minute, he finished what he had to say.

"Joe, I will live my life as a Trappist monk and die at Gethsemani Abbey in the presence of God, because I want to. I want to more than anything in the world."

Joe smiled at his friend and said quietly, "I'm happy for you, man." After a few minutes he added, "We're sure gonna miss you, though. Once you go, we won't ever see you again."

After a few silent moments, Joe changed the subject. "So what do you think you'll want to do before you go in? You know, like your last meal before they put you in the chair?"

Dick laughed, pondered the question and then turned his head to grin at his friend. "Chicago." It would be a good diversion from waiting for a letter from Gethsemani.

The next morning six of them caught the early train on the Rock Island Railroad that got them to the city in time for the late morning movie at the Chicago Theatre. "The Tall Men" was playing that day, with Clark Gable, Jane Russell and Robert Ryan. They all agreed Clark Gable was almost as good as John Wayne, the king of western stars. They also loved the voluptuous Jane Russell, and covered Dick's eyes during the sexier scenes. Dick pushed their hands away because he loved looking at her, too; he wasn't in the monastery yet. After the movie, the Crew Cuts performed their newly-released hit, "Earth Angel." Dick's buddies teased him about his vocation and the fact that he would never have an Earth Angel of his own.

"Or maybe you'll turn into an angel yourself, Dickey boy!"

After the show, the group took the elevated train to Wrigley Field and ate hotdogs and drank beer as they watched the Chicago Cubs, then headed west on a bus to the Riverview Amusement Park. They rode the parachute ride, a water ride called "Shoot the Shoots," and "The Bobs," one of Dick's favorites. It was an old wooden roller coaster and at times Dick genuinely feared the cars would fly off the tracks. It made some of the boys queasy, but another one of their friends, Jim Wimbiscus, rode it with him, over and over. They stayed at Riverview until it closed, then caught the "milk train" home to Peru. Life was good.

Over the next few weeks, Dick did as many of the things he enjoyed as he possibly could, including a going-away party at the Starved Rock State Park. As he drank beer with his friends, listening to the car radios in the hot summer night, he realized how much he would miss them. A couple of nights later, he drove with Art to one of Chicago's south side blues clubs, loving the smoky environment and the music by the Negro performers. It disturbed them both, though, that the Negroes in the audience were charged twice as much as Whites for beer, especially when most of the performers were colored, too.

As part of his "final days on earth," as his friends had started calling this time, Dick also went with the gang to the Les-Buzz Roller Rink in Spring Valley. Every two weeks the owners turned the skating area into a dance floor and featured shows by big-name entertainers like the Everly Brothers, Louie Armstrong, Dick Jergens Orchestra and Guy Lombardo.

"Hey," said Art. "You know that new singer, Elvis Presley? I heard he wanted five thousand dollars to play here."

"Five thousand? Les-Buzz would never pay that kind of money!"

One day Dick and Joe drove over to the Trompeter home where Art was hanging out with Duke and Jim Wimbiscus whom the boys teased with the nickname, "Wimbie."

"Hey, let's take a ride out to St. Bede," suggested Wimbie. "I haven't been there since graduation. It seems like a long time ago."

St. Bede Academy was set back off U.S. Route 6, in the countryside. A long lane lined with trees led to the beautiful campus. The young men talked about Dick's older brother as they drove past the football field, baseball diamond, tennis courts and handball alleys, and Dick started to think again about the effect St. Bede might have had on his vocation. The monastery and school were joined by a cloistered walk, and, even though the monks had never overtly tried to talk the boys into joining them, the exposure to the lifestyle must have had an influence.

Between classes, the boys would see the lay brothers in their brown habits working on the dairy farm where St. Bede had about thirty purebred Holsteins. In the fall, the brothers harvested grain and hay, and the boys helped them pick apples. The monks who were priests and teachers often played croquet on the lawn and fished on the Illinois River, an activity they called "the apostolic sport." When a monk died, the whole school attended the funeral where the monks chanted the Funeral Mass. Afterwards, the students joined with them in the procession to the gravesite.

They had all enjoyed their high school years at St. Bede where there were about 350 high school students. Day students like Dick made up about half the population. The other half came from Chicago and its surrounding communities. Those "Boarder rats," as Dick and his friends teasingly called them, lived together in large dorms, sleeping in single beds with iron headboards and footboards.

The boys got out of the car, walked around the outside of the school and leaned against the railings under the brick-faced Roman arches that lined the exterior walkways, enjoying the hot summer day. They compared the monks who had been their teachers and all agreed that Father Gregory was one of the best. He taught literature, which included Thomas Merton's writings. Then there was Father Peter, the freshman Latin teacher. Dick shuddered as he remembered how the priest used to rant and rave, throwing blackboard erasers at students who made mistakes. The boys laughed about the amount of chalk dust Dick used to collect in his hair.

Later, as Dick dropped them all off at Art's, they suggested another going-away party.

Dick shook his head. "I don't even know for sure when I'm leaving."

"Yeah, well we better have the party soon, just in case!"

He smiled and agreed, then drove home to check the mail. His mother noticed his disappointment. "How long has it been since the interview, dear?"

Dick sighed. "Over two months. Do you think they got the address wrong?"

"I doubt it," said Betty, wishing the letter would never come, yet wanting her son to be happy.

That weekend, Dick and his friends got together at the State Park for another farewell party. They all tuned their car radios to the same station with the volume cranked up as they drank beer and swayed to the Crew Cuts' "Sh-Boom, Sh-Boom, Life Could Be a Dream." A little later in the evening, Dick stepped behind a bush to relieve himself and, on the way back, overheard a conversation among some of the girls. Susie Kane was saying she wished she had a boyfriend. The girls all agreed it would have to be someone from outside their group of close friends, and Susie said her mother recently suggested she go out with Dickey Sanders. As Dick stared at her from the darkness, mesmerized by her neck and her breasts under the tight white sweater, he cursed himself for the physical urge that came over him. He breathed deeply and slowly, praying for it to pass, but could not bring himself to move. Then Susie spoke again.

"He's nice, but, like I told my mother, if we went out, we'd probably spend the whole evening and never speak!"

Dick walked away, his feelings doused by her comment, and then smiled to himself – she was probably right. He got another beer and joined the original group, laughing and joking in the warm summer night.

By the time Dick got out of bed the next day, the mail was already there, including a letter postmarked Trappist, Kentucky. He opened it excitedly, but his mood changed quickly.

"You would get lost in a corner with all that's going on here," wrote the novice master. "There are other Trappist monasteries opening up that are smaller but even so, you are young to be making a commitment like this. Also, I noted your Latin grades. I suggest you attend college for a few years, include Latin in your coursework, and then come see us again."

Dick threw the letter on the couch and went into his room to pray, needing reassurance that the Trappists were truly his calling. He also felt some resentment. Gethsemani had so many men applying that they could pick the cream of the crop, and he was apparently not part of that elite group. Then he stopped himself as he realized he was angry with men of God whom he wanted to join more than anything in the world.

"God, why do I have this strong desire to spend my life in your presence, yet am being kept from the thing I most want to do?"

Then he called his brother. Jim had a friend who taught a semester-long crash course specifically for men entering the priesthood, at Loyola, a Jesuit University in Chicago. About a week later Jim sent him a copy of the letter he had received from Father Henderson that said he could get him in and would see about a complete scholarship.

Betty and Dick Sanders, 1955

Just in case it didn't work out, Betty encouraged her son to start junior college at St. Bede while he waited to hear about the scholarship. Money was tight, so he worked part-time. In late November he received a letter that said he could start the Latin course in January. He took it and for a semester he did nothing but attend Mass, eat, sleep and study. Years later he would write of it to Father Henderson, thanking him for an experience that was like an introduction to monastic life. "We learned how not to talk (no time), how not to go out (no time) how not to eat between meals (no time), how not to sleep too much (no time), how not to eat too much (definitely no time for indigestion.)"

At the end of the semester, he passed with a "B" and that June, 1956, he wrote an impassioned letter to Father Louis, literally begging to be allowed to enter Gethsemani. A few weeks later, a reply again said no, but that, because of the apparent strength of his vocation, there was another option. Five other Trappist Abbeys had sprung up recently due to the large numbers of men entering monastic life. The most recent "daughter house" was Our Lady of Mepkin, located in Moncks Corner, South Carolina. It was founded in 1949 and had only recently been raised to the status of abbey, and it was less crowded there. Mepkin would take him at a younger age because they needed men to help get the monastery established.

Dick immediately called Mepkin Abbey, his sense of urgency so great he did not want to wait for letters. His heart sank when Mepkin's vocation director said he had never heard of him.

"But my letter from Gethsemani said you would take me."

"Oh, no, my son," said the kind voice. "They can't make that decision. I'm sure Father Louis was just giving you options. Send us a letter explaining your vocation. We will need references, too."

Dick was disappointed and frustrated – he had already done all that. The vocation director said he would have to do it again, and if everything looked good, Dick would have to make a trip to South Carolina. All monasteries were different, with different needs, people and personalities. The monks at Mepkin would have to decide for themselves if Dick would fit in. And Dick had to know that he would be comfortable with them.

Dick hung up the phone and sat down, stunned, feeling a combination of confusion and anger. This meant starting all over at square one. What was wrong with these monasteries anyway? He prayed for patience. "God, is this a sign that you really don't want me? What kind of vocation do I have, that is being blocked at every turn?"

Then, feeling guilty about challenging his Creator, he walked over to St. Mary's, lit a candle at the statue of Mary Immaculate and knelt, looking longingly at her sweet face. He prayed a rosary, focusing intently on each Hail Mary, and then made his plea with a silent, anguished cry. "Dear sweet Virgin Mother, show me the way to your Son. Get me into the abbey and I promise I will adore you forever. Help me, please!"

Almost immediately he felt reassured, and the anger and frustration left him. Thanking Mary profusely, he went home and wrote a new application letter. Over the next few days he got new letters of recommendation, wishing there were some way he could have made copies of the first ones. Then he told Jim Wimbiscus the story, frustrated at the recent turn of events yet hopeful about the new option to become a Trappist. "Anyway, I sent the stuff off and have to go for an interview. Then I'll be back and will still have to wait again to see if they'll take me."

"They'll take you," said his friend, reassuringly. "Before you go, though, we better have another party!"

CHAPTER FOUR –
OUR LADY OF MEPKIN – 1956

Not knowing when he would hear back from Mepkin, Dick worked at the Rec. Department and continued to be the excuse for parties. When the letter came, it was good news – they wanted him to come for an interview.

Dick took a bus from Chicago to Charleston, noticing obvious signs of racial prejudice when the bus reached the southern states. At their first stop, the driver told the colored people on the bus to move to the back, and those boarding from that point on walked directly to the rear without being told. When they stopped for gas there were separate restrooms and drinking fountains, one marked, "Whites Only" and the other, "Colored." The colored facilities and fixtures always looked more rundown and older than those for Whites. Though Dick had heard about segregation, he had not seen it in real life except for the blues joints in Chicago with their two-tiered pricing based on skin color. He would make colored people a regular part of his prayers at the monastery.

When the bus arrived in Charleston late the next morning, he took a taxi from the station to Monck's Corner and to Our Lady of Mepkin Abbey. After stopping at a small white cement block building, they drove up the half-mile lane to the monastery. Though the grounds were beautiful, Dick was disappointed with the architecture. These simple buildings were a far cry from Gethsemani.

The novice master met him in the parking lot. Older than Dick by about ten years, "Father Master" reminded him of the actor, Anthony Quinn. He took Dick on a tour of the abbey, explaining its history. The Honorable Henry R. Luce and Clare Boothe Luce had purchased the property in 1936 and later donated it to the Diocese of Charleston for a religious community.

Mrs. Luce admired the Trappists because she had read Thomas Merton's books shortly after her conversion to Catholicism, so the Bishop offered the 3,000-acre property to Gethsemani for a new monastery. When the founding monks arrived in 1949, there was only a gardener's house, a few guest cottages and a two-story building that had been the Luce's home. Since then they had worked unceasingly to build the monastery. Dick and Father Master spent the next hour touring the grounds and work areas, then joined the others for

When the monks left for supper, Dick went back to the guesthouse for a simple meal of bread and vegetables. Later he returned to the church for Compline when the monks chanted the closing prayer of the day. Afterwards, the abbot blessed each man during their procession out, and Dick longed to be among them.

He fell asleep surprisingly easily and slept soundly until the bell rang at 2:15 a.m. Resisting the urge to roll over and sleep more, he pulled himself slowly out of bed; he had a feeling the novice master might count his appearance at church as part of the interview process. He stood sleepily in the balcony of the chapel watching the monks chant Vigils, spent some time in silent prayer, then Lauds, Angelus, and a series of private Masses and sacred reading.

That afternoon he went to meet Father Master, more convinced than ever about his vocation. In a kind but firm voice, the novice master asked questions similar to those of his counterpart at Gethsemani, including "Why do you want to be a Trappist?"

Dick groaned inwardly, wishing again that he had taken the time to develop an appropriate answer. "I told Father Louis, 'It's the most I can give to God.'" Then he added quickly, "...and get."

The novice master looked at him skeptically so Dick decided to just tell him. "To be completely honest, Father, I've never figured out how to say it. All I know is that I am called to this life. God is calling me here, so strongly."

The monk nodded, looking pleased, then asked about Latin. Dick hesitated and decided that, again, the truth was the best course. "I didn't do that well in it in high school, but I took a course for priests at Loyola and got a B."

The novice master smiled and handed him the same psychological test he had taken at Gethsemani. Though still surprised that all this was not centrally coordinated, Dick took the test without comment. Maybe I'll do better the second time, he joked to himself. A half hour later, the older monk returned. Dick managed to sing another scale pretty much on key, and then Father Master walked him to the parking lot and told him they would be in touch. Dick's heart sank as he thought about another several-month wait, but prayed that this time the eventual answer would be yes.

The letter arrived from Mepkin Abbey in late November, suggesting he join them after Christmas. When he read it, Dick yelled aloud, then sank to his knees in praise and thanks to God and the Blessed Virgin to whom he would dedicate the rest of his life, as promised. The long wait was finally over. He had to have a physical and dental examination and settle any financial obligations, which he didn't even have, and then he could go.

When the time came, his friends threw another going-away party, accusing Dick of deliberately delaying his departure because the parties were so much fun. At the end of that last long night, though, he said goodbye, knowing he would never see them again.

Dick woke to the smell of his mother's coffee and groaned as she shook him awake, laughing. "Didn't you tell me they get up early in the Abbey? I think you might be in trouble there!"

"Yeah," said Dick, sleepily. "I never thought I would think of 6:00 a.m. as 'sleeping in,' but I guess this is the last day I'll ever do it."

"Forever," said his mother, with only a slight show of emotion.

She would drive him to the train station in Peru so he could catch a train to Chicago where he would spend the night with his brother before flying to Charleston. Before they left the house, she fixed his favorite "big breakfast," fried eggs, bacon, sausage, home fries and toast.

Betty had finally come to terms with Dick's leaving and supported him as she always had. There were no more tears, no more wondering aloud what would happen to her when he left. Jim was in Chicago now and allowed more freedom than before, so she would be able to see him more often, she could visit Dick once a year and he would be happy. She assured him that was the most important thing.

It was a bright sunny day and Dick drove the Kaiser for the last time, listening to Perry Como sang, "Dream along with me, I'm on my way to a star." As he looked over at his mother who seemed comfortable now, he thought about their conversations, going to Mass together, playing cards after dinner and all the things she had always done for him, like his laundry, cooking and cleaning.

"I'm gonna miss you, Mom."

"I'll miss you too," she said softly, turning her head to the window.

When they reached the train station, Dick pulled up to the curb and got out. They hugged for a long time and she held back tears until, abruptly, she got into the car and drove away.

As he sat on the train, Dick's thoughts turned to his friends as he remembered their many trips to Chicago. He had a moment of hesitation as he thought again about how his life would change. He would never again sleep late, eat big breakfasts, smoke cigarettes, drink chocolate malts or go to parties. This would probably be the last train he would ever ride. They had just passed one of the last gas stations he might ever see. It might be the last time he'd see anything outside the monastery and its grounds, possibly ever. The monks called it "turning your back on the world." He was transitioning into another state of being, like a rebirth – yet only now did he realize it was deathlike, too.

"What am I thinking?"

The thought came more as a self-condemnation than a real question. A kind of panic overtook him and he realized he was truly afraid. What was he doing, for God's sake? His heart beat faster and it was hard to get air into his lungs. For God's sake. With that thought, he caught himself and blew out a long, deep breath. Yes. That was it. It was for God's sake. He realized he was doubting, and remembered that even Christ doubted, as he hung on the cross, dying, asking "My God, my God, why have you forsaken me?"

"How small my life seems compared to His," thought Dick as he refocused on the monastery. "He loved us enough to die for us, and in the end, even He was afraid."

Dick thought about spending his days thinking about and getting to know Christ, really know Him, to be in His presence, in His world, close by, every day, forever... and the doubting left him.

II

LAUDS

1957 - 1969

CHAPTER FIVE –
WELCOME, MY SON – 1957

To get to the abbey, Dick made a trip more complicated than the one Thomas Merton outlined in *The Seven Storey Mountain*. As planned, he had spent the night with his brother Jim in Chicago, having one final discussion about his vocation. The next morning, Mass went late and Dick had breakfast with his brother, so his cab driver left without him and he barely made his plane. After a flight that stopped in four cities, he finally arrived in Charleston and took a cab to a bus stop where the bus drove right past him. Later that evening, from a motel, he wrote to his mother about the trip.

> I went into a gas station near where the bus was supposed to have stopped and got talking to an old fellow in there who was having his car fixed, battery problems. He was going through Moncks Corner and would be glad to give me a ride. They say you shouldn't accept rides from strangers but I jumped at the chance. We got about five miles from Moncks Corner when his battery went dead again and the lights went out but the motor kept running. We were promptly stopped by the state police. I had to keep my foot on the break so we wouldn't run downhill (and you think you need a new car!) We took off again for Moncks Corner, without lights. He stopped at a gas station to get the battery charged and I walked down the road to a general store.
>
> When the people at the store found out that I was going to Mepkin to stay, they got more inquisitive, wanted to know how long I would be stationed there, if I could leave if I didn't like it, and how often I could get into town. They seemed to know

more about it than I had expected and are very curious, which is good. However, there are very few Catholics down here and in general the people treat the idea as though it is a wax museum.

When we were talking about me entering the abbey, one fellow mentioned that he was going to join a nudist colony once, as though the cases were quite parallel.

All for Jesus – through Mary with a smile, Dick.

He arrived at the abbey mid-morning. The Novice master met him with the words, "Welcome, my son," and showed Dick to the building where he would stay temporarily with the family brothers who were not Trappists but oblates who lived in the monastery under different rules from the monks. They took care of most of the buying and selling, and anything else that required contact with the outside world. Dick would wear his street clothes until he was accepted into the community, at which time he would be given a habit and his religious name. Father Master walked him to the novitiate building, mostly classrooms and meeting rooms where Dick would study with eight other choir novices, those who were or would become priests. Eight lay brother novices studied separately in their own section. The reason for the two types of monks was that the early Cistercians attracted brothers who had limited education but wished to enter the abbey and spend most of their time in manual labor. The lay brothers at Mepkin worked eight hours each day, the choir monks only four. They slept in the same room with the choir monks and followed similar sets of prayer hours, but many of their prayers were said outside, wherever they were working. It was like a separate community within a community. In the early days, lay brothers were mostly illiterate, which was no doubt where the concept of two social classes developed. Today, however, the distinction struck Dick as odd and even unfair.

They walked out to tour the abbey's work area in more detail than they had last time, to determine what job Dick would be assigned. The monks built or grew just about everything they needed, according to Chapter 48 of the Rule of St. Benedict: "When they live by the labor of their hands, as our fathers and the apostles did, then they are truly monks."

First they walked past magnolias and live oak trees, so called because they kept their leaves all year long, to banks of the Cooper River. Dick noted what seemed to be stars on the water, created by the afternoon sun. Following on a dirt walkway that led to the working section of the monastery, he continued to take in his new surroundings. The grounds were largely timberland but included an extensive and beautiful terraced garden, left by the Luces. Ancient live oaks, some eighty feet tall and almost as wide, hung with graceful Spanish moss and exotic palms anchored the wooded areas. Bushes and shrubs, some flowering, dotted the expansive lawns. Southern yellow pine trees, tall scraggly cousins of the pines in Illinois, grew up from the banks of the river.

In the nursery, the monks grew camellias and azaleas that they sold to help support the abbey. As Dick and Father Master skirted the edges of a plowed field, he saw that Mepkin had a sophisticated irrigation system for the dry winter months.

When they reached the edges of another plowed area, this one as large as a football field, they viewed the work buildings in the shape of a horseshoe around it, where Dick counted about twenty monks working in the various buildings, and all of it looked difficult. Though choir monks didn't work as much as lay brothers, Dick would still have to do some manual labor. He inhaled a nervous breath as he understood more clearly why they were interested in taking him. Mepkin needed men to continue to build the monastery, not just spiritually but physically.

They visited the building where they made cement blocks, then the machine shed and then the blacksmith shop. All of it looked like heavy work. Next they entered the sawmill where the monks processed southern yellow pine trees. The sawlogs or tree trunks were cut into lumber and used for building. The upper trunks, branches and thinner trees were trucked to a local pulp mill to be made into paper products. Dick watched the sawmill process carefully, determining the function of each piece of mechanical equipment, fascinated as always with how things worked. He was also impressed with strength of the men working there. As he watched them, Dick suddenly felt faint; it was hard to breathe in the thick pine dust, especially with the heat and humidity, and the high-pitched whine of the saw was so loud he wondered how the sawmill-monks could hear God's voice in the racket. Then he chided himself; God's voice could certainly be heard over a saw. He liked the sweet smell of the pine resin, but prayed that God and the novice master would keep him out of the sawmill.

Just ahead, another area was being prepared for additional farming by a monk who used a backhoe to clear the stumps left by the lumberjack-monks. At the head of the horseshoe-shaped complex, a barn housed Jersey cows. This, too, would soon be expanded as Mepkin's brothers had begun to rear their own cattle; calf pens were already being built behind the dairy barn. They also grew and harvested the hay and grain the cows ate. Nearby, inside a hen house, about three dozen white Leghorn chickens pecked in the dirt for seeds; they were the abbey's source of eggs. Dick noted that the hen house, like the cow barn, was adorned with a white wooden cross. Just beyond it, across the field from the cement block shed and blacksmith shop, stood a large water tower with yet another wooden cross on top. Dick was suddenly moved – he would spend the rest of his life focused on those crosses.

He looked at the men working, his new brothers. Like the monks at St. Bede, most of them wore monastic habits, white with black scapulars for the choir monks and brown for the brothers. He saw one he knew from Peru, a friend of his family's, who knew Dick was coming. Frank smiled and made some signs to welcome him, indicating with a facial expression that it was about time Dick had gotten there, and then walked silently away. A few of the others smiled and nodded; they would be introduced later. We have plenty of time, Dick thought to himself, noting the calming effect the abbey was already having on him. We have the rest of our lives.

After the tour, the novice master motioned Dick to follow him to a classroom. He offered a mimeographed copy of a schedule that Dick had seen on his interview weekend. It varied a little on Sundays and feast days, and the Choir monks and the Brothers had different schedules, all shown on the same page. It was already 1:30 in the afternoon, so Dick would start late – his new brothers had been up for almost twelve hours. The novice master suggested that he walk the grounds or pray in the church until Vespers at 3:00 p.m. At 5:15 would come supper and then spiritual reading, and at 6:15, more spiritual reading. The day would end with the prayers of Compline, Angelus and Examin (of conscience), and at 7:00 p.m. the monks retired for the night. The schedule seemed more challenging now that Dick would have to do it every day, significantly different from following it for a weekend. He liked it, though. It was freedom from the cares of normal life. There were no decisions to make, no plans to attend to, and nothing to think about except the prayers of each moment, the time of which were noted by the ringing of bells. Later, he would describe the life in a letter to his mother as "living by the bells."

Father Master interrupted Dick's thoughts when he looked up from his notebook. "I'm just checking to see where you will work."

Dick's heart almost stopped as he prayed to himself, "Please not the sawmill, please not the sawmill," and he breathed an audible sigh of relief when he was assigned to the gardens. The novice master reminded him only to offer his work to God, and to keep God constantly in his mind. Dick nodded seriously, thinking again of the white crosses on the abbey's buildings.

He learned about the probationary time he was in at the moment. After a few days, he would be accepted as a postulant, which meant he would move into the dormitory, eat in the dining room and sit with the monks in choir, but he would still wear his lay clothing. He could stay for a month to get an idea of how the Trappist life might suit him.

"At the end of that time, if you decide to stay," the novice master paused for significance, "and we decide we want you... you will be given a religious name and a white postulant's habit."

Assuming all went well during the few months after that, Dick would present a petition to the abbot to become a novice and if the abbot and a committee approved, Dick would receive a novice's habit, similar to a postulant's but with a hood. Then he would study for another two years about monastic life and the meaning of the vows he would take later on. At the end of that time, the monks would vote on whether Dick could join them permanently. If the vote was 'yes,' he could take simple or temporary vows and be a junior professed monk for three years. Then, if all went well, he would take solemn vows and finally be a professed Cistercian of the Strict Observance, O.C.S.O. It would be at least five years before he would be a "real" Trappist, and at any point along the way, they might reject him. He wasn't worried because he was quite sure he would fit in, but then, he had been sure he was that he would get into Gethsemani, too.

Father Master smiled. "You'll be surprised at how little the concept of time matters here. If you are meant to be here, you will be, and you'll stay until you die."

Dick had another question, prompted by the reference to dying – he had not seen a graveyard. The novice master explained that they did not have one, re-emphasizing the young age of Our Lady of Mepkin Abbey. No one had died here yet.

The only other thing Dick wanted to know was when he would begin his studies for the priesthood. The answer was yet another lengthy time period. He would begin studies in theology and philosophy near the end of his time as a junior professed monk, but would not study for the priesthood in earnest until after solemn vows. The studies for the priesthood would then take another three to four years, so it would be eight or nine years before he would be a priest. He would turn twenty the coming summer, so by the time he had achieved all the milestones, he would be at least twenty-eight years old. Not so old, he realized then, thinking of the time it was taking his brother. Jim was still not ordained.

Dick walked the grounds and prayed; he and the novice master would meet again later, in the church. He again thought about the words, "...and we decide we want you..." He had only a month to prove that he had what it took to be a Trappist.

As he walked, he found himself again drawn to the strangely shaped live oaks that shaded large areas of the property. Some were six or seven feet around, he estimated, with branches that began low on their trunks and grew in almost unnatural angles. Their beauty rivaled the sprawling sycamores at Gethsemani. He walked down to the river, still amazed that he was actually here, as the afternoon sun cast a glow over the grounds. Frogs croaked in chorus from the river and Dick began to feel as if he were in a dream. Soon, however, a swarm of God's winged creatures surrounded him and he hastily made his way back to the church.

The first structure built by the founding members of Mepkin, the church had a two-story ceiling and a small balcony for visitors where Dick had prayed when he was here for his interview. Wooden stalls with seats lined the left and right sides where each choir monk was assigned a permanent place, based on seniority. When the bells called the monks to Vespers, he watched them from the balcony.

As he had learned, Vespers was the second of two most important 'offices' of the monastic day, the first being Lauds, which was observed in the morning. After the prayers of Vespers and fifteen minutes of silent meditation, the bells called them to *Lectio Divina*, sacred reading.

At 5:00 p.m., the monastic schedule indicated fifteen minutes of "mental prayer," and then supper in the refectory. The novice master pointed him to the table in the back; one's place at table was yet another symbol of seniority. The abbot and two others sat at a separate table at one end of the room.

Supper that day was bread and a dish of mashed fruit, which Dick ate hungrily. He had already begun to feel at home. When the monks took their plates to the sink, he did the same, and then looked for Father Master who nodded for Dick to follow him to the Chapter room. It was the family room of the monastery where the abbot gave spiritual conferences and sermons during the week to the choir monks and on Sundays to the whole community, including the lay brothers. It was a single-story room with low, white beamed ceilings and wooden benches, hand-made at Mepkin. For a moment, Dick wondered what it would have been like had he been able to enter at Gethsemani as he originally planned, but decided it was better to be here at Mepkin with 40 monks than at Gethsemani with 270. The numbers for the novices were even more dramatic – Mepkin had only nine novices, while Gethsemani had 70. The abbot, whom Dick had not yet met, introduced him to the group using his full name, Richard Edward Sanders. When the abbot began his sermon, Dick hardly heard, still in awe about the fact that he was beginning his contemplative life.

At 6:00 the bell rang again and they processed to the church for Compline, the final communal prayer of the day. Dick noticed how the monks moved together seamlessly, as one body. Just before the *Salve Regina*, Hail Mary, the lights were dimmed and all that remained lit was the statue of the Virgin and the Infant Jesus and the voices rose wondrously in the glow of the sun that was just descending in the western sky. Dick felt a surge of excitement as he waited for the monks' chanting that expressed their love for the Blessed Virgin of Nazareth whose motherly love was the path to Jesus.

Salve, Regina, Mater misericordiae

Hail, holy Queen, Mother of Mercy,
Our life, our sweetness and our hope.
To thee do we cry, poor banished children of Eve;
To thee do we send up our sighs....

Finally, the monks prayed their thanks for the love and faith they had lived this day, trusting that they would awaken with the dawn but prepared at any moment to join their God in heaven.

The next morning Dick stayed awake during the first five hours of prayer, and at about 7:00 a.m., the monks processed out to go to work. Dick followed the novice master to where the novices studied in the mornings rather than going out to manual labor. They met every day but Sunday and feast days in the classroom where they studied Scripture, liturgy, monastic sources, the Cistercian patrimony and the vows they would one day take. Dick sat down with the others who nodded their heads in greeting. The novice master addressed all nine of the novices together.

"You must learn to accept yourselves as you are and then to be 'no one.' Set aside any ambitions and learn simply to 'be.' Keep Jesus in mind as a role model, and remember how often He sought solitude apart from others to enter into prayerful communion with His Father."

Next, the novice master explained the job of the abbot, who guided them on St. Benedict's Rule. Father Abbot was their leader, as Christ was the leader of the Apostles, and he prayed constantly for guidance to help discern God's will for all of them. He was responsible not only for the lives of the monks, but for their souls. It was an important position. Dick thought about the power the abbot would hold over his future.

He was given a copy of the *Rule of St. Benedict*, one of the few things he was allowed to have as his own. It contained St. Benedict's message to new monks.

Are you hastening toward your heavenly home? Then with
Christ's help, keep this little rule that we have written for
beginners. After that, you can set out for the loftier summits of
the teaching and virtues we mentioned above, and under God's
protection you will reach them. Amen.

He was also given a copy of a pamphlet that explained the Trappists' focus on Mary. When class was over, Dick tucked both under his arm and walked down to the river, feeling gratitude for his life to come. Then the bell rang and he hurried back to the church for the little hour of Sext. After entering the refectory in an orderly line, the monks stood at their seats and chanted Psalm 118, verses 97 – 128, and Dick took this time to get another look at his new brothers as a group. They were of varying ages, and all tonsured, shaved bald with a "crown" of hair around the outside, above the ears. His would soon be the same. He wished he had a monastic habit already because in his street clothes he felt like he was there for a weekend retreat. But then, this was part of becoming "no one."

The monks seemed to pay no attention to each other, and it didn't seem rude, just comfortable. Dick sat quietly as food was brought to him that had been prepared by the abbey's cook, who smiled broadly at the new man.

Later, Dick fell in behind the others as they processed out to work – he went to the gardens. The Luces' beautiful gardens had led to one of the monastery's first businesses; flowering bushes and trees for wholesale sale. Brother Gardner taught Dick what to do through sign language. First they took cuttings from the existing plants, rooted them in the green house and then set out in beds for early growth. The cuttings that had already grown some were then planted in regular rows till they were a year old, when they were "balled' – dug up, roots wrapped with burlap, and sold. It required weeding, hoeing, and mixing special dirt combinations, fertilizers and peat.

After work, he took advantage of a brief amount of free time and walked down by the river. He had lived through twenty-four hours as a Trappist. Reflecting on the life, he realized the complete order of it, and that the monks seemed to decide nothing at all. None of the activities and business of the world existed here. He was impressed by the order of the life, the sense of meaning, certainty and stability. He only had to follow the rules and focus his thoughts on God. How could life be better than that?

He spent a few minutes continuing a letter he had started to his mother.

> I smoked my last cigarette about an hour ago. I ran out.
> I can hardly wait for you to come down and see this place. The flowers are blooming; they seem to be mostly flowering bushes. I don't suppose the others will bloom until spring. It is said that the Luces spent about $75,000 about twenty years ago to landscape the place and you can imagine what $75,000 would do twenty years ago, especially in the South. It is one of the oldest plantations in the South.
> I will write again in a week. Please remember a special intention in your prayers. It's starting already, isn't it? I assure you that you will get many letters asking for prayers, only four letters a year, but eight this year.

All for Jesus – through Mary – with a smile, Dick

Then he joined his brothers for Vespers, went for supper, more spiritual reading, and then to the church again for Compline, Angelus and the Salve Regina.

At 7:00 p.m. as he tried to fall asleep, he thought about the words of the pamphlet that explained the Trappists' devotion to Mary, written by the Abbot General of the Cistercians of the Strict Observance, the Most Reverend Dom Gabriel Sortais, in 1953.

> Do not have any fear of loving Mary too much, nor of giving her too large a place in your contemplative life..... Will Jesus tell us that we loved His Mother too much? Why then did He wish that she should also be our mother? And why did He make her so beautiful, so good, so loveable, if He did not wish our hearts to be taken by her...?

Dick prayed that he would soon stay asleep each night in the arms of Mary Immaculate with the monks' final prayer:

May the almighty and merciful Lord grant us a restful night.
And a peaceful death.

CHAPTER SIX –
I GRANT YOU PEACE

On his third day, Dick found a note under his napkin that said the abbot wished to see him that afternoon. He anticipated the meeting with trepidation, still fearful that he might not be accepted. He didn't even have a habit yet and already the abbot wanted to see him. What if this meeting was bad news? Could he go back to his former life, rejected again? How could he live in the outside world when monastic life was so perfect for him?

He knocked on the door and was calmed a little by the friendly voice that told him to come in. As he had been instructed, he knelt next to the abbot's desk and waited. The abbot turned, offered his ring to be kissed, blessed the young monk and then motioned for him to sit down. He asked how Dick liked the life so far, and what he thought about the differences between Mepkin and Gethsemani. Dick assured him that, though he had originally wanted Gethsemani, Mepkin was perfect for him. They talked for about a half hour, with Dick shyly answering probing questions about his family and religious life. He thought about holding back but felt so comfortable that he just started talking, telling how his father was swindled out of a business deal with a Kaiser/Fraser car dealership, having invested most of his life savings and ending up with only a car. Not long after, as Dick's father was driving home from work, the son of one of his good friends darted out from between two parked cars and Bill hit the boy, causing permanent brain damage.

Shaking his head sadly, the abbot asked about Dick's brother Jim, the Jesuit and asked if Dick had ever had thoughts of joining the same order.

"Oh, no," Dick replied, quickly. "I'm not smart enough. I didn't do well in school, and Jim and I are just different. He's more outgoing and confident, he's a great athlete, good looking, popular, smart." Dick shifted nervously in his chair and looked out the window, then stammered, "I'm not anything, really. I mean, nothing important.... I mean, I just wouldn't want to be a Jesuit."

When the abbot asked about the death of Dick's father, Dick looked down at the floor as he brought up a blurry yet painful memory that he usually pushed from his mind with prayers. Something about the abbot, though, made him comfortable with sharing the story. One of the chanted psalms came into his mind.

Laboravi in gemitu meo...
I have suffered and wept...

He told the story of his father's illness, death and funeral, sobbing aloud, as the abbot's caring nature told him that releasing the pain was finally permitted. When he recovered his composure, Dick sat back in the chair, regretting his tears. Would the abbot think he was too emotional to be a Trappist? He was reassured, however, when the abbot looked at him tenderly, raised his right hand toward him and said, "I grant you peace."

After a minute, the abbot changed the subject again and asked how his mother felt about Dick entering the monastery. Dick paused and thought for a moment. "She was sad, I guess, but she always supported everything Jim or I wanted to do, so she's fine with it."

"Is she a religious woman?"

"She's a committed Catholic. So was my dad. But they were pretty normal." He shifted again, nervously. "I mean, we didn't grow up thinking our parents wanted us to become priests or anything. After Dad died she got a job as a clerk in her sister's clothing store. She had never worked outside of the house before, and it surprised everybody how she took hold of things. She did well for herself financially and personally. I helped her some, but really she pulled herself together."

When the abbot said he looked forward to meeting her, Dick took it as a sign this talk was going well. The abbot looked back down at the file and asked about Jane. As Dick described the older sister he had never known, sounding as if he had, it became clear to the abbot that the family had always considered Jane part of the family, even after her death. The abbot sensed the emotional pain that Dick was not aware of but must have felt from his brother and parents. The grief of losing a child could not be hidden, and it never healed. The abbot also believed that most people are not born shy. Dick's quiet demeanor no doubt came at least in part from sadness his mother, father and brother felt, all of his life.

They sat in silence for some time and then the abbot said he would look forward to their next meeting. "Next meeting." Dick's heart soared – he had made it past the first hurdle. He smiled to himself as he knelt for the blessing.

He was assigned a "guardian angel," a novice who was appointed to help Dick get him used to the routine. Dick wrote about him to his mother. "I was quite surprised find out that I was not even allowed to talk to my guardian angel. You are shown where to get the book on sign language, where to sleep, and where to eat, the rest of the time you follow your guardian angel around and try to do what he is doing."

He wrote letters a little each day or two, because there was little time for writing and because mail was only sent out once a month, anyway.

> The popular conception of us sitting around and contemplating all day could not be farther from the truth. We are actually quite busy. Aside from about eight hours of spiritual exercises, we are also working people. We have to raise or buy food and all the necessities (including soap, we do wash.) Around here it is not a question of what to do first, you are told what to do first, even in your 'free' time, and the extras are squeezed in wherever you can find a minute. Father Master says that around here there are only forty minutes in an hour. I am sure of one thing, there aren't any more than that.

He was limited to two large sheets of paper per letter, so he wrote carefully on both sides using a fountain pen and bottle of ink, which took some getting used to. When he neared the end of the back of the second page, he wrote "Well, the bottom is coming up."

> It's 3:50. I just came back from work. Got your letter last night, also got one a week ago today. I got the one from the gang on Tuesday. I was glad to hear from them, too, and it didn't bother me a bit, even though they wrote it at a party. Please tell them if you see them that it makes no difference how wet the glue is, they are opened before I get them anyway.
>
> The food here is quite good and plenty of it. We only get one meal, and of course breakfast and supper. (That is all I ever got and I am still quite alive.) For breakfast, one quart of hot chocolate, all the bread you can eat, and I get butter (I suppose I will until I am twenty-one). For dinner, one quart of a barley drink, which I don't drink. I tasted it and decided I am not that much of a saint yet, but I guess some of them like it. I drink water. Two hot food portions (each is about a quart),

one of vegetables and the other is soup, usually made with the
vegetables you didn't eat yesterday. (That is why I eat all my
vegetables and wish the others would, too.) Also all the bread
you can eat, and all get butter, also desert, either canned fruit or
pudding. (We got cake once.) For supper, one quart warm hot
chocolate, bread, butter, and cheese or fruit. If I go hungry here
it is my own fault.

As he adjusted to the schedule and the sense of being in a different time
and space, he experienced both emotional and physical reactions. He was
homesick and missed his friends and his mother. He suffered withdrawal
symptoms from cigarettes, intense cravings and headaches, and had coughing
fits, all of which left after a few days, except for the cravings. The other monks
seemed sympathetic. The new diet of high-fiber vegetarian food affected him
too, and for the first week, he had indigestion and bouts of diarrhea. The
2:15 a.m. awakening was a struggle that was even worse on Sundays and
feast days when they rose at 2:00. Then there was the corresponding early
bedtime and his inability to fall asleep. He quickly learned to nap standing
up and no one seemed to notice. He wondered how many of the others
did the same thing, but then realized that, if all the monks slept on their
feet, there would be no chanting. He described the mosquitoes as one of
the biggest challenges. "There are numerous wild animals around here but
by far the most fierce is the *Diptera Culicidae*. I have been bitten by them
numerously since I got here and I think it is one of my greatest crosses. They
don't seem to bother the others."

After a while, however, the mosquitoes were no longer a problem, and he
attributed their lack of interest to the monks' vegetarian diet. He still had to
adjust to the weather, however. "Whenever the sun isn't out it is quite damp
and the sun is out only about seven hours a day, 11:00 a.m. to 6:00 p.m. It
seems very strange but when I get up the sky is usually clear and stays so until
about sunrise. It then suddenly clouds and doesn't clear until about four
hours later. When the sun is out it is about 75 to 80 degrees but as soon as
evening comes it drops into the 50s and the horrible dampness. I have a cold
now and it can only be from the dampness."

A few weeks later he let her know that, though he was generally happy,
he was not always certain he would stay. "I have had twenty mornings here
and I am sure that in at least fifteen of them I was seriously tempted to leave.
But I just call to mind a resolution I made on the first morning I was here: I
will leave only if I make up my mind when the sun is brightly shining and the
temperature is between 70 and 80 degrees. That way I will be sure it is not
just the inconveniences that are driving me away."

Soon it was time for him to formally enter the community as a novice. He would make an eight-day retreat and then "receive the habit" and his religious name on March 3, 1957. He would be named for Saint Robert, the first abbot of the Cistercian order, not Robert Bellarmine, a Jesuit saint, he reminded his mother and brother in a letter. "Robert died at the age of 93 so you can see what I have to look forward to. As Abbot he retired four times. Finally the Pope told him to get back to work. I think he was 87 then. Of course, I don't have to worry about that, I will just do what the Abbot tells me for the next 73 years. I expect to be pulling weeds most of the time."

Soon after, in a ceremony in the Chapter Room, he was clothed by the abbot and novice master in a white postulant's cloak. "Richard Edward Sanders" disappeared into the hidden world of the monastery, and "*Frater Mary Robert*" took his place.

Now that he had the habit, everything he had been doing seemed new. He joined his brothers in this choir stall, the last one at the back. When the day ended and Compline was prayed, the abbot blessed each man and *frater* Robert followed in his turn. Then, as if for the first time, he walked silently with the others to the dormitory.

At the top of a central stairway three wings radiated out from a central platform. Altogether there were about forty "cells," small areas about 7' by 5', separated by plywood on two sides, open on the bottom and the top, with a curtain in front like out-patient examination rooms in over-crowded hospitals. It was tight, but not as bad as the boarders' dorm at St. Bede; at least here they had some visual separation from each other. Robert's appeared to be identical to the others, with a cot and straw mattress, covered with a green blanket. Hooks in the plywood on both sides provided a place to hang his habits. A Bible sat on a small shelf.

There was shower area downstairs in the same building. He followed the other monks, washed up and then went back upstairs, sat down on the rude straw mattress and looked around at his cell. Through the open screened window, he heard the bullfrogs singing and listened as the breathing of the other monks grew steady and then some of them began to snore. He lay awake for a long time and then thought about Mary who would bring peaceful sleep and lead him to her son in the morning.

At 2:15 a.m. a brother walked through the dormitory, ringing the bell. Robert woke sleepily. Later he wrote, "When the bell rings, I go."

Having a monastic name and habit made him feel more at home, but he began to realize something he had not expected. Life at the abbey was not only sheltered from the world but was sheltered in time – it was medieval Europe rather than Twentieth Century United States, like living in a foreign culture. He described the feeling in a letter to his brother. "It's hard for me to think of the meaning of time anymore. That must seem strange but in a certain sense we seem to live in eternity. We do about the same thing every day but without it getting monotonous. Everything is a continuation of doing the Will of God, rather than a repetition of doing the same things over and over."

Little things became significant; a cutting grew roots, flowers bloomed, new plants took hold and grew stronger. Differences like the High Mass became exciting changes to the routine. He found incense more intoxicating than ever, as it took him further back in time with the monastery's medieval setting, especially coupled with the monks' Gregorian chants.

In the mornings, he and the other novices learned details of the Rule of St. Benedict. Though he had seen it before, Robert found it fascinating to study it in the context of the reality of the monastery. Called the "Rule" because it "regulates the lives of those who obey it," almost everything in it pointed to a quote from the Bible and it was from this perspective that the novices studied it. The monastic life, as outlined by St. Benedict, consisted of three things: prayerful reading of Scripture called *Lectio Divina*; the communal chanting of psalms and other prayers at specified times of the day, called *opus Dei,* Divine Office or Liturgy of the Hours; and work. Robert was amazed at the level of detail the Rule contained and how applicable it was to his day, even stating the time monks should rise and retire, what they should eat, clothing, footwear and various jobs at the abbey. It also contained concepts such as the fact that monks were forbidden to own anything, based on Acts 4:32.

> Now the multitude of the believers were of one heart and one soul, and not one of them said that anything he possessed was his own, but they had all things in common.

Most of it just made sense. The Rule of St. Benedict was the guidebook to the abbey, to the life Brother Robert loved.

He also continued to be amazed at the beauty of his new home. Unable to communicate the inward changes that went along with the life of a silent monk, he wrote mainly about his surroundings in his letters, sitting at his desk in the scriptorium in front of a set of corner windows.

> Looking out my window I can see a small valley, thickly wooded, about a hundred feet away and to the other side, the Cooper River. Right here it is about three times the width of the Illinois River but much of it is shallow. It runs down to Charleston and there into the Atlantic. Being so close to the Atlantic, it varies slightly with the tides. There goes that bell again.

> I was just called to Vespers and then Collation (supper.) It
> is now about 6:00 p.m. The sunset is beautiful. I can see it from
> my desk. The sun is like a ball of fire going down behind the hill
> across the river.

Betty forwarded it on to Jim, with a note: "It was nice talking with you. Just finished a letter to Dick. I feel so close to both of you. The good Lord is really taking care of me. He lets me feel very lonely, then seems to give me the strength to overcome it. I have so much to be thankful for. All my love, Mom."

Over time, Robert learned Trappist sign language. Deliberately not complex, it was created only for basic communication and therefore limited gossip and other discussions not focused on God or immediate work. He explained to Father Henderson in a letter.

> The sign language is coming along alright. I think I could even
> do better in Latin but I haven't missed anything yet (except for
> a few jokes.) It is wonderful, actually. No gender, number and
> case, in fact, not even any parts of speech. Of course with that
> loose a language it is possible to be misunderstood, but if we are,
> so what, what we have to say is never that important.

Overall, Robert found himself comfortable in the world of mostly silence that contrasted beautifully with the prayers of the hours they chanted throughout the day. There were times, however, when he wished he could know more about his new brothers. The novice master said he had been with monks for years and never learned even the smallest details about their backgrounds. They did, however, learn about each other in a different way, in a way that people in the outside world never touched. Robert thought it might be similar to the heightened alternate senses of the blind or the deaf, as he noted the way different brothers looked at the sunrise, sang in choir or laughed at the joy of their work. At the same time, he became aware of himself through these new senses, seeing himself as a monk yet very human.

The only other downside of the silence, he realized over time, was that the men did not express animosities they felt toward each other, and small irritations could become large concerns because they were never aired. After a few months Robert's own awareness of his brothers came more into focus and he began to notice signs of conflict. A coffee cup set on the refectory counter with more force than needed, squinted eyes, furrowed brows, tensed shoulders became easy to read.

He was personally happy, though, and had no problems with any of them. In one letter to his mother he described his life as "fine and happy and just floating along on a cloud."

That August, a new postulant, frater Mary Joachim, joined them in the novitiate. The new man was about his own age, quiet and serious, but had a subtle sense of humor, discernable through the silence. He was also assigned to the gardens, and Robert appreciated how hard Joachim worked, with no sign of complaint.

When he wasn't working, praying the Liturgy of the Hours or sacred readings, Robert immersed himself in his studies and was amazed at how much he loved it. It was more complicated than he had anticipated, though, and he began to understand why the formation took so long. Using St. Anthony of Egypt as a guide, he worked to attain the state of being "no one," to be in a state of nothingness except for that part of him that sought the supernatural knowledge of God.

> That prayer is most pure in which the monk is no longer aware
> of himself, or of the fact that he is praying.

One of the things he loved most was the Trappists' focus on the Virgin Mary and he chanted her praise along with his brothers.

> *Virgo Dei Genitrix...*O Virgin Mother of God,
> He Whom the whole world does not contain,
> enclosed Himself in thy womb, being made man.

In September, Betty Sanders visited Mepkin for the first time. Family could come for one three-day period each year. Brother Robert still had to take part in all prayers but he was released from study and work while she was there. Robert walked over to meet her and smiled shyly when he saw his mother's reaction to his monastic habit. She was smiling and crying at the same time as she stood back, taking in the new image of her son. "Let me look at you!"

She looked much the same as she had when they hugged goodbye nine months ago, in a purple dress with open-toed pumps. He complimented her on her tightly-curled brown hair and new horn-rimmed glasses. Then Betty took his arm and they walked the grounds. She marveled at the beauty and asked questions about the plants and trees. After a few minutes, she told him carefully that she had sold their home and moved into an apartment. It was the biggest thing she had ever done on her own. "I just couldn't see living alone in that house with nothing but memories."

Brother Robert felt a pang of guilt about being only a memory, but realized that of course she was right. In terms of the house on Rock Street, or anywhere else in the world, he was just a memory. He wondered what she had done with his things, and Jim's, but did not ask. Things were not important.

"Jim comes down from St. Ignatius once in a while to visit, and I drive up to Chicago to see him sometimes. Last week-end we went to dinner and a play called *My Fair Lady*. It was wonderful, Dick!" He could almost hear the words she did not say: "I wish you could come with us sometime."

For the next two days he went to the guesthouse after morning prayers and spiritual reading, to walk her back to the church. Betty sat in the balcony, watching her son chanting prayers from his choir stall.

When she left Brother Robert disappeared again into the timeless world of the monastery as the days settled back into what had come to be routine. The most unusual thing that happened was in November, when the monastery changed to daylight savings time.

> We went on it in the beginning of October when Rev. Father got back from the General Chapter. He wanted to be sure it was OK before he tried it. I don't know how long we will be on it. The brothers were having trouble getting in the hay and other things. It wasn't dry enough until after noon to start taking it in so they had to work late and didn't get in to eat until the rest of us were going to bed. Rev. Father, being a very wise man and not wishing to deceive anyone, did not set the clocks back but rather set the schedule ahead. We now do everything an hour later, we don't get up until 3:00 a.m. The first night we got an extra hour sleep but no one could sleep that late.

Robert had worried about feeling homesick over the holidays, especially Christmas, but found the time with his new monastic family so wondrous that he did not miss home at all. They had four days without any work, beginning at noon on Christmas Eve. All prayer hours and the rest of the monastic schedule remained in place, however. The only thing he was worried about was that his mother would be worrying about him. She had written she was having problems with high blood pressure. In an effort to reassure her, he described his Christmas in a letter.

> We (novices) put up our crib Wednesday. We have only three images but that is alright. There are four cribs around and all fixed nicely...

Father Anselm played some Christmas music on the organ before Mass. Christmas is the only time all year that the organ is used except to accompany singing. We have also been celebrating in the refectory according to limited means. Christmas for desert we had spiked ice cream. We make our own and are likely to find most any flavor in it. We have been having candy and cookies for a week now. Believe it or not, we started with your cookies. They were as good as ever. I had two cinnamon stars, almond loaf, two chocolate macaroons, a moon & crescent and some pieces of the pressed cookies that unfortunately broke in shipping.

Thank you for the card you sent. We have all our cards strung around the room here. They are all very beautiful and add to the Christmas spirit.

About New Years, he wrote only, "It's January 1 and no one around here has a hangover!"

After the Christmas season, months passed and continued to be blissfully happy. "I just wonder how happy one can get. This life is wonderful, especially in that everything is done for the same One and then there is no change in happiness, no waiting for something special that is coming or for some special part of the day that is more enjoyable than the rest."

He reported that the monks were making changes to their Office and the Cistercian rites, simplifying changes that had been made over the centuries that now received some "housecleaning." Also, in a move Robert approved of greatly, the lay brothers were now allowed assist at the Divine Office in choir on Sundays and feast days, instead of saying their own office. "They are bringing our Brothers more and more into the picture, *Deo Gratias*."

The highlight of the spring was when three of the professed monks were ordained. Robert wrote to his mother: "It will be tremendous to suddenly be serving Mass for them instead of with them, and to receive Jesus from their hands."

On July 29, 1958, Brother Robert passed his twenty-first birthday. He didn't even notice the date until three days after. He wondered if he should feel different now that he was officially an adult, but quickly decided that age was not important, especially here. The only days that were noted by the monks were anniversaries of name days, solemn vows and ordination. He thought briefly of the party they would have had if he were still at home, at the Starved Rock State Park, imagining himself there in his regular clothes, toasting his friends and laughing about how old they all were. But Mepkin was his home now. Betty had sent an angel food cake that was shared by the

51

community and Robert smiled; she always baked angel food cake for family birthdays.

Mail was delivered on August 15th as it was every three months. His mother and brother had sent birthday cards, and there were a few from old friends. Jim's card mentioned how much he was enjoying his studies at the Jesuit facility in West Baden and what a good time he was having. Robert remembered visiting there with the family and the beautiful swimming pool as he thought, "What I would give for a swim!" They had plenty of water around Mepkin but swimming was not allowed. Betty had sent a present, too, one of Thomas Merton's recent books, *Thoughts in Solitude*. Apparently the abbot had given permission for the book to be delivered, but Robert would bring it to the library when he finished reading it. Although the book was about the pleasures of the solitary life and silent meditation, it began in a way that chilled him.

> There is no greater disaster in the spiritual life than to be immersed in unreality, for life is maintained and nourished in us by our vital relation with realities outside and above us.

Brother Robert's thoughts went to his own situation. He was happier than he had ever been, but at times he felt something like guilt, as if it were wrong for him to stay in this peaceful, mystical unreality, while others dealt with and suffered in the world.

Over the next few weeks those feelings grew and he encountered his first crisis as a monk. He was never sure what caused it: his twenty-first birthday, the intense summer heat or the small hopping chigger-sized bugs he picked up working in the flower gardens that itched like crazy. Whatever the cause, suddenly being so far from everything he grew up with, so immersed in a world of unreality, caused him to question his vocation and, for the first time, none of it made sense. He prayed for guidance and discernment but could not shake the feeling that something was wrong.

The early morning coffee was too weak or too strong, the novice master's teachings were boring, the weather was too hot or too cold, the chanting of the psalms was monotonous and his decision to seek the face of God spiraled downward into a bitter tolerance of monastic life. The brothers for whom he had developed an idyllic, holy love but whom he did not know at all in the conventional sense, suddenly irritated him. He grew tired of Brother Joachim's constantly pious face and wished he would display a normal emotion once in a while. Brother Gardner kept giving Robert the hardest, dirtiest work that made him rush to clean up before spiritual reading and left him stressed to the point that he could not focus on the readings at all. During free time he paced, wishing for a cigarette or anything that he remembered as "normal." He began to think he was crazy for ever coming here.

Finally he decided to talk to the novice master about it, even though the man's curt manner was starting to bother Robert, too. He knocked on his office door, entered when bidden, put his two index fingers to his lips and then brought them down to his chest, asking for permission to speak. The novice master nodded.

"I have a problem," Robert began, awkwardly. The novice master had, of course, noticed Robert's mood but knew this was part of a monk's growth as a contemplative. "I don't know what's wrong with me, Father. Nothing has changed, except that I was happy before and now I am not. This is the life I wanted, and still want, yet I feel depressed and irritated all the time. I don't know what it is, or how to fix it."

The novice master explained gently that there was a likely reason for Robert's feelings, that it was normal for monks to experience periods of doubt. In fact, they usually happen much sooner than this. "You've spent the better part of two whole years now on an extended 'honeymoon.'"

Robert found the metaphor interesting. It was true that he had been extremely happy ever since he came in. The novice master mentioned St. John's "Dark night of the soul."

"John wrote that in the dark night, 'God secretly teaches the soul and instructs it in perfection of love without its doing anything or understanding of what manner is this infused contemplation.' The experience is for many a necessary part of spiritual growth. It is a part of being 'nothing,' that Thomas Merton talked about. You may have reached the 'nothing' point, Brother Robert, and will hopefully soon climb up to the point St. John described when he said, 'they may arrive at the state of the perfect, which is that of the Divine union of the soul with God.'"

Robert jumped at the thought of his soul united with God, but was so depressed he could not see it in his future. "But I've had these feelings for so long, now."

"What, a few weeks? That's not a long time. It just seems that way because you're still young. Another man, 'St. Paul of the Cross,' had one that lasted forty-five years!"

Robert looked at him skeptically and the novice master smiled. "Presumably yours won't take that long. I suggest that you start listening more closely. Just listen. God is aware of your discomfort and will guide you out of it if you just listen for His voice. If it is truly a 'dark night,' you should emerge in a light greater than anything you have ever experienced. Some people pray to be brought into a dark night like this, just so they can be strengthened and emerge in the light of God's love."

Determined to get back to the peace he had come here to find, Robert took the words to heart and prayed devoutly to God and Mary Immaculate to help him lose his focus on himself, gain humility and be happy again. When he started to think about the things that irritated him, he closed his mind and listened instead for God's voice. Though wishing their schedule included more time for private contemplation, he used the time allocated to focus more intently on *Lectio Divina*, slow, sacred reading of the words of God. He found it remarkable that he could actually spend time pondering one word from the Gospels at a time or the beauty of a single phrase. And he prayed constantly for relief from the depression. "Speak, Lord, I want to serve you. Please let me know how to be happy again in your love." One day, in the middle of one of these desperate pleas for help, his answer came.

It was in his love for others that Robert found his way – in the path of service to his brothers. They were all looking for the same thing, and by that desire were bound to each other in search of a communion, a consciousness of God in which they could remain for all time. Rather than expecting things of others, he would, in some humble way, try to assist them in their search for God.

He became not only less needy but more helpful, thinking often of the novice master's typical response when asked to do something: "Here am I, Lord!" When Brother Gardner motioned for him to take a load of plants to the hothouse, Robert took Joachim's plants, too. When there was not enough food for the new men who had come in after him, Robert took less. His search for the spiritual union with God for himself and his brothers now occupied his entire mind, in choir, study and work, and, little by little, the depression lifted. The humidity dropped, the coffee was the right strength again, and he looked forward to seeing Brother Joachim's pious countenance each morning.

CHAPTER SEVEN – MEN, NOT SAINTS – 1958 – 1959

One day in the spring of, 1958, work in the vegetable garden was added to Robert's tasks. The garden, about two acres in size, produced enough potatoes, sweet potatoes, tomatoes, carrots, melons, squash, peas and carrots to supply the abbey year round. Robert joined the brothers in vegetables during planting and harvesting and the rest of the time tended to the flower gardens.

In September, his mother came for her annual visit. She did not have any significant news from home; most of Robert's friends were off at college and she was busy working. Finally, Betty gave up trying to talk and contented herself with walking at his side. On the last morning, they attended Mass together and shortly after, she left.

Soon the monks were occupied with prayers for the leader of the Catholic Church when October 9, 1958, the abbot announced that Pope Pius XII was dead. A picture of this pope had hung on classroom walls at St. Mary's elementary school and St. Bede Academy, and Robert and his friends had prayed for him every school day of their lives. Nineteen days after the pope's death, on October 28, white smoke at the Vatican announced the election of Cardinal Angelo Roncalli who would take the name Pope John XXIII. The choice was a surprise to many because Archbishop Giovanni Montini of Milan had long been the assumed successor. Because of conflicts with conservative Pope Pius XII, however, Montini had never been made a Cardinal. The new Pope John was seventy-six years old, and the other cardinals reasoned that, by the time he died, Montini would be a cardinal and would then become the next pope. In fact, one of Pope John XXIII's first acts was to raise Montini to the rank of cardinal. What the monks of Mepkin and most others did not expect was that this "interim" pope would capture the affection of the world's Catholics and non-Catholics with his personal warmth and kindness.

Robert had now been at the abbey for nearly two years and enveloped himself increasingly in the peace of work and silence. He observed his brothers in a different way now that he was committed to assist them, and developed a heightened sensitivity to their moods. He began to smile softly when others passed, rather than just nodding. One day, however, it seemed one of his smiles was misinterpreted. It was an afternoon not long after Christmas, and Robert had just finished work.

He was walking quietly and prayerfully through the woods, far from the abbey's buildings, enjoying the cool weather and the solitude. He heard footsteps behind him and turned to see Brother Melchior, a few years older than Robert, about the same height but little heavier, with a round face and bushy eyebrows. He hurried to catch up. Robert felt confused – the monks were not permitted to walk together. However, he had made his decision to be kind to every monk so he smiled and nodded.

They walked quietly for a time, and then Brother Melchior put his left arm around Robert's shoulder. Robert grew rigid as he noted a look in the other monk's face that made him feel sick; the look was lust, or something like it. Robert pulled away and started to walk faster, but Melchior moved with him and put his arm around him again, then stepped in front and blocked his way. As Melchior looked deeply into his eyes and moved closer, Robert stepped back sharply, jerked his hands up in front of him in a "stop!" motion, and ran back to the abbey buildings, not turning to even see if Melchior was behind him. Robert went straight to the church and knelt in prayer, wishing Vespers would start and return his sense of normalcy. He tried to analyze his own reaction, which was something akin to revulsion, yet he loved Brother Melchior as he did all of his brothers. He sat back in the pew and tried to intellectualize the experience, easier than dealing with it on an emotional level.

Was Brother Melchior a homosexual? Robert had never met one before, but of course had heard about them. He was curious, not personally but in general, about these people whom many perceived to be perverts with an aberrant affliction. But maybe Melchior was not homosexual at all; maybe he was just lonely. Hidden away as they were from the world and forbidden even to speak to each other, perhaps the other monk had acted on a simple longing for intimacy.

When the bells rang calling the monks to Vespers, Robert joined them in his choir stall but avoided eye contact with Brother Melchior. Days passed, and several times Melchior tried to approach, but Robert warned him away with a stern frown and shake of his head. The experience still made him feel sick. Not long after, however, he began to chastise himself for his own lack of compassion. Clearly, all the men at Mepkin had come here to seek God and therefore avoided sin and near occasions of sin. Homosexual or not, Melchior probably felt as disgusted with his own behavior as Robert felt toward him – perhaps more so. Who am I to judge? Am I God? No, I am as frail and weak as we all are. For the first time, he realized, "We are men, not saints." Then he thought more about the homosexual issue.

Robert understood how difficult it was for heterosexual men to give up contact with people, with women. He had had enough of his own urges, when in the company of young women in Peru, but believed that celibacy was a sacrifice for God and also that denying the feelings could lead to higher things. But St. Benedict was specific in Chapter Seven:

> As for the desires of the body, we must believe that God is always
> with us...We must then be on guard against any base desire... For
> this reason, the scripture warns us, 'Pursue not your lusts.'"

Getting back to his original mental discourse, Robert realized that if men like himself struggled with lust in an environment where women were almost never seen, how much more difficult the vow of celibacy would be for homosexuals, surrounded here by the gender to which they were naturally attracted. It was a comparatively enormous sacrifice and Brother Robert began to feel compassion for men of that persuasion who were called to monastic life. He began to look at Melchior directly again when he saw him, noting the intense sadness on the other monk's face.

One morning after Mass he nodded for Melchior to walk with him. Melchior hesitated for a moment and then hastily followed. They stopped at the statue of the merciful Christ that stood atop a pedestal of bricks, Jesus' hands extended in mercy. Robert looked at Melchior closely, noting the guilt and sadness in his face. Melchior opened his palm toward Robert with the index finger pointed back to his own chest: "Forgive me." Robert was moved with compassion; he remembered hearing somewhere that God not only forgives, but forgets. Determined to do the same, he knelt alongside his brother and prayed. The incident was forgotten, and soon life at the monastery became normal again.

Information about the burgeoning civil rights movement appeared on the bulletin board outside the refectory where the abbot posted articles he thought were relevant. Robert was not sure why he cared so much about this issue, but the evilness of prejudice touched him strongly. It seemed bizarre to him that people could be separated and even persecuted based on the color of their skin. His sensitivity was exacerbated by the abbot's frequent reminders that Mepkin Abbey was originally a plantation worked by Negro slaves. The monks shared the past of the land on which they lived, good or bad, because they shared in what the land offered in the present.

For the most part, though, Robert was occupied with the news that he would soon make his simple profession, or temporary vows. In January, he wrote to his mother about it.

> I asked Rev. Father for a definite date so I could tell you, so it is set for the feast of St. Joseph, March 19, 1959. I am looking forward to it with great joy...
>
> Be sure to unite with me on the feast of St. Joseph in my profession. You are giving your baby to God (what a big baby, too.) Remember that our Blessed Mother offered her Son on Calvary and there would have been no earthly joy in that; it was the will of God. That knowledge alone upheld our Mother. Our offering is indeed much less but united to Jesus and Mary they have real meaning and worth. There can be no doubt also that you have a real part in my profession just as our Blessed Mother had a real part in Calvary and that through the church my little profession has a real part in Calvary.
>
> I got your card the other night with the $5.00. Thanks loads. Turned it in to Rev. Father and asked to have a Mass said for our Blessed Mother's intentions then told Her to be sure to take care of us all. Also the Mass this morning was for Her intentions then I asked Her to take good care of you and Jim and a whole bunch of others. As you well know, I learned to take a Mother for all she is worth. Strangely enough, they seem to like it that way, at least I always got plenty out of you with a great big smile, too. If it worked with you I figure it will work with our Blessed Mother all the more. Sad to say I fear I don't thank Her much more than I ever thanked you, but Mothers also seem to understand that...
>
> Love in our Infant Savior and His Most Blessed Mother,
> fr. M Robert OCSO

News from the Holy Catholic Church was read at chapter meetings. On January 25, 1959, Pope John XXIII, who was expected only to maintain the status quo of the traditional Church, had called for an *aggiornamento*, the first Church Council to be held since the First Vatican Council nearly ninety years earlier. Trained as a historian and previously assigned to various countries as Apostolic Visitor and then Apostolic Delegate, John XXIII had seen firsthand the changes in the world and saw the need for a renewal to address them. The council would cover a wide range of topics including developing countries, arms negotiations, changing women's roles, civil rights and the need for greater awareness of human dignity. Perhaps considering his own mortality, the pope pushed for haste in the preparations, but still the council would not begin for three years, in the fall of 1962. The reason was the enormous preparation that included thousands of documents on issues and proposals. Little known at the time, "Vatican II" would reshape the face of Catholicism and change the lives of tens of thousands of priests, brothers and nuns, including Jesuit priests and Trappist monks.

After petitioning the abbot and waiting anxiously for the community vote, Robert was accepted and permitted to take temporary vows. It changed things, and not only inwardly. A full-length black scapular and black belt was added to his white novice tunic, and he felt a real part of the monastic community. He tried to describe it in a letter to his mother.

> There isn't much I can say beyond the fact that it was the happiest day of my life and I am still very happy and know I will always be. I now belong entirely to God and though I go on doing the same things and thinking the same thoughts and having the same distinctions (plus a few new ones as always) somehow there is a difference. I was happy here before but am even more so now.
>
> The profession took place in chapter, I guess it was about 8:30 or 9:00 a.m. Placing my hands folded in Rev. Father's while kneeling before him sitting in his abbatial throne, I promised him and his successors obedience according to the rule of St. Benedict. Then I read, standing in the middle of chapter, a longer form of the profession and signed it and gave it to Rev. Father.
>
> Then I knelt down before him again and he took off our novice's cloak, cincture and scapular and put on me a black scapular and leather belt and cowl which I have been swimming in ever since. I suppose we will have these habits off for the summer by the time you come so you won't get to see it. It is very big and the only measurements needed for it are the height and the shoulders. The sleeves go down to about a foot from the floor and are a foot and a half wide. It isn't a misfit – that just happens to be our style.

He would repeat those vows annually and was bound by them unless released. The fact that he had been permitted to make them meant that the others had accepted him, at least for now. From Robert's perspective, the fact that he requested to take the vows also meant he had decided to stay.

CHAPTER EIGHT –
SEASONS – 1960 – 1961

The seasons of the Church passed with the seasons of South Carolina as the monks fasted through Advent, awaiting the birth of the Christ child and, at Christmas, celebrated His birth. Later, they fasted through Lent, suffered with Jesus in His passion and then woke to praise the risen Christ at Easter. Through it all, Robert continued to love this group of silent men. In a bizarre yet beautiful paradox, they shared almost every moment of their lives while living in complete solitude.

Changes happened here on the inside, he realized, while the external person hardly seemed different at all. Robert's ability to sense his Creator grew steadily as memories of the outside world faded, leaving his mind free for prayer and contemplation. At times, he felt the presence close by, like the passion he had described to Joe Story in what seemed now to be a long-ago world. Too quickly, though, it would slip away, leaving him hungrily watchful for the next glimpse or the next whisper. He prayed fervently, focused on this search, desiring only to learn to live every moment in God's presence and confident that He would come. All Robert had to do was wait and be watchful.

Though the world outside the abbey was for the most part hidden from the monks, occasional news items on the bulletin board disturbed Brother Robert's peace. On February 1, 1960, just a few hours from Mepkin, four young Negro men sat down at a whites-only lunch counter in Greensboro, NC. Their brave action started a wave of sit-ins across the south. It occurred to Robert, now twenty-two years old, that those students were all younger than he was, and their courage impressed him.

In May, when letters were delivered, there was one from his mother who wrote of the escalating "Cold War," her fear of Communism and of

Cuba's apparent partnership with the Russians. She reminded Robert of his elementary school days when the children hid under their desks during air raid drills. His father had designated a section of their basement as a bomb shelter back then and Betty kept it stocked with canned goods and jugs of water. As she wrote in a stream of consciousness, she went back further in time and described her feelings when she saw pictures of the destruction of the atomic bombs the U.S. dropped on Hiroshima and Nagasaki, killing hundreds of thousands of people and leveling the two cities. She was afraid now, more than she had been then.

Brother Robert felt a sharp twinge of guilt that, because both he and Jim were gone, their mother was alone. He felt better, though, when she went on to say she was "seeing" someone. His name was Gail Gurnett. Robert wondered about the spelling, thinking it should be "Gale," but she had written it clearly. The fact that she planned to bring the man to Mepkin meant the relationship must be serious. How could she replace her husband, his father, with a stranger? He quickly matured in his observation, however, when he thought about how long his mother had been alone.

When she came in early September with her new friend, Robert could not help but stare. A few inches taller than his father, Gail was still shorter than Betty. He was stocky, with a square angular face; his eyeglasses had dark upper rims, giving the illusion of dark eyebrows and he wore his brownish-gray hair in a short flat-top that gave him a military look. Robert observed that he was pleasant and doted on Betty. Though still feeling awkward at the concept of his mother dating, Robert wondered to himself if they would marry, assuming they probably would.

On November 7th at chapter, Robert learned that monks voted. The abbot reviewed presidential candidates and issues and, remembering his father's patriotism, Dick paid close attention so he could make a good decision. They set up a voting booth the next day in the church. Everyone who wanted to vote could do so between breakfast and dinner, then one of the lay brothers would drive their ballots into nearby Monck's Corner. Robert had always been a strong Republican, following in his father's footsteps. He thought of the Democrats as "the war party" because they were in office when World War II and Korea started. Robert was grateful for the abbot's political commentaries, without which he might have voted along his family's party lines for the Republican candidate, Richard M. Nixon.

While Nixon stressed a continuation of the policies of the Dwight D. Eisenhower years, Kennedy campaigned on the promise of change. Kennedy's fresh new attitude, his Catholic faith and his relative youth formed the basis for Robert's decision. He grimaced as he cast his ballot, though, imagining his father turning over in his grave.

The day after the election, the abbot posted two articles on the bulletin board at the entrance to the refectory. It was the closest election in American history – Kennedy had won the popular vote by fewer than 100,000 votes. The close results made Robert aware of how important the votes of a small number of people, like the monks at Mepkin Abbey, could be. He wrote to his mother about the experience.

> Yes, our voting does seem strange... We have about forty-three votes here at Mepkin and the politicians try to get them in any reasonable and "honest" way they can. Dom James of Gethsemani always jokes about the politicians around there because Gethsemani has a couple hundred votes... We have a problem here having our own precinct and due to the fact that we are the first ones finished voting. We get our name in the paper for having the first returns. This year Rev. Father put a clipping on the bulletin board headlined "Monks vote 38 – 5 for Kennedy." It also told that last time we voted, I forget how much, for Ike. Rev. Father had held back the returns so we wouldn't be first but we were third anyway and I guess it was good news.
>
> I agree with Jim. I think it is wonderful to get a Catholic into the White House. Not that it will be a profit to the Catholics but just on the principle of the thing. Also of course, if Kennedy is a good Catholic as I hear that he is, he will be honest and upright and he is supposed to be a good man all the way around. However, I liked Nixon, too. It's true that anything that goes badly will be blamed by some on Kennedy and on the Church but no matter how badly things go many people, especially in the South, are going to find out that the Church isn't mixed up in politics and isn't possibly half as bad as they have been led to believe.
>
> It is truly amazing what these people think of Catholics... Rev. Father said that a store owner told one of our family brothers, who delivers our eggs, that the people around here are all scared now, wondering what will happen with a Catholic President. I'm sure they're not scared about some foreign policy – they're scared what's going to happen to them, what kind of changes the Church will make. They can't be too scared because S.C. went for Kennedy, but these people have very mysterious notions about Catholics.

In late November, he wrote of a new monk. "We have a new choir postulant and he is right next to me in choir. I noticed him shivering this morning at the night office but at prime he had his coat on. He is a Negro priest from Detroit. He was born and raised in Charleston so he should be used to the weather."

He also wished his mother a joyful Christmas, responding to her comments from her most recent letter.

> Yes it is truly nice to have had so many happy Christmases and
> their memory always fills me with joy. I think they were so
> happy because we truly knew what Christmas meant... Before,
> our joy was in what we had. Now our joy must be both in
> what we have in our Christian faith and in what we hope
> for. Someday we shall be together again in the possession of
> unimaginable joy and that, without any danger of ending. Our
> true joy now is at Mass and at the crib with Mary and the Infant
> Jesus.
> I hope that you will have a very joyful Christmas. I will
> be praying for you, especially at Midnight Mass and Holy
> Communion and it is there that we will all be together, you and
> Dad and Jane and Jim and I.
> Love in our coming Savior and His Holy Mother,
> fr. M. Robert OCSO

In January the weather grew cold and a severe ice storm hit South Carolina, so bad that Mepkin lost many of its trees. The southern yellow pine was not strong enough to stand up to the weight of the ice that took off branches and even the tops of some trees. It was the kind of damage that would retard their growth and leave the trees open to insects that would eventually destroy them. The monks would soon look to expand their egg production to make up for the lost income.

Robert remained content in his chosen lifestyle but soon changes in the Church would change him, too. It started on May 15, 1961, when Pope John XXIII issued his first major social encyclical, *Mater et Magistra*. In it, the pope spoke to the need for the Church to help people in a real and physical way, referring back to the historical Jesus:

> He showed His concern for the material welfare of His people
> when, seeing the hungry crowd of His followers, He was moved
> to exclaim: "I have compassion on the multitude." And these
> were no empty words of our divine Redeemer. Time and again
> He proved them by His actions, as when He miraculously
> multiplied bread to alleviate the hunger of the crowds.

The world had changed greatly, and Pope John emphasized those changes as a "radical transformation." As he listened to the reading at dinner, Robert realized that most of the changes mentioned had occurred during his own lifetime: nuclear energy, advances in chemistry, growth of automation, modernization of agriculture, the "easing" of communications through radio and television, faster transportation and the initial conquest of space. Social advances included social insurance and social security, labor unions involved in social and economic issues, increased education, breaking down of class barriers and a keener interest in world affairs by greater numbers of people. The pope also talked about the rise in the world's population.

> According to sufficiently reliable statistics the next few decades
> will see a very great increase in human population, whereas
> economic development will proceed at a slower rate. Hence,
> we are told, if nothing is done to check this rise in population,
> the world will be faced in the not too distant future with an
> increasing shortage in the necessities of life.

Was Pope John considering reversing the Church's stance on artificial contraception? As Robert listened, however, it became apparent the pontiff was only talking about reaffirming the Church's stance against it. Robert was impressed with the pope's perspective on the depressed agricultural sector, poor rural workers, unequal conditions in developing countries and the need for international cooperation in addressing those needs.

Early summer passed without significant world news and Robert continued to love his peaceful home. In mid-August, world news included the fact that Communist East Germany had begun construction on a wall between West and East Germany. The Berlin Wall, guarded by armed soldiers who shot and killed would-be defectors, would become one of the Cold War's most chilling symbols.

In October, 1961, Robert's mother and Gail Gurnett drove from Illinois to visit. Betty hesitated then blurted out the news. "We're getting married!" They planned the wedding for December. Off and on during the visit, Robert felt sad about his father, but sensed that this was the best thing for his mother. Gail told him that he had four daughters, two of whom were nuns.

"Finally there are more members of religious orders in the family," said Robert with a shy smile. He almost wished he could attend the wedding, but of course he could not.

Gail nodded and smiled back, pleased that Robert referred to them as one family. The following February 15th, Robert's mail included a thick envelope of wedding pictures. After an initial sadness as he again remembered his father, he smiled. Betty wore an off-white knee-length dress with a matching veiled hat, and Gail looked like he had when they visited, in a dark suit, white shirt and black tie. Father Gildea conducted the wedding ceremony at St. Mary's in front of several of the couple's friends. Robert's brother Jim went too. She also wrote that they were going to build a house. In the meantime, Gail had moved into her apartment.

Brother Robert wrote back, sent prayers for a blessed life together and said he looked forward to seeing them both again in the fall. Then his thoughts turned to Lent and springtime and he studied harder than ever as he looked forward to taking his solemn, permanent vows.

In mid-May, 1962, Robert's mail included an invitation to his brother's ordination. Again, of course he could not go but he sent his brother a note addressed to "Father Jim Sanders," and wished him a happy and blessed life as a Jesuit priest. The next batch of mail had a letter from his mother, describing the ordination. Robert got the impression that she had finally gotten over any sadness about her sons in religious life, and had developed significant pride in what they were doing. In fact, she was downright enthusiastic.

"Ordination is even a bigger event than I realized," she wrote. "I've never been to one before. Jim had a lot of guests, including Gail and his family plus several of your aunts, uncles and cousins. The following Sunday, Jim said his first Mass at St. Mary's in Peru and we had a reception for him at the Parish hall. It was wonderful! Your brother is going to come with us when we visit in the fall, and we'll bring pictures. I can't wait for us all to come to your ordination someday soon! Love, Mom."

Other mail included birthday cards reminding Robert that he had turned twenty-five. One was from Jim Wimbiscus who was stationed at Fort Bragg in North Carolina, just a few hours away. He wondered if he could come to visit. Brother Robert was happy when the abbot allowed it.

A week later, on a Saturday, the two old friends shook hands and hugged warmly, then stood back from each other, noting changes in their appearances. Robert's hair had recently been tonsured, and Jim looked about the same except for a short Army haircut. Robert was surprised and a bit disappointed that Jim wore civilian clothes; he had wanted to see his friend in uniform.

They went to Mass, sitting together in the visitor's section, and afterwards went for a walk. Jim was a quiet man himself, so the walk was peaceful as they caught up. He was a lawyer now, and had received a draft notice as soon as he graduated. He joined the Army rather than being drafted so he could be in an officer's program.

"What about you?" asked Jim. "Are you still going to be a priest?"

"I'll be working on that after I take my solemn vows. I still have so much to study." Robert grinned and looked at Jim sideways, then added, "And a lot of it's in Latin!" They laughed and reminisced about Father Peter's tirades.

Robert felt even more peaceful than usual with his friend at his side. It was the first conversation he had had in years with anyone besides the novice master, the abbot and his mother. He began to realize that he missed the company of real friends who knew each other in the context of the real world.

Then Jim brought up the war. Robert was aware of a conflict in Vietnam but had not heard much about it. Jim explained that, at first, President Kennedy had only sent equipment, military advisors, support personnel, plus helicopters and pilots, but about six months ago he had sent combat troops to fight the Vietcong and clear vegetation alongside roads. Robert looked seriously at his friend. "It sounds like it could be bad. Will you have to go?"

"Anything's possible, but I'm only signed up for two more years, but hopefully we'll be out of Vietnam by then. I guess monks don't have to worry about that?"

"I'm exempt, classified ministerial, 4-D. We never leave the monastery grounds, never mind going the other side of the world!"

Jim laughed, and then studied his friend. "Are you as happy as you seem? Was this the right choice for you?"

Robert was quiet for a while before responding. "I am happy. It's become my home, and these monks are my family. But sometimes I feel a little selfish because I love it so much."

Jim looked at him questioningly and Robert explained. "When I read about the civil rights struggle, for example, every once in a while I think I should be out there doing something."

"Civil Rights bothers me, too," said Jim. "You remember the racism at home, don't you?"

Robert shook his head. He had never seen a Negro in Peru, Illinois.

"There's a reason for that. There used to be some kind of ordinance, or maybe just an agreement among the hotels and motels, that colored people couldn't stay overnight in our town."

Robert raised his eyebrows as Jim explained how his father, Judge Wimbiscus, had invited a Negro football player from the University of Iowa to speak at the Hall High School football banquet. Duke Slater was one of the first Negro players in professional football; he was later inducted into the football hall of fame. But when he came to give that speech in 1949 he had to stay at the Wimbiscus' house because they wouldn't let him stay in a hotel.

"Wow," said Robert. "Stupid, isn't it?"

"Yes it is," agreed his friend. Then he switched back to the discussion of Robert's commitment to the abbey. "So it bothers you that you're not out in the world working for a cause or something?"

Robert shrugged and said softly, "Yeah, sometimes, a little."

"Well, if you believe in the power of prayer, which I certainly do, then you are doing something. I mean, don't you pray for people all the time?"

Robert nodded thoughtfully. "Yes, we do."

He looked at his friend and remembered how supportive he had always been, and was being right at this moment. Then they both realized it was time for him to go. Brother Robert put his arm around his old friend's shoulder and walked him back to his car.

The warmth of Jim's visit caused Brother Robert to reexamine his relationship with his brothers at Mepkin. The medieval European culture of total silence did not encourage or even permit friendships like he had in high school. An ideal imposed on them externally, from outside and above, made all their decisions for them and there seemed to be little individuality. But then, he thought, that's the point. Men who entered here literally lost themselves to God, to the monastery, to the ideal of constant prayer.

September approached, a beautiful and welcome time as the humidity dropped and the temperatures grew cooler. Brother Robert was excited about the upcoming visit of his mother, especially because his brother was coming with her. When they arrived, he hugged his mother and shook Gail's hand, then stood back, grinning at Jim's roman collar; it looked good on him. The two brothers embraced in a warm hug.

Jim Sanders with Brother Mary Robert, 1962

He and Jim walked ahead together as Betty and Gail deliberately lagged behind to give the boys time to talk. Jim reviewed his Jesuit training as they pieced together how long it had been since they had seen each other; it had been more than six years.

"This might sound strange for me to say, but you've really grown up, 'Brother Robert.'"

"Yeah, 'Father Jim,'" murmured Robert, looking again at Jim's collar. "My hair's even starting to get a little gray."

Jim smiled at his little brother. "My hair is a little grayer than before, too. And the hairline at the temples isn't going anywhere but back."

"Mine is the same, but I don't think either of them will recede much more. Dad's was about like ours when he died."

Thinking of their father brought on a moment of sadness, and the two brothers became silent.

"Do you miss him?" asked Robert, already knowing the answer.

"All the time."

Then Jim changed the subject to the upcoming Second Vatican Council and discussed his hopes for changes in the rules against celibacy for priests and for birth control to be permitted, especially since now the pill was available and many women were already taking it.

"Let's hope Good Pope John is as good as we think he is," said Jim, and then changed the subject. "How are your studies going?"

Robert raised his eyebrows with a smile. "Pretty well, actually."

"Really?" Jim had expressed more surprise than he meant to. He tried to backtrack on the tone of the comment but was awkward about it, unusual for Jim. "I mean, school was never one of your strong points."

"It's OK," Robert reassured his brother. "You're right. It's easier to focus here because there are no distractions. I like studying about monasticism and after my solemn vows, it's all philosophy, theology and other topics related to the priesthood. I think I'll like that even more. I'm becoming quite intellectual."

At that, they both laughed.

The visit passed quickly, but Robert had to get back to his monastic duties. Jim promised to come again soon, but Robert did not expect to see him for some time.

CHAPTER NINE –
THE COUNCIL YEARS – 1962 - 1965

Easter of 1962 was an uneasy time as *frater* Mary Robert anticipated making his solemn vows the following month. Final vows with their sense of permanence and definitiveness brought on some real angst because there was a clearer feeling than ever of making a decision between two worlds. The lifetime commitment he would soon make to the monastery was both exhilarating and frightening. At one point, he thought he might be getting cold feet, like a groom about to be married.

The long-anticipated day finally came just after Easter, and Betty and Gail were permitted to attend. The ceremony was a High Mass officiated by the abbot in the symbols of his position, a miter and shepherd's crook. At the end of the Mass, as Trappist monks had done for centuries before him, Brother Robert walked forward alone with a signed copy of the vows that he presented to the abbot, who nodded for Robert to place them on the altar. Then he lay face down on the floor, the top of his head pressed against the altar's bottom step, focusing on the primary responsibility of a monk, which was to love with all his heart. Betty later told him that she wept with joy and sadness as her youngest son made his final vows.

"I, *frater* Mary Robert, promise my stability, my conversion of life and my obedience until death in accordance with the Rule of St. Benedict, abbot. I do this before God and all his saints, in this monastery of Our Lady of Mepkin, of the Cistercian Order of the Strict Observance, constructed in honor of the Blessed and ever Virgin Mary, Mother of God, and in the presence of the abbot of this monastery."

They were the most meaningful words he had ever spoken. He had made the decision and was finally and formally a Trappist, part of a community that would forever be his home. The abbot blessed the cowl of a solemnly professed monk, and clothed Brother Robert in it as the other monks, beloved brothers in Christ, extended their hands over him and chanted.

God with us, God in us, we are the body of Christ.

His monastic milestones achieved, there was only one thing left for him to accomplish – becoming a priest. Along with Brother Joachim and several others, he began classes for his ordination, which he hoped to celebrate in three and a half years. He found he loved theology and philosophy, was determined to understand the basis of his faith and the thought processes of great thinkers. These classes were almost like those in the outside world. Later they studied dogma, moral issues, canon law, liturgy and the history of the Church.

Robert felt more confident now that he was professed, feeling more responsible to his brothers. He took greater notice of the class differences between lay brothers and the choir monks, something that had always bothered him. One day in the scriptorium, a young lay monk came in, in his brown habit. Robert asked without words if he could help, and the monk wrote out the name of a philosophy book that evidently was not in the lay brothers' scriptorium. Just then, Brother Librarian came up, shaking his head and wagging his finger; lay brothers were not permitted access to the choir monks' books. The lay monk shook his head sadly and started to walk away, but Robert, tired of this treatment of one of their own, got the book from the shelf and handed it to him. The librarian scowled at Robert and stormed off. Robert had no pangs about what he had done, however, and he would do it again if the situation arose.

On October 11, 1962, the much-anticipated first session of the Second Vatican Council began in Rome. Decisions made there would change the face of Catholicism, and not only the liturgy, rules and regulations – it would outline a whole new approach to the world.

Just days after it began, however, the Cuban Missile Crisis overshadowed the Council's activities. It was serious enough that the abbot posted articles on the bulletin board every day because the monks' prayers were badly needed. This was not a threat thousands of miles away; Soviet missile sites had been discovered ninety miles from U.S. shores. The reaction of U.S. citizens was described as "electric tension" as schools closed and churches remained open all day and all night. Calling the Soviet missiles "a clandestine, reckless, and provocative threat to world peace," President Kennedy demanded that they be dismantled. Moscow's response challenged the right of the U.S. to blockade Cuba, threatening the possibility of an all-out atomic war. As Robert read details of this deadliest of dances, the crisis ended, twelve days after it began, when Soviet Premier Nikita Khrushchev ordered the dismantling of the Cuban missiles in exchange for a U.S. pledge not to invade Cuba.

News of the Church was most applicable to the monks' lives and everyone paid close attention to the details of papal documents, especially now that the Second Vatican Council had started. On April 11, 1963, Pope John XXIII issued a major social encyclical, *Pacem in Terris*, Peace on Earth. In it, the pope called for the creation of institutions to promote justice and peace and respect human dignity. He recognized legal, political, economic and social rights of all people, referring specifically to the right to a just wage, the right to emigrate and immigrate and the right of political refugees to migrate. The pope also supported the United Nations and called for an end to the arms race in a strong statement. "Justice, then, and right reason, and consideration for human dignity and life demand that the arms race cease." As Robert reflected on this encyclical, he thought back to *Mater et Magister* that had been released the previous spring. Both documents focused clearly on the role of the Church in helping the poor and oppressed, and Robert foresaw an overall change coming. The role of the laity, another major topic of discussion at the first session, was another sign of the changing Church. Lay people were now considered part of the Church, co-responsible with priests to bring the Gospel to the people. It would not be long before professional lay people worked in parishes, taking over positions traditionally held by priests and nuns.

Other secular news spoke to Robert, too, as in April, 1963, when Martin Luther King wrote his "Letter from a Birmingham Jail." In it, Dr. King criticized the churches for their lack of support for the civil rights movement. His words resonated.

> In the midst of a mighty struggle to rid our nation of racial and economic injustice, I have heard so many ministers say, "Those are social issues with which the Gospel has no real concern."

Robert was certain that the Gospel did, in fact, have concern with social issues, but the abbot and novice master continued to assure the monks of the value of prayer, the greatest contribution they could make. But, Robert wondered, was prayer really enough?

Just before Pentecost, the abbot reported the sad news that Pope John XXIII was dying of stomach cancer. On his deathbed, the pope expressed his hopes for the future and a message that seemed to speak directly to Brother Robert: "It is not the Gospel that changes; it is we who are beginning to understand it better."

Soon after, Good Pope John died, and white smoke from the Vatican on June 21st announced that a new pope had been named. The successor was not a surprise – Cardinal Giovanni Montini took the name Pope Paul VI. Montini's father had been a staunch advocate of social justice, and Giovanni followed in his footsteps. He shared many of John XXIII's modern ideas and committed himself to continuing the work begun by the late pope. Throughout his papacy, he would focus on helping the poor and oppressed.

On September 29, 1963, Vatican II began its second session, and this time, lay people and non-Catholic observers were invited. Pope Paul VI opened the second session with a memorable address in which he begged the pardon of non-Catholics for any fault Catholics may have had for the divided state of Christianity. Robert looked forward to news from the Council, wondering now what changes might affect the monasteries.

News on the bulletin board, the 23rd of November, stopped the monks on their way into Vespers. President Kennedy had been assassinated in Dallas while he was riding in the back seat of a convertible with the top down. The president and his wife, Jackie, were waving to the people along with Texas Governor John Connally who rode in the front passenger seat. Just after they entered Dealey Plaza, a gunman fired three shots. The First Lady was not harmed and the governor was wounded, but the President of the United States was dead. The nation, and many of the monks, went into shock. Two days later, the assassin, Lee Harvey Oswald, was shot at close range and killed, on his way to the Dallas County jail. The president, assassinated? How could such a thing even happen?

Trying now to block out news from the world, Robert did his best to immerse himself in studies for ordination. However, he could not ignore the changes that continued to come from Vatican II. The abbot gave a summary of recent documents and announced that the full texts were in the library.

In *Sacrosanctum concilium*, "Constitution on the Sacred Liturgy," the Council made key strategic changes to the Mass, dictating "full, conscious and active participation" on the part of the faithful with songs and prayers. Lay people would become Eucharistic Ministers and lectors. Altars were to be moved out, away from the wall, and priests would now stand behind them, facing the congregation rather than with their backs to the people. Instead of Latin, the Mass would now be said in the language of the people, so in the U.S., prayers and hymns would soon be in English, even at the abbey. Robert was not sure how he felt about that decision, as the Latin Mass was part of the mystical, medieval incense-filled world that he loved, but still, he thought about how much better it would be if all the faithful of all the churches could understand what was being said. Even the music would soon expand from traditional organ hymns to folk music accompanied by a guitar.

Robert brought back an old memory of a Catechism diagram and realized happily that the steps that had separated Christ from the people were being removed.

On the work side of the monks' duties, he found himself more frustrated with pressures as the abbey's products grew into serious business. One day when he was loading flowers into the truck to be sold, the bells rang for free time and he brushed the dirt off his hands and started to walk toward the dormitory. Brother Gardner followed behind him with a purchase order in his hand, pointing emphatically to the delivery date, today's date. Robert shook his head; he was looking forward to the small amount of time he had for private meditation. Brother Gardner shook his head even more strongly and pointed him back to the truck – the flowers had to be delivered today. For a moment, Robert had a flash of anger and turned to stalk away, but his vows of obedience referred to not just the abbot but to all senior monks, so he reluctantly finished the load.

Part of the papal instructions to the monasteries was to keep the monks more apprised of world news, so dinner readings now included the writings of contemporary religious activists. Dr. Martin Luther King, Jr., who had stepped out as leader of the civil rights movement, was one of them. The January reading was from Dr. King's first book, *Stride toward Freedom: the Montgomery Story*, in which Dr. King related the religious experience he had the night he was released from jail. Brother Robert never forgot his words.

> At that moment I experienced the presence of the Divine as I
> had never experienced Him before. It seemed as though I could
> hear the quiet assurance of an inner voice saying: "Stand up for
> righteousness, stand up for truth; and God will be at your side
> forever."

Robert pondered Rev. King's words as he prayed, wondering about his own decision. How were the monks standing up for righteousness or truth, hidden here in the monastery? The answer came through Mary who reassured him in the night that, no matter what he thought, Mepkin was his home and he would spend his life, die, and be buried here. After a while, the questions passed and he slept peacefully again.

In the library that now contained Catholic periodicals, Brother Robert read more about Dr. King's struggle with his own vocation. King had not sought leadership in the civil rights movement but felt that God had directed him, that he had no choice. How would it feel to love the life you lived, yet be called to follow God's will in a different direction?

Mail was delivered to the monks now as soon as it was received, and in the spring, Robert received a letter from his mother that included a clipping about the wedding of Jim Wimbiscus. It was September before he got around to writing, sending the letter to the most recent Army address he had for Jim.

Dear Jim,

Congratulations to you and your wife on your marriage last spring! My Mother sent me a newspaper clipping about it some time ago and I have been wanting to write this to you ever since. I'm sure you will forgive a monk for not being quite on time.

The picture of your bride (with the clipping from the paper) looks very beautiful. I am so glad for you both. Of course, I can't give you a wedding present, being a poor monk (in more ways than one), but I assure you of my prayers that you will have a long, happy and holy life together, living out the great mystery that you have entered into. As St. Paul teaches us, the mystery of married love is no less than to imitate and exemplify the love of Christ for His Church when He laid down His life for her. I will also pray that you will have a family to be proud of.

I have been wanting to write to you ever since you came down to see me several years ago and the only reason that I didn't is that we are not supposed to write letters very often. I'm glad now to have a good reason to write to you. Needless to say, I enjoyed your visit very much, getting the news from you about some of my other old friends, but especially just being able to talk to you for a while again. Since you are still so close maybe you will come down again some time? I hope so. If you do it would be good to let me know ahead of time. I'm always here but with 3,000 acres it's not always possible to say exactly where. Also enjoy getting your Christmas cards, and hearing what you are doing. Wish I could answer them, but I assure you that you are in my thoughts and prayers.

It sounds like you are making a career of the army, or at least you are in longer than originally planned I think. It ought to be pretty good for one in your position. But then I guess a lawyer is usually in a pretty good position. Don't suppose there is much danger of you getting sent into battle. They can hardly use a lawyer on the front lines. That is not the way they prove things over there.

There is not much new around here, except for the changes in the liturgy, which however are really important. We have daily concelebrated High Mass at which all the non-priest choir and brothers receive Communion under both species. Am hoping to be able to sing the office in English later on. I'm still studying theology and will be for a few years.

Please keep me in your prayers, and I assure you I will do the same for you, both for your family and also for your work in the service of our Country.

Your friend, in Jesus,
Br. M. Robert OCSO

As he read the letter before mailing it, Robert realized again how much he missed the company of real friends. He was glad that the Vatican Council had led to easing of the rule of strict silence at Trappist monasteries. Perhaps now he could get to know some of his brothers in a real way.

The fourth and final session of Vatican II began in September, 1965. To the disappointment of many Catholics, including Brother Robert, a major issue was removed from consideration: the Church's ban on birth control. Instead, the pope created a commission of clerical and lay experts to study it. It made no sense to Robert. With overpopulation and related problems in the world, why would contraception not be an option?

Not long after, the Church issued several documents, the most important of which, especially to the Religious Orders, was *Perfectae Caritatis,* the "Decree on Renewal of Religious Life." The monks listened intently as this letter was read, as it directed religious orders to research their roots and return to the original intentions of their founders. They waited anxiously to hear what it said about monastic life and breathed a collective sigh of relief when the document not only permitted but honored their vocation.

Communities which are entirely dedicated to contemplation, so that their members in solitude and silence, with constant prayer and penance willingly undertaken, occupy themselves with God alone, retain at all times, no matter how pressing the needs of the active apostolate may be, an honorable place in the Mystical Body of Christ, whose "members do not all have the same function" (Rom. 12:4)....

The monks were not left without changes to make, however. They, too, needed to adjust themselves to the ideals laid out by the council.

...Retaining, therefore, the characteristics of the way of life
proper to them, they should revive their ancient traditions of
service and so adapt them to the needs of today that monasteries
will become institutions dedicated to the edification of the
Christian people.

The abbot began a series of discussions in the chapter room to determine
how Mepkin Abbey should change to follow the intent of the Second Vatican
Council. It was through these discussions that Robert first realized how
polarized the monks were in their views, some close-minded and conservative
and others extremely liberal and open to new ideas. Though he had always
seen himself as a conservative Republican, he was surprised to find himself
on the liberal side of many issues. In the first discussions about how they
would reform monastic life at Mepkin, Robert proposed adding additional
time for contemplation, pointing out that the balance between work and
contemplation was off. "We've gotten too caught up in earning a living and
forgotten our purpose here." He spent his free time for about a week, writing
a document that supported his point of view, then posted it on the bulletin
board, smiling as he watched the others try to figure out who wrote it. Robert
was still not what one would call a scholar, and no one ever suspected he was
the author.

A few weeks later, the Vatican issued additional documents. *Dei Verbum*,
"The Dogmatic Constitution on Divine Revelation" called for a more modern
approach to the study of Scripture. God wanted people to know Him and
understand His Word in a real way. In another, *Gaudium et Spes*, "Pastoral
Constitution on the Church in the Modern World," Catholics were directed to
live their faith openly and bear witness to it through the example of their lives.
The term "social justice" began to be used to describe active work on behalf of
the poor and oppressed.

The Second Vatican Council solemnly ended on December 8, 1965 and
Robert reflected on its results. Beyond anything he could have imagined,
it had resulted in a strategic change to the mentality of the Church. When
Robert was growing up, Catholicism was "inside," protecting its priests and
sisters from the "outside" world. Now the focus was shifted, with the laity
more involved in the Church and the religious more directly involved in
society. Vatican II really had turned everything inside out.

CHAPTER TEN –
CHANGES AND CHOICES –
1966 – 1967

After the Council ended, like religious leaders around the world, the abbot held ongoing group discussions about how the monastery should change to follow it. Our Lady of Mepkin Abbey became more focused on political and social issues and the abbot led discussions on how they could become more responsible to the poor. Also, they would make more room to welcome outside people for retreats and open up their prayer services to others. The monks were Christians, and as such were part of the world. Robert had not felt part of the world for a long time.

A new schedule for Liturgy of the Hours was issued that eliminated Prime and included a forty-minute "optional siesta" at 1:00 p.m. and an hour in the evening for "various individual and/or community activities." Limited speech was now permitted during the day; the "Grand Silence" would only be observed at night. They decided to build out the dormitory and add more space so each monk could have a separate room; a real room with a bed and a desk and bookcase and private space. The distinction between "Lay Brothers" and "Choir Religious" disappeared, and lay brothers could now sing in choir and vote on decisions that affected the abbey.

As the monks, especially Robert, struggled to retain their serenity in the face of disturbing news from the outside world, a new perception of God came about from a combination of Vatican II and the ever-expanding space program. When Robert was growing up, God was in a heaven somewhere above or around the earth, and priests and saints were intermediaries that allowed Catholics to reach Him. The new understanding of outer space coupled with the freedom of the Council had led to a new view. No longer unreachable in the heaven above, God was here on earth in the form of His Son, Jesus Christ.

Nineteen sixty-six began with three inches of snow and a severe ice storm. Brother Robert continued his studies for his upcoming ordination, grateful that he was spending his mornings in a classroom instead of working outside. He also spent more time reading, as the relaxation of the rules led to newspapers and more Catholic periodicals available in the library. Publications considered leftist or radical were not permitted, but were often circulated surreptitiously by the monks as they began to focus on social issues.

As Robert played "catch up" with events of the 1960s, he was shocked at how much had changed and how little he knew. It was as if he had been in a coma for years, waking up to learn what had occurred while he slept. A Mexican farm worker leader named César Chávez had led a strike of California grape-pickers to demand higher wages, and those workers became part of a catchall phrase, "The Movement," that described those committed to end racism, the Vietnam conflict and sufferings of the poor. That summer, race riots in the Watts section of Los Angeles killed thirty-four people. U.S. involvement in the war in Vietnam deepened, and, by the end of the year, over 200,000 U.S. troops were stationed there. Protest marches against the war escalated. Had Robert lived outside the abbey, would he have joined them?

The information troubled Robert so much that he almost wanted to return to the days when they were protected from news, but it was too late. The fear and hatred he read in the stories about the Cold War, discrimination against Negroes, the exploitation of farm workers, women's struggles for equality and the conflict in Vietnam all troubled him, particularly since Vatican II had called most religious orders to a more active life. He began to feel more and more that his life choice was contrary to the Council's teachings and the new view of the world he was beginning to embrace.

Ordination was only one month away, however, so he made a greater effort to block out these thoughts. He did not need distractions as he practiced for the final examination before the abbot.

Finally, the day he had waited for all these years arrived. On May 7, 1966, at age twenty-eight, *frater* Mary Robert was ordained a priest. Brother Joachim was ordained at the same time. Betty, Gail and Robert's brother Jim attended. They arrived the day before the ordination and visited for a while. It was a pleasant afternoon; Robert felt happy and at peace.

The next morning he rose with his brothers and chanted Vigils, Lauds and the Angelus. Robert and Joachim attended the Communion without receiving, and remained in the church in prayer while the others ate breakfast. Later they were driven by a lay brother to the Cathedral of St. John the Baptist in Charleston. Robert looked curiously out the window at a world he rarely saw.

Bishop Ernest L. Unterkoefler would officiate at a High Mass. Robert had not seen the bishop before and was impressed with his size; he truly could have been described as a "mountain of a man." After the Alleluia, the bishop called them each by name.

"Brother Mary Robert, Robert Edward Sanders."

"*Adsum*," Robert responded. I am here.

Robert approached the altar and knelt as the bishop addressed the archdeacon. "Is Robert Edward Sanders, Brother Robert, worthy to be admitted to the priesthood?"

"He is."

The bishop addressed the congregation. "The Fathers decreed that the people also should be consulted. If anyone has anything to the prejudice of the candidates, he should come forth and state."

When no one came forth against any of the four, the bishop instructed the men in the duties of the priesthood, then knelt in front of the altar and the four candidates lay face down on the carpet. Then Brothers Robert and Joachim moved forward together. The bishop laid his hands on each of their heads in turn and signaled the attending priests to extend their right hands. He crossed the stole over their chests in another ancient rite and finally prayed a call for God's blessing on the newly-ordained. While the choir sang, the bishop anointed the hands of each man with chrism, the oil of the catechumens.

He presented them with their own chalices that now held wine and water, and their own patens, containing the Host. Robert had selected the chalice and paten, and Betty and Gail purchased them as gifts. Robert's large chalice was silver plate with red stones at the neck and a dark azure-blue base, engraved on the bottom.

DEATH IS SWALLOWED UP IN VICTORY
IN MEMORY OF THE WILLIAM J. SANDERS FAMILY

The paten had a similar engraving that read "In memory of the William Sanders and Gail Gurnett Families."

The bishop finished the Offertory, after which the newly-ordained priests repeated the Mass with him word for word. After Communion, they recited the Apostle's Creed, and then the bishop laid his hands on each of them and said words Robert remembered from his childhood. "Receive ye the Holy Ghost, whose sins you shall forgive are forgiven them; and whose sins you shall retain, they are retained."

When they got to the Eucharistic Prayer, Robert felt a surge of incredible joy as he lifted the Host, heard the altar bell ring and repeated the words Jesus said to his disciples.

"Take this, all of you, and eat it: this is my body which will be given up for you."

Incense filled his lungs and the bell rang again as he lifted the chalice.

"Take this, all of you, and drink from it: this is the cup of my blood, the blood of the new and everlasting covenant."

When the ceremony was over, the four newly-ordained priests waited on a reception line at the altar as their guests approached. Robert almost wept when his mother, with tears in her eyes, knelt before him and kissed his extended palms. Jim did the same, with reverence for the Holy Orders that had now been conferred upon his brother.

The next morning, Father Robert celebrated his first Mass for his monastic family, assisted by his Jesuit brother. Later that day, he walked with Jim on the Mepkin grounds.

"Well, Father Robert," asked Jim, "how did it feel?"

Robert walked for several minutes before he finally answered, and then it was a rush of thoughts. "You know, it really is amazing. I am one of the instruments through which bread can be changed into the body of Christ, and wine into Christ's blood. In fact, I was humbled; humbled at the faith of you, our mother, and my monastic brothers, the fact that everyone believed that transubstantiation took place through my hands. How was ordination for you?"

Jim only said, "About the same."

A week later, Robert received a letter from his mother, saying how proud she was of him. She also admitted that she was enjoying bragging about her two ordained sons. He smiled, happy that she was finally at peace with his decision.

Soon life at Mepkin got back to normal, except for ongoing changes in response to Vatican II. Robert decided to take back his baptismal name, which many of the monks at Mepkin had already done. It felt odd at first, as *frater* Mary Robert became Father Dick Sanders. Father Dick. Father Sanders.

A feeling came back that he had not had in some time. Now that he had been ordained, his faith was stronger than ever, but he had a nagging thought that it might not grow inside the walls of a monastery. This was not a decision about leaving the priesthood; he was certain, now more than ever, that he had been born to be a priest. Rather, it was a choice between a life of contemplation and a life of service. He found himself looking for signs in the Bible, remembering the words of Pope John XXIII: "It is not the Gospel that changes; it is we who are beginning to understand it better."

Freed from the pressure of studying, he worked outside in the mornings and afternoons and also had more free time. The freedom was at once a blessing and a curse, though, as it gave him more time to read about current events. The previous summer, congress had passed the Voting Rights Act of 1965 that banned literacy tests and poll taxes used in the south to keep Blacks from voting. In October, a militant group called the Black Panthers was formed, and Dick wondered where this would all lead.

More of the monks were leaving, now, moving back to the outside world to work among the poor. Dick missed them, but had no real desire to join them. He wrote to his mother and Gail.

> From a theological point of view I really think their move was quite legitimate. Not everyone can see it that way, but I sure do miss them. They were really the best theologians in the house, and we need that badly, so I fear we are going to suffer without them. Too many of our priests are still living in what I consider to be a pre-Vatican II theology.
>
> But in spite of their move, I do think that our life still has a real meaning, even with the changing theology, though there can be no doubt that some of what we used to consider its meaning is no longer valid. That is why I think some are justified in leaving. The reasons they came for are no longer theologically solid, or are at least much weaker.
>
> But for me, our life does still have a meaning so don't expect me home soon!! But please do pray for us because I think there is some danger that we may really suffer from a theological short-sightedness and out-datedness now that we have lost these men. The reason that it worries me is that I do think so much of our life. If I didn't, I wouldn't care too much what happens to it.
>
> Keeping you in my prayers and Masses,
> Love, in our newborn Savior, Dick

A few days later he was reading the newspaper in the scriptorium, and nodded when Father Raymond came into the room. In earlier years they had not had the opportunity to talk, but lately Raymond had shared some stories about his childhood in North Charleston, and Dick had heard firsthand how difficult life was for Negroes in the south, from someone who had lived it. On this day he nodded, put his index finger to his lips, then lowered it out and down to just below chest level. *I wish to speak.* Sign language was no longer needed except at night, but Dick did it for emphasis; he really wanted to talk.

The other priest nodded, and they left the silence of the library and went to the chapter room. The conversation quickly got around again to civil rights.

"In many cases life is not getting better for the black people with the civil rights movement," said Raymond. "Often, the tension makes the discrimination and racist treatment worse than it used to be."

"Then why are you here?" asked Dick, pointedly.

For a moment, Raymond looked troubled, but then regained his peaceful countenance.

"I made a choice," he breathed, quietly.

Father Sanders sighed. "So did I, Father Raymond. So did I."

CHAPTER ELEVEN –
WE NEED A PRIEST! – 1966

As Father Sanders weighed his life choices at Mepkin Abbey, Luis Hernandez stood at a payphone in Naples, Florida, talking to his wife in Texas.

"Corina, *tienes que venir.* You gotta come over here because I need you."

"Luis, you know I'm not gonna go," she replied, firmly.

"But Corina you don't understand. This place is going crazy with work! I never seen nothing like it! They're planting acres and acres. There are big companies here now – majors – not so much the small growers we used to know. They're clearing fields all over the place and they need workers to plant and pick the crops."

His words fell on deaf ears because Corina was barely listening. It was just a year ago the family, with eleven children, had finally settled down in a permanent home in Texas. That year Luis migrated alone and Corina thanked God every day that she and the children no longer had to go.

"But Corina, you don't understand the opportunity. We can make a lot of money."

Unknown to Luis, the opportunity was due to Fidel Castro's takeover of Cuba in 1959. Prior to Castro's nationalization of farms and the U.S.'s embargo on trade with the now-Communist country, large growers bought winter vegetables from Cuba for remarketing in the United States, importing boatloads all winter long. But now that supply had been cut off and the big growers took advantage of the opportunity to replace it by expanding their operations in Southwest Florida.

Luis continued trying to convince his wife. "It's not just Mexicans from Texas here now. A lot of Mexicans are coming from Mexico and they don't speak English. I can get a lot of workers and make a lot of money because I can talk to them and I can talk to the growers."

But Corina was not moved. "I'm not gonna be a migrant again," she told her husband firmly. "I have a home here and I am not gonna come."

When several phone calls over the next few days resulted only in his wife's continued stubborn refusal to go to Florida, Luis drove back to Texas and the next day they visited the priest.

"Look, *Padre*," Luis explained. "I found good work in Florida. There's so much expansion of agriculture there that I can make a lot of money, but my wife won't come with me."

The priest thought it did sound like a perfect opportunity, but Corina disagreed.

"*Padre*, I will not move again. You know I was a migrant all my life and I'm forty-one years old and I have eleven children. Our oldest, 'Lupe, is working with a doctor because she's gonna be a nurse, and the other kids are in school. I will not go."

The priest sympathized but sided with Luis. "Corina, I know how hard this will be for you," he said softly, "but you have to go with him. He's your husband and he needs you."

Tears came to her eyes but she would not disobey a priest. She did not speak on the drive back to their house and Luis knew enough to remain quiet. When they got home, Corina went into their bedroom for a long time and left Luis to tell the children they were moving again. They were all disappointed, and Maria Guadalupe, the oldest, refused.

"I'm not going to follow you anymore," she said, shaking her head. Guadalupe was twenty-one years old and could stay with an aunt and keep her job at the doctor's office.

In the next few days the family packed their clothes, pots, pans, dishes, towels and the pictures of Jesus and Our Lady of Guadalupe that hung on the walls. There was no need for furniture because they would live in *barracas*, housing on the farm where Luis worked. *Barracas*, the Spanish word for huts or shanties, were small cabins or rooms in which beds were usually provided. Martin, the oldest boy, and Luis put the old washing machine with rollers into the back of the pickup truck, then the television and then boxes of their clothes. They put a tarp over everything except the washing machine that stuck out over the top of their other belongings.

Corina started to cry. "We look like those Beverly Hillbillies," she thought, ashamed, especially when her neighbors came out to say goodbye.

When the truck was loaded, the children climbed into the back behind the boxes; the older ones sat on the sides, hanging their arms over the edges, the younger ones on blankets in the center. Corina took two-year-old Luis

Jr. in the front cab. As they drove away, Guadalupe waved goodbye from the driveway and Corina wiped the tears from her eyes. They drove without speaking, north to Houston, east through Baton Rouge and Mobile and the Florida Panhandle, then south on U.S. 41 to Naples.

Corina had spent most of her life as a migrant worker. When she was only ten years old she was already picking cotton in Texas. The small hands of children were better than those of adults at picking the cotton "clean." She had to poke her fingers between the spines of the cotton plant and pick the soft, white cotton out from between them. In West Texas, they used machines to clean the cotton, so they could pick "dirty," grabbing the whole cotton boll. It hurt a lot less to pick "dirty" and her fingers didn't bleed so much, but either way, she and her family had to pick enough to fill a large sack, ten feet long. Together her family would push and pull the sacks down the rows and then take them to the scale for weighing. If they weighed less than one hundred pounds the growers would not accept them; they had to go back and fill some more.

When she got older and married Luis, another field worker, they expanded into tomatoes, cherries and other fruit and vegetable crops. The family had moved between Texas and Florida in the winter, for years. In the summer they headed north from Florida up the migrant stream to South Carolina, Michigan and Indiana.

When Luis pulled the truck up in front of the *barracas* at A. Duda Farms, her husband's friends introduced themselves through the passenger window of the truck and several said, "You got two rooms!" Usually each family was given only one room, no matter how many children they had. "And you got new mattresses, still covered with plastic!"

The people were so nice that Corina did not want to hurt their feelings, so she reluctantly went inside. They were right; there were two rooms with a small bathroom and shower in between. And there were brand new mattresses. Corina, Luis and ten children would sleep in one room and the other would be for cooking, eating, studying and watching television. Corina thought of the home she had left behind in Texas and realized with a combination of disgust and sadness that she was a *migrante* again. Migrant.

She went back outside and asked the people where they went to church. Tomorrow was Sunday, and not just any Sunday. It was the day before the celebration of Our Lady of Guadalupe that the people called *Doce de Diciembre*, the Twelfth of December, the day Juan Diego saw the vision of the young Virgin Mary in Mexico, but no one in the labor camp seemed to remember.

"We don't go to church," they said. "Every once in a while a priest comes out here during the week and says a Mass, but there is no church around here with Spanish services."

The depth of her own faith and her dedication to farm workers made her decide to help the people find *El Señor*, the Lord, again. She climbed back into the truck and refused to do another thing until they located a church. Luis Hernandez was so grateful that his wife and children were with him in Florida that he did not question her demand. He drove out to Highway 41, the Tamiami Trail that ran from Tampa to Miami, to a phone booth at the Indian Food Bank grocery. She called the nearest church and learned there was a Mass the next day at nine o'clock.

The twelve of them took up an entire back pew, conspicuous with their poor clothing and dark skin, particularly when contrasted with the wealthy white congregation of St. Ann's Catholic Church. As the priest said the Mass in English, which Corina did not understand well, she imagined the preparations going on in her home town of Sinton, Texas. There, as with many Texas border towns, white people were the minority and the congregation was mostly Mexican-Americans. Tomorrow, before dawn, the altar there would be covered with flowers and the church would be filled beyond capacity with people singing *Mañanitas*, or good morning to Our Lady of Guadalupe. After the service, young people dressed in Aztec costumes would dance traditional dances and the *Cabelleros de Colón*, Knights of Columbus, would serve hot chocolate, tamales and frijoles. But Corina was not in Texas – she was in Florida, and there would be no *Mañanitas* for her this year.

After Mass, their family lit candles and prayed devoutly while the priest stood at the back of the church, greeting his parishioners. Then the Hernandez family walked out to meet their new pastor.

Luis introduced himself and his wife who smiled shyly and nodded her head. She didn't like to speak English, afraid she would mispronounce words like "sheet" and "beach." Luis explained that they had just come from Texas to work at A. Duda Farms.

The priest turned to the children who waited patiently. "So many children," he marveled.

"Actually there is one more," said Luis.

"Maria Guadalupe," Corina interrupted proudly, no longer shy when it came to talking about her daughter. "She gonna be a nurse. She stayed in Texas. She's working for a doctor."

"You have eleven children all together?" The priest was amazed.

"*Sí*, we were blessed. God gave all of them to us."

The priest addressed the children. "What are your names and how old are you?"

One by one they introduced themselves. Martin, age twenty, shook the priest's hand confidently and said, in a Texas-Mexican accent, "*Mucho gusto*, Father, it's nice to meet you," then, "I'm Juanita but they call me Janie. I'm seventeen." Arturo was fourteen, José thirteen, Yolanda nine, Jesús, called Jesse, had just turned eight, Maria was six, Rita would be five at the end of December and Anita had just turned four. Baby Luis shyly held up two fingers and the priest shook his tiny hand.

The priest asked about farm work and Luis explained the job of a crew leader. He recruited workers and usually had a steady crew. He managed them, provided transportation, brought water during the workday, submitted the numbers of rows planted or buckets of tomatoes picked by each worker to the grower, and paid the workers. Their oldest son, Martin, worked with his father in the fields all week. The other children attended school but worked in the fields on weekends. In order for the family to live in the *barracas*, anyone old enough to work in the fields had to do so, if even for a day or two each week. While they worked, Corina took care of the younger children. She had migrated with the family all their lives but had not done fieldwork herself in years – there were always children to care for.

Then the priest turned to Corina and asked if she could pick up used clothing donated by his parishioners and distribute the clothes to the workers. She did not mention that she did not have a car because Corina never questioned when the Church asked something of her, but nodded, "*Sí, Padre.*"

There were four camps in the area and more would open as agriculture continued to expand. Three were in Naples: A. Duda where the Hernandez family lived and worked; Six L's and Gargiulo. The fourth was in Bonita Springs about thirty miles to the north. Corina sorted the clothes she got from the church by size and gender and took them to all the farms. Once the word got out that someone could bring clothes to the field workers, St. Ann's parishioners collected used clothing on a regular basis.

The camps in Naples were not bad compared to the one in Bonita Springs. Corina was shocked when she first went there. In Naples, workers lived rent-free in small but modern *barracas* with bathrooms, showers and kitchens, and on the grounds they had a soccer field and a basketball court. In the Bonita camp, ironically called "Camp Happy," electrical boxes had exposed wires, propane tanks leaked, windows were broken and the roofs had holes in them. Many of the wooden floors were unsafe, overflowing septic tanks led to raw sewage on the ground, grease traps did not function and the barracks had no bathrooms. Instead, dilapidated buildings housed communal toilets and showers. Corina thought this place was unlivable even for adults, but there were children in the camp, too. If Luis had brought them here, she would have taken the children and hitchhiked back to Texas. What made it even worse was that the owners of these camps charged workers to live there.

In all the camps, however, one thing concerned her – the number of empty beer bottles in the garbage outside the living quarters. Many of the farm workers, especially those from Mexico, were "*solteros*," in the US by themselves without women to make the *barracas* a home for them. She had to do something to bring God back into their lives.

Every few weeks a priest came from Immokalee, about an hour to the northeast, to say Mass in the Naples-area camps. Occasionally a Hispanic priest would drive over to Naples from Miami, but most of the time there were no religious services for the field workers at the Naples or Bonita farms.

The children of the farm workers were receiving no religious education, either, so Corina started teaching Catechism. At each of the four farms, ten or twelve children would come and sit on the ground around her on a blanket. Later she also taught Catechism to Hispanic children in local schools, three days a week. Two of the nuns who taught children in English at St. Ann's began to help her, providing suggestions that Corina would then translate into Spanish for the migrant children.

She began to include a request for a Spanish-speaking priest in her prayers, and also asked visiting priests about it when they came.

"*Padre*, we have so many people here. We need a priest!"

"I understand, Corina," they usually said, "but there just aren't many Spanish-speaking priests who are willing to work with field workers. Most priests want some nice parish with a beautiful church and rectory. Nobody wants to come and work with poor people, saying Mass at night in labor camps."

"But *Latino* priests go to Immokalee, *Padre*. Why not here?"

"*Sí*, Corina, but it's hard to get anyone to go to Immokalee, either. Nobody stays too long. And at least there they have a little church and a trailer where the priest lives. Here in Naples there is nothing."

"*Sí Padre, entiendo*," she said patiently. I understand. "But we need a church close to our people with a priest who speaks Spanish. I'm gonna keep praying. Somebody will come."

CHAPTER TWELVE –
THE PLANS I HAVE IN MIND –
1967 – 1968

Back at Mepkin Abbey, Father Sanders prayed for guidance and discernment. Vatican II had lifted the medieval mist of the monastery and brought the world and all its problems into focus. Even Thomas Merton was speaking out on civil rights and Vietnam, calling them "the two most urgent issues of our time." Why did the monks not seem to know or care what was going on?

"We are capable and should be out there making a contribution," he thought, but then chided himself for judging his brothers. He confessed the sins of anger and pride and later meditated on words from Zachariah: "Let none of you imagine evil against his brother in your heart."

Dick was vocal in open meetings in the chapter room, however. "People out there are suffering," he said often, "and we should be doing something."

The abbot shook his head. Though he didn't seem to know it himself, the desire for an active life among the poor seemed to be growing in Father Sanders' heart. But that was not part of the abbey's future. There were and always would be contemplative monks and the desires of the more liberal monks were a challenge to the peace of the monastery.

When he tried to ignore the outside world and regain his monastic peace, he found that even the Church would not let him. On March 26, 1967, Pope Paul VI issued *Populorum Progressio*, "On the Development of Peoples." It was a response to the global injustice of the poor and hungry and seemed to speak directly to Father Sanders.

The hungry nations of the world cry out to the peoples blessed
with abundance. And the Church, cut to the quick by this cry,
asks each and every man to hear his brother's plea and answer it
lovingly.

Just a few years earlier, he had vowed to remain at Mepkin with his
Trappist brothers, forever. He had promised obedience until death. Could he
simply change his mind and ignore the vows he had made so devoutly? Did
he want to? He prayed to Mary his mother to help him find his answer.

On June 24, 1967, another papal encyclical was issued, this one on priestly
celibacy. First the pope reviewed the arguments for lifting the ban, including
two Dick had discussed with his brother: there was no biblical basis for celibacy
and also, many men felt called to the priesthood as well as married life. The
letter included a related third point that lifting the celibacy requirement might
help alleviate the growing shortage of priests. Like the birth control issue,
however, it became clear that this was yet another confirmation of traditional
Canon Law. Dick was disappointed that the Church was willing to lose so
many good men who might have stayed priests if they could marry.

He wrote to his mother about it, as part of a general commentary about
the Vatican II changes:

> One of our priests is coming back from Rome soon, after four
> years of study over there, and he will be giving me another year
> of studies. He has a lot of good ideas and is quite up to date...
> and that means a lot. There has been a tremendous change in
> the theological outlook in the past few years, and it isn't finished
> yet... The real honest changes in theology and outlook are so
> considerable that they startle many and are confusing to them.
> Of course, many of us younger generation feel and see the
> need for changes and are eager for them. For one thing, while
> the basic elements of our faith certainly are the same, there are
> many things which are not so basic in which there should be
> more freedom, and we can see in the past history of the Church
> and especially in its earliest centuries that there was much more
> freedom and flexibility. Some things may be very good but
> they are not necessary, so it is questionable whether such things
> should be imposed as a law.
>
> Priestly celibacy is a big example of what I mean. Personally
> I think it would be very desirable to have some married priests. I
> feel almost certain that any change in that law would not apply
> to us who are already ordained, so you see, I'm not talking for

myself. There is one former novice from here who is now a Jesuit who told me in his last letter that many disagreed with the Holy Father's recent pronouncement on that subject. Of course everyone knows that it is not an issue of faith. It is a Church law which can be changed by the authority of the Church and it was not a law in the earliest centuries of the Church but many priests didn't marry. So it is a question of whether it is better today to impose it upon all priests or leave it to the free choice of each, as in the Eastern Church. Personally, I wouldn't be surprised if the law were changed within the next 10 years.

But this is just one type of example of the different line of thought in theology today. There are even deeper changes where our understanding of our faith is becoming more rich and it is actually these that are the basis of the others. For instance we are realizing more the real dignity of each Christian, and his closeness to Christ and his total commitment and consecration to Christ through Baptism.

A side effect of this is to realize that there is much less distinction between we religious and a layperson, or between a priest and a layperson than we seemed to think before. The main difference is in the function of each. Some of the practical results of this is to see on the one hand that the layperson has a much more important and active role in the Church and responsibility for it; and on the other hand, that there is little reason for the priest or religious to try to be so different from others and so segregated and protected from the 'world' because all Christians are called to the <u>same holiness of life.</u> Of course, there are a few aspects of the religious life, such as celibacy, which require a certain amount of prudent caution in our way of living, but definitely not the type of separation and apartness from others that there was in the past.

Well, how did I get off on that long comment on renewal? I better end up by saying it doesn't apply to monks in exactly the same way as to other religious and priests. Those in active work have a real mission to mingle with others as much as possible, but our life demands that we have solitude.

A month later, the periodicals talked again of race riots when two dozen people were killed in Newark and later, forty-three in Detroit. If he were out there, he wondered, where would he be, and how could he help?

The New Year ushered in 1968, the year everything would change. Not long after it began, he was told that his brother Jim had requested a visit. It seemed odd. In the ten years Dick had been at the abbey, they had written few letters and Jim had only come to Mepkin twice. He was always absorbed in his life as a Jesuit and was now teaching part time at Fordham plus finishing his dissertation.

When he arrived, the two brothers greeted one another and walked to the river. The weather was brisk, but Dick's robes were warm and Jim wore a coat. Jim commented on his changed appearance, sounding, as always, like a big brother. "You've grown into a man here. Are you happy?"

Dick nodded and looked at his brother seriously. Jim wasn't there to comment on Dick's maturity. "What's going on?"

Jim hesitated. "I'm leaving the priesthood."

Dick raised his eyebrows, looked into his brother's eyes, turned and began walking again. Jim seemed uncertain, something Dick had never seen.

"I've reached a point where it is difficult for me to uphold some of the Church's teachings. I've become more open, more critical in my thoughts about the Church and Christianity. By the time I was ordained six years ago I was already rethinking some of the major dogmas."

Dick looked at him curiously as Jim continued.

"In theology we studied Church history and how Christian doctrines developed over time, and that there were great controversies over fundamental Christian beliefs. How can I be sure the Church is infallible, or for that matter even that Jesus is God? Some theologians are even questioning the Resurrection. More concretely and practically, I can't accept some of the Church's moral teachings, like the ban on birth control. Most of the priests and nuns I know feel the same way."

Jim seemed happy to be able to talk through it with someone who would understand.

"To be honest, I don't really think I like being a priest. I didn't feel like a 'leader of the flock' or anything like that. I love teaching, but I don't like preaching or giving homilies. I've never liked telling people what to do. I feel out of place in the pulpit and frankly, I find all the ceremonies and rituals unreal and even silly."

Dick was surprised at that comment; he loved the rituals. Jim saw his reaction.

"I don't mean to be sacrilegious, but that's how I feel. The only priestly function that seems to suit me is hearing confessions, which I think I do well because I listen sympathetically. But confessions are one of the big problems. How am I supposed to reinforce the Church's position on birth control when I have a poor young mother of four who just wants to make love to her husband but can't do it because she'll get pregnant; yet if she uses birth control she can't receive Communion? I see too many committed young Catholic couples suffering under this questionable moral teaching. Of course, if I reject one principle of Catholic teaching, then where does it stop? If the Church is wrong on even one issue, then it could be wrong on others as well, couldn't it?"

Dick thought almost longingly for the time in which he and Jim grew up, when the Church was infallible and no one questioned its rules. It was a simpler world. Suddenly he got the impression that Jim might want to be talked out of leaving the priesthood.

"Still," he said, carefully, "you could stay in the priesthood and try and work around those issues and hedge the birth control question. I imagine priests do that all the time. Is that the only reason you're leaving?"

"No, there are other things."

Dick had suspected as much.

"I'm longing more and more for a 'normal' life, and envying those who have it. Part of it is that I've been out among students and professors and my beliefs are more liberal than they used to be. And then there's the other thing. For the first time since entering the Jesuits I was thrown into close contact with married couples. While I haven't had any physical relationships, I recently realized how much I don't want to be celibate anymore. I don't just mean sex; I mean intimacy, responsibility for another person, a family, all those things. Didn't you ever want that?"

"No, I never did. I seem to have the same sexuality as any man, but never wanted more than friendship with the women I knew. I'm lucky because God made it easy for me. I'm sure I was born to be a priest."

Jim felt exactly the opposite. "I never really wanted to be a priest. I fought the idea in my later teens because it meant giving up marriage and a family, and I was pretty seriously in love at the time, as you might remember. But at the same time I felt relentlessly called to make this 'supreme sacrifice of my earthly happiness.' I don't know why."

"It's a shame anyone has to make that sacrifice in order to serve God," said Dick, shaking his head as he looked off into the distance. "The Church has suffered greatly from losing good men. Other rules change; why shouldn't this?"

"I don't know," agreed Jim, shaking his head.

Dick had another supportive comment. "We only get one life on earth, you know, and I have no doubt that God wants us to be happy in it."

He could tell Jim felt relieved. As they walked quietly back to the church, Dick thought of the challenges he might be facing about his own future but did not mention it. Instead, he asked a final question. "What did Mom say?"

Jim smiled. "She wanted me to do it with honor, of course, and the fact that I will still be a professor helped. She said, 'I never thought you were really happy anyway.' As usual, she is fiercely loyal – to both of us."

Dick smiled, knowing she would be the same if the time ever came for him to leave the abbey.

He felt better after his brother's visit. At least one of them knew what he wanted to do and was taking action toward his goal.

In February, the civil rights movement came close to home again when the "Orangeburg Massacre" took place only about an hour and a half away. Though it had been four years since the enactment of the Civil Rights Act, the All Star Bowling Alley in Orangeburg, SC, was still segregated. On the evening of February 6, black students gathered there in protest and were arrested. Their numbers grew and, a few days, later, police officers shot into the crowd of student protestors, killing three of them and injuring twenty-seven. All the officers involved were acquitted. Dick was horrified, wondering why there was not more of a national uproar, then realized sadly it was because the dead students were black.

He checked his mail and found a present from his mother, a copy of Thomas Merton's latest publication, *Conjectures of a Guilty Bystander.* Father Sanders took the book excitedly to the library to read, assuming Merton would speak to his soul and bring him peace. As he skimmed on through the book, however, Dick realized he was selecting sections that matched his current state of mind.

> Christian social action is first of all an action that discovers
> religion in politics, religion in work, religion in social programs
> for better wages ... because God became man, because every
> man is potentially Christ, because Christ is our brother, and
> because we have no right to let our brother live in want, or
> in degradation, or in any form of squalor whether physical or
> spiritual.

He read and reread the words and suddenly this new outlook made sense to him. Where would an imitation of Christ be more valuable than in a real, active environment?

As Dick struggled with decisions about his future, events in the world would exacerbate his doubts. That evening, he learned that Martin Luther King had been shot dead as he stood on a hotel balcony. Stunned, Dick went to the library to find a speech Dr. King had given only a few months earlier in which he spoke of his own death and funeral. Brother Martin had said he wanted no long eulogy; he only wanted to leave a committed life behind.

Father Sanders did not care what others would think about his life, but began to wonder about the contribution he would leave. When he died, would he have made a difference?

Two days later, race riots again erupted all over the U.S. and Dick wondered how they could have forgotten that Dr. King stood only for non-violence. Shortly afterwards, Catholic activists stole and burned draft files of soldiers about to be deployed to Vietnam. Then the abbot made another shocking announcement: Senator Robert Kennedy, JFK's younger brother who was running for president, had been shot and seriously wounded. He died the following day.

Local news was no less disturbing. An article quoted a 1966 study that found that the Negro infant mortality rate in South Carolina was fifty per thousand – twice that of whites. Part of the problem was that Negro children were delivered by midwives in unsanitary homes or backrooms of stores, not hospitals, and the nutritional deficiencies were horrendous.

In the summer of 1968, Catholics received the Church's answer about birth control. A new papal encyclical called *Humanae Vitae*, "On the Regulation of Birth," was read to the monks at dinner: the Church would remain opposed to contraception.

Father Sanders shook his head and threw his napkin on the table. Several of the monks shot him disapproving looks, and the abbot shook his head sadly. That evening at Vespers, the brother on his right chanted loudly in harsh tones that seemed to be aimed directly at Father Sanders. He was one of the more conservative and, Dick thought, rigid monks. Apparently this was his way of venting his frustration with the liberals. Soon the yelling became more frequent and Dick began to dread it, especially when they chanted the "raging psalms" like Psalm 73.

> They are corrupt, and speak wickedly concerning oppression:
> they speak loftily.
> They set their mouth against the heavens and their tongue
> walketh through the earth.

The angry chanting was one of many signs of the growing annoyance with Father Sanders and the other restless monks who were disturbing the abbey's peace. In this place of heightened sensitivity, their moods created tangible atmospheres.

Dick, in the meantime, was entertaining the idea that God might be calling him to work among black people in South Carolina. Father Raymond, the black monk who had become his friend, was of the same mind.

As the summer heat lessened and the breezes cooled, more news pushed Dick to choose the poor over the monastery. A new theology was emerging, one that would change his views forever. Pope Paul VI delivered the opening address to the Second General Conference of Latin American Bishops at Medellín, Colombia, where the South American bishops created documents that would come to be known as *Theología de Liberación*, or Liberation Theology. The conference ran for two weeks, and there was news every few days of their progress.

Dick was fascinated with their interpretation of the Gospel, based on the historical Jesus who actively helped the poor and oppressed. According to Gustavo Gutierrez, one of Liberation Theology's founders, "We find the Lord in our encounters with others, especially the poor, marginated, and exploited ones." The conference focused on the need for a change in the Church within this vision, a "preferential option for the poor."

In early October, Dick received a letter from his brother. He hadn't heard from Jim since his visit in January. Jim had moved to Staten Island to take a faculty position at a branch of the City University of New York – and he was getting married. The intimacy and warmth he had been missing would become a reality.

Jim wrote that he had known Joan Lark before he left. She was a member of the Grail, an international Catholic women's movement committed to transforming the world into a global community of justice and peace. The letter included a question that took Dick by surprise.

"We thought the family might be more comfortable with the whole thing if you came to the wedding. Even though a lot of priests and nuns are leaving religious life, a lot of Catholics still haven't accepted the idea."

Dick agreed with Jim's concern that family members and friends might look dimly at Jim leaving the priesthood in the first place, never mind getting married so soon after. Though many men and women around the country had done the same, it was still not generally accepted, and many Catholics felt a sense of shame about it.

Surprisingly, the abbot allowed Dick to attend, agreeing that the family would benefit from the support. The abbot had made a general decision to be lenient in the rules, especially now, in the most difficult year he and many of the monks had ever lived through. He loved the men in his charge and was responsible for their souls. In an effort to avoid losing them, he would break many traditions.

The day before the wedding, Father Sanders put on some work clothes and boarded a plane for Newark International Airport. It felt incredibly strange to be outside the abbey. A pretty young stewardess asked what he would like to drink, and he could only shake his head.

Jim and their mother met him at the gate. On the drive into Staten Island, Dick sat in the front seat and stared out the window intently. Except for a rare trip to Charleston, he had not seen the world in over ten years. He was amazed at how different it seemed.

When they got to the apartment, he met Joan Lark, his sister-in-law to be. She was pretty, with shoulder-length soft brown hair and obvious intelligence. Not accustomed to speaking much, Dick barely talked to her but he liked her immediately. Then Betty stood back, shaking her head, looking at his work clothes.

"You'll need a suit."

Dick nodded and looked down at the floor, then at his brother.

"Don't worry. I'll take care of it."

Joan stayed at the apartment making final preparations as Jim drove into Manhattan with Dick and their mother. Dick followed them quietly into Barney's and Jim found a salesperson.

"How can I help you?"

Dick looked down at the floor.

"My brother needs a dark suit for a wedding," answered Jim.

"Of course," the salesman said and turned once again to Dick. "What size?"

Dick shook his head – he didn't know.

"Well, you look to be about a forty-two or forty-four. Let me show you what we have."

Dick followed silently, keeping his head down as if the cowl were still covering it.

"What color?"

Dick looked up at Jim and then down at the floor again.

"Black, I think," said Jim, smiling now.

Finally the salesman stopped talking to Dick entirely and continued the conversation with Jim, assuming his brother was retarded or had some other mental disability.

"I think he would look good in this one," said the salesman to Jim. Betty and Jim agreed and Dick tried on the suit. He grinned embarrassedly when he came out of the dressing room; except for his work attire, he had not worn regular clothes in over eleven years.

The next day, Jim and Joan celebrated their wedding Mass at their apartment, officiated by a priest friend of Joan's from Chicago. As always, Dick was proud of his big brother and happy for him and his new bride. He returned to Mepkin with the same questions he had when he left, but with a lighter heart, and for a short time, peacefully anticipated the nearing Advent season.

The only news of note was that a group of hospital workers, mostly black women, were trying to start a union in Charleston. They earned $1.30 per hour, significantly less than their white counterparts, and, instead of their names, doctors and nurses called them racial slurs like "nigger" and "monkey grunt." Dick prayed for the workers' success, wondering if perhaps this was a cause for which he should leave the abbey, but felt no strong calling to go right now. He was always happy during Advent.

His temporary peace was darkened with sadness, however, when Father Abbot announced that Thomas Merton was dead. The previous September, Merton had made his first extended trip away from Gethsemani Abbey for speaking engagements, his abbot apparently also bending St. Benedict's rules for the greater good. Merton had even traveled to India and met with the Dalai Lama, then on to Sri Lanka, Singapore and Thailand. On the morning of December 10, Father Louis gave a speech in Bangkok at an international ecumenical monastic conference called "Marxism and Monastic Perspectives." That afternoon, he went to his room to rest and later they found him dead, from accidental electrocution when he turned on a lamp with faulty wiring. The voice that had led Dick to the Abbey and comforted him there during his days of indecision, was silenced.

Each day now, Dick felt only wrenching indecision, torn between the contemplative life and an active one. His faith was so strong that he knew God would never abandon him, yet he struggled in darkness, unable to see the next steps. He felt worthless and then felt guilty for feeling that way. Each night he slept restlessly, hoping that in the morning this would all be gone and he could again be happy as a Trappist, but each morning he faced the same depression. Brother Boniface noticed his mood, which was obvious to everyone, and made Dick's favorite foods more often, including corn bread. Work became more difficult and Dick began to suffer from backaches and weakness. Walking by the river no longer calmed him and the chants that had always moved him sounded empty. At night, Mary Immaculate, who usually calmed and comforted him, was nowhere to be found. He lay awake, alone, staring up at the darkness.

Finally he decided to talk to the abbot. After the blessing, he sat and looked down at his hands. "I don't know why this feeling is so strong or what started it, Reverend Father, but I have this longing to be out in the world, working with the poor, looking for Jesus among them. Yet at the same time I do not wish to leave: I love this life, the prayer, the deep devotion, the peace, and my brothers here – you are my family. But the more I read the Gospel, the more I feel God's call to active ministry, perhaps with poor black people. Working among them seems more relevant and true to the Gospel than what I'm doing here."

The abbot had observed Dick talking with Father Raymond and a few others, and their glances during discussions about civil rights. Unknown to Dick, other monks had already visited this office with similar thoughts. The abbot suggested that Dick continue to pray to discern God's will.

"You might be feeling symptoms of what we call *Acedia*, a kind of listlessness in the heart. However, it is also possible that this longing is a call from God."

Dick looked at him questioningly. He had expected the abbot to talk him into staying and working through the depression. Was he suggesting that he leave the abbey?

"I am trying to navigate difficult waters, here, trying to implement decisions from Vatican II with a group of men who entered years before and sought a far different experience. Within that, there is little room for disruptions to our routine and our contemplation. Your restlessness is noticed and heard. The others have started to refer to you and the others as 'murmurers' and 'protesters.'"

Dick had been aware for some time of looks from other monks, but, he thought, how dare they criticize him when maybe they should be considering going out to help the poor, too? But their life was their choice, was it not, as his choice was his?

"Father Sanders," the abbot's voice brought him back.

"Yes, excuse me."

"You do seem to struggle."

Dick sighed. "Yes, Father Abbot, I do. I don't seem to be able to find peace here anymore. Still, I am afraid of what will happen if I live outside the monastery."

"Trust that God will guide you. It takes discipline to develop a discerning heart, to make decisions like this one."

After Father Sanders left, it was the abbot who got down on his knees. He had hoped to get through these difficult times without losing anyone else. He had to care for the men he loved as well as for his own soul, but he also had to do something about the negative atmosphere the disgruntled monks were creating. After praying for a few more days and seeing no change in Father Sanders, the abbot realized he had to put the needs of the monastery ahead of his love for these few. He called Charleston's Bishop Unterkoefler and together they came up with a plan in which the bishop would find temporary homes in the diocese for the restless monks, so they could discern their true calling. A day later, the abbot asked Fathers Sanders and Raymond Robertson to come to his office together.

"I want you both to go out and work in the diocese for a while," he said, sadly.

Dick looked at him, not comprehending. What was he saying?

"We are sending you to North Charleston to work with poor black people. The bishop will fill you in on the details, but I feel comfortable that you will like the assignment. With any luck, you'll also be able to help with the hospital workers strike."

Dick's heart jumped at the possibility of being of some service in the world, yet was wary of the implications.

"You will be still be monks, but will be what we call 'exclaustrated,' because you have not asked to be released from your solemn vows."

Dick drew in a quick breath and panicked. It had never occurred to him to be released from his vows. As Dick and Raymond listened, almost in disbelief, the abbot continued.

"We will still carry you on our roll, but you will be outside, away from your monastic family. If you decide to remain out, you will have to ask the bishop to be incardinated into the diocese."

Incardination meant "adoption" or becoming "flesh of the diocese." Though Dick somewhat agreed that leaving for a time might be a good idea, he did not want to be officially part of anything but Mepkin Abbey. He breathed a sigh of relief at the abbot's next words.

"Mepkin will be your home. Come back to us if it seems right, or even if it doesn't."

Then Raymond asked about the other restless monks. "Are they going too?"

"Not yet. There may be other ways of helping them. You two, however, are clearly feeling called to active service, and I want you to try it. If you change your mind, you can come back. You have to figure out what God wants for you."

Later, after Vespers, Dick skimmed through the Bible and happened on Jeremia 29:11-13.

> For I know well the plans I have in mind for you, says the Lord,
> plans for your welfare, not for woe! Plans to give you a future
> full of hope.
> When you call me, when you go to pray to me, I will listen to
> you.
> When you look for me, you will find me.
> Yes, when you seek me with all your heart, you will find me with
> you.

The next day, as he packed his few belongings, Dick had a sudden wave of panic that this was a bad decision. It was all happening too quickly. It reminded him of how he felt when his father died, a sudden, desperate stab of intense grief: "Wait! Wait! Don't go!" He thought back to his first day at Mepkin; it seemed like yesterday. A world and a Church had changed since he entered. How could everything have come out so drastically? He knelt for a final discerning prayer, then stood and finished packing.

Dick took his suitcase down to the front entrance where Father Raymond waited. One of the lay brothers would drive them to Charleston. The abbey grapevine had let the other monks know what was happening, and several came to say goodbye. The novice master and the abbey's cook were two that Dick had hoped to see. They embraced him warmly, each in turn.

The old cook winked and said, "Don't forget. The corn bread will be here when you come back."

The novice master said nothing, but smiled gently and gave his student of many years a long hug. The abbot did the same, with tears in his eyes. Then he blessed them each with the Sign of the Cross and added his own wish.

"*Pax tecum.*" Peace be with you.

Father Sanders felt another moment of panic as he looked around at the grounds and the buildings. This place was his home and he would be back, yet the separation tore at his heart. As the station wagon made its way down the long drive, however, the abbot's final blessing bought to his mind comforting words.

Let not your hearts be troubled, neither let them be afraid.

III

TERCE

1969 - 1974

CHAPTER THIRTEEN –
ECHO HOUSE AND PROTESTS – 1969

Soon Dick and Raymond were sitting across the desk from the bishop, who was polite but to the point, telling them the story of the place where they would be assigned. A few years earlier, the bishop had read an article in Catholic Extension Magazine about a program run by the Sisters of St. Francis of Rochester, Minnesota. Following the instructions of Vatican II, the sisters had gone back to the intent of their founders to work with the poor. They created a program for poor inner-city Blacks in Chicago where they taught typing, homemaking, sewing and crafts. By the end of the summer, the program had decreased juvenile delinquency by 35 percent. Bishop Unterkoefler contacted the major superior of their order, requesting them to set up a similar program in Charleston. Sister Maigread Conway came with about twenty sisters and began SAIL (Summer Achievement in Learning). The bishop continued negotiations with the sisters to not only continue summer programs but to come and work full-time with the poor.

He told Dick and Raymond that God had pointed him to the location for the sisters' full-time ministry when his driver got lost taking him to the airport. Not knowing where he was, the bishop's observation of the impoverished area told him this area needed assistance, and he said to his driver, "This is where I want the sisters to work." At first, the sisters' white skin plus the fact that they were Catholic made the people in the neighborhood nervous, but they gradually became welcoming as an empty house on Echo Avenue became their center of operation. The bishop got used sewing machines, and the sisters began to teach.

Sister Maigread's real priority, though, was to do all in her power to see that the children attended school – difficult in a state that had no compulsory school attendance law, and in an area where many parents were illiterate and money for clothes, let alone food, was scarce. The sisters contributed time at an interdenominational clothing center to access clothing for the children and, once the children were in school, pushed for books and free lunches. Because it was late in the school year, children were behind in their work so a need for after-school tutoring came up, and the sisters soon added basic adult education. The children called the new center Echo House, because of its location on Echo Avenue.

Then the bishop got back to the role of the restless monks. When the abbot of Mepkin called Bishop Unterkoefler about where to put them, the bishop asked the sisters if there was anything they could do in Union Heights. There was – providing transportation for the people to medical facilities and government offices, plus they could develop some kind of program for the teens, especially the boys.

Dick waited to hear more, but the bishop moved on to logistics. The diocese had rented a house for them, two blocks from Echo House. Their new home was actually an old grocery store with a large downstairs, now empty, and living quarters upstairs. "Hopefully you can start something in the building that will help the community. We're providing you with a car that you can share, and my secretary will give you some money – you'll need clothes and toiletries, I imagine, plus food of course."

He was right. The two monks had nothing except the work clothes they wore, plus vestments, chalices, patens and Bibles.

"We'll put you on a monthly stipend for the future. Any questions? Fine. My secretary will give you a map. Good luck to both of you."

The abrupt conclusion surprised both of them. Dick and Raymond got up, nodded to the bishop who had already started reading papers on his desk, and left.

After picking up money and car keys, Raymond drove to Union Heights. Dick rode in the passenger seat and watched intently out the window. The houses were small one or two-story rundown structures that had probably not seen paint since the 1920s or 1930s. Electric wires hung from poles that leaned in various directions, and Dick noted outhouses in some of the yards. Only two of the streets in the area were paved – the rest were dirt roads. In the distance, on either side of the twelve-square-block community, he could make out smoke stacks of chemical factories that left an acrid smell in the air. Black children in faded, worn clothing played in the dirt streets and several adults walked slowly on the sides of the roads. They stared at Dick as the two men drove by.

He raised his eyebrows at Raymond. "Apparently, they don't see a lot of white people here!"

They parked in front of a two-story white frame building at the corner of Comstock and Adams, that reminded Dick of St. Mary's convent in his home town, but older and in bad shape. They walked up the faded wood stairs and unlocked the front door to a 3,000-square-foot empty space. Dick noted long, parallel indentations on the floor, signs of shelving, and rectangular marks where meat and produce cases had probably stood. There were only a few windows, in the front and the back, and the place smelled of mildew. They walked up the creaky side staircase to their new living quarters that contained a kitchen, small living room, two bedrooms and a bath.

Dick let Raymond select his bedroom, and then went into the other that overlooked the area they had just driven through. He suddenly became concerned about their day-to-day living needs; his mother had always cooked for him at home and Brother Boniface and others made the food at the abbey. His new partner reassured him. Raymond had been on his own quite a bit before he entered Mepkin. They found a grocery store south of the river and stocked up. Dick made sure they bought bread, cheese and tomatoes so at least they could make sandwiches. He bought ham, too, excited at the thought of eating meat again. At the checkout, he hesitated, then smiled.

"Pack of Pall Mall's, too, please – and some matches?"

He didn't know how long he would stay "out," but while he was here, he was going to do some of the things he had missed.

It was mid-afternoon by the time they got back to their new home. About fifteen young people had gathered in front of the house – apparently word had gotten around about the white man moving into the Heights. The two men smiled as they walked up the steps and the young people nodded, hesitant but curious. After unpacking the groceries Dick ate a ham, cheese and tomato sandwich. The ham was delicious, but he would have liked anything because he was hungry. They hadn't eaten since breakfast at the abbey, early that morning. Could it have just been this morning that they left? It seemed impossible. They had come out to an entirely different world.... the real world, Dick reminded himself. But then, was he sure about that?

They walked over to meet Sisters Maigread Conway and Colleen Waterman and the curious young people followed them. Dick looked back at them and smiled but the kids kept their distance.

The sisters' building was a small house with several rooms and a couple of porches. It had a large kitchen where the sisters served coffee and offered donuts that Dick ate gratefully.

Sister Maigread had a round, full face and kind eyes and Sister Colleen, the younger of the two, was thin and pretty with brown hair. As she explained what they did at Echo House, Dick was conscious of how pleasant it was to be in the company of women again.

Colleen explained that tutoring adults was a big part of their work. "You would not believe how many of these people are illiterate and have no education at all. We've been tutoring them because Charleston doesn't have basic literacy programs unless people have completed seventh grade. Many of the people are originally from the South Carolina islands and speak only Gullah. It is a level of poverty we'd never seen before. The parents are ashamed that they can't read, so when the children bring forms from school to be signed, their parents make believe they lost their glasses. Many of the kids can't get free lunch programs because the parents don't sign the forms. The diet is a big problem. A lot of these people are so poor that they eat clay, and that causes a lot of birth defects in the children. The lack of decent nutrition also causes congenital defects like deafness."

The sisters went on to explain that they helped the parents register their children for school, got them books and tutored the kids after school. Because so many of them didn't have decent clothing, they had also opened a used clothing center.

Sister Colleen said that many of the adults did not know how to get to the Medical University Hospital where they could get health care for themselves and their children. They also were ignorant about things like social security, which they had paid into all their lives but didn't know they were entitled to collect. Transportation would be a great service to the community.

"The other thing," she continued, "is that the area needs something for the teenagers to do. We have some of the girls here in sewing classes, but we can't handle the boys."

As he and Raymond walked home, Dick pictured the empty grocery store and wondered how long it would take to make it into a community center. Later that evening, he went out to the front stoop. It was dark now, and the young people who had followed them earlier were gone. Sitting alone, Dick smoked his first cigarette since 1957. At first he coughed and felt sick, but soon he enjoyed it as much as he always had. He went to his room and prayed the psalms of Compline, then lay down and ended the day as he had and always would: "May God grant us a restful night, and a peaceful death."

He fell asleep an hour later than monastery time, but woke at 3:00 a.m. Happily, however, he rolled over and fell back to sleep. When he awoke again at 4:00, he lay back, taking in his new room. Part of him cherished the solitude, the silence of being just by himself, but another part felt empty and he missed his family of brothers. He was glad Raymond was there in the next room. Living by himself would have been too lonely.

As the priests adjusted to their new life, they found they worked well together. Dick enjoyed talking to people more than he remembered – not really talking, but listening. He was impressed with how respectful and confident the young people were. When he asked what they did with their spare time, they replied, "Nothin'. Ain't nothin' to do."

Not long after they started, the priests and sisters met with Catholic Charities about organizing and expanding their programs. Fathers Sanders and Robertson were introduced to Father Thomas Duffy who ran the organization, as the group sat down to discuss future plans. Father Duffy reiterated the need for teenage activities and transportation to medical facilities and the on-leave monks were happy to help.

"Father Dick" did most of the driving and got a closer look at many of the poor homes of the families in Union Heights. Most notably, the people seemed happy and unaware of their poverty. Personally he was happy too, surprised at how easily he adjusted to being out in the world. He missed the peaceful routine of Mepkin but enjoyed sleeping until 6:00 or 7:00 a.m. for the first time in over a decade. He started smoking regularly, enjoying it so much he was amazed he had ever quit. He let his hair grow and within two months it was back to the tall flat-top he wore in high school.

When he wasn't working, he walked around the neighborhood. Across from the rear of their house was a sweet shop called "Ida's Snack Bar." It was a small place, twelve feet by twelve feet, and Dick liked to talk with the young people who congregated there, particularly Ida Singletary. She was twelve years old, thin with short tightly-braided hair, intelligent, confident and well mannered. Both her parents worked, apparently having decided that Ida was mature enough to be trusted with the business. He watched as she talked to the driver of the soda truck, ordering enough wooden cases to last until the following week's delivery. He ordered a Coca-Cola and she efficiently popped off the cap with a bottle opener nailed to the counter. Then he asked what it was like for her, growing up in "the Heights."

She thought for a minute before answering. "You know, Father, I guess you'd say we're poor; but I don't really notice it because everybody's poor. I love it here."

"Are there many white people?"

"Not many. My mother is a cook at a school and white folks work with her. Some white folks come into the Heights to sell life insurance so if somebody dies you can get a little somethin' to help bury them. White guys sell furniture, cleaning supplies and hair products. You order stuff and they bring it to you later. So yeah, we see some white people. Not many though, and none like you, walking around in the streets. Talking to you is the most time I've ever spent with anyone who's not black."

"How is it?"

She nodded and smiled. "It's fine. You're a nice white man."

Ida volunteered that the neighborhood was safe and the other kids agreed. Dick was curious about prejudice and discrimination and Ida answered simply.

"Like I said, we don't see that many white people. The closest thing I can think if is, there's a shopping center a few miles away where I go sometimes with my mother. As soon as we walk in, this white woman follows us looking all suspicious like we're gonna steal something."

"Doesn't that bother you?"

Ida shook her head. "Nah, I know who I am. And Mama taught me that people like that aren't bad, they're just ignorant."

He nodded, impressed with the wisdom and forgiving nature of the girl's mother.

It wasn't long before Dick and Raymond had supervised the build-out of the downstairs of their building and opened it as the Union Heights Community Center. They got funding from the diocese for tools and materials, and volunteers from the neighborhood did the work, adding walls for several classrooms and leaving the large center area for meetings. At first it was just a gathering place for the young people, but soon it expanded.

Content with his work with the adults and getting to know the teens, Dick remembered the black women hospital workers and wondered if he might get a chance to be involved in their strike. He got his answer the morning of March 21, 1969, while teaching an adult reading class at Echo House, when Sister Colleen brought in a copy of a telegram faxed from the bishop's office.

MOST REV. ERNEST L. UNTERKOEFLER:
MANY HOSPITAL WORKERS MAINLY WOMEN AT
MEDICAL COLLEGE BEATEN AND JAILED. MORAL
SUPPORT URGENTLY NEEDED. PLEASE ATTEND
EMERGENCY MEETING FRIDAY 4:00 P.M. 655 EAST BAY
STREET.
ISAIAH BENNETT

Colleen explained that Isaiah Bennett had been working with the hospital workers for about two years. Since the last time Dick had read about the strike, the twelve original union members had been fired and the bishop wanted the clergy to support them.

The priests and the sisters drove that Friday afternoon to the church where the meeting was being held. In a side kitchen, Father Thomas Duffy explained why Charleston had not had race riots like those that took place in many other cities. It seemed there was an agreement in Charleston, spoken or unspoken, between the white and black leaders, that they would continue the status quo and not make waves that could upset the city. That balance was being upset by this strike, however, and the bishop was worried about violence. He hoped that having the clergy involved might help prevent it.

Dick thought back to the "Orangeburg Massacre" of the previous year. If we had been there, he wondered... then the guilt came back as he visualized himself at that time, peacefully living at Mepkin. If he and other priests had been at Orangeburg, those young people might still be alive. He made a silent vow to do all that he could do, in whatever amount of time he would be out in the world before returning to the abbey.

Then Isaiah Bennett, a serious young man with extensive experience in organizing workers, took over the meeting and explained that the Charleston hospital workers had recently gained the support of New York Local 1199 of the Retail, Wholesale and Department Store Union. They had helped set up picket lines at the hospital and around the old Slave Market to point out how similar the working conditions were to slavery. About 500 workers were involved in the strike so far. Reverend Ralph Abernathy had visited recently, spoken to 1,500 striker supporters and had organized several marches that were coming up soon. He had been a close friend of Martin Luther King and had helped Dr. King start the Southern Christian Leadership Conference, which Abernathy now ran.

Dick was grateful that he had temporarily left the abbey at this particular time. He felt rejuvenated and inspired as he and Raymond and the sisters from Echo House joined picket lines, attended rallies and marched in the streets with the workers.

One night, Raymond reminded him that he was supposed to go and see the abbot periodically, to update the abbot on his progress. Dick had gotten so involved with the strike and development of the community center that he had forgotten. He went to Mepkin the next day. Driving up the long lane to the monastery, he realized that his whole being was still a monk, yet at the same time he felt so worldly now. He parked and walked to the church, kneeling by himself in the silence and a sense of peace enveloped him. How long had it been? Over two months? He could hardly believe it. Part of him wanted to put on a habit and stay, but the other part couldn't wait to tell the abbot about what he had been doing.

The abbot blessed him, smiled and motioned to the chair across from his desk. Dick thought about how often he had sat there.

"Do you have any regrets?" The abbot's voice was soft and supportive.

"Uh, actually, Reverend Father, no, not so far."

The abbot asked about how he was maintaining his religious faith. Dick thought about eating meat, smoking cigarettes, sleeping late and drinking an occasional beer, but realized that was not what the abbot meant. "I don't spend as much time praying as before, of course. And we don't always say Mass, at least not every day, but we're pretty busy."

Then Dick got a rush of excitement and told the abbot about the young people of Union Heights, the optimism of their parents and his activities with the strikers. "I miss the abbey and the routine, the constant prayer, and everything, really, but for right now it feels like I made the right decision to take a temporary leave." Then he remembered how the change came about. "Uh, I guess you made the right decision, Father Abbot."

"Maybe God had a hand in it. Do you think you might end up staying out and becoming a diocesan priest?"

"Oh, no," said Dick, quickly. It had never occurred to him to stay out. "I just feel that right now, it's important for me to be doing this work. It feels like I was called out to do it – but just for now, not forever. My home is here, at Mepkin Abbey."

As he drove back down the lane, Dick wondered how it would feel to spend a whole weekend there. Part of him did not want to risk it. He was committed to the work he was doing and afraid the monastic life could call him back too early He wanted to at least make some contribution in the world before he returned.

Soon the number of strikers and their supporters grew to over six hundred and Father Sanders and other members of a group called Concerned Clergy stood with them. Dick was disappointed there weren't more priests and ministers involved, but Father Duffy explained they were afraid; several priests had tried to support the strikers in their sermons but white parishioners had angrily stalked out of their churches. Other priests came out against the clergy's support of the workers and Dick began to understand the subtleties of prejudice and how it could be hidden underneath patronizing comments.

As tension in the city mounted, Charleston's mayor sent out press notices asking citizens to remain calm. Bishop Unterkoefler issued another statement of support for the strikers and designated Sunday, April 27 as a day of prayer "for peace and harmony among the Catholic citizens of Charleston."

That Sunday, Dick joined Father Duffy at a peaceful, mid-afternoon rally. About seven hundred people gathered at the Zion Olivet United Presbyterian Church and the rally went on for two hours, led by Rev. Jesse Jackson who denounced South Carolina's governor for calling out the National Guard. When the crowd left the church they formed a line of three and four abreast and marched to Rutledge Avenue. By the time they got to the Medical College they numbered close to one thousand. Hundreds of National Guardsmen, state troopers and Charleston city police had already surrounded the hospital. Hesitant at first, fifty protestors moved forward and formed a picket line.

Fathers Sanders and Duffy went with them. The picketers got on their knees in the street. As he knelt there, singing "We Shall Overcome," Dick felt a combination of fear and exhilaration; he couldn't believe he was doing this! By the end of the work day, the police chief announced through a megaphone that the picketers were violating a court order that limited picketing to ten people spaced twenty yards apart. No one moved.

The chief shouted, "Do you want to be arrested?"

Dick's voice was part of a loud response: "Yes!"

The police began their arrests at the back of the line to avoid the priests – they did not want publicity involving white clergy. When Father Duffy got up and moved to the back of the line, Father Sanders followed him. They were handcuffed and taken to jail along with the black picketers, all charged with demonstrating without a permit.

As he posed for a "mug shot," Dick thought about how far he had come from Mepkin Abbey. By this time of day, his brothers were finishing supper and processing out peacefully for spiritual reading. His thoughts were interrupted by a deputy who pulled him roughly by the arm, heading toward a side room. Dick was alarmed but quickly relieved when the sergeant stopped the deputy. "No need to search. Give them jail clothes and take them to a cell."

The two priests changed and were escorted into a cell in which there were four cots. A few hours later, they had offers of bail, but Fathers Duffy and Sanders decided to stay for a few days as a form of demonstration. That night Dick slept restlessly, awakened often by noise from the other cells. He finally got to sleep around 2:00 a.m., not long before his brothers at Mepkin would be waking up.

The next day's *Charleston News and Courier* featured an article by Stewart R. King that headlined, "47 Arrested In Hospital March." A photograph of the kneeling picketers accompanied the article and, clearly shown in the front of the line, were Fathers Duffy and Sanders.

> A mass march on the Medical Hospital here Sunday afternoon
> was climaxed with the arrest of 47 demonstrators, including two
> white Roman Catholic priests. Among those joining the Rev.
> Ralph David Abernathy behind bars at County Jail were the
> Rev. Richard Sanders, a native of Peru, Ill., and the Rev. Thomas
> Duffy.....

Dick felt a combination of pride and embarrassment when he thought about the article being posted on the Abbey's bulletin board. The next afternoon, they were joined in their cell by two other priests who supported the strikers, leading to another headline about "Militant Clergy."

The other priests were released a few days later but Dick refused to go. Many of the black people did not have bail. At the end of four more days, however, a judge released Father Sanders without bail and he went peacefully. The teens in Union Heights needed him.

That evening, as he sat on the steps of his Union Heights home, several of the local young people approached. Ida Singletary was with them after closing the snack bar for the night. They were all excited about him being in the newspaper.

"How did it feel, Father? Were you scared, Father? What was it like? Are you going back?"

He laughed as he tried to answer their questions in order. "It felt good to stand up with people who are standing up for themselves. No, I wasn't scared. Well, maybe just a little. What was the next question?"

"What was it like in jail?"

Father Dick hesitated on this one and then said, "It's not any place I ever want to go again. But I'm definitely going to continue to support the strike."

On May 11, he was out on the streets again with more than 12,000 people in a Mother's Day March. The governor had again called out the National Guard to control the crowd and Fathers Sanders and Duffy were again at the front of the protesters. The sisters from Echo House were there, too, and this time it was really frightening – guns and tanks were aimed at them, and each time the people moved, the tanks came toward them. As he stood facing armed soldiers from his own country, Dick thanked God his father was not alive to see this. Fortunately, the march went on peacefully without incident.

After more protests over the coming weeks and months, the International Longshoremen's Association ended the strike when it threatened to close down the port of Charleston if the hospitals did not give in. By the time it all ended on July 26, 1969, the strike had lasted 113 days.

While he had enjoyed the experience of standing up with the oppressed, Dick gratefully returned to his work in Union Heights. He turned thirty-two a few days later, feeling on track for something but still not sure what it was.

CHAPTER FOURTEEN – UNION HEIGHTS COMMUNITY CENTER – 1969 – 1972

The Union Heights Community Center was busy all the time. In addition to the inside classrooms and meeting room, the priests cleared a playground in the back of the house and added monkey bars and a metal slide that the children poured water down, to cool it from the sun. Then the people of the neighborhood paved the yard on the side of the building and put up basketball hoops. Dick mixed concrete in a wheelbarrow and poured it as he had learned when they built a hothouse at Mepkin the previous year. Teenagers spread the concrete and local masonry laborers smoothed it.

Most evenings, neighborhood folks met at the basketball court and watched the games, officiated by volunteer coaches from local high schools. Raymond contacted other communities and their teams came to Union Heights to play. Though still not interested in sports, Dick enjoyed how happy they all were with the facility.

In late August he heard about Woodstock, a music festival billed as "Three Days of Peace and Music." As he read the articles and looked at the pictures, he thought how different young people were today from when he grew up. He liked some of their values, especially the focus on peace and love. He also liked the look of long hair and beards, and decided to let his go the same way.

In September, he spent his first week-end retreat at Mepkin, wearing black clothes with a Roman collar. Most of the other monks nodded when they saw him and several smiled, but a few seemed blatantly annoyed at his presence there.

"Get over yourselves," thought Dick. He could see now, though, how disruptive he had been to them. He could also tell that some of them were confused, wondering if he were coming back. He couldn't have given them an answer if they'd asked because he didn't know yet himself. Over the course of the weekend, as he walked the grounds and took part in prayer hours from the back of the church, he began to realize how much he missed monastic life.

He talked again with the abbot, hoping to avoid the issue of being incarcerated, but the abbot had a copy of the article with the picture of Father Sanders kneeling with the strikers on their way to jail.

On late Sunday afternoon he was still there, finding it hard to leave. He strolled down by the river and watched the dancing stars on its waters, remembering his first day at Mepkin. When the bells rang for Vespers he automatically turned toward the church but then longingly watched his brothers as they processed in together. It was not time for him to join them again, at least not yet – he had work to do.

When he got back to Union Heights, he noticed for the first time how much hotter it was than on the expansive grounds of Mepkin, and the Community Center had no air conditioning. The next day he bought one of the hugest electric fans he or any of the young people had ever seen. About five-feet square with a cage around it, it was bigger than some of the smaller children. They would walk toward it and then stumble backwards, making believe they were blown back by the wind. He was grateful as always when the fall came and the temperature and humidity dropped. When he asked the young people about Thanksgiving, they looked at him, amused.

"Same ol' thing, Father. Grits and beans, maybe some po'k rinds. There's no money for no Thanksgiving dinner, if that's what you mean."

Later, Dick talked to Father Robinson who handled most of their administrative work.

"Do you think you could get money from the diocese or other churches for some turkeys, sweet potatoes and stuffing?

Raymond nodded. "I bet we could get some churches to cook, too."

"No, no, no. The people here should cook. That way it's not just charity. Oh yeah, ask for pumpkin, apples and mincemeat, too."

Raymond shook his head and laughed. Together, they held a Thanksgiving dinner for 150 people at the Center, cooked by the people of Union Heights. They sat at tables Raymond borrowed from a school and thanked God for their country and the food they were about to eat.

Christmas was like Thanksgiving when it came to money, and Father Robinson petitioned several of the wealthier Charleston churches to take up a collection for toys. He and Dick bought a tree, the young people decorated it as part of a holiday party and they served a Christmas dinner. As the young people sang about the Christ Child, the smiles of the children and their parents made Dick think this might be the most beautiful Christmas he had ever spent. They were no longer "poor black people" to him. They were good, gracious and loving people who happened to be poor and black.

The next day, he flew to Staten Island to spend the rest of the holidays with his brother and Jim's wife, Joan. Their mother flew in to be with them, too. She doted on Dick, frying eggs and bacon, his favorite foods, every morning. Joan, concerned about nutrition and healthy eating habits for her own family, voiced a complaint. "You shouldn't be feeding him that."

Betty smiled and said, "But, look how much he loves it!"

Dick grinned and nodded enthusiastically. His mother was enjoying being able to cook for him after so many years. He was also glad to see his brother with a family; the life really suited Jim. As Dick observed them together he noted that Joan's value system was similar to Jim's and that, except for sports, they had many shared interests. Later, Dick surprised the family by telling them he was involved with a basketball team.

"You?" Jim's mouth fell open in shock.

"Well, not really involved," Dick clarified, smiling. "Raymond is the sports guy. I just like watching the people."

He developed a close friendship with his sister-in-law and grew to love her. She spent so much of her time working, though, that they barely had time to talk. She was editing a book for her employer, Sadlier Textbook Publishers. She took time out, however, to play board games with him. One afternoon they sat at the table and he won a game of Chinese Checkers.

"I love winning," he said, laughing. "Especially when I can tell you're trying your best to beat me!"

Joan laughed, too. "How can I feel bad about losing when you're having so much fun?"

They talked for a while about his calling to work with poor Blacks. She, more than anyone, seemed to understand his feelings about the injustices of the world. She wanted to know more about Union Heights and was fascinated with his explanation of the different shades of prejudice. He explained what he had learned in the strike planning meetings.

"Isaiah Bennett called it a 'paternalistic' attitude, where some white people see Blacks more like children than adults."

"So that's why white people call black men 'boy'?"

He nodded. "Exactly. In the Memphis sanitation worker protest, the strikers confronted that issue directly by carrying signs that read, 'I am a Man'."

"What did the signs say in Charleston?"

"We had an additional factor of gender because the workers were black females. Their signs read, 'I am Somebody'."

He asked her about The Grail, the organization she was still part of, now as a married member. Joan was enthusiastic about it. "It's a feminist lay order of women, founded by a Jesuit in the Netherlands in 1921, originally called the 'Women of Nazareth.' Our founder wanted to bring the contribution of dynamic Catholic lay women into the Church and the world. We focused on deepening our understanding of Christianity and its social implications. Grail women are dedicated to making a difference through faith and actions." She went on to explain that she grew up in the full-fledged emergence of Women's Liberation and that going into the Grail was, for her, a part of that movement. The Grail provided an outlet for young Catholic women who wanted to be liberated and to do something religious, but not join a convent.

He smiled gently when Joan paused and she stared at him, noting his quiet intensity. "Dick, I envy you because you always seem to be in this deep place of peace, as if you walk in the presence of God, the way St. Paul described it: 'Him in whom we live and move and have our being.' You exhibit that peace in such a real way. It's like you don't exactly carry God around, but you float *in* God."

"I guess that comes from spending so many years in the abbey – we strove for that awareness." He paused, and then lightened the mood. "They say you can take the monk out of the abbey, but you can't take the abbey out of the monk!"

When he returned to South Carolina, Dick went to Mepkin for a retreat, contemplating Joan's comments and praying about his future. While there he spent more time with the abbot, grateful for his patience.

"Take as much time as you need, Father Sanders. Our Lady of Mepkin will always be your home."

The following spring, 1970, a young black man named Stanford Williams came to the Community Center. He looked to be about eighteen years old, and Dick was impressed with his presentation and maturity.

"I'm with a government organization called United Farm Workers Commission. It has a youth program that finds part-time and full-time jobs for high school students in the summer, and full-time jobs for high school graduates. We wondered if you had kids here who might like to get involved."

Raymond asked, "What kind of jobs?"

"All sorts of things. For instance, if somebody wants their lawn cut, we provide the manpower and equipment. If someone needs light office work done like filing, we train a young person to do it. We provide transportation, too; that's mostly what I do. If they don't have a way to get to the job, we take them and bring them back."

Dick was confused. "I don't get the connection with the Farm Workers Commission. What's this have to do with farm work?"

"I think the funding is really more kind of general, for the training and advancement of any poor young people. I work with black kids. We do other stuff, too, to raise their consciousnesses."

Dick smiled to himself. "Consciousness-raising" was a popular term these days, particularly used by feminists but related to all of the social movements. Stanford continued.

"We have 'rap' sessions, to talk about racial issues. We take trips to retreats down in Beaufort County and meet with white kids at a place called Camp St. Mary's. It's enlightening for everybody; it was sure new for me."

Dick enjoyed the summer when it came, because the young people were around all day long. One day when he and Raymond came down from their kitchen after lunch, they noticed that most of the kids were still there. A few of them had sandwiches that they shared with their friends and others bought snacks at Ida's Snack Shop, but many simply skipped eating. Dick chided one of the young men he saw eating a candy bar. "You're going to spoil your lunch!"

"Father, this *is* my lunch!"

Soon Dick understood that many of the people could not afford lunches for their children. The kids got hot lunches during the school year, but not in the summer. He suggested that Father Raymond contact the government and make the Community Center a distribution point for a feeding program. Soon they had the authorization and were able to ensure that each child, aged one to eighteen, received at least one hot, balanced meal. They priests paid Stanford Williams a part-time salary to pick up the food in downtown Charleston.

The program brought more young people in to the Community Center, and Dick and Raymond began to include drug prevention education in their programs. Drug abuse was a particular problem in poor areas like Union Heights and Dick could not bear the thought of these beautiful young people losing themselves to drugs.

He also spent more time at the Snack Bar, chatting with Ida Singletary. She had great insight into the people of Union Heights.

"I'm really impressed that the kids here are so well-behaved," he began.

"We have to be, or else!" laughed Ida. "Seriously, though, we have a good sense of family and were taught to respect our elders. I remember I had a bicycle when I was a kid and was only allowed to ride it two blocks. The other kids would tease me because I couldn't could go further, but I wouldn't do it because my mother said not to. I didn't resent it or talk back. I did what I was told. And I just loved those two blocks!"

He asked her about segregation and she seemed to accept it as part of normal life.

"I went to an all-black elementary school, except we had a visiting art teacher who was white and a white assistant principal for a while. Back then we could choose what school we wanted to go to, but now, going into eighth grade, we don't have a choice anymore; we have to go to Chicora High School. It's part of a bussing program."

She was less than thrilled. "My friends and I really wanted to go to the black high school, Bonds Wilson. We wanted to be 'Cobras!'" Then she grinned, raised her eyebrows, tilted her head and shrugged. "But they're sending me to Chicora High, so that's where I'm going to go. I'm sure I'll like it. I'll make it a point to like it.... like I liked my two blocks!"

Later Dick thought more about what Ida had said, and the wisdom in the young girl's words.

In 1970, news of struggles continued and Dick tried to understand it in the context of the living scriptures. He often sat reading both the newspaper and the Bible at the same time as he drank his morning coffee, trying to find parallels between today's world and the time when Jesus walked the earth. He found himself intrigued by the activities of Cesar Chávez, working on behalf of the Hispanic farm workers. The grape boycott was successful as many California growers were signing union contracts with the workers. There was bad news about the war, however. On April 30, Richard Nixon announced that U.S. and South Vietnamese forces had invaded Cambodia, claiming it was necessary step toward ending the Vietnam conflict. A few days later, students at Kent State University organized a demonstration against the move. It went on for four days, until Monday, May 4, when National Guardsmen fired into the crowd of students, killing four of them and wounding nine others. The photo of a girl screaming in horror as she knelt over a young man's body was one of the most moving images Dick had ever seen.

Contrasted with the upheaval in the greater world, the time he spent in Union Heights was good. Stanford Williams started spending more time at the Community Center, and he and Dick became good friends. They discovered they both liked jazz music and would spend evenings listening to recordings on eight-track tapes. They also went together to watch local jazz saxophone players. One evening, Dick asked about Vietnam, realizing as he spoke that the war had cast a shadow over the entire country for years, and showed no signs of stopping.

Stanford blew out a quick breath and looked at the ceiling. "I'm in the Navy Reserves, so I'm not supposed to have to go."

"Would you want to go?" Dick realized how stupid the question was before the words were out of his mouth.

"I don't think so," said Stanford, stretching out each word for emphasis. "Vietnam is pretty 'hot' right now, especially with this new Cambodia invasion, and active duty doesn't sound too good. I'd end up in a psychiatric ward by the time it was over, with all the crazy stuff goin' down over there."

Then Stanford asked, "Are you going back to the monastery?"

"Yeah," he nodded.

"When?"

"I don't know. I'm just taking it a day at a time."

Dick learned that the Charleston Naval Base had a huge pool and gymnasium so he called and asked if he could bring some of the young people to use the facilities. The next day, he called the kids together.

"How many of you like to swim?" When only a few hands went up, he paused and asked, "How many of you know how to swim?" The same hands went up. One of his jobs at the Rec. Department in Peru was giving swimming lessons, so he asked again, "Who wants to learn?" A few more hands went up, hesitant but willing. "Well, even if you don't, there's an indoor basketball court, too. How does that sound?"

"You mean, basketball, in air conditioning? We're there, Father!"

Raymond got the bishop's approval to purchase a used school bus, and every Wednesday Stanford Williams drove the priests and a busload of kids to the Naval Station. Stanford and Raymond were the adult supervisors, alternating between the pool and the courts, while Father Dick spent most of his time in the pool teaching the youngsters and later, swimming alongside them. He enjoyed the water more than he remembered, although swimming was more difficult now. It was hard to catch his breath and he couldn't swim fast or very far. He figured was out of shape and tried over the summer to increase his stamina. It didn't improve much, though, so he settled for slow laps back and forth while the young people he had taught sped by him.

Back in Union Heights, Dick and Raymond again increased activities at the Community Center as they began to focus on the upcoming election. Raymond filled him in on the political situation. "In the last statistics I saw, South Carolina had more blacks per capita than any other state – 32 percent. We should have a lot more political power than we do."

Dick thought about the lesson on the importance of individual votes he had learned at Mepkin, when the paper reported specifically how the monks voted and how close the Kennedy/Nixon election was. He was puzzled. "You're right; they should be a major voting block..."

"Yes," said Raymond, "but that's the challenge. For years the south has kept Blacks from the polls with bogus literacy tests, poll taxes and threats of violence. As a result, the people of Union Heights have no experience voting; many of them have never even registered."

"What about the Voting Rights Act of 1965? Wasn't it supposed to stop all that stuff?"

Raymond nodded approvingly. "Yes, it was supposed to. That act applied specifically to states and counties where more than half the residents of voting age did not vote, and South Carolina was among them. Statewide, only just over half of eligible Blacks were registered. Other Deep South states were worse, like Alabama, where less than a quarter of Negroes were registered, and Mississippi it was under 10 percent. In spite of the Voting Rights Act, those numbers haven't changed much. The Act also required Federal examiners to oversee election procedures, but a lot of the people are still afraid."

In the weeks before the 1970 election, Dick and Raymond held meetings at the Community Center to discuss the issues and the candidates that would appear on the ballots. Dick began with an overview.

"There are two candidates for governor. Albert Watson is an open racist. John Carl West, the opposing Democratic candidate, is more open and progressive. As Lieutenant Governor, he has spoken at NAACP rallies and fought to keep desegregated schools open. It's important that you all get out and vote."

As Raymond had predicted, some of the people who had lived with Jim Crow racism all their lives resisted the idea.

"Maybe it's best to leave things like they is," said one of the older men, and several of the others nodded.

Dick was disappointed and annoyed with this lack of interest. "Like they are! Where black people are paid less than whites for the same jobs, where you are still kept in separate waiting rooms and there are still restaurants that won't serve you?"

Raymond shot him a cautionary look and another man, heavy set, about fifty years old, spoke directly to Dick. "They talked about all this in 1964, but nothin' changed. Father, I know you can't see this yet, but they ain't gonna let us vote"

Dick realized he would get further with a gentle debate than judgment. "Why do you think that?"

"Never did befo'," said a woman, about sixty years old with a Gullah accent. "They said we could vote, but when we try, they keep us 'way. Made excuses so we *cyan* vote, threatened us when we go to the votin' place."

"We'll make sure they let you this time," assured Father Raymond.

The younger people were more receptive and the older ones came around as the priests went over sample ballots and reviewed election issues. On voting day, Dick, Raymond and Stanford alternated driving people to and from the polls all day long. The man who drove stayed at the polling location to make sure there were no problems.

John Carl West won the election, 52 percent to 45 percent. While pleased with the results, Dick was surprised that the other candidate could have garnered so many votes. He led the people in prayer that the 1970 election would be the last openly racist campaign they would ever see.

Not long after, Father Robinson announced that Governor John Carl West was coming to the Community Center to talk to them. Dick had made the suggestion to Raymond but never ceased to be amazed at what his priest-partner could accomplish. Afterwards, Stanford Williams said, "That was the first time anything like that had ever happened in Union Heights!"

When the elections were over, the priests' involvement in civic activities continued. They took the people to Charleston County government meetings and encouraged them to speak up about issues that affected their community.

Father Dick was happy over the next year, immersed in helping the people of this community yet spending a lot of time at Mepkin. It was like going back and forth between two realities.

Though he still planned to return to the abbey permanently at some point, his active position was often reinforced by new papal documents. One such document, *Octogesima Adveniens*, "A Call to Action," issued in May, 1971, pointed to the role of Christian communities to fight injustice and work for the transformation of society. Dick knew by now that he was on the right path to do that. He just did not know where it would lead him, or for how long.

The following May he received a letter from the bishop. Father Sanders was being transferred in June to St. Peter's Church, a middle-class white parish in Columbia, about two hours northwest of Mepkin. Dick could have the car; Father Robinson would get another and remain in Union Heights. Bishop Unterkoefler said he felt that Father Sanders should have the experience of being a regular parish priest, and they needed another man at St. Peter's.

As far as Dick's personal goals went, it made no sense. Why be outside the abbey if he couldn't help the poor? When he protested, however, the bishop suggested he was welcome to go back to Mepkin.

Dick considered it, but knew that he had other things to do – he just wished he knew what they were. A few weeks later, after a sad good-bye party at the Community Center, he packed his things and drove to Columbia.

CHAPTER FIFTEEN –
HOW SHALL I SERVE YOU? –
1973 – 1974

He went directly to St. Peter's Church and found the front door open and a few people praying inside. It was a huge, cathedral-like structure with what he estimated to be a five-story high nave and a stone lectern with a winding set of steps, framed by imposing stained-glass windows of St. Peter and other saints. At the rear, a polished oak choir loft ran in a semi-circle the full width of the nave, with one of the largest pipe organs Dick had ever seen. He couldn't imagine how it would sound when played. He was also intimidated at the thought of saying Mass at that great altar and giving a sermon from the top of those stairs.

He walked over to the parish office and was greeted by Father "Jimmy" Carter. He recognized Father Carter but the other priest showed no sign of knowing Dick.

"We were ordained together," said Father Sanders. "I guess I looked a little different when I was tonsured."

Father Carter looked at him closely, then laughed and patted him on the shoulder. "Ah, you were one of the monks! That long hair and beard sure has changed your appearance!"

Father Carter was an unusually handsome man with auburn hair that reached down over his ears, and a neatly trimmed beard. Father Sanders' hair had gotten thicker and wirier as it grew and his scraggly beard reached down past the center of his chest. He had gained a little weight in Union Heights and had a mid-section 'spread' that he usually didn't think about but noted now, because Carter was in such good shape. He figured Jimmy must work out in a gym every day of the week. Self-conscious, Dick sucked in his stomach and stood a little taller as they talked.

They spoke for a while about their ordination and Bishop Unterkoefler, whom Dick now learned was known as "The German Shepherd." Father Carter explained that the bishop had reluctantly approved a Vatican II-inspired experiment requested by the priests in Columbia, that they move out of the rectory to live like the people they served.

"There are four of us here now, including you, and we all live by ourselves. You'll meet the others soon."

He told Dick about a couple, Bill and Mary Lundy, who did a lot to help out in the parish. If Dick needed help living on his own, he should go see Mary and Bill.

The next day Dick rented an old trailer. At age thirty-five, he would live alone for the first time in his life. He did not like the feeling of it.

As for his work, he was involved with activities of most parish priests: visiting the sick, a little prison ministry, confessions, Mass and sacraments. The first time Father Sanders celebrated Mass at St. Peter's he was relieved that he didn't have to say his sermon from the top of the winding staircase after all. He did feel strange, though, preaching to a group of people who were not monks or nuns. He had never done this before and had so little life experience - what could he tell them? Also, he was shy and uncomfortable speaking to that many people. He relied on the priests' homily guide and gave the sermon awkwardly, just grateful to get through it.

After Mass, he stood outside the church shaking hands and introducing himself. The people were warm and welcoming, and a few even complimented him on his sermon. These are kind folks, he thought to himself. The last to come out were the choir members and their families. One of them, a tall man with wavy light gray hair and a firm handshake introduced himself. "Welcome, Father, my name is Bill Lundy. This is my wife, Mary, and our boys, Kevin and Terry."

The boys seemed confident and friendly as they shook his hand. Dick guessed that Kevin was about fourteen and Terry maybe six.

"Father Carter told me about you, Mary," he said, looking her in the eye. "He said that if I had questions about living on my own, you could help me."

Mary laughed. "Of course! I don't suppose Father Carter told you I even had to teach him and the others how to fry eggs!"

"He didn't mention that, but come to think of it, I don't know how to do that either."

"Well, we'll take care of that soon enough. By the way, speaking of living alone, would you like to come to our home for dinner tonight?"

Dick jumped at the chance. He had only been in Columbia a few days and so far had eaten out with the other priests or made sandwiches in his trailer. He got directions and looked forward to one of the first home-cooked meals he had had in a long time. Father Raymond's rudimentary cooking in Union Heights wasn't good enough to count.

Then Father Carter came out. He had been in the pews for Father Sanders' first Mass. He commented on the fact that Dick did not sing.

"You're at least supposed to at least chant the Doxology," he said. "Didn't you have to do that at the abbey?"

Dick explained as they walked together back to the sacristy. "Yeah, I did, but something happened there that caused me to stop singing. I must have irritated this one brother more than most, and he happened to be in the choir stall next to mine. When he was really mad, he would shout the psalms at me in loud, angry tones. Ever since then I can't bring myself to sing."

"I don't blame you," laughed Jimmy.

That night Dick drove to the Lundy's home, looking forward to spending time with a family. Their house was a new ranch-style home with a vaulted beamed ceiling. Father Sanders was quiet but enjoyed their conversation. He complimented Bill on his musical ability and asked where he learned it.

"I never had any lessons on an instrument or voice. In fact, I can't really read music. But I love it."

"It comes through," said Dick. "What kind of work do you do?"

"I'm a purchasing agent for a company that manufactures heavy machinery like rock crushers. We were living in Milwaukee when my old company was purchased by Hewitt-Robbins. Upon the recommendation of the manager, I transferred to Cincinnati where a new plant was under construction. After a year or so there, the manager decided to give my job to a friend of his. They offered me a chance to transfer to Sandusky, Ohio or to a new plant they were building here in Columbia. I drove down here in our 1955 Chevy on Labor Day weekend, 1969, and commuted among the three cities until November, when the plant here was opened.

"Mary didn't come until November, but when she got here, the pastor who was here at that time hooked her into parish work right away. I came back downstairs from the choir loft the first weekend she and the boys were here and the four of us passed in front of him. That priest gave her a big smile and said, 'Hello Mary, I've heard so much about you.' Then he leaned over and said, 'And this must be Kevin and Terry.' After that, every time there was something going on he'd call her or catch her after Mass and say 'Mary, you know we've got a problem, or 'We have to have a party,' or, 'We have to do something about this,' and 'Mary, would you mind taking care of that for me?'"

Dick laughed. He would remember that if he ever needed to get people involved in parish work. Mary spoke up.

"The first big project I did was to be the organizer for the reception for the first Eucharistic Minister classes for lay people. I said, 'That's not so hard. Just get two hard workers and the two prettiest women in the parish to pour coffee and you'll have people flocking in.' It worked!"

Soon Dick asked them to please stop calling him so formally. "Call me Dick," he said. "That's my name."

A few weeks later, Bishop Unterkoefler came to join the priests for their monthly Sunday afternoon meeting. As usual, he was gruff and intimidating and the priests were unusually serious in his presence. He seemed pleased at how well Dick seemed to be adjusting to parish life. Dick wished he could explain again how he really felt, that he would rather be working with the poor, but he'd heard that the bishop didn't like to be confronted, so he kept quiet. The bishop celebrated Mass that morning, and that evening, Bill Lundy talked with Dick about the bishop.

"You won't believe what Terry did when he first met him. The bishop was talking with some of the wealthier parishioners after Mass. Terry went up, right smack in front of him, looked up and poked him in the tummy with his index finger. 'Bishop,' he said, seriously, 'I'm Terry Lundy. You haven't met me yet.'"

Dick laughed. Terry was only six years old and had more nerve than most of the priests in the diocese.

Soon Father Sanders began spending time in a new "mission" of St. Peter's, the daughter congregation that still lacked a church and a name. It was temporarily called "Irmo-St. Andrews Catholic Community" and they held their Masses at local schools. Dick got to know others including Marge and Bill McCollam, John and Mary Chapiesky and a woman named Margaret Shull who was also deeply involved in the parish. She wrote for the parish newspaper, "Holy Smoke," and would be the director of religious education for the new church. Margaret was about the same age as Dick's brother, a heavyset woman with curly grayish-blonde hair. She shared his deep faith and was equally convinced that God was active in today's world, in the people who served Him and each other.

As the months went on, he spent some time with St. Peters' only black parishioner, Clay Normand, helping him start up a Boys and Girls Club. Dick also did a little work at the Baptist Gospel Mission shelter across the street from the parish office but did not like working with alcoholics. For the most part, however, he was bored, wondering what he was doing here. He visited Union Heights every few weeks, spent time at Mepkin and thought more often about returning to the abbey. He missed the routine and the silent peace he had known there, although it did seem like a long time ago. He couldn't shake the feeling that there was more in the world for him to do, but he wasn't going to find it at St. Peter's.

He didn't like living by himself, either. He enjoyed quiet time in meditation and prayer, but it was lonely without others around. Therefore, he spent evenings at the homes of parishioners, often with Bill and Mary and their boys. The couple joked that as soon as the oven timer went off, Father Sanders pulled into the driveway.

A bright spot in the news came on January 27, 1973, when the Vietnam Peace Accords were signed in Paris. President Nixon praised the agreement as the fulfillment of his promise to bring "peace with honor" to Vietnam. Dick shook his head sadly, wondering where the peace was for the 58,000 dead Americans, more than 1,000 missing in action and 150,000 wounded soldiers. Also, the nearly 1,000,000 dead military in North Vietnam and 250,000 in South Vietnam, plus hundreds of thousands of civilian deaths. He said prayers of gratitude that the war that was never declared was finally over. It had cast a shadow of deep pain over the country for a decade and a half.

That May his mother flew down from Illinois. She stayed with him in the trailer, thrilled to spend more than a few hours once a year with her son; she mentioned it several times. He took her to visit Mepkin and then to meet some of his friends in Union Heights. Ida Singletary was there at the snack bar. She said she was happy at Chicora High School, the school that was more white than black. Another white man had come to work at the Center, she told him. They called him, "White Mike." When Dick asked about Stanford Williams, Ida said he had been called to active duty in the Navy. He held his breath, hoping not to hear bad news.

"He was sailing in the waters off the shores of Vietnam just when the peace accords were signed. He's still in the service, but stateside now, and should be home soon."

Father Dick said another silent prayer of thanks for Stanford's safety.

World news affected Dick directly in October, 1973, when Arab oil-producing nations cut back on oil exports, starting an embargo that would last until the following March. He drove past gas station after gas station with signs taped to the pumps: "NO GAS." When gas was available, he waited on lines for hours to buy it. This meant Dick could visit Mepkin and Union Heights less often, so he made an uneasy effort to adjust to being a regular parish priest.

The gas shortage continued through the winter into March, and, as a result, Dick spent more time in his trailer reading publications like *NCR, The National Catholic Reporter*. He read more about Liberation Theology, the movement focused on the historical Jesus Christ and His relationship to real-life issues. The term "social justice" was used more often, a catchphrase for those who focused on following Jesus in caring for the poorest members of society. For nuns and priests who had entered the world and workplace looking for jobs in which they could serve humanity, *NCR* also contained employment listings. Dick began to read the paper backwards, looking for an assignment with the poor. When nothing struck him, he continued to wonder why he had been called from monastic life.

In late March, the question became more paramount. The abbot of Mepkin resigned to become a regular monk, and, within a few weeks, Dick received a letter from his replacement. It was kind but to the point, explaining what he already knew – the monks who were out in the diocese were still affiliated with the abbey with their vows. The previous abbot had allowed this "on leave" status to go on for years, but the new abbot could not.

"You need to make a decision," he wrote. "Either come back and stay here at Mepkin or be incardinated as a diocesan priest."

Though he had known this day would come, Father Sanders was not ready to face a final good-bye to the abbey. He called Father Raymond to see what he was going to do.

"I'm going back."

Dick hung up the phone, blew out a long breath and dropped to his knees. He still felt called to help the poor, yet maybe this white middle-class congregation was all there was for him out in the world. If so, he would return to Mepkin to finish out his life in peace with his brothers.

"Here am I, Lord," he prayed. "I need to know, how shall I serve you?"

Then he opened his Bible to a random page. Catholics were discouraged from using this type of divination for answers, but Father Sanders hoped something would speak to him. He found Jesus' commands to Peter in the Gospel of John.

"Feed my lambs, Peter. Take care of my sheep."

"What lambs, Lord, what sheep?"

Unanswered, he struggled with the decision in sleepless nights, wondering what his options would be if he left the abbey permanently and changed his mind later. He remembered clearly St. Benedict's Rule number 29, on this topic.

> If a brother, following his own evil ways, leaves the monastery but
> then wishes to return, he must first promise to make full amends
> for leaving. Let him be received back, but as a test of his humility
> he should be given the last place.

He grimaced at the description, "following his own evil ways," but knew he could deal with making amends and being put in last place. Finally, he decided not to decide, and ignored the letter. There were still too many unanswered questions.

A few months later, Bill Lundy asked him to celebrate Terry's First Communion at their home because the Church of Our Lady of the Hills had a name but no building. They would have a Mass at the church in September, to commemorate all of them together. Twenty-eight young people were receiving that year. Bill commented on the large number. "That's because of the 'northern invasion!'"

When Father Sanders looked at him quizzically, Bill explained. "We never had that many kids around here. It's because of all the companies moving their plants down here to escape taxes."

Dick frowned jokingly as he remembered that Bill's company had transferred him to Columbia only a few years earlier, to work at a new plant. "You're part of the invasion!" he laughed.

The evening of Terry's First communion, Dick sat in the family room with Terry and Kevin and talked to the boys about the meaning of Holy Communion. A little while later, he dressed in his vestments, took out his chalice and paten, and prepared the Host, water and wine. He had written a special service for Terry and made copies for those who attended.

> Whenever something exciting happens to us, we always want
> to share it with others. Jesus' coming to be with us was such
> a very special event that we want to keep celebrating it – like
> Christmas, and birthdays, and parties and anniversaries.
>
> Before Jesus went back to his Father, He told us how we
> could keep on celebrating and remembering Him. He told us to
> come together and share food and drink just like he did with his
> friends at the last supper.
>
> Tonight is a very special celebration for Terry who will, for
> the first time, join his parents, Bill and Mary, his brother Kevin,
> and all of us gathered here, to receive Jesus in a very special way.

As they sang hymns, Dick suddenly realized he would miss them, but it was time for him to go. The next day he called the bishop's office, asked for a meeting and requested a transfer to a place where he could again work with poor black people. He was surprised when the bishop seemed willing, and said the diocese supported a place down near Beaufort, about two hours south of Charleston. Camp St. Mary's, run by Sister Ellen Robertson, was home to an alternative high school for teen-aged mothers, most of whom were black. Noting Dick's long hair and beard with disapproval, the bishop assured Father Sanders that he and Sister Ellen would get along well. At least Dick was on his way back to a life that might make it worthwhile to be out of the abbey.

On Friday, June 7, 1974, the Church of the Hills congregation held a farewell reception for him and on Sunday, Father Sanders celebrated his last Mass in Columbia. That evening he had dinner with the Lundys who assured him they would stay in touch and even visit. Camp St. Mary's was not that far away.

After dinner, Dick went to his trailer to pack, anticipating his new assignment. He prayed to the Virgin Mary for guidance. If this third location outside the abbey did not turn out to be his calling, he would return to Mepkin. That night he rested peacefully in Mary's arms, trusting God for the final answer.

IV

SEXT

1974 - 1978

Chapter Sixteen –
Camp St. Mary's – 1974 - 1975

Father Sanders headed south to Ridgeland, home of Camp St. Mary's and the "Low Country Human Development Center." After leaving the highway, he drove through a remote area with only small, dilapidated shacks made of weathered wood and rusty tin roofs. Union Heights was poor, but this was another world. Black children playing in the dirt near the road stared blankly as he drove by.

Soon he arrived at his destination, a beautiful spot on a bluff along the Okatie River. In many ways it was like Mepkin, but sandier and without the gardens. Camp St. Mary's was natural Low Country. Sister Ellen Robertson greeted him in the driveway and invited him into her office. She was a large woman with a pleasant face one could call jolly. Her short white hair contrasted with round, dark-rimmed glasses and she wore white pants, a plain blue shell and a pewter cross around her neck. He noted two telephones on her desk and explained that she liked to deal with situations efficiently so she often spoke on both of them at the same time. She was an Adrian Dominican Sister. Dick was always interested in histories of Religious Orders.

"We go back to the thirteenth Century with St. Dominic," she explained. "Like most orders around the U.S. we revisited our constitution after Vatican II and a lot more of us started working in social justice. We take St. Dominic seriously as we 'scatter and sow seeds of change'."

Sister Ellen surprised him by telling him she was often not easy to get along with, and that she, like many of her Dominican sisters, was a no-nonsense, hard-working, risk-taking woman, deeply devoted to her work. She said it with what Dick judged to be justifiable pride and he sensed she also meant it as a bit of a warning. Ellen and her staff were turning Camp St. Mary's into a place of active social justice by helping children and teenaged mothers. When she first arrived two years ago, the camp was not even being used.

Sister Ellen Robertson, Camp St. Mary's

"When the Bishop integrated the camp in 1966, the white kids stopped coming and the black kids' parents couldn't support it, so it closed."

Dick asked if a young man named Stanford Williams had ever brought young black kids dhere for "rap sessions" with white kids. She did not remember, but had heard about meetings that took place shortly before the white kids disappeared.

"How did you get here?" he asked.

"My blood-sister Mary Anne, an Adrian Dominican sister, too, was working nearby in one of the poorest areas in South Carolina. Father Thomas Duffy showed Mary Anne this place, hoping she would consider directing a program here that would use the existing abandoned buildings. Have you met Father Duffy?"

Dick smiled. "I guess you could say we've met. We spent a couple of nights in jail together."

Ellen looked at him sideways and smiled. "That's one story I'm going to want to hear soon! Anyway, Mary Anne wasn't interested, but she suggested me. I was in transition at the time – also too long of a story for right now – and I jumped at the chance. That was about a year ago. When we got some money, we started a child development program here for small children, and we also take care of Hispanic migrant workers' children in the summer. As we started to learn about the older black kids, we found that 25 percent of them couldn't read and some of them had graduated high school that way! The problem is that most of their parents are uneducated and they speak only Gullah, the language of the Sea Islands. When the kids start school, that's the only language they know. The white teachers can't understand them and the children can't understand the teachers."

Dick knew a little about Gullah from the people in Union Heights, but the children there all spoke regular English, too.

"Do you speak Gullah?" he asked.

"A little. Some of the mothers of the children in our daycare speak it when they tell stories to the children. It's a Creole language, an adaptation of West African languages to English, like Jamaican Patois."

Dick had never heard of Patois but said nothing, reminding himself of how little he knew about the world in general.

"The parents can't read, and therefore they never read to their children, can't help them with homework, etc. And there's no motivation for the kids to stay in school because the parents don't see any future for them anyway. They figure they'll end up picking crab or shucking oysters, two of the main jobs for poor Blacks around here."

Dick mentioned that he had some experience tutoring kids and adults.

"That will come in handy. How about if I give you a tour?"

As they walked, Father Sanders noted the pool, arts and crafts room, large dining area, church and concrete block cabins. There was a dock where they fished and crabbed and a beach for public swimming. Behind one of the buildings sat an old "hippie van" that came with the camp, a 1964 Ford Econoline painted in psychedelic colors.

Ellen smiled. "I used this van the first year to go out and get the children, but soon there were so many that we had to get buses."

They sat on a picnic table and she explained one other program that had become more meaningful to her than the others.

"I mentioned young mothers. Last fall, one of our teenagers was expelled from high school, so we brought her in for tutoring. That was the beginning of our alternative high school for teenaged mothers. Most of them have dropped out of high schools or been kicked out."

"Isn't it a law that all children have to go to school?" He had some familiarity with this, too, from Union Heights

She nodded. "South Carolina has a Mandatory School Attendance Law, but it exempts children who are pregnant or have had a child out of wedlock. Essentially it says that a child with a child is an adult and therefore doesn't have to go to school."

Dick frowned.

"That's why we decided to take them here" she nodded. "We go out and pick them up every day, forty of them now, in about a fifty-mile radius in two counties."

Dick wondered if any of them lived in the kinds of shacks he had passed on his way here, guessing that they did. Ellen continued.

"I insist that they at least finish high school and that they learn parenting and other life skills. We teach everything here that they learn in regular high schools, using the same books, but this is a more forgiving environment. If they don't complete a course, we don't fail them; we just make them finish it the next quarter. If they do a paper and get less than a 75 percent grade, they have to do it over. We also teach life courses like sewing, budgeting, how to apply for a job and so on, and of course, how to avoid drugs and alcohol abuse."

"It's great," said Dick, wishing he had thought of an alternative high school when he was in Union Heights. He decided to call Raymond about it, but then remembered that Raymond had gone back to Mepkin. It was a strange realization. Ellen continued.

"We give the young moms and their babies the only decent food many of them get all day – breakfast and lunch. Oh, I almost forgot; we also have grade-school children who come on Saturdays and during the summer for education, culture and recreational programs and teenagers in the evenings. And we have a swimming pool and try to make time for swimming lessons."

Dick smiled again. There was plenty for him to do here. He looked forward to learning more about the practical application of social justice theories. Bishop Unterkoefler had been right about one thing – Dick and Sister Ellen were going to get along just fine.

"How are you funded?" he asked.

She shook her head, remembering how they struggled. "While we tried to figure out what to do with the place, I worked as a counselor at the Mental Health Department, going into the public schools to help teachers cope with problems caused by integration."

Dick would like to have heard more about that but Ellen was focused on efficiency as she kept talking. "I learned there that federal grant money was available to offset the effects of segregation, so we applied for it. We also did some fundraising, and we charge sliding fees for our services based on what the families can afford. I can't tell you the number of meetings with local county councils and state agencies I sat through, trying to get them to pay more attention and provide money for programs for poor Blacks."

Ellen said he could start as soon as he moved in. They had housing for volunteers, but Dick had a different idea. He had gotten used to the old trailer he rented in Columbia, so he called and asked if he could buy it. The bishop approved the purchase price and Dick borrowed a truck, hooked the trailer to the back and towed it Beaufort the following week. He set it on the banks of the Okatie River.

He got to know some of the teen mothers, mostly through tutoring or teaching them to swim. When there was time, the older girls told him stories that chilled him, about incest and violence, poverty and hopelessness. For many of them, Camp St. Mary's was just a safer place to be. One of them told him how hard it was for pregnant girls to stay in high school.

"I lost my friends, my family was mad, my father disowned me. Everything good was over... until I got here."

He also worked in the daycare, teaching the little ones the alphabet and their numbers and, in the afternoon, taught them to swim doggy-paddle. On some days he drove the young mothers home on the bus. Ellen once asked if he would pick them up in the morning but he groaned so loudly at the idea that she gave up. "I thought Trappists got up early!" He just groaned again.

One afternoon as was taking some of them home, a pretty young girl named Anyika asked if he would help carry her baby and books into the house. He pulled over in front of the one-room unpainted shack and saw a heavyset, barefoot black woman dressed in ragged clothing standing in the door. "That be my mom," said Anyika.

The woman had a boil over her right eye, her mouth looked parched and the dead look in her eyes suggested a kind of dull pain. She moved slowly out of the way as Dick carried the baby inside. Newspapers were pasted on the walls for insulation, and cardboard material hung down in spots from the ceiling. There were no windows, lights or plumbing, just a wood burning stove and two kerosene lanterns. Four young children lay on a double mattress on the floor and Anyika put her baby next to them. A pot of what appeared to be a mixture of grits and peas sat on the wood stove. Dick was visibly shaken at this poverty and could not pretend otherwise. Anyika let out a long sigh.

"Yeah, Father, this is it. Now you know why we love Sister Ellen."

The following week, Dick sat in the dining room with the newspaper, reading more details about President Nixon's resignation after the Watergate scandal and Gerald Ford's pardon of him. Though no longer a fan of Nixon's, Dick thought both were wise moves. The country had been through enough.

When one of the teens came and sat with him, he set the paper down. She was pretty, in a rough way, about fifteen years old, tall and thin, her hair held in place by a braided rag headband. She sat without speaking, looking out the window with a scowl on her face. He tried to talk to her but her words and the tone of her responses communicated only contempt. Dick then remembered why this one was here; she had been expelled from school for repeated bad behavior that included disrespecting and threatening teachers.

A crying baby and a voice from the other room interrupted their talk before it even began. "Sawny, your baby's crying. Come in and feed him!"

"Yazz'm," she called back sarcastically, and then turned to the priest. "They make me feed my baby breast milk, and they say it don't hurt but I think it does. My mama says the baby can eat grits."

"Your baby is only a month old!" said Father Sanders. Even he knew babies that young could not eat solid food.

"Mama says she knows better. She doesn't want me coming here. She says I think I'm better than everyone else, thinks the baby is too good for them, should be eating the same food I ate and my brothers and sisters ate. She thinks, too, that I should be out workin', but I know I need education. If I don't get it, I'll be living poor just like my mama."

"What do you want to do?"

She shrugged. "I don't know. But I know if I don't finish high school I can't do nothin' but work in rice or in crab factories or worse yet, shuckin' oysters. My older brothers and sisters never finished, and that's what they do. I want more than that for me and my baby." She paused for a moment and her attitude softened, but just then the voice called again from the other room and the baby's cries grew louder, so Sawny left without another word.

As time went on, Father Sanders spent more time with her and the other girls and prayed for their success in school and in life. He and Ellen continued to get along well, too. He liked her directness and her passion for helping women and children. One night after dinner they took a walk down by the river and sat at a picnic table. It was a beautiful night, the rippling water reflecting an elongated image of the almost-full moon. Dick asked Ellen how she had been led to a path of social justice.

"As a teenager," she said slowly, "I had a strong sense that God had something important for me to do. I believe I followed His will in developing this school. Before that, I was working in education but it never seemed like the perfect fit."

Dick nodded, wondering when he would find his perfect fit.

She asked, "Do you miss the monastery?"

"Sometimes," he nodded.

"I understand how you feel. The Adrian Dominicans are heavily rooted in contemplative prayer, and I wish I had more time for it. Ideally, we could mix it with our social justice work, but there's always so much to do."

Though he grew more comfortable at Camp St. Mary's, Dick could not shake the nagging feeling that this was not his destination. He made frequent trips to Mepkin, still trying to decide when to return to monastic life. Being there recharged his faith and gave him renewed energy as he waited for God to make His plans known.

Chapter Seventeen –
The Migrants

One day in April, 1975, Sister Ellen reminded him about the migrants. Every summer, from late May to mid-July, the staff members who worked with the teen mothers also provided daycare services for Hispanic farm workers.

He got to know them a little at a time because he was not yet out of bed when they dropped off their children early in the morning, but he enjoyed having the Hispanic children around during the day. They got along well with the children of the black girls and Dick spent as much time as he could, playing with them and teaching them. When the parents returned in the late afternoons, he noted they were dirty and exhausted, yet treated their children so gently and with such love that Dick was moved. Most of them were from Texas and spoke at least some English. The more he saw of these interesting people, the more curious he was about their lifestyle.

"Where do you go when you leave here?" he asked a man one day as he helped put three children into a truck.

"We go north – we call it 'up the road' – to North Carolina, Delaware, and New Jersey. Some even go all the way up to Maine, and work all summer. Others go to the Midwest to pick apples. In the fall, we head back to Florida. My family goes to a place called Naples where there's work in tomatoes and other vegetables in the winter. They have pretty good housing for us there, too."

"What do you do about attending Mass when you're traveling?"

The man looked uncomfortable, shuffled his feet and turned his hat in his hands. "We don't go."

Another man continued the answer. "We're not comfortable in white churches, Father. People stare at us, looking down at us. Also, even those of us who speak English still prefer to worship in Spanish – that's our first language – and there are no Spanish-speaking churches in most places."

"Hey Father, maybe you could say a Mass for us in Spanish?"

Dick shook his head. "I don't know Spanish. Sorry."

The man nodded and raised his eyebrows. "Could you learn?"

There was something about the way he asked the question that showed Dick how important faith was to these people, and how much they missed celebrating it.

That night, he thought about their work. He knew about vegetable farming from Mepkin, but the migrants worked at an entirely different production level. What would it be like to plant, weed, tie or pick crops all day long, every day? The only similar experience he had was when he was a teenager, something he had not thought about in a long time.

When Dick was growing up, for a few weeks every July, corn farmers on the outskirts of Peru/LaSalle hired teenagers to remove the tassels from corn. The farmers planted rows of a different kind of corn in the same fields, and later the wind blew pollen from those plants into the detasseled plants, mixing the two into hybrid corn seed. He hated the corn rash that looked and felt like bad sunburn, but soon he learned to wear long sleeved shirts, pants and gloves and a bandana around his neck and chin. The farmers only paid minimum wage and the work was hot and miserable, but Dick's mother said it would build character. Dick worked ten hours a day in the hot sun for three weeks in two summers but as soon as he was old enough to work at the Rec. Department, he never de-tasseled corn again.

He kept the image in mind when the migrant parents came to Camp St. Mary's to pick up their children. He also noted tee-shirts with pictures of Our Lady of Guadalupe. There were decals of her in the back windows of some of the trucks, too. He asked a woman named Maria if she would tell him the story. She and her husband were on their way back to their camps and she suggested Father Sanders come with them so they could have time to talk. They all had to make dinner first and do other chores. He followed on dirt roads through field after field until they came to a housing compound of wood *barracas*. Families with children stayed in one room each, and young single men bunked together in groups.

He was impressed with the people's warmth and kindness as he sat in the front of the *barraca* of Maria's family, watching the men and women go about their evening tasks as the children played in the dirt. After about an hour, Maria brought him a plate of chicken tacos and sat down with him on the step. He hesitated as he assumed it was spicy food, but it was delicious and quite mild.

"Spicy is Mexicans from Texas," she explained. "I came from Mexico, and our cooking is not so *picante*."

He nodded as he took another bite. There was also a delicious white cheese and beans and rice on the side. As he ate, she told him the story of *Nuestra Señora de Guadalupe*, Our Lady of Guadalupe.

"It was a very long time ago, not long after the Spanish conquered our country. Early in the morning an *Indio*, Indian man named Juan Diego was on his way to church. You see, he had been converted to Christianity. He was fifty-seven years old. Suddenly he heard the most beautiful songs of birds and then he saw a vision of a young girl, glowing in sunbeams. She called to him sweetly, like he was a little child, *'Juanito, Juan Dieguito.'*"

The vision was the Blessed Virgin Mary, she explained, still pregnant with the Christ Child. "You could tell that by the sash she wore; it was marked in the Indian way that told when a woman was with child. She told Juan Diego to go and tell the bishop to build her a church right there on that spot, a rocky area in the middle of nowhere. He was afraid because the bishop was Spanish and Juan Diego was just a poor Indian; he knew the bishop would never see him. Our Lady assured him that they would let him in, but as it turned out, Juan Diego was right. The bishop's servants turned him away."

By now a crowd of children had gathered around Maria and Father Sanders, wondering what he was doing there.

"*Sientate*," she told them. "Sit down and listen to the story of *Nuestra Señora.*"

Dick was charmed when they squatted down in a circle and listened attentively as Maria continued.

"Then someone told him his uncle was sick. He went back to his village and his uncle was actually dying, so Juan Diego went to the priest to bring him for the Last Rites. That meant he had to go right past the spot where he first saw Our Lady. He went around the back of the hill, hoping to avoid her, but she appeared there in front of him, glowing like before. When Juan Diego told her his uncle was sick, she said her famous words: 'Do not be afraid of anything. *¿No estoy yo aquí, que soy tú Madre?'*"

Maria turned to the children as if she were their teacher. "Now what does that mean, in English?"

One of the older girls answered, "It means, 'Am I not here, who is your mother?'"

Maria smiled. She took Father Sanders' empty plate inside and while she was gone, he looked at the children and the other people in the camp. He felt comfortable, as if he were with a large extended family, and completely at home. Maria returned, drying her hands on a dish towel.

"OK, where was I? Yes, so Our Lady told Juan to go home again, and Juan found his uncle there, completely cured. She had given his uncle the same message: 'Do not be afraid of anything. Am I not here, who is your mother?' Then Juan put on his cloak, called a *tilma*...."

One of the children interrupted to clarify for the priest. "*Padre*, a *tilma* is like a cloak and a big apron, together."

Dick smiled at being called "*Padre*." He liked the sound of it.

"So he went again to the bishop," continued Maria. "This time the bishop wanted to believe him but said he would need a sign so he could be sure it really was the Blessed Virgin. Sadly, Juan Diego returned to Our Lady with the bad news. She was not concerned and told him, 'Up on the hill you'll find Castilian roses.'"

Dick was impressed with how well Maria told this story, with vocalizations and gestures; she could have been an actress. The children were still listening attentively.

"Flowers didn't grow in the winter in that area, and Castilian roses did not grow yet in the New World at all. Still, Juan went up to the hill and found the roses all cut and ready for him and he gathered them up in his *tilma*. When he got to the bishop, the roses spilled out on the floor. Then the bishop knelt down in front of Juan Diego, staring intently at Juan's chest and midsection."

Maria motioned to the front part of her shirt and the children nodded.

"Juan was afraid. What was happening? Why was the bishop kneeling in front of him?" She looked again at the children. "What was it?"

"It was the image of Our Lady of Guadalupe!"

"What a great story!" said Dick. "How beautiful!"

"*Sí, Padre*," she nodded, looking at her fingernails that were stained from picking tomatoes. "But there's more. That painting on his *tilma,* they put it in a frame and hung it in the church. One time the church burned down but the picture was not damaged, and another time, during one of the wars, the whole building was bombed but the painting was still perfect."

Dick applauded Maria's rendition of the story and the children clapped along with him. He spent the drive back and the rest of that evening thinking about the story and the devotion of the migrants to Our Lady of Guadalupe, the Mexican manifestation of the Mother of Christ. When he got back, he looked up the history in an encyclopedia. It said that, because the young Mary appeared with the Christ child still in her womb, Our Lady of Guadalupe was also believed to be the protector of the unborn, and women who were pregnant prayed to her to keep their babies safe.

He did not know why, but he felt drawn to these people. He went again to the camps and met more of them, and more of them asked, "*Padre,* why don't you learn Spanish so you can say a Mass for us?"

The thought was tempting until he thought back to how he struggled with Latin – he dreaded the idea of learning another language. Anyway, these people were only here for a little over a month each year. He had enough work to do with the girls and children at Camp St. Mary's.

The next day, however, he found himself thinking about the migrants. He went to the camp again the following Saturday evening and spent more time with Maria and her family. She introduced him to several others, and they spent the evening drinking coffee. He was fascinated with their stories of moving from place to place, following the crops.

It was not long before he realized he was happiest when he was with them. Being there made him feel good about himself and particularly about his priestly vocation. One day he brought a card table and the accoutrements and offered to say a Mass in English in front of the *barracas*. Not many people attended, but there were a few. Maria explained that, even though many of them spoke English, Spanish was their first language. They didn't relate to the Mass in English and they didn't know the prayers. He also noted that no one received Communion.

"We would never do that, *Padre*," explained one of the men shaking his head strongly. "Not without Confession first. Mexicans won't go to Communion without Confession."

The following Saturday he went earlier and heard a few confessions. Still, as with the Mass, he could tell that the people had trouble expressing their sins in English.

One late afternoon when the migrants came to pick up their children, he asked a group of three men if he could go to the fields with them, just to see what it was like. They raised their eyebrows and grinned at each other, then checked themselves, not wanting to offend him.

"Uh, *Padre*, I don't think you'd do too well out there," said one.

Another drew lines in the dirt with his boot.

"It's pretty tough work, *Padre*, and early. We're on the bus at 5:00 and by 6:00 we're in the fields, set up and ready to start picking."

Dick had not thought about the early hour. "Could I just come out and meet you later in the day? Maybe I could help you."

They shook their heads, trying not to smile. "Uh-uh. The farmers won't allow people to just come out there; you'd have to spend the whole day and we work eight to ten hours. Even some of us get sick from the sun, and our backs are killing us all the time. It's hot, and there's never enough water, plus we're working so fast..."

The man seemed unwilling to finish the sentence so the third man picked up where he left off. "We get paid by the bucket, so we're really hustling, bent over, picking as fast as we can or running along side the trucks, throwing the full buckets up, catching the empty ones and filling them again." Then he said what the others had been afraid to say. "No offense, *Padre*, but you'd probably just be in the way."

Dick sighed, knowing they were right.

At the end of June the migrants headed north. South Carolina's work was done for them until next summer. Father Sanders was touched when they asked him to bless their trucks before they left. The trucks, he realized, were critical to their lives; without them, they could not move from place to place for work. The vehicles safely transported the workers and their children, and provided a place to sleep if they did not make it to the next farm on time. He sprinkled each truck with Holy Water and blessed them.

"*Padre* Sanders" sadly said goodbye to those he had come to know and then focused again on the young black girls and their children. The migrants stayed with him, though, in his thoughts and prayers.

As he got to know Sister Ellen better, he became more impressed with her faith and trust in the role she filled; she was certain she was carrying out God's will for her. They talked often about how important it was to work among the poor in order to imitate Jesus on earth.

Unable to shake the Hispanic migrants even though they had gone north, he decided to study a little Spanish so he could talk to more of them the following summer. Maybe he could even learn enough to say Mass. In the fall, he took a night class at the nearby Naval Reserve Marine Air Station, relieved that it was easier than Latin and that his knowledge of Latin was helpful. In fact, to his amazement, he picked it up faster than the other students. Maybe this is the Holy Spirit, he thought, giving me this ability. Maybe I'm getting help because I'm supposed to be here.

He talked to Sister Ellen about his idea of taking Mass in Spanish to the camps when the migrants returned.

"Great idea, Dick, but it could turn into a lot of work. You've only seen a few of the camps. There are a lot more of them out there."

"Could you help me?"

"I could come once in a while," she said, carefully, "but the teens and children here are what God has called me to do. You'll have to figure out how to get help somewhere else."

He was used to her bluntness, and of course, she was right. She did have a suggestion, though. "You might want to think about getting a volunteer to assist you. If you could find someone fluent in Spanish, all the better."

"Good idea." He would run an ad in the National Catholic Reporter. He also decided to study Spanish full time. Ellen mentioned MACC, the Mexican American Cultural Center in San Antonio. "They have classes in culture combined with Spanish, plus I'm sure you could study more about Liberation Theology there."

That fall, 1975, Dick drove home to attend his twentieth high school reunion. He stayed with his mother and Gail in the home Betty had designed. She didn't seem to have her normal energy and Dick worried that she was getting sick or depressed. Later in the week, however, he decided it was just her age. That summer he had turned thirty-eight and didn't have all that much energy himself.

During the day on Saturday, he drove to the homes of his close old friends, spending time individually with Joe, Jim, Art and Duke, and they reviewed the changes in their lives. As they talked, Dick wondered for a moment what it would have been like to have lived a more normal life, but could not visualize it. He was happy with his choices. Then his old spiritual friend, Francis Kasperski, came in and Dick greeted him warmly. They talked for a while about their different experiences in the priesthood. Francis was pastor of a parish in LaSalle.

Saturday night was the formal reunion dinner at St. Bede. Most of the alumni wore ties and jackets. Four of the graduating class of 1955 had become priests and three of them wore Roman Collars. Dick wore an un-collared button-down shirt, open at the neck, with a jacket. No need for formalities. He was also the only one with long hair and a beard. He noted that the same order of sisters from Mexico still cooked. Now, he was able to talk with them a little, and explained in rudimentary Spanish how the boys had always appreciated their work.

That night before falling asleep, Dick thought about how much of his conversation had been about the migrants. He loved how they seemed to all be part of one extended family, helping each other at the camps and driving in caravans "up the road" to the next state and the next farm. Then a larger connection dawned on him. It was their devotion to Our Lady of Guadalupe, Mary Immaculate, the Blessed Virgin.

Still, he was not sure if this was a calling or a passing interest. He prayed for guidance and found another part of his answer in simple logic. The Blacks were mostly Protestant, the Hispanics were mostly Catholic and he was a Catholic priest. Where could he help more? He fell peacefully asleep, thinking of Juan Diego and Our Lady of Guadalupe.

CHAPTER EIGHTEEN –
YOLANDA'S CALLING – 1976

As Father Sanders studied Spanish and tenets of Liberation Theology at the Mexican American Cultural Center, a woman in Charleston was awakened from a deep sleep. The message was loud yet gentle.

"Yolanda, work with my people. Help my people."

She became lightheaded and felt as if she had been lifted up out of her body, felt the greenness of the blades of grass, the wetness of dew, like being taken into an unbelievable heavenly embrace. She knew it was a message from God.

"What people, Lord? What people?"

"My people. My migrant people."

Her husband woke from his sleep and stared. She was sitting up, staring at the ceiling with an almost angelic glow around her head.

"Ron, I felt something, or heard something."

She was sweating and breathing rapidly and her husband, a registered nurse, was concerned. He leaned up on one arm to look at her more closely. "You don't think it was a dream?"

"No, I swear this was a message. I think it was a calling from God."

Filled with religious fervor himself, Ron knew his wife and the strength of her faith. If she said this was something, it was something.

She lay back down on the pillow, her long brown hair framing her face, smiling as she relived the feeling, such beauty, such peace. Ron had never seen her like this. She was excited to know what the message meant, yet still felt so lightheaded that she could not make sense of it.

"Ron, the voice said, 'Help my people, my migrants.' What could that mean?"

"I don't know," said her husband, gently. "Migrants like farm workers are the only kind I can think of. But what could that mean to us? Do you have any migrant farm worker kids in your school?"

"No, I don't know any around here. There were migrants outside of Miami when I was growing up, but I never saw them."

Ron and Yolanda had moved to Charleston, South Carolina, the previous July. She had a job teaching eighth grade and he was a nurse at the Veteran's Administration.

"Go back to sleep," he said. "See what you think in the morning."

She lay back down into the perfect peace, remembering the sound: "Yolanda, help my people, my migrants."

The next day she awoke, still marveling at what had happened. She and Ron decided she should pray about it so she went as usual to her teaching job. As she walked up and down the rows of students, checking their work, she became lightheaded again with the same beauty she had felt the night before. She sat down at her desk, flushed, and told the class to work problems. She needed time to think. What kind of message was this that came so strongly? Was she ill? Hallucinating?

She finished school trying to keep the voice out of her mind, but could not wait for the day to be over. She wanted to talk more with her husband, the love of her life, her counselor, her friend.

"It sounds like a calling to me, Yolanda," said Ron as he took a forkful of *chiles rellenos*. "But how can you do it?"

"I don't know. Maybe it's just some weird thing, and not a calling at all. But it was so real, and so beautiful."

"Go see Father Hanley. This might be something."

The next day Yolanda drove to their church. Father Frank Hanley was in his office, planning his sermon for the following Sunday. He knew Yolanda because she and Ron were Eucharistic Ministers at the church.

"Father Hanley, the weirdest thing happened."

She told him about the feeling, the connection, the perfect peace. He was skeptical but also open to the possibility that this was a calling.

"You need to pray about this, Yolanda. Messages from God are sometimes real, but we have to be careful to interpret correctly and to be sure it was really His voice."

"Father, I'm sure it's real. Otherwise I don't know where something like that would come from. My husband Ron thinks it's real, too, but we're both confused about how I can do work with migrants here in Charleston. Are there even migrants around here?"

"Actually, there are a lot of them here, but only in the summer," explained the priest. "They come in late April, early May and stay through June to work in the fields down around Johns Island, just south of Charleston. Then they move on up the road to Maryland and New Jersey, I think, and in the fall they go back to Florida or Texas. It seems more of them come, every year."

He looked at his watch and realized he needed to get back to work.

"Pray, Yolanda," he said gently. "If it truly was God's voice, He will guide you."

Not long after, she found an envelope from Father Frank in her mailbox. In it was an advertisement from *NCR*, the *National Catholic Reporter* – a little ad from the Help Wanted section.

"Bilingual volunteer needed for work among Mexican migrant people in Beaufort, S.C. Room and board will be provided. Call or write Father Dick Sanders."

Yolanda wrote a letter.

"Dear Father Sanders: I have a copy of your ad requesting a bilingual person to help you work with migrant farm workers. I was born in Cuba so I am fluent in Spanish. I have three children but I could spend the summer in Beaufort if I could bring them. They are eight and a half, six and a half and the baby, Aaron, will turn two in May. My husband is a nurse at the Veteran's Administration but he could come on weekends and help, too."

Every day she checked the mail for a response. This would be the best possible answer to God's call to help the migrants because Beaufort was only an hour from their home, but she heard nothing. She tried the telephone number a few times, but it was either busy or didn't answer. Finally she decided this ad was not the answer she sought, and went back to praying to discern God's will.

Then one night in early May the phone rang.

"Yolanda?"

"Yes, this is Yolanda."

"This is Father Dick Sanders."

She paused for a moment, not recognizing the name.

"I ran the ad in NCR that you answered."

Her attention returned immediately. "Yes, Father, I remember. I sent you a letter a month and a half ago. I tried calling but never got through."

"I'm sorry. I went to San Antonio to study Spanish at the Mexican American Cultural Center."

"*Sí*, MACC," she said. "I know it. *¿Habla Español?*"

"*Sí, poquito*," he said shyly. A little. "I took an intermediate class to improve."

"Father, I am so strongly called by God to do this work. I actually heard Him. Then I saw your ad and decided it was a sign …."

She spent several minutes telling him about her life and her family and the calling. At the other end of the line, Father Sanders thought how perfect she would be for him; she talked a lot and he hardly spoke. He was certain that Yolanda was the answer to his prayers. In the back of his mind he heard the chanting of a psalm.

> You have put gladness in my heart,
> more than when grain and wine and oil increase.

"....then I got the ad from Father Hanley and I was so excited because it seemed so perfect. My husband is OK with the idea, he's a very religious guy......"

Dick interrupted gently.

"Yolanda, please come. The migrants start pulling in next month and I need you."

He gave her directions and the following Saturday she arrived at Camp St. Mary's. Sister Ellen met her in the driveway and brought her in. Father Sanders looked up from where he sat on the floor, playing with the one and two year-old babies of the teen mothers.

Sister Ellen smiled, "It's a shame he never had kids."

Dick laughed. "No thanks. I like to play with them but I like to give them back!"

"*Hola*, I'm Yolanda," said his new volunteer.

"*Mucho gusto*," he said, standing to shake her hand. It's nice to meet you.

"*Igualmente.*" You, too.

He noted that she studied him and wondered what she saw. He had trimmed his beard and his hair was a little shorter now than before, though both were still long.

She introduced her children who said hello and then started playing with the black children on the floor. Dick took Yolanda on a tour. His trailer was older and more rundown now than it had been when he bought it, but it was a beautiful location. He showed her the small house behind the trailer where volunteers lived. Dick explained that he had come to work with the black children and their mothers, but felt now that he might be called to Hispanic ministry. "The migrants aren't here long, though. They start coming in mid-May and most of them leave by the end of June."

"Where are they from, Father?"

"Call me Dick," he smiled.

"OK, Dick," although he could tell she wasn't comfortable calling a priest by his first name. "What should my kids call you?"

He thought for a moment. "How about 'Uncle Dick?'"

As part of the explanation of what he needed he showed her a map that he had started working on, to help him locate the camps. "What do you think?"

"Well, it sounds interesting," said Yolanda. "My husband works, so I would have to bring the kids with me."

"Maybe they could attend the camp," he offered. "I like children. You could stay overnight with the kids in the apartments where the volunteers live. During the days the older ones could play around here and the little guy could go into the daycare."

Yolanda agreed and came again the following week with her three children, this time to stay for a month. Her husband would come on weekends. More volunteers had come the previous week to work with the teen girls, so the place she was originally going to stay was full, so Father Sanders moved Yolanda's family into his trailer and he moved to one of the bedrooms in Sister Ellen's home. While they waited for the migrants to return, Yolanda helped with tutoring the teen mothers in math.

When the farm workers arrived a few days later, Dick and Yolanda had breakfast with the young mothers and their babies, then went out to find more camps. Some of them were a lot worse than the *barracas* he had seen before, just little ten-by-ten-foot cement platforms with tin roofs and no walls, indoor plumbing or electricity. The first couple they came across was sleeping on a thin mattress and the woman was in advanced pregnancy, going into labor. Dick and Yolanda had the same reaction to the couple – they were like Mary and Joseph.

"I know about the church and about Jesus," said Yolanda, "but I truly feel like I am meeting Jesus in these people. This is horrible; and yet they never seem sad, they never complain."

Yolanda started going with him to the camps on Sunday afternoons and most evenings to say Mass on the card-table altar. When the people sang it sounded beautiful, and Yolanda developed a little songbook for them. The migrants asked to keep the booklets, so she left them.

A few weeks later, Dick received a letter from the bishop's office. Because of the ever-growing shortage of priests, he needed Father Sanders to move to Blessed Sacrament Church in Charleston. It was yet another white middle-class church, and Dick was once again being torn from ministering to the poor. Without mentioning it to Yolanda, he drove to the diocese and asked to be allowed to remain at Camp St. Mary's. The bishop greeted him with a frown, probably displeased with Dick's hair and beard, but Dick ignored the look.

"I'm not sure exactly how or why," he explained to the bishop, "but I know that I am called by God to work with the poor. Can't I stay where I am?"

The bishop shook his head. "I need someone at Blessed Sacrament. All the priests in the diocese move when transferred."

"But I am really helping the teen mothers and their children, and also the Hispanic migrants, when they come. Can I at least stay until the end of June when the migrants go north?"

Reluctantly, the bishop agreed. "But don't worry about missing the migrants. There are farms closer to Blessed Sacrament than you might think. In fact, I will put you in charge of migrant ministry there, if it will make you happier."

Dick was grateful. "It will, Bishop, it will. Thank you."

He and Yolanda continued their ministry, bringing the word of God to many more migrants over the next few weeks. He even baptized a few babies at nearby Holy Spirit Catholic Church.

After he blessed the pickup trucks and vans and the last family left to go north, he told Yolanda about his transfer. She accepted it better than Dick had.

"It's not that far, only an hour and a half north of here," she said. "It's actually better for me because it's closer to where we live. And we can still come back here next summer when the migrants return."

Sadly, Dick packed and said goodbye to his old trailer. Then he returned to the building to say goodbye to the girls, he realized he would miss them, especially Sawny, who was turning into a lovely young woman.

"You're the first person who ever really believed in me, besides Sister Ellen," she said. "I'm gonna miss you."

Sister Ellen felt bad that he was leaving, but the bishop's decisions were usually final. They said goodbye and Dick drove up to Charleston, wondering what direction God would send him in next.

Chapter Nineteen – Cuernavaca– 1976 – 1977

The Church of the Blessed Sacrament was an imposing, modern structure, golden-tan in color with two huge towers on either side of the multi-story stained glass windows in the front. The priests lived at the rectory and Dick was given a two-room suite with a separate entrance. The back room contained a bed and a dresser, and in front was a small office that doubled as a living room and kitchen.

He liked the pastor, Father Nick Bayard, and the other associate pastor Father Robert "Bobby" Fields. The three of them got together once a week to coordinate their work. In addition to offering Mass and celebrating sacraments, Father Bayard worked with the marriage encounter program, Father Bobby was the representative for the parish school and Father Dick would work with migrant ministry.

"That means you have to say more Masses and sacraments when the migrants aren't around," said Bobby. "and we'll cover for you in the summer when they're here."

He confirmed what the bishop had said, that there were migrants closer to Blessed Sacrament than Beaufort. In fact, Johns Island, only about fifteen minutes south, had many tomato farms that used migrant labor. Until they returned the following summer, however, Dick would once again minister to a white middle-class population.

Dick and Father Bobby were about the same age and became good friends. Bobby was a little shorter than Dick and a little heavier, with medium-length brown hair and a closely-trimmed beard.

The main thing he liked about Bobby was his sense of humor. He complained about almost everything but never seemed to lose his humorous attitude, except in the face of injustice. They agreed on many things, including the evil of prejudice. Bobby, born and raised in South Carolina, had grown up with segregation and had vivid memories of Blacks being tormented for no reason.

"Once, when I was about ten, I saw a drunken white man throw a Coke bottle at a young black boy driving by on a bicycle. He threw the bottle so hard that it shattered the boy's head, knocked him off his bicycle and he died, right there on the sidewalk. That's when I first thought of becoming a priest, hoping to do something about hatred like that."

Bobby was less active than Dick in social justice because he was more conservative and less of a risk taker, but he listened intently when Dick told him about his activities since he left the abbey. Bobby had worked at Camp St. Mary's when he was still a seminarian, as a camp counselor.

"Were there black kids there then?" asked Dick.

"Nope, just white. That was just before they integrated the camp."

Some of the priests in the diocese were involved with the National Federation of Priests' Council (NFPC), a controversial group that tried to follow the intent of Vatican II by responding to the world's needs. In its early days, the NFPC had challenged the church's stance on birth control and issued a call for removing the ban of celibacy for priests. Dick heard about the NFPC's work with homosexual rights and an upcoming convocation on the topic of Gay Ministry. Remembering Brother Melchior, he was curious. When he mentioned it to Bobby, his friend looked at him sideways and smiled.

"OK, we're talking poor Blacks, teen mothers, Hispanic migrants and now homosexuals? I guess if any group is subject to prejudice, you're gonna be involved?"

Dick liked the description. He raised his eyebrows and shrugged. "I guess." Then he paused and thought for a minute. "Really, though, I do have strong feelings about anyone who suffers discrimination or rejection because of who or what they are. From what I've read, homosexuals' identity within the Church is filled with guilt and their guilt is often reinforced in the confessional, rather than absolved. I'm glad the Priest's Council is doing something for them. We should check it out."

Bobby was skeptical. "But homosexuality is banned in the Bible, isn't it? In the Old Testament, at least I think it is. I don't know if I'm comfortable with it, frankly."

"Tell me why you feel that way," said Dick.

As Bobby talked, sorting it out as he articulated his thoughts, Dick listened carefully and asked pointed questions. Finally, he asked his friend, "How do you think Jesus would feel? Would Jesus discriminate against them?"

Bobby finally sighed, "Of course not." He raised his eyes toward the ceiling and shook his head. "OK, OK, I'll go!"

Two week-ends later they drove to Atlanta to attend the Convocation on Gay Ministry. While there, Dick was able to see how the Church had failed these people. The evening before the conference, they sat with a homosexual couple, Danny and George.

After some light conversation, Dick asked a pointed question. "I'd like to know about your faith, and how you view the Church."

"Well, you could say that it seems a lot of priests would rather see us burned at the stake than talk to us!"

Dick looked at him seriously. "We don't feel that way."

George spoke next. "We were both raised Catholic, and we still go to church. But unless we act straight, we're not wanted. They even preach against us from the pulpit. It's horrible."

"Yeah, well, what can you do?" shrugged his partner. "It's not like anyone believes we're God's children, now, is it?"

"I do," said Dick, gently, and then nudged Bobby with his foot.

"Me too," said the other priest, quickly.

Then Bobby had a question. "How long have you been gay?"

Dick shot him a frown and noted that both men were annoyed at the question.

"I'm sorry," said Bobby. "It was an ignorant question."

"It's OK. Do you really think somebody would choose to be gay, to be a pariah of society, discriminated against, people saying we will spend eternity in hell?"

"No, of course not," said Dick. "And by the way, we don't think you're going to hell, either. Even the Church hierarchy seems to be leaning toward acceptance of homosexuality, but not homosexual acts. It still says sex is only for procreation, so anything that does not potentially produce children is not allowed. Even masturbation and sex between married men and women using a condom are forbidden."

Saturday during the day, speakers at the convocation talked about the issues. The bishops encouraged open and frank dialogue, looking for a consensus that would allow the Catholic Church to be supportive to its homosexual members yet fall short of endorsing sexual relations between them. They wanted something that would be acceptable to the Vatican.

On Saturday night Dick and Bobby attended a service at the Metropolitan Community Church, a church that accepted all people regardless of their sexual orientation, gender, race or religion. At the pre-dinner blessing, the pastor explained that the church had been founded in 1968 in response to the cry of a desperate homosexual man: "No one loves me – not even God!"

Dick thought about the men they had met the night before and reaffirmed his own thinking, that all people were God's children.

Dick found the homosexual issue worthwhile but felt no sense that his destiny was related to it. He continued to think about the Hispanic migrants, and started to plan what he would need to serve them when they returned in the spring, and researched places in Mexico where he could study their language and culture. He would have time that winter because retired priests came down to the Charleston Diocese for a few months in winter, happy to take over masses.

He learned about a place called Cuernavaca, Mexico, and a school called *El Ideal.* In addition to Spanish, they had courses in culture and in Liberation Theology. He discussed it with Bobby, who had heard of the place.

"I've heard about people who went there and came back unhappy with their current positions. It's gotten to be a suspicious destination, people asking, 'What's going on in Cuernavaca? What are they teaching?'"

Dick smiled. "That's one of the reasons it appeals to me."

Bobby looked at him in mock exacerbation as Dick said, "But they have fine programs."

"I don't disagree," said his friend. "I'm just telling you what I heard. It seems to be a kind of catalyst that changes people to the extent that they go off and do some other kind of ministry or find some other ways to do ministry. So you might have a problem getting the 'German Shepherd' to approve Cuernavaca."

After Bobby's comments, Dick was pleased and a little surprised that he was given permission to go to Cuernavaca for three months. That January, he flew into Mexico City and took a bus to Cuernavaca, about an hour south. The capital of the state of Morelos, it was known as the "City of Eternal Spring" because it had year-round temperatures of between 75 and 80 degrees. The school he attended was a Spanish-style three-story pink building that sat on the side of a hill, and he stayed with a Mexican family that spoke little English and supplemented their income by taking in students from language schools. Maria and José had three young children. They gave him one of their two bedrooms; the children would sleep with their parents. They all had to use the single bathroom but that was no problem for Dick who had shared bathroom facilities with forty men. He was also welcome to have meals with them but avoided doing so because they had so little money. Under normal circumstances, he would have enjoyed spending time with them, but their schedules were such that he felt he should out of their way as much as possible.

After he put his clothes in the small closet, he walked outside and up on a hill that overlooked the city. Cuernavaca was beautiful, filled with multi-colored buildings, palm trees and spectacularly blooming bougainvillea. Looking at his guidebook, he realized he could see the cathedral with its rounded atrium that dated back hundreds of years, and the round castle turret of Spanish explorer Hernán Cortéz' summer palace that had recently been opened as a museum. Dick read with interest about Cortéz' greatest yet dubious achievement, certainly in the mind of many Mexicans. By befriending and later betraying them, he conquered the Aztecs and their capital city of Tenochtitlan. Dick also learned that, contrary to what he had always thought, Moctezuma was not the last Aztec emperor. In fact, there were two others. The last one, Cuauhtémoc, was killed by Cortéz after surrendering, ending the Aztec Empire forever. Dick would visit the palace during his time there, as well as the almost 700-year-old *Teopanzolco* Pyramids.

Mostly, however, he would study, almost all in Spanish, in three different classes each weekday, plus he signed up for a class in English on Liberation Theology. In it, he learned with interest about base Christian communities, one of the building blocks of Liberation Theology, called in Spanish *comunidades eclesiales de base* or *CEBs*. In Spanish, "base" meant "grassroots," and in base communities, lay people used the scriptures to address questions of social injustice. The base communities also increased the numbers of lay people in leadership positions within the Church. It appealed to Dick, particularly since he knew the migrants were afraid to go to church half the time, never mind take part in it. He talked with other priests there about applying the concepts of Liberation Theology in the United States.

"I don't know if you can do it in its true sense," said one of the men who worked in Nicaragua. "The United States is such a rich country. I don't think you can truly experience what it's like to live without basic utilities like electricity and water, or with the government oppression that we have in a lot of Latin American countries."

Dick thought about the killings of the Blacks and the students not so long ago in the U.S., but decided it was still nothing like living with violence and oppression on a day-to-day basis.

His Spanish improved during the time he spent there, and he learned more about Our Lady of Guadalupe and the symbolism in the vision. Her image, brilliant with light, standing on the moon with stars on her mantle, matched the prophesies of the Book of Revelation, 12:1: "A great sign appeared in the sky, a woman clothed with the sun, with the moon under her feet, and on her head a crown of twelve stars."

On weekends, he went to different communities to see the sights. One Saturday he rode with three other priests to Aztec ruins not far from Cuernavaca. They were a spectacular testimony to civilization long gone, and Dick felt a sad empathy with the people who had lived there. He looked around at the lush valley surrounded by mountains filled with strangely-shaped formations, like Indian faces peering out through the mist.

As they walked back to their car, three Mexican men stopped them. One of them appeared to be nervous as reached his right hand inside his jacket. "*Tengo una pistola*, I have a gun right here, and you better give me your money."

The other priests were frightened, but Dick was not. He felt sorry for the man who said he had a gun. It was obvious that he was not a professional *bandido*, so Dick spoke slowly, clearly and softly to him in Spanish.

"*Mira*, look, you're gonna kill yourself with that gun. You're shaking! Do you know why? Because you are attacking priests. We are all priests."

That made the man shake even worse. "Just give me your wallets!"

"*Señor*," pleaded Dick. "We don't have any money in our wallets. We just have our identification there. But wait, I have a few pesos in my pocket. I will give them to you and will you please then leave us and do not do this again. You will hurt yourself and your soul."

Dick was filled with compassion as he watched the men scurry hastily away with such little money. The other priests were stunned.

"How did you do that? I couldn't even speak I was so scared."

"He didn't have a gun," said Father Sanders sadly. "He was just probably looking for money to feed his family. Pray for him."

They drove back into Tepoztlan and had lunch that included several beers as the other priests calmed their nerves, then strolled through the town's narrow, crowded streets and visited the central market. A brightly-colored assortment of vegetables and fruits greeted them, and they spent another hour looking at native clothing and crafts.

The time passed too quickly and Dick found he did not want to return to South Carolina. On the plane on the way back, he realized he was completely entranced with Mexico and its culture. He had learned a great deal in addition to improving his Spanish. The concepts of Liberation Theology were becoming more concrete in his mind, especially the combined ideals of Gospel-based reflection and action and of freeing the oppressed in both body and soul. He had also gotten in touch with the reality some of the migrants had left behind.

Back at Blessed Sacrament, he was a regular parish priest again, looking forward to the migrants' return. At the beginning of Lent, he thought back to his old life at Mepkin, with restricted food and constant prayers related to suffering during this season. He decidedly did not miss that part of the monastic tradition. This year his biggest sacrifice was to give up drinking alcohol. Bobby decided to do the same. Instead of going out to a bar or having a few drinks at the rectory, the two of them went to the local Krispy Kreme, drank hot chocolate and ate donuts.

CHAPTER TWENTY –
FINAL DISCERNMENT – 1977 - 1978

That summer, Dick and Yolanda and took Masses to the migrants on Johns Island, not far from Blessed Sacrament Church. One of the crew leaders, Adán Hernandez, later called his sister.

"Rosa, we got a priest up here who came to the camp."

Rosa had not gone up the road for many years because she had a full-time job as housekeeper for the priests in Immokalee, Florida, but she looked forward to hearing how things were going. There was camaraderie when they met up at different camps and, in many ways, she missed it. But not the actual work. Fieldwork was backbreaking and exhausting and she was grateful she didn't have to do it anymore.

"What do you mean you got a priest?"

"He came over to me last week in the parking lot by the store where all the Mexicans stop to pick up lunch. Somebody pointed me out to him, I guess, because he knew I was a *Jefe*, a crew boss. He came over and talked to me about if I had any crew in the area and if he could come and visit. I told him where my camp was located and then he asked if it was OK for him to come and give a Mass at the camp. I said yes."

"Nobody ever did that before, did they?" asked his sister.

"No. At least I never seen nobody do it. So on Sunday I prepared the people who were around my camp and we waited for the *Padre*."

"Is he Mexican?"

"No, *gringo*, but he speaks Spanish. Not great, but you can understand him. He came with a woman, too, Yolanda. I think she is *cubana*. She speaks perfect Spanish, but with that accent they have over there. There were two other people, too. They came in a white station wagon, I think it was a Dodge. The woman, she called him 'Dick.'"

"Dick?" Adán could feel Rosa blush through the telephone. She stifled a giggle and he could picture her eyes rolling. "Doesn't that mean…"

"*Verdad*. True. It must be his name, I guess."

"Well, what were they like?"

"The first impression of him was that he is very serious, quiet, conscientious, dedicated. She's real lively and talks a lot. It was Sunday afternoon so nobody was working. You remember the house where we stay, with the two trailers on the side? The one on Benjamin Jinkens Farm?"

Rosa remembered. Their family had worked tomatoes on Johns Island for many years.

"Well, in the back under that big oak tree where the benches are, where we sit and relax after work, he made an altar. He took a card table from his car, covered it with a white cloth and took out a crucifix and a chalice for communion. He even made a couple of confessions before Mass."

Rosa asked to hear more.

"He talks soft and is cautious to speak, but he made the readings make sense to us. The service was dedicated to the people, to each individual, not to the crowd or not to the crew leader or the boss man, it was dedicated to all of us. I liked him. You should see the attention that he put personally in each one of our people there. He stayed long enough for me to detect his *manera de ser*, his 'way.' He's got a *carisma*, a way to reach us, a way to reach the people. He talked to every single one, asking where they came from, about their families, everything. Before he left, he talked to me again and asked me how I liked the service, and I said I enjoyed it."

The next time they came to say Mass, *Padre* Sanders asked Adán about other camps and was pleased to learn there were many more within driving range.

"*Sí Padre*, there are other groups in different places all over the island. I mean, when I first came to Johns Island in 1957 just a couple of farmers were farming here, and then suddenly a lot of farmers started growing tomatoes. There are thousands of acres planted here. So lots of people come to work the fields."

Yolanda expanded the map based on Adán's directions and soon the little ministry group was going to all the camps on the island. They found fourteen and knew there were more, but didn't know how they would find time to visit all of them even once a week. *Padre* Sanders tried inviting them to attend Sunday Mass at Blessed Sacrament. Not many came, and when they did, they sat in the back rows. The English-speaking community was not receptive to having the migrants there and it seemed many of them openly resented the presence of the farm workers. Bristling at comments about their poor clothing and dirty fingernails, Dick finally gave up and focused on ministry in the camps.

Yolanda was almost always with him, sometimes with a few volunteers, and once in a while, Father Bobby. Bobby complained, although never without humor. The insects hardly bothered Dick, for example, but Bobby seemed to be constantly swatting them. "Dick, how can you stand these bugs? I've never had such ugly-looking bugs come onto my body in my whole life!"

Dick also had to listen to Bobby's complaints when the camp Masses went late. They would arrive at 7:00 p.m. but sometimes the Mass wouldn't even start for two hours.

"Well at least I know what the word '*mañana*' means," Bobby laughed. "You know, Dick, you cause the delay, going around talking to everyone you see. I have to get up and say the early Mass, when you'll still be sleeping!"

The little group went to the camps on Saturdays and several evenings during the week until late June when the migrants left to continue their journey north. When Dick came on the last Sunday the migrants were packed up, ready to leave right after Mass and the blessing of their vehicles.

Padre Sanders sprinkled holy water, made the Sign of the Cross and said, "May God guide you safely on your journey."

As Dick and Yolanda watched them pull out in a long line, a young man hurrying out to catch his ride and was accidentally hit by one of the trucks. He was badly hurt but the men he was riding with couldn't wait; work had already started in Delaware.

Yolanda and Dick took the young man to the hospital. His name was Miguel Sanchez, he was seventeen years old and he had come from Mexico the previous year. He was alone here.

"My family saved up so I could cross the border and send money home to support them. I hooked up with a couple of guys and paid for gas money so they let me ride with them, but now they're gone."

The injury turned out to be a compound fracture of his right leg.

"Oh my goodness!" said Yolanda. "They're all leaving and this guy can't work. He's gonna need someone to help him. Where is he gonna stay?"

Dick looked at her as if the answer were obvious. "At your house."

Yolanda took Miguel into her home and he stayed with her family until his leg healed. She contacted his mother in Mexico who was beautiful with her thanks on the telephone. Later she wrote Yolanda a letter. "I hope that if your children are ever anywhere in the world and in need, that someone will take them in like you took in my Miguel. God bless you."

Birthday with Yolanda and children

That fall and early winter Dick returned to his parish duties and in January spent another month in Cuernavaca. He saw Yolanda periodically and they both looked forward to the return of their migrant friends. Yolanda went back to teaching school but lined up a position for the following summer through the Charleston school system as "Migrant Coordinator." Dick was pleased that the educational system was paying some attention to migrant children.

The second week in May, Adán and his wife Maria came to Mass at Blessed Sacrament Church. Father Sanders noticed them halfway through his sermon and smiled happily. Afterwards they waited to see him.

"*Hola, Padre,*" smiled Adán, shaking Dick's hand.

"*¡Buenos Días, Adán y Maria! Mucho gusto de verle otra vez.*" I am happy to see you again. "How is everything?"

"*Bueno, Padre.* Now that we're back can you come to the camp and have a Mass for the people?"

"*Claro que sí,*" said *Padre* Sanders, smiling warmly. "Of course."

When Dick and Yolanda arrived at the house on Jinkins farm, Adán invited them into the house for coffee. Maria offered *pan dulce*, a sweet Mexican bread that Dick loved.

"How are things in Immokalee?"

"Good," said Adán. "We had a good year there and now we're back for the tomatoes."

"And Our Lady of Guadalupe Church?"

"Well, that's something I wanted to talk to you about, *Padre*." Adán paused and took a bite of his *pan dulce*. "What do you do when we're not here? The migrants are only here for this short time in the summer and then we move on."

"Regular priest stuff," Dick replied, with little enthusiasm.

"*Con bolillos*, eh?" said Adán, using a teasingly derogatory term the Latinos used among themselves to describe Anglos. It was the name of a white doughy pastry.

"*Sí*," said the *Padre*, laughing. "*Con bolillos*."

"But you prefer *Latinos*, yes?"

"I prefer everyone, but I must admit the *Hispanos* have a special place in my heart."

"So why don't you come down to Immokalee?" asked Adán. He had talked to his sister Rosa about this and had given some thought about how to present the idea to *Padre* Sanders.

Dick sat quietly for several minutes before speaking. "Priests can't just go where they want to go, Adán. Besides, you have a priest already, don't you?"

"*Sí*, but we almost always have two priests and now *Padre* Pedro is alone there. The Immokalee parish is a lot of work. It's growing like crazy because of the agriculture and we really could use another priest. I've been there for fifteen, twenty years now and it's always the same – the priests come, stay for a while, but then they get tired or worn down and they go. Some of them develop problems with alcohol and the others just get depressed. It's not easy ministering to poor farm workers because they have so many problems and they all go to the priest for help. *Padre* Pedro could really use some help."

Dick nodded and took a sip of his coffee.

"Hey *Padre*, I brought you something," said Adán, changing the subject. "I saw you don't have any missalettes, Mass books, in Spanish up here and in Immokalee we have ours in English and Spanish but we get new ones every year. *Padre* Pedro said I could bring the old ones here to use for our Masses."

"*Excelente*," replied *Padre* Sanders, "but you should take them with you when you go up the road."

"There's no other place where a priest comes. You might as well keep them."

After confessions, Mass, coffee and pastries, Yolanda led the people in more songs and they sounded like two hundred chanting monks. *Padre* Sanders leaned with his back against a tree, took a long drag on his cigarette and slowly and deliberately blew the smoke up into the starry night sky. He smiled as he remembered describing his search for God to Joe Story, so many years ago. "This kind of 'connection' came over me, like, the world was huge and beautiful yet at the same time it was small and safe, completely and lovingly warm. And it was, like, all mixed up together with this intensity – you wouldn't believe how intense it was, and at the same time, I felt perfect peace, just for that instant." He had never been happier.

One night after saying Masses at the camps, *Padre* Sanders drove back to Blessed Sacrament with Yolanda. It was late, and he was unusually pensive.

"Yolanda, I've been praying and I feel the Lord is calling me to do full-time migrant ministry. What do you think?"

"Well, I think you're called to that too, but you can't do it here. You'd have to go to Florida or Texas because that's where the migrants are most of the time."

"I know," he said quietly, "but Mepkin Abbey is here, and that's my home. Even though I'm with the migrants in the summer and the Blessed Sacrament parishioners the rest of the year, I still spend a lot of time at Mepkin. It's where I get my strength. How could I move far away?"

"Well, it's not that far of a drive from Florida, or you could fly back. You could come back for retreats."

"It's a really tough decision." He shook his head sadly. "I need to pray for discernment. Mepkin will always be my home and I really want to stay nearby, but the lives of these people are so hard and they have so few priests."

Yolanda looked over at him and shivered. It was no longer Dick sitting there. She saw Jesus! She looked out the window, shaken, and did not speak for several minutes. Finally, she whispered, without looking at him again, "Are you Jesus, reincarnated?"

Dick rolled his eyes and smiled. When Yolanda looked back, she saw her friend again.

"*¿De qué hablas?*" he laughed. What are you talking about?

She was not laughing. "Dick, I swear when I just looked at you it wasn't you sitting there, it was Jesus. I saw Jesus!"

He needed to talk to her more about her visions one of these days, but he was embarrassed and changed the subject.

"Have you heard of a conference called the *Encuentro*?"

"I heard a little about it. It's a Catholic Hispanic thing, focused on getting more Latinos involved with the Church, yes?"

"*Sí.* They had one already, in 1972, but there's a second one coming up."

He explained what he read in the promotional material. The first *Encuentro* was considered the infancy stage of Hispanic ministry in the U.S. Its goal was to "encourage wider participation of Hispanic Catholics in the life and mission of the Church; include Hispanics in leadership positions and in decision-making processes; and to establish specific structures to serve Hispanics."

"It sounds perfect for us," said Yolanda.

Dick nodded. "Bishop Flores from Texas, the first Hispanic Bishop in the U.S., will be there. Maybe I can talk to him. Can you come?"

"*Sí,* of course. Let me just check with Ron about watching the kids."

They drove together to Trinity College in Washington DC for the *Encuentro* on August 18, 1977. Twelve-hundred people attended from across the United States, plus from Latin American countries. They included cardinals, archbishops and bishops, teachers, health-care professionals and farm workers. The conference proceedings were in Spanish but there were translators. Dick knew within moments that the decision to attend was one of the best he'd ever made, beginning with the convocation.

"We must do all we can," began Archbishop Joseph Bernardin, "as a matter of strict justice, to help people in their struggle to overcome everything which condemns them to a marginal existence: economic injustices, inadequate education and health care, substandard housing, political powerlessness and a host of other evils. But this effort, to be truly productive and life-giving, cannot be divorced from the Gospel."

Other speakers talked about the purpose of the *Segundo Encuentro,* Second Encounter Conference, which was to make sure the Church knew that the Hispanic faith and traditions of worship were different from those of U.S. Catholics, but in no way inferior. "We must continue to preserve the treasures of our heritage and the identity of our faith and culture. For if we begin to lose the richness of our culture, we will then begin to lose our faith, because, for the Hispano, his faith is essential to his culture."

Another speaker talked about the Latino culture coming face to face with the Anglo culture of the U.S. "We have much to learn from the North American people: practical sense of life, their capacity to organize, their work ethic... But I believe that we also have a great deal to give; that we also have values which we must not lose... These include our spontaneity; our joy of life; our richer and deeper sense of family... our devotion to the Virgin Mary."

This confirmed what Dick already suspected, that the devotion to the Virgin Mary was part of what attracted him to the Hispanics. Our Lady of Guadalupe was now the vision of Mary who comforted him as he slept.

"We must become a part of the country in which we live, love it, feel its problems, give it our best efforts. At the same time we must continue to be what we are. We must not lose our own identity." The speaker also reminded the attendees that "the Church is one and the same throughout the world. Wherever we go, the bishop of that diocese becomes our pastor. We must feel that the local Church is our own."

Dick looked at Yolanda. They were both thinking about the fear the migrants had of attending white churches.

There were many happy moments during the *Encuentro*, as attendees relaxed between sessions and Dick and Yolanda joined them on the lawns. Poets read poems, musicians played guitars and bongos, people sang and others danced to songs like *"Somos un Pueblo Hispano,"* We are a Hispanic community. In the evenings there were musical galas and *fiestas*.

Dick was particularly moved when he and Yolanda took part in a huge march of the 1,200 people who attended. The group walked in rows of eight across, arm in arm, from Trinity College to the Basilica of Our Lady. The closing liturgy was celebrated at the National Shrine of the Immaculate Conception. It was a breathtaking experience and solidified even more Dick's thought that he was called to migrant ministry. Later that day, he talked with Bishop Flores of San Antonio, hoping to line up his future. The Bishop was pleasant and understood Dick's desire to work with Hispanic migrants, but unfortunately did not need anyone in Texas.

"I can call Archbishop McCarthy in Miami for you, though, if you like. He's getting inundated with Cubans, plus a lot of Mexicans who are coming to do farm work in southern Florida. I bet he could use someone like you."

Dick enthusiastically accepted the bishop's offer for the contact but did not mention it to Yolanda until they were driving home.

"Yolanda, you know me better than anyone and I respect your opinion. I need to know what you think. I want to go to Florida with the migrants. I love these people and I don't want to leave them. I want to be their priest, wherever they are."

He didn't have to say he was afraid to leave South Carolina, to be so far from. He felt like a little boy asking his mother for advice: "Do you think I should go?"

"*Sí*, Dick." She smiled reassuringly, knowing how much she would miss him. "You should go."

He smiled and breathed a deep, satisfied smile, knowing his long period of discernment was finally over. His vocation had been cemented. Now he just had to wait for God to tell him where to find it.

Jesus, our lord, hasten the day we fulfill your work.

A month later, Dick frowned as he read an article in the September 2, 1977 issue of NCR. A thirty-man papally appointed International Theological Commission charged that "Liberation Theology is often tied too closely to politics and to questionable sociological and ideological theories, especially Marxist-Leninist ones." They were challenging a theology that said people should live like Jesus, with a preference for helping the poor and helping the poor help themselves.

Even though his personal decision was final, there was still a lot to do before he made the change. He talked with the abbot at Mepkin. Dick was still a Trappist in his heart and had never really thought about making a final break with the abbey. Then Dick thought about Our Lady of Guadalupe and her words to Juan Diego: "Do not be afraid of anything. Am I not here, who is your mother?"

Relieved that the first step had been taken, he spent the rest of the week-end in the guesthouse at Mepkin. On Monday he spoke with Bishop Unterkoefler about a move to Florida and the bishop approved. Next, he called Archbishop Edward A. McCarthy who had already heard about Father Sanders from Bishop Flores. The Miami Archdiocese included all the parishes in southern Florida, both east and west coasts. With the increasing expansion of agriculture, the Hispanic population had grown tremendously and they could use more Spanish-speaking priests.

"In fact," said the bishop, "a devoted and persistent Hispanic woman in Naples has been requesting a priest for years but I couldn't find anyone. Perhaps something could be worked out for you there. Rest assured I can use you. I just have to determine where."

While he waited, Dick asked the Bishop of Charleston if he could return to Cuernavaca to continue his Spanish language studies. This time he would go for three months. By the time the course was over the migrants would once again be in South Carolina, so the move to Florida would wait one full year. The delay was not a problem for Dick. Change did not come easy to him and it was going to be difficult to leave South Carolina. He thought back to the different lives he had lived in the past nine years, moving from Mepkin Abbey to Union Heights, protesting for black hospital workers and getting arrested, starting a community center, working with a white middle-class parish in Columbia, helping poor black teen mothers at Camp St. Mary's and then the Hispanic migrants.

After the first of the year, 1978, he flew again to Mexico City and returned to the same school. In addition to Spanish, he studied more Liberation Theology and was exposed to more discussions of the work of several theologians, most notably Gustavo Gutiérrez who had been a major force at the Medellín council in 1968.

In Spanish, Gutiérrez' work was called *Teología de la Liberación*, published in 1971. *Theology of Liberation.* Dick had read the English translation but now struggled with the Spanish, comparing it to the English version to make sure he understood it properly. It was a brilliant and passionate work, more so in the language in which it had been written, and explained Liberation

Theology as a practical and radical challenge to the contemporary church. The concept, explained Gutierrez, was built upon the way Pope John XXIII opened Vatican II when he said, "...the church is called to be a church of the poor." Gutierrez called for supporters to help with a *concientización* or "awakening" of the people. He said that the world would see authentic Liberation Theology "...only when the oppressed themselves can freely raise their voice and express themselves directly and creatively in society....when they are the protagonists of their own liberation." Father Sanders prayed fervently to someday become a catalyst for this kind of awakening among the farm workers he would serve.

In mid-January he wrote a Christmas letter from Cuernavaca that he did not get around to copying and mailing until mid-March.

> Dear Friends,
>
> Wishing you a late Merry Christmas and a very Happy New Year. I am sure that for most of you this is the only time you have received a letter from me. (Hope you can withstand the shock.) However since I am in the process of moving again this seems an appropriate time to get in touch.
>
> This past nine years I have been working in the Charleston diocese and enjoying it very much. Among the various things I have been doing has been a ministry with the Migrant Farm Workers. The past three years I have been involved with this each summer. This is work that I have truly enjoyed and also there are all too few involved in it. Therefore I have decided to work full time with Migrant Farm Workers. To do this I will be moving to southern Florida which is the home base for the Migrants on the East Coast.
>
> As you may know, the majority of the Migrant Farm Workers are Spanish-speaking Catholics. They are referred to as migrants because they move with the crops, not because they are immigrants. Actually, most of them are U.S. citizens by birth coming from the Spanish-speaking areas of the Southwest or from Puerto Rico though some of them are from Mexico. My intention is that I will be working in a parish in a farming area in Florida during the winter and then in the summer, when many of the workers move on to other areas on the East Coast to pick the crops, I will move with them.
>
> I am at present trying to polish up my Spanish at a language institute here in Cuernavaca. This is a beautiful city about 50 miles out of Mexico City and being down here is a lot of fun. I plan to be here till about March 10th so I will be using the

above address until then. After that I will be going to Florida but I don't have an address there yet, however the mail will be forwarded from my last address: 0 Moore Drive, Charleston, S.C. 29407. Please say a prayer for the success of my new work.

Peace, Dick Sanders

V

NONE

1978 - 1981

CHAPTER TWENTY-ONE –
IGLESIA DE SAN PEDRO – 1978

A few weeks after the migrants went north from South Carolina, Father Sanders drove south to Miami where he met with Archbishop McCarthy, signed incardination papers and drove west across the state to Naples. He took "Alligator Alley," a desolate eighty-mile strip of highway that cut through the Everglades. Two hours later, he arrived with his few belongings, mostly clothes and books, at the rectory where Father Mike Murphy welcomed him. Mike shared his passion for helping the Mexican population but had never had time to master Spanish.

In addition to being the priest to the migrants, Dick would help Father Murphy with English Masses. The white population in Naples was growing as rapidly as the Hispanics, but for different reasons. Mike explained that the Anglos were mostly from the Midwest, moving down to a tropical paradise to retire or to a winter home. Hispanics were coming because vegetable fields promise an opportunity to earn money.

He handed Dick a copy of the August 18, 1978 Naples Star. A front-page article headlined, "The Rev. Richard Sanders Has Come to Town." Dick smiled. He had never been in the newspaper before except for announcements of his vows and ordination. Oh yes – he almost forgot about when he went to jail in Charleston. It seemed like a long time ago. This article was based on an interview he had done with reporter Moira Schanen.

> Because of the large population of migrants in South Florida, he
> asked to be transferred here to continue his work year-around with
> the people… He will supply the basic services of the church in
> their own language, something, he says, all people are entitled to.

The article went on to say that Father Sanders intended to serve not only migrant workers, but the growing numbers of year-round Hispanic residents in the Naples area. Masses for his mission would be held in St. Peter the Apostle Church. He would offer Masses at migrant camps during the week and travel back to South Carolina with the workers in the spring, at the end of Southwest Florida's growing season. "Migrants are not always made to feel very welcome,' the article quoted him as saying, 'but with my contacts in South Carolina I hope to change that.'"

Dick smiled awkwardly as he handed the paper back to Father Murphy, embarrassed by the attention yet happy the migrants were front-page news.

The two priests talked as they ate dinner at a seafood restaurant. Dick loved being so close to the ocean. St. Peter's was a brand new church and Father Murphy was its first priest, reassigned there from St. Ann's. He explained that they would soon have five English Masses, but that there was nothing formal for the Hispanics. Father Pedro Jiménez came from Immokalee when he could, usually with a Guadalupana sister, and celebrated a Spanish Mass in the Lely High School. Pedro also sometimes said Mass in the camps in the evenings, and there was a Spanish-speaking priest in Miami who came over about once a month, but that was it. Dick thought about the opportunity he had been given and said a quick prayer of thanks.

Father Murphy explained that he was trying to develop a social consciousness attitude in dealing with the Hispanics, something where the two cultures could come together. He also talked about Corina Hernandez, saying he knew her from when she took second-hand clothing from St. Ann's to the farm workers. Corina and her daughter Rita taught Catechism to the Hispanic children in the Avalon and East Naples Middle Schools. They also went out to the farms to teach ten or twelve kids at a time, on blankets outside the *barracas*. Corina used her own car, a pretty old one, too, and paid for her own gas. They had prepared a lot of Hispanic children for their First Communion last year.

When Dick asked about Corina's salary, he learned she was a volunteer. He raised his eyebrows because it sounded like a lot of work. Father Murphy explained that, in addition to her work with the migrants, Corina was responsible for Dick coming here. St. Peter's church was built partly with the money she helped raise through *reinados*, hoping that one day a mission church might be started here, with a Spanish-speaking priest. Dick smiled thoughtfully, thinking of the steps that had led him from Mepkin Abbey to the fields of Naples, from monk to migrant priest.

The next morning, he drove to St. Peter the Apostle Catholic Church, his new church that would now offer services in both English and Spanish. Only about ten miles from the major farms, the 6,500 square foot multi-purpose building sat by itself on five acres. It was different from other churches Dick had seen, somewhat modern-European in design. The large double front doors were glass with windows on either side. As Father Murphy opened them, Dick saw the spectacular two-story stained-glass window in the far right corner behind the altar. It was a giant tabernacle, one of the most impressive pieces he had ever seen. Father Murphy credited the hard work and generous financial donations of the parishioners.

Dick walked toward the altar that was diagonally positioned on the right on a platform in front of the stained-glass window, his eyes focused on the glass image and five-foot wooden crucifix that hung in front of it, suspended by two chains. Long oak pews lined diagonally across the front half of the church.

The rear half of the large room had a lower ceiling, and chairs were set up there in rows. It held 735 folding chairs, Dick would later learn from St. Peter's maintenance man. The cathedral-ceilinged front and the fourteen-foot back of the church were lit by beautiful round chandeliers with radiant incandescent bulbs. All the floors were covered with a deep red patterned carpet. The effect was stunning.

The glass accordion doors between the front and the back half of the church could be closed, creating a chapel plus a multi-purpose room for classrooms, meetings and parties. At their immediate left were confessionals and next to them, a kitchen and then a hallway that led to the sacristy and offices where Father Murphy worked and where Father Sanders would now join him.

Father Murphy had business to attend to so Dick took a walk around the outside. On the west wall hung a wrought-iron sculpture of St. Peter overlooking a long flower bed that hugged the building, filled with purple Mexican petunias. As he came around the back, he looked up and stopped in his tracks. In the corner where the stained glass window took up two stories, a diamond-shaped roof extension jutted out from the building and a fifteen-foot cross hung through it, as if huge fingers had dropped it from the sky to pierce the pointed roof. About one-third of it, including the vertical beam, was on top of the roof extension while the other two-thirds hung down from underneath. Still staring, Dick moved backwards a few paces so he could see it better.

"Impressive, huh?"

The voice startled him because he had been so intently focused. He turned and saw a Hispanic man who looked to be about ten years younger than he was, probably in his early thirties, about 5'9", with thick curly black hair, eyebrows and moustache. His darkened skin and muscular hands told the story of many years of hard work in the sun. Dick knew immediately he was talking with a field worker. He was gentle and quiet yet gave Dick the sense that he could be powerful if needed.

"*Sí*, impressive." Then Dick introduced himself.

"*Sí, Padre*, I know who you are. My mother has prayed for you for years. I am Martin Hernandez, the parish maintenance man. *¡Bien venido!* Welcome! My mom is waiting at the front of the church. She's really excited that you have finally come to us."

Dick went back to the front of the church where Corina Hernandez stood talking to Father Murphy.

"*Mucho gusto de conocerlo, Padre*," she said shyly. I am happy to meet you.

"*Igualmente, Corina*." Likewise.

He held her hand and studied her carefully. She could not have been more than 5'2" tall and had skin that showed that she, too, had spent much of her life in the sun. Her shoulder-length brown hair was curly and her round face showed signs of a hard life. He judged her to be about fifty or so, but she had a youthful energy and, like Martin, exuded an impressive combination of humility and resoluteness. Standing in the doorway of the church with the sun setting behind them, her substance and deep faith were obvious. Without speaking, they walked together toward the altar, genuflected on one knee, made the Sign of the Cross and sat down in the front pew.

"*Entiendo que....* I understand you've been praying for a priest," he said softly in Spanish.

"*Sí, Padre*, we have waited a long time."

It was several minutes before Corina spoke again. She was pleasant but practical and to the point, asking Dick if he planned to say Masses in the labor camps in addition to the church. He could tell she was still not sure she believed they actually had a priest.

"*Sí*, Corina. *¡Claro!*" Of course. Are Masses in the camps set on a regular schedule now?"

Not really, she explained. "When a priest can come from Immokalee or Miami, they try to go to a different camp each time."

"What do the people do when a priest doesn't come?"

"They don't do nothing." She frowned and shook her head. "I say to them, 'That's not good, just working, working and you forget about God.' But they don't do nothing."

"If they can't get to church, we will bring the church to them. I will go four days a week, once to each camp, every week, on a schedule. Will you come with me?"

She nodded. "Me and my daughter Rita, too."

"Could we visit one of the camps today?"

"*Sí, Padre*," she said, delighted. "There aren't many people here yet, but some are back to start preparing the fields. We can go right now."

Dick sat in the passenger seat of her van as she drove south and east on the Tamiami Trail about ten miles to the Six L's Farm, making a left turn onto a dusty dirt road that led to the workers' camp, about a mile in on the farm. It was a fenced-in area of about two square acres, with a guard shack at the gate.

"Most of the people aren't back yet so they don't have the guards now," she explained.

"What are the guards for?" Dick asked, frowning. He had not seen this before.

Corina reassured him. "It's not to keep the workers in; it's to keep people out. The workers make their money in cash and they keep it in their houses. The guards keep robbers from coming in. Also there are guys who come, trying to sell worthless things or bringing in prostitutes and the workers spend all their money. They work too hard for that."

The camp was made up of several rows of small one and two-room buildings. It was nicer than any of the *barracas* he had seen in South Carolina. At one place two men were hanging clothes on a line. At another, a man sat on a step, drinking coffee. He nodded as they drove by. A woman worked in a small garden in front of a third house while children played around her.

"Her family gets the same place every year," explained Corina, "so she treats it like her home and keeps this garden."

They stopped to talk with the woman whose name was Maria. Dick was beginning to understand that almost every Mexican woman was named Maria, after the Virgin Mary, although many of them used their middle names in speech. Maria's husband was working today while she got their winter home in order. They had come originally from the city of Guanajuato in Mexico, and now migrated up and down the U.S. east coast. Her garden was simple yet beautiful, with cactus, purple bougainvillea, bromeliads, an aloe plant and flowerless rose bushes. As Dick admired it he had a sudden image of himself as a young novice, tending the gardens at Mepkin. It made him miss the abbey, but he shook the thought out of his head.

He turned to Corina, already viewing her as his assistant. "I like to have fresh flowers in church. Only real flowers for the altar of God."

Corina nodded.

On Sunday morning, Father Sanders assisted Father Murphy at the English Masses at St. Peter the Apostle Church. That Sunday evening, at the same altar, Father Murphy assisted *Padre* Sanders as he said the first Spanish Mass at the *Misión de San Pedro* – with real flowers at the altar.

News of the new priest had circulated through Naples' Hispanic community, but only about one hundred attended the first Spanish Mass. *Padre* Sanders looked at his new parishioners as he stood in the back before processing to the altar. They looked like the people he had known in South Carolina, with dark hair and various shades of tan or brown skin. The men wore jeans or white denim pants, cowboy boots and white or checkered shirts. Most of them held cowboy hats in their laps. The women wore plain dresses and what Dick's mother used to call "sensible shoes." Some of the older women wore mantillas, light lace scarves, over their hair.

Most of them sat in the back of the church in folding chairs. Only about twenty sat in the pews near the altar, most of whom were Corina Hernandez and her family.

From the altar, before beginning the Mass, *Padre* Sanders asked in Spanish for the people in the back to come forward. No one moved. He asked again and still no reaction. He knew right away it was the same here as it had been in South Carolina – they were intimidated, thinking it was not appropriate for them to sit near the altar in what they perceived to be a wealthy white-people's church.

Then Corina stood up slightly from her seat in the second pew, her knees bent, trying to be inconspicuous yet letting the people see her. She turned toward the back of the room and quietly motioned with her right hand. Slowly, they all got up and moved.

Saying Mass at St. Peter's

Padre Sanders spent the following day getting forms about his transfer finalized, a job he detested. That evening he drove with Corina and Rita to the A. Duda farm, a little farther south than Six L's. Corina noted the worn condition of his 1970 Dodge.

"This car is my old friend," he explained. "She has taken me to camps in South Carolina, lots of them. It shows!"

Rita, sixteen years old, smiled happily. She looked a little like her mother, like a sweet young angel.

"Rita's gonna be a nun," Corina told him proudly.

Padre Sanders was impressed. "What a beautiful vocation. I hope you do it!"

He had brought with him the card table that served as a portable altar, and all the accoutrements for saying Mass. He walked through the camp ringing a bell to announce the start of the services. Only about fifteen people came over, but *Padre* Sanders said the Mass and stayed afterwards and talked with all of them.

In the following weeks, word spread that this priest was assigned to them permanently, and gradually the crowd at the Sunday evening Mass picked up. Also, more workers returned from the north, and they came to church, too.

One day Dick talked again with Corina's son Martin, the parish maintenance man. "How many generations has your family been in the United States?"

"I'm the fourth."

"You worked in the fields?"

"*Sí, Padre*, most of my childhood. All of us did."

"Did you go to school?"

"Sure, *Padre*, my mother made sure of that, even though we were migrating. I was taught in English."

"That's why your English is so perfect."

"I guess, *Padre*. Thanks."

"What was it like to be a migrant worker?"

"To tell you the truth, sometimes I think those years were the best ones of my life." Dick's interested look urged him to continue. "We were all together, our family. Then there was this warm feeling of people working together, singing together at night in the camps. When we moved on to the next place, a lot of the same people came too. It was like a big extended family in a lot of ways."

"What about the war? Did you have to go?"

"Sure did. I got drafted when I was twenty-two, in 1968. I spent a year in 'Nam."

They talked more and Martin told the *Padre* some of his experiences in Vietnam, things he had never shared with anyone. Dick blessed Martin and prayed that the country would never see another such war.

Recognizing her significant role with the farm workers who would be his parishioners, Father Sanders gave Corina the official title of *Ministro Pastorál*. Pastoral Minister. It was a volunteer position, but it pleased her to be recognized. She had worked for a long time with little appreciation except from the people she helped, and now she had a title.

Chapter Twenty-two – The White Doors – 1978

One day in late October, Dick received a call from Pat Stockton from the Miami Archdiocese offices. Pat ran the Rural Life Bureau, RLB, a department started by the late Archbishop Coleman Carroll in 1970 to coordinate mission churches in agricultural areas. She wanted to come over and to familiarize him with what they did.

He was outside in front of the rectory when she drove up in a Volkswagen Beetle that showed its age. Pat was about 5'7", thin, with short neatly-trimmed hair. She had a pleasant smile and he liked her immediately.

"I travel all the time to the migrant parishes," she smiled. "This helps with gas mileage. I'm gone so much, though, that sometimes I think I should have a camper!"

He commented on her slight Spanish accent.

"I was born in Peru."

His eyes lit up. "Ah, you're Peruvian! Me too!"

She looked at him sideways and he started to laugh. "I was born in Peru, Illinois!"

As they talked, she told him about herself and her work. "I was hired originally to act as Religious Education Coordinator for the migrant parishes, but as I got into doing the work I realized that you can't do religious education in a vacuum. You have to address all the issues that that affect their lives, like their working conditions, health, general education, everything."

Dick agreed and was grateful there was someone else with the same ideas.

"It's not just me," Pat continued. "The Rural Life Bureau is a coordinated effort on the part of the archdiocese to support churches in towns where there are large numbers of migrant farm workers. A lot of them are designated 'mission churches,' technically not parishes because they don't have the funding to support themselves."

Dick nodded.

"Most of the churches are in towns in the agricultural heart of South Florida. You'll get to know them because we have meetings at a different location every month." She showed him the towns' locations on a map. "They're in Indiantown, Pahokee, Belle Glade, Clewiston, Moore Haven, LaBelle, Immokalee, Naranja, Pompano Beach, Delray Beach and now Naples. My job and the purpose of the Rural Life Bureau is to help priests, women religious and lay leaders connect with one another, and to provide a liaison with other mission groups so you can help each other. Ministering to the farm workers with their lifestyles and poverty comes with whole a set of issues of its own, social issues, and it can get a little overwhelming sometimes. The meetings will give you a sense that you're not alone."

"I'll look forward to meeting others with the same vocation that I seem to have gotten."

Pat shook her head. "Some of the priests in these towns are really happy, but others seem to feel they are sentenced there like a punishment or something. Those guys seem so tired. I remember talking to one priest when I first visited his parish. I had all this energy, saying, 'Oh Father this is so wonderful, I just love this and the place is so beautiful.' He looked at me like he was thinking, 'This woman is nuts!' When I started calling them together in meetings, though, the priests responded well because they were finally were getting the attention they never had, and spending time with other priests who were dealing with the same realities. You will see how wonderful it is to meet regularly with them, the sisters and the lay leaders, the energy and the vitality, the sense of commitment to the Gospel of Jesus that is there. It is an experience of the Church at its best. The Rural Life Bureau is here to support you as you go about being the presence of Jesus to our brothers and sisters in the fields. Just call if you want a presentation or training, or if you are looking for any materials at all for your mission here."

"It sounds like you love the work."

Pat smiled. "I feel this is my calling in life, what gives me meaning and a sense of purpose. I am inspired by the farm workers lives, the sisters, the priests whose hearts and souls are with the workers, like Frank O'Loughlin over in Indiantown and some others, plus the women religious who are so dedicated and giving. They are so involved that it's almost like the workers' lives are their lives."

Dick smiled.

"So yes, you're right," she agreed. "I do love the work. I even got to work with Cesar Chávez for a while."

"You met Chávez?"

"He was here in Florida with his brother Manny a couple of years back, trying to get the workers organized. There was a great movement in the Miami area that supported him. Then I guess he had so much going in California that he had to leave with not much accomplished here. But it was wonderful to meet him."

As they chatted, Corina's name came up and Pat told Dick how impressed she was with the volunteer who had been the faith leader of the Naples Hispanic community for many years.

"She has charisma," said Pat, thoughtfully. "When she speaks, the people listen."

Dick smiled, remembering how Corina had moved the people from the back to the front of the church with a simple motion of her hand.

"I think she is a born leader," Pat continued. "She can say the toughest things with a smile on her face. There's a childlike quality in her, too, together with a strength that I think comes from having suffered."

That comment reminded Dick that he had not heard much of Corina's story. They were always so busy, and when they were together it seemed they only talked about the needs of the migrants.

That evening, Pat joined them at Mass at the A. Duda camp were they set up the makeshift altar in a sandy area. A number of small children played nearby. Just before Communion, one of the children bumped into the card table and spilled the consecrated wine and hosts all over the sandy ground. Pat gasped because the wine and bread had already been transubstantiated into the body of Jesus Christ, but Dick and Corina calmly picked it up, Host by Host, brushing the sand off and returning it to the ciborium.

"It's part of saying Mass in labor camps," smiled Dick. "Anyway, it was children who spilled it, so Jesus wouldn't mind."

Pat spent the night at the rectory and the next morning continued her explanation of the mission parishes.

"Most of the priests work together with nuns who, for the most part, run the religious education programs. A Mexican order called Missionary Guadalupanas of the Holy Spirit sent sisters here to help with the Mexican farm workers."

"Are U.S. orders involved in the parishes, too?"

Pat nodded. "There are quite a few providing services like distribution of clothing and food, emergency funding, day care, health care and legal assistance. A lot of nuns from the School Sisters of Notre Dame, S.S.N.D.s, do that kind of work here, plus other orders. Some of them even follow the workers when they go north."

"I wonder if we'll get any sisters here," mused Dick.

"Right now it seems that Corina Hernandez and her family fill their role pretty well."

One evening, *Padre* Pedro Jiménez called from Immokalee and asked Dick if he could cover Masses for him the coming weekend. Dick could go Saturday afternoon, say the evening masses in Spanish, spend the night at the rectory, say the three Sunday morning masses and still be back in time for the evening Spanish Mass in Naples. That Saturday he followed the directions, taking County Road 951 north to Immokalee Road and heading east.

"Immokalee is where the road ends," Corina had told him. "It actually keeps going, but you'll know when you're there."

On the drive Dick passed field after field of winter vegetables that were just starting to grow, then gladiola fields and then swamps. He saw a sign for the Corkscrew Swamp Sanctuary, then citrus groves and then more vegetable fields. Finally, he came to Immokalee's Main Street. Corina had been right; he knew when he was there. The wide street had no median or streetlights and was lined with wooden buildings, restaurants and shops with faded paint, many signed in Spanish. He noted many apparent indigents along the side of the street. Though only an hour and a half from downtown Naples, it seemed cut off from the rest of Collier County, like a different and poor country.

After making a left onto 9th Street, he saw the rectory and church plus two large buildings, one with a pitched roof and another long, rectangular one. Across the street were vacant overgrown lots.

He parked his car, got out and looked around, holstering the fingers of his left hand into his pocket and hooking his thumb through his belt loop. Then he looked down and noticed an inscription in the sidewalk: "Rev. P.J. 1979." Dick smiled. Pedro Jiménez had put his initials into the cement when he built the rectory.

The church grounds consisted of about ten acres, partly grassy but mostly sand. Saw-palmetto bushes dotted the landscape, a few cabbage palms housed air plants on their spiked trunks, and grey Spanish moss decorated the live oak trees.

He stopped to say a quick prayer at a rustic grotto of Our Lady of Guadalupe and then walked to the front of the church. It was less than half the size of St. Peter's, at least twenty years old and showing its age. The door was open and he stepped in. The inside was like the outside; small, poor and rectangular with simple lines. He judged that it would hold about three hundred people if a third of them stood up. Dick wondered if he would even need a microphone to say Mass, but noted that they had one. He looked up and saw ceiling fans, hoping they had air conditioning, too.

Two of the Guadalupana Sisters he had heard about were decorating the altar with flowers. The sisters, dressed in habits, introduced themselves in Spanish and then quietly continued their work. Later, he said the Saturday afternoon Mass and afterwards, as he greeted people on their way out, a woman approached him.

"Are you the same *Padre* Sanders that was in South Carolina?"

"*Sí*, I was in South Carolina."

"My brother is Adán Hernandez. He said that *Padre* Sanders said Mass for them in Johns Island."

Dick laughed delightedly. "I just moved to Naples to start a Mission for the farm workers. Adán used to talk about his sister, Rosa. You are the housekeeper for the priest, *sí*?"

"*Sí, Padre*" she said, proud that he knew of her.

"*Mucho gusto*, Rosa. I am happy to finally meet you."

"*Padre,* why did you go over there to Naples? Why didn't you come to us? You could work here with *Padre* Pedro. He is alone here."

"But there's nobody at *San Pedro* either, Rosa. Not anyone to even say a Mass in Spanish. And there are a lot of field workers there. They need me."

"*Sí, Padre, claro*," she said, disappointed.

The next day Dick drove back to Naples, grateful that he had not been sent to such a remote area. He would soon learn that some of the churches in agricultural areas were even more remote and rustic. His mission in Naples was one of the nicest among the Rural Life Bureau churches.

"*Padre*, do you want to come for dinner?" asked Corina one day.

Father Sanders loved sharing the lives of the people he worked with and served, so he enthusiastically accepted the invitation. He liked Corina, Martin and Rita, and there were still many more of her children and her husband to get to know. He had only said hello to them. They were all adults except for Luis Jr. who was probably eighteen or so.

The *Padre* arrived a half hour late. Corina's husband, Luis, welcomed him and offered him a beer.

"*Gracias*," accepted Dick. He did not drink often or much anymore, but he still enjoyed Mexican beer. The men sat in the modest but comfortable living room while Corina and three of her daughters finished preparing dinner. On the walls hung a crucifix, a painting of Our Lady of Guadalupe, a photo of Luis in his army uniform and wedding pictures of the older children. Corina brought in some Guacamole and tortilla chips.

When they sat down to eat, *Padre* Sanders said grace. Then Luis asked him a question in English.

"*Por favor,*" responded Dick. "*Hablen siempre en español. Tengo que practicar.*" Please speak always in Spanish. I have to practice. "*Y por favor, llámanme 'Dick.'*" And please call me Dick.

Luis Jr. smiled sideways at his older brother Jesse until a stern look from Corina stopped him. Dick realized that his name apparently didn't translate well into Spanish.

The conversation was lively as the Hernandez "children" interrupted each other and their parents. At one point they asked the new *Padre* who he thought would be the new pope. Pope Paul VI had died on August 6th and his successor had not been named. *Padre* Sanders began in Spanish to tell them about the voting process and the white smoke that would announce a new pope.

He began carefully. "*El proceso para elección la Papa...*"

Rita started giggling and soon the whole family was laughing. Dick smiled, puzzled about what was so funny.

"*Padre*, the Pope is *El* Papa! You said '*La* Papa.' That's a potato!"

They all started laughing again and now Dick laughed with them. He would never make that mistake again. As they finished their meal *Padre* Sanders looked seriously at the family of his volunteer Pastoral Minister. "I have an important question."

He paused for emphasis and the family leaned in, wondering what it could be. Then Dick smiled and looked directly at Corina. "How on earth did you get so many children?"

The family burst into laugher, interrupting each other again as they all tried to give their explanation. Finally Corina said firmly that she would tell the story and the rest of them became quiet. She spoke Spanish but slowly, so the *Padre* could understand.

"In 1944, when I was nineteen years old, I married Luis. Then they called him to the army in 1945. I was already pregnant with my daughter, Guadalupe. When Luis came home from the war we had Martin and Janie. Martin came out feet first."

"Breech," said Father Sanders in English, frowning. He remembered this from Camp St. Mary's. "One of the young girls I knew in South Carolina had a breech birth, and they had to do a Cesarean delivery."

With Corina it was different. "They didn't do Cesareans back then, at least not in the hospital we were in. I had this baby the natural way."

Father Sanders stared sympathetically, amazed that such a thing could even happen.

"It hurt me," said Corina, remembering the pain. "I was awake and then I was unconscious. They took me in the cab. My mother asked if she could stay with me. The doctor said, 'Yes you can stay but you're gonna sit down in that corner over there.' And my mother sat there and said the rosary the whole time. It was terrible for me."

Padre Sanders cringed, imagining the pain of childbirth, something no man could possibly understand.

"And then I went."

He looked at her sideways. "*¿Qué?*" What?

"I don't know what happened but the pain was gone. And I saw the hand of my mother with the rosary following me. I went straight and I saw a bright light and white doors opening for me. I was being drawn toward the doors, so beautiful!"

Dick leaned in on his elbows as Corina told the rest of her story in her broken English because she thought he would understand better.

"*Sí.* But when I was closer, the doctor told my mother, 'Go with her, get in her ear and talk. Because she's not hearing us but she's gonna hear you.' And my mother told me, '*Hijita*, my little girl, you have a beautiful baby boy. The one you wanted. You have a boy.' And I went back and I no enter the white doors. And I'm not feeling the pain, because I was dead. But after that, it hurt. Oooohhhh, it hurt."

"You were really dead?" Dick was fascinated. "Medically proclaimed dead?"

"That's what the doctor said later." Luis confirmed it with a nod.

"How did you feel about the white doors? Did you want to go through them? Did you want to keep going?"

"At that time it was so beautiful I can't describe it, but I just heard my mother call 'come back, come back.' So I came back."

Dick listened in quiet amazement as Corina continued her story.

"The doctor told my mother I could not have more children because I would be paralyzed or something. He wanted me to get my tubes tied."

Padre Sanders thought this would have been a good idea but said nothing as Corina explained that her mother was a strict Catholic who did not believe in contraception for any reason.

"She always told me, 'If you're going to get married, you're going to have children. This is why marriage is and that's why God made men and women, to be together and to make children.' So when the doctor wanted to tie the tubes, my mother said to my husband, 'No!' She said, 'Luis, the doctor is not God to tell my *joven*, my daughter, that she cannot have more children. She's gonna have as many children as God's gonna give her. This is why marriage is!'"

Luis obeyed his mother-in-law and there was no tubal ligation. Corina recovered and had seven more children. Even though the next child, Janie, was another breech and delivered at home, it was easier than with Martin, and all the children were healthy. But Corina never forgot the white doors.

CHAPTER TWENTY-THREE –
JESUS AS ROLE MODEL –
1978 – 1979

One Wednesday night in November when they arrived at the Six L's Farm, Dick was delighted to see a man with a guitar. The musician introduced himself and the other singers. He was Miguel Flores and they were his father, brother and uncle.

Miguel spoke like an educated person, which made the *Padre* curious about his background. After Mass, he asked the young man why he was doing field work.

"I was in school in Mexico, in the university, but I came up here to learn English and make some money. My plan is to go back as soon as I have enough to complete my education."

Padre Sanders asked if Miguel and his family would sing at the church on Sunday evenings in addition to playing at the camp. Dick was thrilled when they agreed to do it – the *San Pedro* Mission now had a band. Soon, Miguel was accompanying *Padre* Sanders and Corina to other camps during the week, too. They became a standard trio, Dick saying the Mass, Corina assisting and Miguel playing and singing.

Though Miguel was twenty-one years younger than Dick who was now forty-two, they quickly became friends. He told Miguel to call him Dick but Miguel stuck to "*Padre.*" He seemed more comfortable with it. Then he asked Miguel to always speak to him in Spanish.

"*Pero talvez no me entiende,*" protested Miguel. But maybe you won't understand me.

"*No, está bien*, it's OK. I can understand you."

"*OK, Español. Pues bien, dígame,*" said Miguel. Tell me about yourself. "Where are you from?"

"Illinois, originally, and then I was a monk in South Carolina, and then decided God's will for me was to work in social justice. I started working with poor Blacks but then met some Hispanic migrant workers and felt drawn to serve them, so here I am."

Miguel tried to ask more questions but the *Padre* deflected them, changing the topic to something he had been meaning to ask.

"Do you know the songs from Nicaragua, from the Revolution?"

Miguel shook his head.

"I have a book of the music, from Cuernavaca where I studied Spanish. Can you learn the songs if I give you the book?"

"*Sí*," nodded Miguel but then was curious. "Tell me more about Nicaragua. I've heard things but don't really know details."

"Just before I came to Naples, the Sandinista rebels took over in Nicaragua, supported by Cuba, Venezuela, Panama and Costa Rica, plus Nicaragua's own middle and business classes."

"Wow, you really know this stuff," said Miguel.

"I read it carefully because what happens in Central America today has a direct effect on what will happen here tomorrow. The poor people will come to us, looking for safety and work."

"Guatemalans are coming into Mexico now because of the war in their country," said Miguel. "The Mexican government doesn't want any more refugees, but the Mayan Guatemalans can pass for Indians from Mexico's southern states, Oaxaca and Chiapas."

Dick interjected, "They will likely make their way to the U.S. and perhaps here, soon. The Nicaraguan situation has been going on for a long time, like many of the other countries including Guatemala. As a matter of fact, Somoza, head of the political dynasty in Nicaragua, was part of the coup that took out the best president Guatemala ever had, at least for the poor people and Maya Indians."

"Jacob Arbenz," nodded Miguel. "That was a U.S.-backed coup, wasn't it?"

"*Sí*, the CIA. We supported the United Fruit Company down there. Part of the justification for removing Arbenz in Guatemala was the fact that he allowed some communist-linked political parties in his government."

Dick was impressed with Miguel's knowledge as their conversation led them from one Central American country to another, hard to avoid as their events were often closely entangled. They also discussed the image of Latin American nations publicized by the dictators. Many of the countries appeared to be thriving, but in reality most of the people were dirt poor and the countries filled with disease and malnutrition.

As the *Padre* continued to say Masses to growing numbers of workers at the camps, the Sunday evening Spanish Mass at the church grew, too. Dick got money from the diocese to buy a used school bus, the kind crew leaders used to take their workers to the fields. It had been painted blue, and held sixty-five people. He sent Martin Hernandez for his chauffeur's license and then Martin started picking up the farm workers on Sundays at 5:00 p.m. Father Sanders also asked Martin to pick up the teenagers for religious education classes.

After a few weeks, Martin came to his office. "*Padre*, we got a problem with the bus."

"*¿Que?* What? Something you can't fix?"

Martin smiled at the compliment. "Not mechanical. The problem is that there's another bus."

Dick looked at him curiously as Martin explained. "The Assembly of God Church has started sending a bus for the workers, too. Most of the people are Catholic, but they can't tell the difference, so they just get on the other bus."

"Well, then you better start getting there earlier."

One day in late November, Dick looked at the stacks of papers on his desk and realized he needed help. He didn't like paperwork and therefore rarely did any, but he had not expected it to pile up so quickly – Baptisms from two months ago had not been entered in the registry. He talked to Corina and then hired her daughter Maria, a bright, vivacious seventeen-year-old, as his part-time secretary, two days a week. He was much happier ministering to his people than taking care of paperwork.

One day Corina came in to see him. "*Padre*, now that we have you and a church we can celebrate the *Doce de Deciembre*, the day Juan Diego saw the vision of Our Lady of Guadalupe. We have never had a real celebration for her here."

Her excitement was contagious.

"*Diga*," he said. "Tell me what happens."

"Well, we have to get there real early, like 3:00 in the morning."

Dick's eyes opened wide and he looked at her sideways. "What time?"

Corina looked at him crossly. "It's only one day a year!"

"OK, OK!"

"We bring flowers to the church, cover the altar with them to remember the miracle of Our Lady and Juan Diego. Then we sing *las Mañanitas*." Little songs of the dawn.

"Would Miguel know those songs?"

"Oh, *sí*, everybody from Mexico knows them. All of us Mexicans from Texas, too."

On December 12, Dick arrived at about the proscribed hour, hating the early hour but looking forward to this celebration. He was shocked to see the church parking lot already filled with trucks and vans. More farm workers and other Hispanics came than he had ever seen in the church before. They sang and prayed until dawn, and then went back to the camps to work. Later that evening, the *Padre* said a Mass that had almost as many people as there were in the morning, deeply moved by the devotion to Our Lady of Guadalupe.

Just before Christmas, Dick sent out a Christmas letter.

Naples, Fla. 33942, December 24, 1978.
Feliz Navidad! Merry Christmas!

Dear Friends,

Greetings from sunny Florida. As you may or may not know I moved into Naples in late July of this year to work here with the Spanish speaking, and am working out of St. Peters Church or as we call it *Iglesia de San Pedro.*

The work here is off to a good start. This is the continuation, or deeper involvement of the ministry I started in Beaufort and Charleston, S.C. with the migrant farm workers. I followed them home. The majority who go up the east coast to pick the crops, work in the winter harvest here in Fla. There are about 3,000 migrant farm workers here in Naples from October till April and some of them stay longer than that. There are also at least 300 Spanish speaking families who live here in the town all year. Before I came there were no Spanish-speaking priests working here in Naples so we are really starting from scratch. There is a good but small group of people who are very actively involved so we form a good team, but there is a tremendous amount to do. Please keep this ministry in your prayers.

I am doing fine, though a little worn out at the moment. Naples is a beautiful town on the southern Gulf coast. It is growing very rapidly as a winter resort town, but somewhat high priced. Christmas afternoon I will be flying to New York to spend a week with my mother and brother. The change in climate at this time of the year will be a bit of a shock, but I'm really looking forward to seeing them and it will be a much needed break.

Please forgive me for not being able to add a personal note but there is just no time at all. However, the thought is there.

As you know I don't usually get anything out, so I'm improving
some. I pray and trust that you will have a very joyous Christmas
and that the deep peace and strength which Christ brings will be
yours. Peace, Dick Sanders.

A few days later, Pat Stockton sent him a copy of an article that had
run in the Miami Herald on Sunday, December 17. Dick smiled as he read
it, happy that the migrants were getting attention again and amused that
he had apparently become Hispanic in the eyes of the press. It headlined,
"PADRE TAKES MASS WHERE THE FAITHFUL ARE." The article
included a picture of a young Hispanic mother and her toddler, and one of
Dick breaking a Host as he said Mass at one of the farms. The writer, Bella
English, referred to Dick as "Father Ricardo Sanders." It was a well-written,
compassionate look at the challenges of farm workers and the beauty of their
simple and deep faith.

> ...with little money and no transportation, Spanish migrants
> have, for the most part, remained isolated from the Catholic
> Church. Until Father Sanders came to St. Peter's Church in
> Naples.
>
> Wednesday nights are reserved for The Six L's Camp in the
> eastern part of the county, not far from Marco Island. Father
> Sanders is late on this Wednesday and the Dodge flies down the
> dirt road, rattling like a train....
>
> "Padre, padre," a chorus cries, as Sanders and his car pull up at
> the camp's tidy day care center. Children of all sizes converge on
> the car....
>
> Inside, Sanders makes careful, even tender, preparations. A
> bookcase covered with a sheet and a multi-colored Mexican
> serape becomes the altar. A 19-year-old youth with his beloved
> but battered electric guitar becomes the church musician...
>
> "They don't have the distracting comforts that others have,"
> Sanders says later of his migrant worshippers. "The only
> meaningful things they have are their families and their religion."

What about the noise from the kids? "What noise?" Sanders
asks. "I think it's great the kids come to church. I love it."

Christmas week was indeed a much needed break which Dick appreciated.
Jim and Joan were now back in Staten Island and Jim had finished a book
on the history of the Church in Boston. They had a beautiful condominium
from which they could see the Statue of Liberty. Dick thought about the
millions of immigrants who had seen her welcoming lamp as they sailed into
the New York harbor.

Their mother flew in from Peru, looking a little weak and kind of gray.
Dick asked about her health.

"I'm fine, dear, just a little tired these days."

For Christmas, Jim gave him a recently-translated book on Liberation
Theology called *Christology at the Crossroads* by a Jesuit priest named Jon
Sobrino. Dick had tried to read it in Spanish, but it was a little dense and
he never got very far, so he was grateful to have the English translation. He
began to read it at Jim's to help him fall asleep, but the book was so thought-
provoking and matched Dick's own feelings so perfectly that he could hardly
put it down. He stayed up half the nights during Christmas, reading, and
during the days he talked about it with Jim who was still amazed at having
intellectual discussions with his little brother.

"Sobrino starts about mid-way through where Gutierrez got in *Theology
of Liberation,*" Dick explained. "In order to have real, first-hand knowledge
of Christ, you have to seek the historical Jesus. Once we understand Christ
in the history of the time when He lived on earth, then we can understand
him being alive during different periods of history."

"Including our own," surmised Jim.

"Exactly."

They talked through Sobrino's review of seven traditional starting points
to Christology, including knowing Christ as a divine person with two natures,
Christ as teacher and Christ as savior.

"Sobrino focuses on an eighth view," explained Dick, "that of the historical
Jesus who is the focus of Latin American Liberation Theology, because of
how similar current conditions in many Latin American countries are to
Jesus' time. Jesus criticized the people in power, including the Pharisees, legal
experts, the rich, the priests and the world rulers. Sobrino says that Latin
America is moving from a traditional, abstract kind of faith to a new, more
practical faith that truly liberates people here on earth."

Jim followed the logic immediately. "So Jesus' faith can be viewed the
same light; more than just faith in God, but faith in a mission."

Dick continued reading the book on the plane, almost disappointed when he landed in Ft. Myers because he didn't want to put it down. But Miguel was picking him up and he looked forward to seeing his friend.

"So, *mi amigo*, tell me about your Christmas."

"It was good," said Miguel. "People at the camp put up a few Christmas trees and I had a nice dinner with my father, brother and uncle. We gave presents – I got a hat!" He reached into the back seat and put on new brown cowboy hat.

"It looks good on you," smiled Dick. He was glad to be back.

A few weeks later, Maria came in to tell *Padre* Sanders that his mother was on the phone.

"She sounds shaky," she told him. "Usually she has this sweet voice that says, 'Is Dick there?' But now she sounds different."

Dick picked up the phone warily and Betty told him she had to have heart surgery. He was always amazed at how calm and collected she was in the face of crises.

"One of my arteries is clogged, dear. The blood can't get through it like it should. I've been kind of tired lately, then last week I had trouble breathing and... well, anyway, they did tests and I'm going to have an operation to fix it. That's the good news. They're going to take a heart valve from a pig and replace one in mine with it."

Dick interrupted, frowning skeptically. "A pig?"

"Yes, dear, calm down. They do it at the University of Iowa Medical Center. I'm scheduled for next Tuesday."

"I'll be there, Mom. I'll coordinate with Jim and I'll see you soon. I'll be praying all the way."

"Good," she said. "I'll rest easier if you're here."

"I love you, Mom."

He called his brother as soon as he hung up. They would meet at the airport in Iowa City.

"This is serious," explained Jim. "It's not a bypass but they still have to saw through the breast bone, open her up, stop her heart, etc. It's a big deal. I'm glad you're coming, too. We can share a hotel room at the same place Gail is staying."

"I almost forgot about Gail. How's he taking it?"

"He's pretty broken up. Mom is handling the whole thing a lot better than he is. It will be good for him that we'll both be there, too."

Dick hung up and sat there, stunned. The thought of losing his mother was unbearable. After making a plane reservation he went into the church and prayed to the mother of God. Our Lady of Guadalupe seemed to reassure him with her words, "Do not be afraid of anything. Am I not here, who is your mother?"

Two days later he flew to Iowa City and met Jim at the airport. They drove directly to the hospital and were relieved to find their mother sitting up in bed. Gail was already there, holding her hand and looking worried. Betty, however, was her optimistic self, accepting as always what life sent her.

On the day of the surgery, they arrived early enough to be able to reassure her with their presence.

"I'll be fine," she smiled, already groggy from the pre-operation sedatives.

Dick waited for hours with Jim and Gail for the operation to be over. Then the doctor came out and said they could see her in Intensive Care, warning them first that it would be a shock because, for some time after the operation, they needed to keep her heart and her lungs going with a machine. Dick stood back from the bed. It was gruesome, his mother's chest heaving up and down from the machine and tubes coming out all over. Gail went to pieces when he saw it and started sobbing. Dick and Jim prayed with him for the woman they all loved.

Later, the news was worse. Betty had had a stroke connected with the operation. The doctors said it was temporary, but it was horrifying for Dick, Jim and Gail to see her with one side of her body totally paralyzed. Dick tried to imagine what it would be like to be in her condition and wondered what it would be like to be aware of your surroundings but unable to move. He spent much of the time in the hospital chapel, praying, while the medical staff did therapy by rubbing and massaging, trying to stimulate the nerves. After only a few days, like a miracle, Betty made a complete recovery. Dick thanked God for sparing her. After losing his father at such a young age, losing his mother would have been devastating. By the time he left to go back to Florida, she was sitting up, happily talking with everyone who came into the room.

When he returned to Naples, life thankfully settled down and Dick refocused on the migrants. As he got to know them better, he continued to think of ways to inspire and empower them.

That spring, 1979, the parish held the now-annual *reinados*. *Padre* Pedro came from Immokalee, and Dick was impressed with the amount of activity in and about the rectory related to the event. In the end, Corina's daughter and his secretary, Maria, was the winner. She was truly beautiful, body and spirit, but she won because the family had raised the most money.

Reinados with Maria Hernandez, "Queen," seated in front of Padre Sanders

To celebrate the *reinados*, *Padre* Sanders held a Mass at the *Iglesia de San Pedro*. Afterwards Martin Hernandez and two of his brothers closed the doors between the main part of the church and the back where the people had hung drapes and created a beautiful archway of real ferns and roses, with a white bow attached to the top. The seven girls who took part in the contest processed in, wearing full length hoop-style embroidered evening gowns that swept out and away from their bodies in circles as wide as the girls were tall. Their escorts, young men of their same age, about fifteen, wore tuxedos with colored formal shirts that matched the girls' dresses. They were accompanied by music from Miguel and his family,

"Isn't this amazing?" Dick whispered to Pedro. "Corina got all this together and runs it every year now."

Pedro agreed. "It's how she got the money she hoped would bring you here, if I remember correctly."

Dick smiled and Pedro continued. "If you think about it, it's a strong expression of an individual's faith. Here you have a woman who was the mother of eleven children and yet she found time to sit down, examine herself and figure out what she wanted to do with that life from that point forward. It's not as if she did nothing before. Picking cotton and raising all those children is enough for a lifetime, but she didn't stop there. She is an agent of change, prodding others and eventually getting what she believes in."

Dick presented the trophies and placed tiaras on the heads of the girls who won, beginning with the runners-up and ending with Maria Hernandez.

As he presented her trophy, he whispered, "I hope you won't be hard to work with, now that you're a queen!"

The coronation did not go to her head, of course, and she continued to be of help to him in the office. The money from the *reinados* was given to the church to continue to pay off the building fund.

One day the following week, Father Sanders left the office, leaving two hundred dollars from the collections on his desk. He locked the door behind him but later Corina came in and saw that someone had broken in the door and the money was gone. Father Murphy was angry. When Dick returned, Mike raised his voice in frustration.

"Dick, you can never leave money out in the open in the office like that! The bishop is going to find out about this and there'll be trouble!"

Father Sanders looked at him and shrugged. He was used to upsetting bishops.

"Michael," he said gently. "Maybe whoever took it needed the money."

Father Murphy shook his head, threw up his hands and walked out of the office. Dick shook his head, too, wondering why Mike didn't understand.

Evenings Masses at the camps continued to be Dick's favorite times. Afterwards, he spent time with the workers as he had in South Carolina, drinking coffee and asking about their lives.

Two men he had not met before leaned against a building, eyeing him curiously. They wore weathered tee-shirts, jeans and dusty cowboy boots. Near them, a third man sat on a step with his elbows on his knees.

"*Buenas noches*," he said, nodding to them.

"*Buenas, Padre*," one of them said, seemingly speaking for the group.

"*¿De dónde vienen?*" Where did you come from? How long have you been here?"

The *Padre* continued the conversation in Spanish, sitting down next to the seated man and lighting up a cigarette. His probing questions put the men off at first, but they quickly seemed comfortable enough to talk.

The man sitting next to him, Cirillo, had been in the U.S. for three and a half years, working up and down the migrant stream. There was no work in his hometown outside of Michoacán and he had come to the U.S.. When he left home, unemployment was close to 50 percent, and half of his friends had already gone to the United States. Dick had noticed more Mexicans from Mexico in the fields now than when he first started working with migrants in South Carolina. These men all hoped to return to Mexico soon. Cirillo would go after he had enough money for his family to build a real house instead of the shack he was raised in.

"*Padre*, we lived in an adobe hut with a dirt floor. We tried to grow some vegetables and raise a few chickens, but there's no way to survive down there. The year I came up here, there was a drought and even the chickens died."

"How much money can you send?"

"Sometimes as much as three hundred dollars. At first my mother used it for food and to get the younger kids into school, plus they needed clothes and shoes. Then they started working on a real house. Last month she said they had finished the foundation. She's waiting for me to come home and help them paint the walls. But *Padre*, I can't go yet or we won't have money to buy the paint!"

They all laughed.

"Do you miss your family?"

"*Sí, Padre, mucho.*" He shook his head, pushed aside some dirt with his boot and then looked up again and grinned. "But mostly my girlfriend! We're gonna be married if I ever get back there."

"I'll pray for you to make lots of money so you can go home soon."

"*Gracias, Padre.*"

Dick asked more probing questions, always fascinated by the stories. The two who were standing had come together the previous year. They hired a *coyote* at Piedra Negras, Mexico and swam across the Rio Grande with about twenty other guys.

"How much does it cost now?"

"Five hundred dollars to get across the river. It covers a place to stay on the Mexico side of the border until the right time for the crossing, a van pickup in Texas and a place to spend the night while you wait for a 'ride' to Naples. The ride was another two hundred dollars. I should be able to pay it off over the next six months, working up and down the east coast."

"Why did you come here, to this place?"

The man looked at Dick quizzically.

"Work, *Padre*. There's work here."

Sometimes the workers had questions about getting religious education for their kids or help with emergency needs. Dick would suggest they visit him at the rectory, but he soon realized that, rather than come to him, they went to the home of Corina Hernandez. After a while he understood that they were intimidated by the rectory and Father Murphy, whom they saw as the priest who ministered to the white people. Seeing the need for a place where the Hispanics could feel welcomed, Dick asked the bishop if the archdiocese would purchase a house for him. He did not mention that he also wanted a place for migrants to stay when they first arrived in town and had nowhere else to go.

As soon as the concept was approved, Corina and Maria found a two-story house in Naples Manor with three bedrooms on the second floor and a living room and kitchen on the first. On the south end was a single-story family room with a separate entrance that would be their office. In the back was a screened-in porch and next to it, a sunroom. The house had a Latin American look to it, painted an almost primitive azure blue, with arches in front of the entry way. Corina found a housekeeper whom the *Padre* hired to cook and clean for him.

Soon the house was filled with Spanish-speaking people.

"This is not my house," he would tell them. "It is God's house, a house for all of us."

The *Padre* allowed families to stay in the sunroom for as long as a week or two, whatever it took for them to get on their feet. Single men and women could use the spare bedrooms on the second floor. He also often gave them money for food or doctor bills.

Maria told him she was worried because she did the books and knew how little he made. "A lot of people think you have money because they think the house is your own, not realizing it's owned by the diocese, so they think it's OK to ask you for money. You can't afford to keep giving, *Padre*. And what about your car? You're gonna need to get a new one, one of these days."

She had a point about the car. The 1970 Dodge had 160,000 hard miles on it from driving on dirt roads and into potholes on his way to the labor camps.

"But she's still running," he smiled. "I'm not ready to give up on her yet!"

He welcomed everyone. When Jehovah's Witnesses knocked on the door, Dick would talk with them for hours, surprising his young secretary.

"How can you do that, *Padre*, discussing things with them so calmly? They're not Catholic."

"It's OK," he smiled gently. "We're all working for the same cause."

Having his own rectory gave him a little extra time for reading, so he had a chance to finish *Christology at the Crossroads*. He came across a section he had missed, in which Jon Sobrino said the kingdom of God could become a utopian symbol for a new way of living, here on earth.

Dick thought back to the diagram in the Catechism from when he was a child. The Christ who sat on the top step inside the cloud had come all the way down to the bottom rung and was Jesus, a man about Dick's age, with long hair and a beard. That Jesus would be his role-model.

CHAPTER TWENTY-FOUR –
EMPOWERING THE PEOPLE –
1980 – 1981

After Dick moved into his own rectory, the farm workers felt more comfortable coming to see him, and, as a result, he worked harder and longer. He stayed up late, slept poorly and struggled to get up in the morning. Often Maria was already at her desk by the time he came down from his room. He seemed to get more tired during the day, too. Not wanting to take time for long naps, he would go upstairs, set his alarm, sleep for fifteen minutes and be back downstairs before Maria knew he was gone.

Dick loved having people at the rectory, though. The migrants often came to him before they contracted for work with a grower, sometimes arriving in the middle of the night. He would feed them soup and sandwiches and put them up in the family room.

On Saturdays, Corina and Rita taught Catechism on the back porch, bringing more people and filling the house with the laughter of children. *Padre* Sanders grew closer to Corina. Her love for the Hispanic farm workers was like his. They also shared an intense dislike for paperwork.

"Papers, papers, papers," she complained. "Nobody does nothing, just making papers."

Every time there was a Baptism, he asked Corina to take pictures. "When they are grown and married," he told her, "they will be happy to have the pictures."

The nights when he said Masses at the camps were often long evenings, as *Padre* Sanders would insist on visiting everyone in the *barracas*. They served coffee and *galletas con coco*, a cookie similar to coconut macaroons. Corina's daughter, Rita, would get tired. "*Padre* it's time to go, it's time to go." But Dick wanted to talk to all the workers.

Soon it was time for the migrants to go up the road. Dick would follow them in a few weeks, but, in the meantime, he would read more about Mexican culture. He dug out a book he had studied in Cuernavaca, *The Labyrinth of Solitude* by Octavio Paz, a philosophical history of Mexico told from an intellectual, cultural and sociological perspective.

Dick skimmed the book again and found the thoughts he was looking for. Paz talked about how Mexico's relationship with the United States impacted the Mexican self-image. He had studied enough Mexican History to remember that in 1848, the Treaty of Guadalupe Hidalgo was signed, ending the Mexican-American War. While Americans lauded the resulting acquisition of Texas and California and parts of other western states, Mexicans mourned the loss of nearly half of their country.

The main theme of *The Labyrinth* was the solitary nature of the Mexican male, something Dick could relate to from his monastic background. It was a desire for solitude that Paz defined as a "nostalgic longing for the body from which we were cast out ... a longing for a place." Paz used Mexicans living in the U.S. as a starting point for an examination of what it meant to be Mexican, using the word *pachucos* to describe them, a word that literally meant "weak or drooping." These *pachucos,* according to Paz, felt ashamed of their origin yet did not wish to surrender their identity to fit into the gringo culture, so they went inside themselves.

Dick spent many hours in contemplation, pondering the meaning of these words and how it affected their faith. *Padre* Pedro visited one evening and they discussed it. Pedro had a similar congregation in Immokalee. For several hours, the two priests talked about the culture in combination with the importance of adult religious education, needed because the migrants were at a "pre-evangelization level." Listening intently, Dick thought that Pedro would make a good teacher.

"They are people with no personal knowledge of Jesus Christ, no knowledge of what the Gospels are and no experience of what it means to be part of a faith community. They go through the motions, they go to church, they sit there, and their faith is strong, but there's no backbone to it."

Dick began to realize how much work it would take to make his people a faith community. They needed to be unified, or worship would become hollow. It was important that the people themselves make it their quest to get to know who Jesus Christ was, what it meant to be a Christian, and what it meant to be involved in the church. He read again about Liberation Theology's "base communities" and became even more determined to create one in Naples. Perhaps he could get the people together in the evenings for a program focused on understanding basic tenets of the Church. He knew it would be asking a lot, considering that they worked until late in the day, but without that understanding, he could they truly live their faith? Without confidence in themselves, how could they ever do anything beyond field work?

He observed Corina and noticed that, in spite of her calm inner strength and deep faith, she had great insecurity, too, so he made it a top priority to increase Corina's confidence in herself. She did God's work so beautifully, but still felt inferior because she had been a field worker and had little education. Although they were in Spanish, she would never do readings at the masses, for example, even at the camps. Dick knew she was capable. She had learned enough from her mother to read in Spanish. He praised her skills and offered to help her practice but still she protested.

"No, I can't do the readings because I never learned nothing. I can help you but I cannot do the readings."

"Yes, Corina, you can do it."

"No, I cannot."

But he would repeat again, "You can do it!"

He spent time helping her and had her practice reading to him, and soon she was doing the readings. Then he expanded Catechism in the fields to include adult religious education, which he taught with Corina's assistance.

After a few weeks, Dick followed the migrants up to South Carolina. He had hoped to go farther, but would not have time. There was a growing population of Hispanics who, like Corina's family, had settled in Naples, and they needed their priest.

He stopped first at camps south of Beaufort and then went to Johns Island. Yolanda met him there and together they visited the people they loved. Yolanda was now six months pregnant, looking happy and healthy, and it was wonderful for Dick to be with his old friend again. He told her about his work in Naples and about Corina Hernandez.

"It sounds like she replaced me," said Yolanda, teasingly.

"Replaced you? Well, in a way I guess she did, but it's different, of course."

They spent the night at Camp St. Mary's catching up with Sister Ellen and visiting the girls.

"How's Sawny?" he asked.

"She doesn't come anymore," said Ellen. When Dick frowned, she said, "Oh no, it's nothing bad. She has a job."

He frowned, hoping Sawny was not picking crab or shucking oysters, but Sister Ellen smiled.

"Sawny finished high school and is working – in an office!"

Dick also stopped to see Father Bobby and then spent a few days at Mepkin Abbey to rest and "recharge." By early July he was back in Naples, thinking more about how to empower his people.

He got to know the altar boys who assisted him at the Spanish Mass, including "Junior" Hernandez, Corina's youngest. He took them on trips like the Miami Seaquarium or up to Tampa to Busch Gardens. On the way, the *Padre* taught them about doing right and being good, being like Jesus, how to be honest and grow into men that he and their families would be proud of. It was easy to convince the boys they could be like Jesus because they were so open. He wished it were that easy for adults.

On July 20, 1979, Dick received a telephone call from an excited Ron Wohl, Yolanda's husband. "Nicholas Martin Wohl was born today!"

"Hah, haaaaa!" Dick laughed out loud. Ron started laughing, too.

"We tried to get him to wait a few days to be born on your birthday, but I'm pretty sure Yolanda is glad to be done with the delivery."

Yolanda got on the phone, sounding weak but happy. "Dick, he's so beautiful. Wait 'til you see him."

"How was it?"

"At the end it was incredibly painful. I couldn't even breathe in between the contractions. But he's beautiful and healthy. We named him after Nicolas, the patron saint of children and St. Martin de Porres."

St. Martin de Porres was one of Dick's favorite saints. An illegitimate mulatto Dominican brother, he worked with the poor and persecuted in the country of Peru in the sixteenth century. Martin believed that all men and women were his brothers and sisters because they were all God's children, so he provided food, clothing and medicine to farmhands, Blacks and Mulattos like himself. St. Martin also had the gift of bi-location, of being in two places at once.

"I wish I had St. Martin's gift right now, Yolanda. I would love to be there with you to help welcome him into the world."

A month later, Yolanda called him again.

"Dick," she began, and then was silent.

He had hoped to hear from her about the baptism of Nicolas Martin, but the sound in her voice indicated a weightier topic. She was trying to control tears.

"*Dime*," he said softly. Tell me. "Is it the baby?"

"No, the baby is fine. The problem is mine. I have cancer."

A pain went through him as if he had been shot.

"I haven't been feeling well lately, and I had a mole that appeared during the pregnancy on my right upper arm that itched. I got it taken out three days ago. I didn't think too much about it. Today they said it is a malignant melanoma, level four out of five. They're going to do massive surgery, cutting from the top of my right breast to my back. They're going to take out the underarm glands and everything."

"I'll leave tonight and be there tomorrow," he said without hesitating.

When he arrived at the hospital in Charleston, the surgery was over but the news was worse – the doctors said Yolanda had six months to a year to live. Dick's closest companion, his beautiful friend who had shared his life with the migrants and guided him through his discernment, was dying. He stayed at their home and prayed deeply into the night.

"God, please leave Yolanda here. I don't know what I would do if she were taken from me, taken from the earth."

When she came home from the hospital he celebrated a healing Mass in Yolanda and Ron's living room with all their friends, people from church and teachers from her school. Then he had to go. He needed a brief visit to Mepkin and then had to get back to Florida.

"Yolanda, whenever you need to talk, I want you to call me. I don't care if it's the middle of the night, just call. I will always be there for you."

She nodded, gratefully. "Tell the farm workers, OK? Tell them I need their prayers."

He drove up to Mepkin and prayed for Our Lady of Guadalupe to beseech God to spare the life of his friend. Then, with a heavy heart, he headed back down to Naples.

In November, 1979, *Padre* Sanders went as usual to say Mass at Six L's Farm and, as usual, Miguel was there getting set up to play. He had learned two of the songs from the book of Nicaraguan Revolution songs, and sang them that evening.

After Mass and his usual chatting with the farm workers, he and Miguel went out for breakfast. Dick loved to eat breakfast at night.

"Miguel, I haven't seen your father in a while."

"He got a different job, working at a French restaurant on Fifth Avenue South, so he moved away from the camps and got a place in town."

"*Bueno.* And when are you going to do the same thing?"

"I don't know, *Padre.* My English still isn't that good, and I don't know how to do anything besides field work. Besides, you already know I just want to make money and go back to Mexico."

"But wouldn't you rather be in some other kind of work, something easier, and maybe make more money?"

"Sure," said Miguel. "If they would hire me, sure."

Not long after, *Padre* Sanders talked to a man at Naples Lumber Company and learned they were looking for someone to stock and load lumber. Dick drove Miguel there. English wasn't a priority, the man explained, he just needed someone strong who would work hard. He hired Miguel on the spot. Next, Miguel would need a place to live because people could only live in the labor camps if they worked on the farm. Dick helped him find an apartment within walking distance of the lumber yard, and loaned him money for the deposit.

Miguel continued to borrow Dick's books and the two friends spent hours discussing them. Most were by Latin American authors, written in Spanish, which were easier for Miguel to read. Dick read them in Spanish but struggled at times, and Miguel would help him translate.

They read two types of books: some from the Latin American "Boom" period of literature of the 1960s and 1970s and others from the Mexican Revolution. Dick had picked up most of them during his studies at Cuernavaca.

"What does 'Boom' mean?" asked his friend.

Dick explained what he had been taught. "From a literature standpoint, 'Boom' authors cross traditional boundaries, experiment with language, and mix different styles of writing in their works. But they have a much bigger effect than that – political. Their books are considered rebellious in a lot of Latin American countries because they expose the problems and injustices common in countries run by military dictatorships, with economic turmoil and Dirty Wars."

"You mean they tell the truth about what's going on there."

"*Exactamente*," said Dick. "I also learn a lot about the emotional and cultural structure of Latinos from reading them. I particularly like the ones they call 'Magical Realism.'"

Miguel was not familiar with the term.

"It refers to stories that include impossible events, but the books' characters never even notice anything unusual. My favorite magical realism book is a novel called *One Hundred Years of Solitude* by Gabriel García Márquez."

Miguel knew that book as *Cien Años de Soledad*. He had read it years before.

"Did you read it in Spanish?" he asked the *Padre*, prepared to be impressed because the book was a brilliant but complicated fantastical story of a family that lived one hundred years in a place where people flew on magic carpets and the dead came back to life.

Dick shook his head. "No way. I tried, but it's so filled with metaphors and magical images that I had trouble following it in English!"

The book had an emotional effect on both of them because of how beautifully it portrayed the betrayal of the innocence of Latin American people by industrialized nations, ending with how the massacre of the banana workers had been erased from Colombian history. The two friends wondered about how much of history simply got erased, depending on the government in power.

In general, life as priest to the migrants was agreeing with Dick and he felt happy almost all the time. The only thing he wished he had was a little more energy. It seemed he was always tired. One night he drove the Mass group to the Bonita camp, Corina in the passenger seat and Miguel in the back with his guitar.

"Dick," said Corina, in the firm yet compassionate voice he had grown to love. "You have to rest."

"Corina, I'm fine."

"Pull the car over," she said firmly. "I'm gonna drive now."

He took a short nap sitting up in the car and by the time they reached the farm he was ready to hear confessions and say Mass.

People at the camps would often remember him from South Carolina.

"*Padre*, what are you doing here?"

He was grateful for his memory that allowed him to recognize each one of them. He was delighted to see them, asking how they were, how were their families and how their work was going. He felt as if they were all his close friends.

"*Padre*, come in for coffee."

"*Padre*, I made *galletas con coco*."

"*Padre*, come and say hello."

Rita, who had taught Catechism and then helped with the Mass that evening, rolled her eyes and looked sideways at her mother. She knew the *Padre* would not only have coffee with the person who asked, but that he would visit every family in the camp, talking and talking while Rita was waiting and waiting. Often they did not return home to Naples until almost midnight.

Chapter Twenty-Five –
He Was Ours – 1981

One of the things *Padre* Sanders continued to wish for was that more of his people would get off the migrant circuit and settle down. Also, he had heard about the number of migrant students that dropped out of high school – only about 30 percent of them graduated. Between leaving school in the spring to go up the road and returning after classes had started in the fall, they couldn't keep up and eventually dropped out. The saddest thing about the dropout rate was that it meant the students would likely become full-time farm workers.

One night when Corina invited the *Padre* for dinner, her second daughter Janie was there, now about thirty years old. They got talking about migrant life when they were young, living on the farm in Naples and why they finally left the camp and moved into a house. It was Janie who had pushed them into moving. She had three issues: one, the school buses only stopped on Tamiami Trail, far from the camps, and they had to walk out all that way. Two, they were the only Hispanics on the bus and the white kids stared at them. She was certain that, in addition to their darker skin, part of the stares had to do with the fact that they were "just" farm workers. Three, and most importantly, they never got to stay in school for the whole year.

"I picked cotton in Texas and we used to do tomatoes, and cherries. It was the hardest work and you could never get ahead in school because you were always moving."

As Janie talked, her voice became increasingly impassioned.

"After we moved here, the oldest kids, especially me, got fed up and said, 'This is no life for us! What are we doing? Is this the future for us? Picking tomatoes?' I was gonna be a senior in high school but I threatened that I would quit school because I didn't want to be moved around from state to state and have to start over all the time."

Finally, following Janie's lead, the children pressured their parents into moving into the city of Naples. They had no trouble convincing Corina, Janie said.

"We lived on the farm for four months and then we moved. Dad stayed there working on the farm because he was a mechanic, but we all moved over to a house we rented in Naples Manor."

The house they found was only a few miles from the farm where Luis continued to work, and it was closer to the schools and to the church. They felt lucky to find it because they had ten children with them. The rent was fifty dollars per month. After they had the house, Corina's eldest daughter Maria Guadalupe, who had stayed behind in Texas working in a doctor's office, called and said she wanted to join them. She missed her family. They sent her an airplane ticket and were happy to have 'Lupe back with them.

Now that they had a home, however, there were many more expenses. To make extra money, the children went from house to house in Naples Manor, selling tomatoes. One couple that had some money and no children helped Maria Guadalupe get her first car, a Mustang. Because she had a car, she was able to get a job at Naples Hospital. A doctor she worked with was so impressed with her work and her drive that he helped her get a scholarship to attend the University of Florida. Dick's understanding of the educational challenges of migrant workers grew along with his appreciation of their potential when given a chance.

The friendship between Miguel and *Padre* Sanders grew, too, as the season progressed and Miguel continued to help Dick enhance the Mass through music. Miguel got to see a side of him that many did not see, noticing that, while Dick was generally quiet, he could get quite irritated when facing injustice

One day they went into a Radio Shack to buy a jack that Miguel needed for his guitar. Dick was wearing a white guayabera, an embroidered button-down shirt with front waist-level pockets and short sleeves, so there was no sign that he was a priest. Though he and Miguel were the first people at the counter, the clerk first waited on someone who came in after them – an American man. Then another white man came through the door and the clerk waited on him, and then a white woman.

Miguel waited patiently but *Padre* Sanders became agitated at this blatant discrimination.

"*Padre*, don't worry about it," Miguel said calmly. "I was born in Mexico, remember? This doesn't affect me because I know who I am."

It reminded Dick of Ida Singletary's answer in Union Heights when he asked her about discrimination, but still he became agitated as Miguel continued to be ignored. Miguel tried again to explain.

"I mean, if somebody acts like they are looking down at me it doesn't affect me because I just say 'You don't know what you're talking about.'"

Dick understood but did not accept Miguel's attitude.

"Forget it, Miguel," he said loudly, so that the clerk would hear him. "If they're not going to wait on you, let's go somewhere else!"

"*Padre*, I can wait," said Miguel quietly. "It's no big deal. By the time we go somewhere else it will take longer than waiting here, and I need the jack."

"Things like this really get under my skin, Miguel," said Dick, even louder than before, to the point that other people in the store stared at them. "We don't have to stay here and put up with this. Now let's go somewhere else where they know how to treat people!"

Finally, the clerk turned to them and Miguel breathed a sigh of relief. He bought the jack and they left, but Dick smoldered and fumed about the incident all afternoon.

Dick often wished he had the time to work on the issues of prejudice but his normal pastoral ministry duties kept him busy. He was also constantly learning how to empower his people, beginning with those closest to him, Corina and Miguel.

"There's a meeting in Jacksonville with the Department of Labor," he said one day. "I want you two to come with me. It's about service to farm workers. We're going to represent the Church."

Miguel said fine, but Corina protested that she would not be valuable there because she did not speak English well and had no education. Dick overrode her and the three of them drove up together. The meeting focused on housing and wages. *Padre* Sanders attended the sessions but did not speak. Instead, he pushed Corina and Miguel to talk.

"These people don't need to hear from me," he told them. "They need to hear from you, the people who lived and worked in the fields."

Padre Sanders was different from the other Anglos at those meetings. The others talked while the workers they had brought with them were silent. Dick, on the other hand, leaned quietly back in his chair with his hands behind his head, listening intently. Miguel looked at him several times, expecting the *Padre* to at least interject something or make a statement, but he only spoke when the discussions occasionally got heated, to calm things down.

Violence in Central America continued to dominate his reading. Later in the spring, Dick read that Archbishop Romero, a convert to Liberation Theology, had been killed in El Salvador. Romero had originally been a conservative but later became a major leader on the side of the people and ended up a martyr for their cause. Dick, who had no wish to die, was happy he could be of service to Latin American immigrants in the United States. Still, he greatly admired priests and nuns who worked in countries like El Salvador.

A few weeks later, the Mariel Boatlift officially began. By the time it ended, it would bring 125,000 Cubans to Southern Florida. It was a major strain on the Miami archdiocese, since most of the Cubans lived there. Dick sometimes saw Cubans in the fields in Naples, but found it curious that, for the most part, they bussed over from Miami and returned there at night.

In May, Yolanda called to let him know she and her family were moving back down to Miami as soon as she finished chemo therapy, probably in late June. He was grateful that she would be closer to him now. They had talked once a week all winter, but this time she had a different sound in her voice, almost as if she were giving up. It had been almost a year since they found the cancer.

"Has the chemo gotten any easier?" he asked softly.

"No, I'm still so sick all the time, and it doesn't seem to be helping. I just want to be in Miami so I can be near my mother and family until..." She could not say the words "until I die," but her voice was filled with such sadness that Dick choked back a sob on the other end of the phone.

"Maybe there will be a miracle, Yolanda. The farm workers are praying for you, and they have taken the word with them to South Carolina to others who knew you there."

"*Sí, un milagro,*" she said, without much conviction.

"I'll be over to visit as soon as you move down. *No te preocupes, amiga.*" Don't worry, my friend.

In the meantime, inspired at how well the Jacksonville meeting had gone with Corina and Miguel, *Padre* Sanders began to work harder to find opportunities to empower his people. He prioritized Corina Hernandez because of her influence over the farm worker population. He pushed her to do more and more readings in Spanish, but realized that she also needed self-confidence in the English-speaking world.

One day he received a request through the diocese from Washington DC for delegates to the upcoming White House Conference on Families. It would start on Thursday, June 5, 1980 and run through the weekend. Dick immediately decided to recommend Corina Hernandez. When he talked to her about it, she looked at him as if he were crazy.

"I can't go there," she protested. "I don't speak English good."

"That's OK, Corina," Dick responded, by now used to this argument. "They will have a translator for you."

"*Pero,* I have no education."

"No, Corina, you have learned much more than most people by the experiences in your life."

"*Pero* that's the same weekend as Rita's and Anita's graduation."

213

"Don't worry about that. I will go with your husband to the graduation. You need to go to Washington."

"*No, Padre,*" she protested even more. "I have never been away from my family. I've never even been in an airplane."

"You have to go, Corina," he finally said, firmly. "I'm going to take care of the kids and your husband. You have to go."

"*Pero porque?* But why? Why would they want me?"

"Because they need someone to represent the Spanish-speaking people and the farm workers."

Corina's firsthand experience as a field worker and mother of eleven children was exactly what the organizers wanted in the mix of delegates. A quote in the conference workbook explained why they particularly wanted Hispanics: "There are many things the Anglos could learn from us. Hispanic families have a strong support system for their members. They seek out help first from the family, and family members will often drop what they are doing to help each other."

Two thousand people attended three conferences, and Corina Hernandez was one of them. When Dick picked her up at the airport, all she could say was, "I met the president! I met the president!" President Jimmy Carter had come to talk to the group during the conference and some of them met him on a reception line.

Dick laughed, thrilled at her excitement. "So tell me about it."

She explained that in one group they talked about parents and children, family violence, caring for old people and families. She was shocked to have learned that many Anglos put their aging parents in nursing homes, with only strangers to take care of them. Dick could see what a contrast this was to the Mexican people who cared for their relatives at home.

"Then another committee talked about education, health, housing and child care. They wanted to know about how migrants took care of all those things. They were really interested in what I was saying!"

"*Sí,* Corina," he smiled. "I told you. That's why they wanted you!"

Dick noted that she carried herself with more confidence after that meeting. More importantly, the Hispanic farm workers now had a role model for advancement and success – Corina Hernandez had met the president of the United States! Her reaction made him more determined than ever to empower the people, beginning with training in their faith that would start next season.

Later in the month, Yolanda called and said they were in Miami. Dick drove over to see her, looking gently at his old friend and companion.

"The Lord is asking a lot of you, Yolanda. I think you're going to come through it, though. Just keep praying."

Yolanda was not so hopeful but found comfort in his support. That summer he spent a lot of time driving back and forth, visiting her. When the migrants returned in the fall, he got busy again.

The second Sunday in November, 1980, *Padre* Sanders was Immokalee covering Masses for *Padre* Pedro. He saw Rosa Hernandez who asked the same question she always asked.

"Hey *Padre*, why you not come to here?"

"Rosa, I am happy that you want me, but I am needed at *San Pedro* Mission, so I have to stay in Naples. I know the people down there and we are all happy, working together."

"But *Padre*," she persisted. "We need you here."

"Rosa, I can't leave my people at *San Pedro*. They need me, too."

"OK, *Padre*, that's it," she threatened, jokingly. "I'm gonna write a letter to the bishop and ask him to send you here."

Rosa was *una obrera*, a worker, a housekeeper, a Mexican immigrant who came to Immokalee originally to pick tomatoes. She was certain that if she ever wrote a letter to the bishop, he would tear it up and throw it away, so of course she never wrote it. Dick returned to Naples that evening, happy to be back among the people he loved.

In December the violence escalated in El Salvador, and Dick wondered when he would start seeing Salvadorans in Florida's fields. This time it included three American Catholic sisters who were protesting the genocide of over 10,000 Salvadorans.

That winter in Naples, the temperature grew cold and a freeze was predicted. Corina was busy but appeared calm as always, collecting warm clothing and blankets for the workers. The migrants were busy, too, covering the crops to protect them from the cold and hastily harvesting what vegetables they could. After that, however, it would be only cleanup – salvaging any vegetables that escaped damage, pulling up the stakes and plowing the destroyed crops under. Dick and Corina worried about the workers who lived day to day on their earnings. Often, if they did not work, they didn't eat. And it went beyond them. If they did not work, there would be no money to send home, and families in Mexico would go hungry, too. Fortunately this freeze was over quickly, but not before the crops had sustained extensive damage. Dick spent more time at the camps, encouraging the workers not to give in to despair.

Not long after, he sat down at his desk and saw a letter from Archbishop McCarthy. After reading, he dropped it onto his desk in disbelief.

It read, "We are transferring you to Immokalee."

Why, when he had finally found his place, would they move him? He thought about how long he had prayed for discernment to make this move and how perfectly it was all working out. He remembered back to other times he had been comfortable yet not certain he was where he was supposed to be: Union Heights, Columbia, Beaufort and Charleston. With those moves, he had been sad to leave but able to accept that the changes were God's will for him. This time, however, he did not trust that this was God's will at all. He was in the right place and the archbishop was making a mistake. The separation anxiety that had plagued him all his life came on strongly and he grew more depressed than he had been during his last year at Mepkin Abbey. Why would they move him, now that he had finally found his place?

Corina was even more upset than he was. "The archbishop knows how hard I prayed to get you here! We raised money, and I kept calling the diocese, year after year, 'We need a priest!' 'We need a priest!' Now we have you and you are perfect for us... and they want to take you away?"

"I don't know what to do," he sighed sadly, slipping into silence.

Corina even forgot her insecurity and called the archbishop, asking him in English to please not take *Padre* Sanders from them because he was such a good priest for the migrants. The archbishop agreed that *Padre* Sanders was a good priest, but his job in Naples was done. *San Pedro Mission* had been created, and Father Sanders would be replaced with another Spanish-speaking priest. "I'm sorry, Corina, but the people in Immokalee need him more than you do, now."

When she told Dick about the conversation, he grew even more despondent than before. She sat for a moment and then had an idea – she would make a petition. Later that afternoon, she returned with a simple document that read, "Please don't take *Padre* Sanders from us. He is our priest." The next few evenings they took the petition to the camps and also circulated it among the Hispanics that were permanent residents of the area. Many of the women cried when they heard the news and some of the men reacted angrily, but everyone signed.

Then Father Sanders drove to Miami to deliver the petition personally. Surely they would respect the people's wishes and leave Dick where he was. The archbishop looked at it thoughtfully, thumbing through the pages of signatures, then shook his head and handed the petition back.

"Father Jiménez is being transferred and Immokalee has no priest. I need you there."

"Of course they need someone," said Father Sanders, feigning understanding while feeling none. "But I am so happy at *San Pedro*, doing work that I love. I have spent the past three years getting to know the farm workers and developing ideas to empower them, and those plans are just now starting to come to fruition. I need time to put them into action."

He started to explain further but his superior stopped him cold.

"I know and I'm sorry, but the truth is that I have another priest who will take over in Naples. I can't get anyone to go to Immokalee."

Father Sanders said nothing for several minutes. His heart was racing and he felt panicked. He tried with all his mental strength to take his mind back to the peace of the Trappists but could not do it. As he stared at the floor, the archbishop said finally, "Dick, you have to go."

Stunned, Father Sanders stood up and left, numb with disbelief. When he got back, Corina saw his face and knew immediately what had happened.

His mind switched to a practical matter but with a bitter tone. "Corina, don't forget this house is for everybody because it's owned by the diocese. It's not just for the priest. Make sure the new priest knows that."

With a frustration and anger he had not felt before, Dick prayed and received no answer. Finally, he decided this move was simply unfair and that he would not do it. He wasn't sure where he would go, but he wasn't going to put up with this. He went to find Miguel at the lumber yard, to say goodbye. Miguel knew right away that something was wrong.

"*Hasta luego*, Miguel," Dick said to his friend. "I'm leaving."

Miguel was shocked. "What are you talking about?"

"They transferred me to Immokalee. They are taking me away from my people. I have prayed for guidance and found none, so I'm quitting. That's it."

Miguel knew he was not just talking, that he would do it. *Padre* Sanders was stubborn when he made up his mind. But then Miguel started to laugh. Dick frowned at his reaction.

"Why are you laughing?"

"Because you are *loco!*" Miguel laughed even harder as the absurdity became clearer. "Immokalee is what you *want*! You wanted to help people and help the farm workers. You can help many more people and do a lot more work in Immokalee than you can do in Naples! Immokalee is a whole community of migrants!"

Years later, Corina would say, without bitterness or judgment, "He was ours, but they took him from us."

VI

VESPERS

1981 - 1984

CHAPTER TWENTY-SIX –
LIGHT YEARS AWAY – MARCH 1981

The drive seemed to take forever as *Padre* Sanders realized again how remote Immokalee really was. The road was in bad shape and narrow in many spots, especially on the two main ninety-degree turns, yet people sped along as if it were a highway. He ignored them and let them pass. He needed to think, to reconcile the move in his mind. Miguel was right, of course, that Immokalee should be the ideal place for him. Maybe he just needed time to adjust to the change.

As he passed the first tomato field he thought about something else he'd been considering, remembering how often Mexican people smirked or looked at him strangely when they learned his name was Dick. As long as he was making this move, he might as well start using his baptismal name again. From now on, he would be Father Richard Sanders. *Padre* Sanders. Richard.

When he turned left on Main Street, he noted the lonely streets. Late this afternoon when the buses returned from the fields, they would be filled with pedestrian traffic: farm workers walking back to their homes, shopping for groceries, doing their laundry. He drove to 9th Street and parked at the rectory.

He wore a light blue guayabera, a style he had started wearing more often because they were comfortable and hid his expanding stomach. His beard still covered his face and he had started wearing his coarse, wavy hair a little long again so it hung over his ears and touched the back of his neck. He was only forty-four but already all were speckled with gray.

It was early afternoon and the weather was perfect. The temperature was in the mid 70s with low humidity. A cold front was predicted to move in later that evening, though. You could never tell what March weather would do in Southwest Florida.

He walked directly to his new church, pausing at the grotto of Our Lady of Guadalupe to pray for Yolanda. He had not lost hope that *La Virgen*, the Virgin would beseech her Son to spare his friend. Still, he submitted to God's plans: "Not my will, but thine be done."

Built many years ago from limestone rock, the grotto had turned gray from rain, heat and humidity. The white statue of the young virgin stood on a stone ledge and at her feet were cactus and yucca plants. The words, *"AQUI ESTOY YO QUE SOY TU MADRE,"* cut from individual pieces of thin wood and painted white to match the statue, were affixed to the stone in an arch that framed her head. The Immokalee interpretation of her words was a slightly different from the ones he had heard before, a statement rather than a question. It translated to, "Here I Am, I Who Am Your Mother."

The church grounds looked different now that he was pastor. His reaction to the difference between this church and St. Peter's was as dramatic as when he had first arrived at Mepkin Abbey, expecting it to look like Gethsemani. He walked toward the street so he could study the church from the front. Made of painted rose-colored stucco, it had a slightly pitched roof with worn grey shingles. On the left was a rectangular bell tower half-again as tall as the rest of it. Mexican petunias in the planting boxes on both sides of the tower made Richard think of Martin Hernandez and how much he would miss seeing him every day. The front facade of the church had three thin rectangular jalousie windows, each protected by a security bar in the shape of a cross. Dedicated on December 12, 1957, the feast day of Our Lady of Guadalupe, this was the first and still the only Catholic Church in Immokalee. Before it was built, Masses were celebrated by out-of-town priests at the Kent Theater on Main Street, or in camps at the farms.

Two Mexican men stood near the entrance to the church, wearing cotton shirts and jeans. He said hello and they greeted him with, *"Buenas, Padre."*

"How did you know I was a priest?" he asked.

"We heard someone was coming and you're the only *bolillo* who has come to the rectory lately."

Richard smiled. He had not heard that term since Adán Hernandez used it years ago in South Carolina. He talked with the men for a while and then walked up three steps under the arched entryway and tried the double wooden doors, but they were locked. For a moment he wished they were glass like Saint Peter's so he could look inside. The difference between Our Lady of Guadalupe and St. Peter's struck him again. This church, these grounds, the main street he had just driven to get here all might have been in Mexico or some other Latin American country. Rather than fifty miles, he could have been light years away.

As he walked around to the side, two shadows sped by on the ground and he looked up, startled, to see large birds, gracefully and precisely gliding parallel with the ground, rising up into the air, then circling and gliding again. They were elegant raptors with a wing-span of about four feet, twice the size of their bodies. Their heads and undersides were white as snow but tipped with black. One of the men he had just talked with came over and explained that they were kite birds that spent the fall and winter in South America. They came to Florida in the early spring to mate, weaving their nests of sticks and Spanish moss in the tall pines. Richard smiled at his welcoming committee of "migrant birds," then walked slowly back to the rectory.

Rosa Hernandez came out to greet him. "Oh, *Padre*, you have finally come to us!"

"Rosa, this is your fault," he smiled wryly, with a twinkle in his eye. "They sent me here because of the letter you wrote to the bishop."

"But *Padre*," she confessed, "I never sent the letter."

But from that day forward, when anyone asked *Padre* Sanders how he came to be in Immokalee, he said, "Because Rosa wrote a letter to the bishop."

She called to a young man who was mowing the scrappy lawn on the side of the rectory with a manual push mower. *"¡Ven, Casto! Ayúdele con sus cosas."* Help him with his things.

Casto was a slight young man with brown hair and fine features. He smiled shyly as he wiped his right hand on his pants leg and then offered it to the *Padre*.

"Bienvenido, Padre, welcome, I am Casto Reséndiz."

Richard took his hand and shook it. *"Mucho gusto, Casto,* I am happy to meet you."

He studied the young man, liking the way he looked, plain, gentle and intelligent. Casto stood quietly, waiting for the priest to speak again.

"You work here?"

"Monday, Tuesday and Wednesday. I mow the lawn, take care of the trees and flowers and do little repairs."

He nodded and stared silently until Casto offered to help him.

"Sí, gracias."

Together they emptied the car of the suitcase and a few boxes and put them in the bedroom where *Padre* Pedro had lived. It was in the far right corner, just past a small living area that contained a television, a couch and two chairs. In the center in the back was the kitchen and, past the kitchen table, sliding doors offered a view of the corner of a yellow building, sand, scrub brush, palmettos and tall scraggly pine trees. Across the living room there were two smaller rooms with a bathroom in between, a window in each bedroom with a side view of the grotto of Our Lady of Guadalupe and beyond it, her church. *Padre* Sanders' room contained a single bed, small sofa, two small book cases, a chest of drawers and, just inside the door, a desk. It reminded him of his room in Union Heights, except that this one had two windows and a private bathroom. He moved the bed to face north, hoping sun in the mornings would help him wake up.

He got the key from Rosa and walked past the grotto again, unlocked the plain double wooden doors and studied his new church. The roof was supported by wooden beams and floor-to-ceiling columns that had been stained dark maple and varnished. The altar was plain wood with vertical, dark-stained pine boards behind it, beautiful in a rustic kind of way. On the left was a small indoor grotto with a statue of Our Lady of Guadalupe on a ledge that came out from the wall, surrounded by about fifty prayer candles, many of which were burning. One the right side of the altar, a five-foot crucifix rested on a stand.

He couldn't help but compare it to St. Peter's. There was no stained glass, imported or otherwise, no stunning image of a tabernacle and no Jesus suspended from a chain. The altar had been designed and built by local carpenters, not an Italian architect. The pews were badly worn, the floor was linoleum and the lights were can-shaped fixtures rather than chandeliers. He scratched his head and patted the hair back in place, then smiled as he realized that he loved everything about it.

He walked to a pew about halfway to the altar and knelt to pray, then went back to the rectory and unpacked his books and clothes. When he came out Rosa offered a cup of coffee.

"*No, gracias.*" He sat down at the table in the corner of the kitchen and lit up a cigarette. She was still washing dishes, facing out the window.

"Rosa, I know your brother but I don't know you. *Cuénteme de usted, por favor.*" Tell me about yourself.

"Like what?"

"Well, where and when you were born?"

Rosa was not used to this kind of direct questioning but she dried her hands on a dishtowel and answered. "I was born in Tampico, Mexico, in 1936. I came to the US in 1953, to Texas when I was still a teenager. My sister had a baby and I helped her. In 1957 my family came to Florida to work in the fields. We picked tomatoes in Homestead: my father, mother, my brother Adán and another guy. The work was good there, but we had to live in a tent with nothing on the sides and no walls. There were no beds, no nothing. We slept on the floor. It was terrible!"

He shook his head with a frown. She started drying the dishes as she continued her story.

"Then we came to Immokalee and for a while we lived on a farm outside of town here. They had *barracas* that were nicer than Homestead, but the horses had ticks, and we got the ticks. So my father came into town and rented a room for us. We paid ten or twelve dollars a week, something like that. It was OK except that it only had cold water and our beds filled the whole room. We lived there four years."

"Did you used to go 'up the road,' too?"

She nodded, still amazed that he was interested. "But it was years ago. I started here as the housekeeper with *Padre* Singleton in 1972 and I've been here ever since."

She got back to her work and Richard decided to go and see the sisters at their convent. Rosa drew a simple map. "It's about five minutes away." He would soon learn that it seemed everything in Immokalee was about five minutes away. He drove into the north side of town. Years before, the north was the "white" side of town and the south side the "Colored" section, and most fieldwork back then was done by black people. When the Mexicans from Texas came to work the fields, they moved to the black section because that's where the buses picked the workers up in the morning and dropped them off at the end of the day. Our Lady of Guadalupe church was built on the south side to be close to the Mexican-American and Mexican people it served. There were a number of black protestant churches on the south side too. Many of the white people in town were Protestant – their churches were on the north side.

The convent sat on the left side of East New Market Road, a plain, single-story ranch-style house. The Guadalupana sisters were busily preparing for the weekend Masses, the Charismatic group, choir practice that evening and thirteen baptisms that were scheduled for Sunday, but they stopped when Richard knocked on the door. He sat with them at their kitchen table, assuring them that he would not stay long.

Sisters Manuela and Octavia, whom he had met before, introduced him to Sister Carmen. They spoke only Spanish which was fine with Richard. They also still wore habits, different from many U.S. orders. In addition to planning and coordinating parish liturgies and religious education, Sister Carmen ran the youth groups, Sister Manuela led the choirs and Sister Octavia was the floral arranger.

"If you ever can get yellow roses, *hermana*," said *Padre* Sanders, "they're my favorite."

"*Dificil, Padre*, difficult to find around here, but I will try."

When he returned to the rectory, Richard was grateful for the sisters who would make up for the priest-partner he would not have. He was still not thrilled with the transfer to Immokalee, but gradually he began to see it as a sign of the bishop's confidence in him.

In the early evening he wandered around the church grounds feeling lonely. Several apparently indigent people, mostly white, sat on picnic tables between it and the grotto. One man was clearly a victim of mental illness. Wounded more psychologically than physically in Vietnam, Thomas now spent his life tracking traces of himself to prove he existed: church records, newspaper mentions of similar names, notes from people who remembered him. He carried this proof with him in a folder secured with string.

Another was a woman who was looking for her daughter, the only person she had left after a tragic accident took the other members of her family. The daughter was somewhere in Immokalee but Susie was not sure where. She would spend this night sleeping on the ground behind the church, wrapped in a blanket she kept hidden in the palmettos. This was different from the lifelong poverty Richard had seen before. These people used to have normal lives, but lost them. Their condition struck him as a sad dream.

Several others were drinking from bottles in paper bags. *Padre* Sanders stopped to talk with a few of them but was disquieted by their drunken state. He had always had trouble dealing with drunks, especially obnoxious drunks. "Give me your heart, sweet Jesus, so I can have more compassion for these people."

Soon the Charismatic group started to arrive, chatting as they entered the CCD building. He followed them inside. The building was just four walls that they divided up when they had classes. Sister Manuela introduced him and he nodded hello, then sat quietly in a chair on the side and observed the people singing and dancing. A pretty young Hispanic woman named Lucy Ortiz came over and said in perfect English, "*Padre,* you need to get into this. You need to sing and dance and well, be Charismatic!"

He shook his head. "I'm afraid I'm a little traditional for it, but I'm glad you all seem to enjoy it." She smiled and went back to her dancing.

After a while he left quietly and walked over again to look at the church. Noting the scraggly yellow pine trees outlined in the graying sky, he felt as if he were back at Mepkin Abbey, seeing God everywhere he turned. The air was cooler now, sixty-five degrees according to the thermometer nailed to the back of the church. All was quiet except for the peeping of the tree frogs and the low murmurs of the indigents on the picnic benches. The western sky was filled with clouds that looked like painted brush strokes, glowing softly from the sun setting into the far-off Gulf of Mexico.

Our Lady of Guadalupe Church, Immokalee, Florida, circa 1981

Later that evening, *Padre* Pedro arrived from Miami, as he would do each Friday for the next month during the transition. They sat in the living room and started to review the "Run-down of the Parish" that Pedro had prepared for him.

Saturday evenings they held a Mass at 5:30 and another at 7:00 p.m. followed by pre-baptismal classes in the parish hall at 8:00 p.m. On Sundays there was an 8:00 Mass in Spanish, a 10:00 in English and an 11:30 in Spanish. Baptisms were done all together, once a month on Sundays, after the last Mass. Then there might be a wedding at 1:00 or if that wedding coincided with the communal baptisms, they scheduled the baptisms first, then the wedding, and if there were *Quinciñeras* they came later. Almost everything happened on Sunday because, when the season was in full bloom, the people worked on the other days. There was also a daily Mass for the sisters, alternating one week in English and the next in Spanish. He went over the schedule of religious classes for young people, meetings with parents and sponsors, youth groups, one in Spanish and one in English, and special retreats.

Richard started to feel concerned, conscious of his own waning energy level, but Pedro reassured him that the Guadalupana sisters would support him. "I've made it a point to always work with them as a team – we plan, execute and evaluate everything together."

Richard said a silent prayer of thanks for the sisters as Pedro continued.

"Immokalee is different from what you've been doing at San Pedro, serving a population that was largely based in the camps. This is a whole community of farm workers, and it's growing like crazy. We have around 25,000 people here in the season and half of them stay during the summer. New Mexicans come every week, plus others from Central America, and right now, as we speak, more Haitians are arriving in town. The Haitians are not only desperately poor, but are refugees from political violence too, and we don't even speak their language."

When they got back to the rectory, Richard, unable to sleep, walked the church grounds again. The number of inebriated had increased, replacing the mentally ill. He walked back to the rectory, read the Bible and prayed long into the night, feeling overwhelmed and inadequate for the job. Still, he sensed that Jesus was here in Immokalee with him. Jesus walked in the fields with the farm workers, in the streets with the homeless and in others he had not met but already loved. When he finally turned off the light he greeted the Virgin Mary, Mary of the Latinos, Our Lady of Guadalupe. Finally, he fell asleep with his final prayer:

> May the almighty and merciful Lord grant us a restful night.
> And a peaceful death.

CHAPTER TWENTY-SEVEN –
SONGS OF SION – 1981

On Saturday morning Richard was awakened by the crowing of roosters and the light of the sun, but he covered his head and went back to sleep. By the time he emerged from his bedroom at 8:30, *Padre* Pedro was up and dressed, had made coffee and gone to get the Naples and Ft. Myers papers and the Immokalee Bulletin. He had also stopped by *La Favorita* Mexican Bakery.

Richard poured orange juice and coffee, took some *pan dulce* and sat down in the living room where Pedro was scanning the Naples Daily News. Pedro pointed out an Associated Press article from March 18 that headlined "New Haitian Influx Feared" and read the first few sentences aloud.

> The weather in the Florida Straits is clearing and the regime of President-for-Life Jean-Claude Duvalier is getting tougher, so immigration officials are bracing for a new influx of Haitian refugees. State Department officials predict this year's Haitian influx could surpass the record-setting 14,000 refugees who sailed across treacherous seas to South Florida last year in rickety, unsanitary boats.

"Fourteen thousand!" exclaimed Richard.

"*Sí*," said Pedro. "That's what I was talking about. Close to a thousand of them came here. There's a corner in Little Haiti in Miami where people can get a ride to rural areas. The Haitians do it among themselves. A guy from here drives over, picks people up and brings them back. He doesn't charge them anything; they just chip together for gas and give him a few dollars if they have it or when they can get it."

They both scanned the papers now for other items that might affect Immokalee. President Reagan was preparing to cut economic aid to the Nicaragua's Sandinista government, partially for concern that aid to Nicaragua could end up supporting guerillas in El Salvador.

"The poor people in both those countries don't know this is going on, yet it affects them directly. They can stay there and risk their lives, caught in between the government and the guerillas, or they can work their way up to the U.S. I don't know if we'll get them or California or Arizona. It all depends on their grapevine and where they hear they'll find work."

"Do most of them stay?" Richard was thinking about the number of Mexicans and Central Americans he had met in Naples who planned to return home.

"Most of them would rather go back but they just can't survive there. Some go home every few years, but it's dangerous and expensive to come back here, so after a while, they just stay."

Soon there was a knock at the door and a pretty Mexican-American woman with a cheery voice came in, smiling. Pedro introduced her to *Padre* Sanders. "This is Lucy Ortiz."

Richard smiled. It was the woman who tried to get him to join in the Charismatic activities the night before.

"*Bienvenido, Padre* Sanders," she said happily. "Welcome – again."

"Lucy is one of the more active people in this parish," said Pedro. "She belongs to several of the groups, attends parish meetings and, most importantly, she does the books!"

"I've been here for a while," smiled Lucy. "*Padre* De la Calle approached me because I worked at the bank. He was paying twenty-five dollars a week to the archdiocese to do the books for him, but he said, 'If you could do it here, I could pay you twenty-five dollars and it would save me a trip to Miami.' So I got to know all the priests, from *Padre* de la Calle to *Padre* Pedro – and now you."

Richard studied her without speaking. "At least I hope you still want me to do it," she said, uncomfortably, mistaking his silence for hesitation.

"Of course," he nodded quickly.

After Lucy left, Pedro told Richard how much he would miss her vibrant, talkative personality, her beautiful smile, her love for everyone and her strong faith in God. Richard had a more practical question, however. "Having someone do the books is one thing, but how did you manage without a secretary?"

"I should have hired one, but I was always trying to save money. I did all my own records, typing, filing, everything. The only thing I didn't do was clean – Rosa has always done that. In earlier years when I lived in the trailer I mowed the lawn, too! Did you have a secretary in Naples?"

"I couldn't function without one. Corina Hernandez' daughter Maria was my secretary." Richard thought for a moment how much he would miss Maria, Corina, Rita, Miguel and the rest of his Naples friends. They were not so far away, but he suspected he would see them less often as time went on; everyone was so busy. He changed the subject to the availability of services.

"What organizations exist here to help the poor, besides our church?"

Pedro explained that it was a short list: Collier Health Services Clinic, Immokalee Neighborhood Services, Florida Rural Legal Services and RCMA.

"RCMA rents space in our education building, right over there," he nodded to his left. "They run a preschool center for migrant children."

"A daycare?" Father Sanders brightened, remembering the children at Camp St. Mary's.

Pedro smiled. "Yes, and the kids are great. They also have two facilities down in Farmworker Village, a migrant housing community just south of here."

"What do the initials stand for?"

"Redlands Christian Migrant Association. Some Mennonites from Pennsylvania started providing childcare services in South Florida in the late 1950s and later they partnered with a man named Wendell Rollason who turned it into RCMA and runs it now. You'll meet him. Their offices are over on North 1st Street, some of the poorest offices I've ever seen. He's amazing, like working with Cesar Chavez or something. Rather than fighting the growers, RCMA works with them, focused on the welfare of the children."

"Why do they call it Redlands?"

"The soil down there is more like red clay. 'Christian' refers to their basic values, and Migrant is obvious. But most people just call them RCMA."

As Pedro continued talking, Richard looked forward to seeing the children, happy they would be just in the next building. But the conversation moved to more immediate information.

The organization that Richard would be most involved with was run by the parish. It was managed by Sister Eileen Eppig, whom Pedro had hired the previous August to do social work. Her job was to coordinate efforts of the church with local agencies, figure out what the people needed by visiting their homes and to be aware of issues and problems.

"But lately she seems to spend most of her time helping the people with emergency needs: money, food and support. Eileen will keep you up to speed on what's happening in the community, although she's really busy. She and I agree on the fundamentals. You know the saying, 'Give a person a fish and you feed them for a day. Teach them how to fish and you feed them for a lifetime.'"

Padre Sanders nodded and smiled, wondering how many people in Immokalee had to be taught to fish and how many he would have to help feed.

Pedro explained how, in the 1950s and early 1960s, migrant workers were mainly U.S.-born Blacks, some Whites, and Mexicans born in Texas like Corina, called *Tejanos*. When agriculture really started to take off in the 1970s, migrants started coming in from Mexico, some legally, some not. For the first few years the Mexican-born Mexicans lived in the camps on the farms. When agriculture grew to a point that more workers were needed than could be housed in camps on the farms, they started living in town. That's why the Guadalupana sisters came.

The new *Padre* clasped his hands together and continued to look calmly at Pedro without speaking.

"I hope this doesn't sound rude," said Pedro, "but that 'silent thing' you've got going can be a little unsettling."

"I'm sorry. I guess living in silence for almost a decade will do that to you."

Pedro laughed and explained how Sister Eileen came to be there. "There were so many people coming to the rectory for a little money for this, or for that and always for important things like food or gasoline, something toward their rent. Many of them came to this country with the clothes on their back or in a bag. A lot of them are single guys but there are also whole families with small children. I would give them a sandwich or a little money or something when I could, but I had a million other things to do and we make very little money, as you know. So now Sister Eileen helps them, too."

That afternoon they drove to her home on New Market Road and Richard saw that Eileen was a young, petite, pretty, soft-spoken woman. She was just leaving to visit some of her clients who needed food, but she would come to the rectory on Wednesday morning after Mass.

Later that day, Pedro and Richard walked over to the church to get ready for the first Saturday evening Mass. Cars and pickup trucks in the parking lot showed that people were already gathering. Some of them prayed at the grotto. The priests entered through the back door.

Casto came in and started to put on his robes; he was an altar server in addition to being the maintenance man. Then two young boys entered, who also began to don their robes for Mass.

"*Hola*," said the new *Padre* with a smile.

Jose and Cory said hello but seemed nervous, hurriedly donning their white robes.

"Take your time," said Richard. "And if you make mistakes don't worry. Everything's going to be OK." Relieved, they smiled and nodded.

The small church was crowded. Pedro explained that, during the growing season, the Spanish masses were standing-room-only. "People end up out in front of the church listening to the Mass on the speakers, standing or kneeling in the parking lot. Their faith still amazes me."

They walked around to the front door and processed down the aisle toward the altar. Someday, Richard thought, looking out at the people, we're going to need a new church. And more priests.

After the evening Spanish masses, he and *Padre* Pedro stood at the church door to greet the people. They seemed welcoming to Richard though they expressed regret that *Padre* Pedro had been transferred. Pedro mentioned later that about half of them were born in the U.S. but almost all were of Mexican ancestry. *Padre* Sanders greeted each one of them warmly.

Back in the sacristy, he talked with the altar boys. "Have you ever been to Busch Gardens in Tampa? Or the aquarium in Miami? Or the Florida State Fair?"

They shook their heads.

"I love to go to those places. Would you like it if we got a bus sometime and we could all go together?"

The boys' faces lit up like it was Christmas. "*Sí, Padre*," they replied, excitedly.

Richard and Pedro had dinner and talked long into the night about the needs of the community.

"As you know," explained Pedro, "it's not really a parish, just a mission, and we're not even technically called pastors. The thing that bothers me most is that I feel like a second-class citizen when I go to meetings with other priests from the Archdiocese, especially the ones with large, wealthy congregations. It's like they think we're not as good as they are because we don't have 'real' parishes."

Richard had heard similar innuendos from other priests at Rural Life Bureau meetings. He didn't have a problem with the attitudes because his focus was entirely on his people and was used to being "no one." He turned the subject back to Immokalee.

"The Haitians. How many did you say are here now?"

"There are just about a thousand of them, I think, and more come every day. Just last week Father Tom Wenski visited. He runs the Haitian Catholic Center at the church of *Notre-Dame d'Haiti* in Miami. Tom brought in a team to help us get a more accurate head-count and to encourage more Haitians to come to church."

"How many come now?"

"Not many, because we don't have anything in their language. Some of them show up at the Spanish Masses but you can tell they feel out of place, and they understand almost nothing."

Richard thought of the irony – in Naples and South Carolina it was the Hispanics who felt out of place in white churches.

"Father Wenski has agreed to be here once a month to say Mass and administer sacraments. Either he or another Haitian priest named Gerald Darbouze will come. They do the same in other migrant mission areas."

Richard asked, "Do you speak Haitian Creole?"

"No, but if I were staying, I would learn it. I'm sure you're going to see a lot more of them. Thousands came from Haiti at the time of the Mariel Boatlift last year. They figured that if the U.S. was taking Cubans, we might take them too, so they got into all kinds of boats, even rafts, to try to make it to U.S. soil."

Pedro explained what Richard had already read, that the Haitians were suffering under the regime of Jean-Claude Duvalier, "Baby Doc," and the *Touton Macoutes*, thugs authorized by the government that terrorized the Haitian people. Richard nodded seriously.

"I don't think Creole is too difficult," continued Pedro. "I've learned a few words and phrases. There's a guy named Fanoly who leads the Haitians in prayer services sometimes. Maybe he can help you."

Sunday morning they concelebrated three Masses, two in Spanish and one in English. After each, Pedro introduced the new priest as he did the evening before. There were so many people. Even with his memory skills, Richard wondered how he would remember them all.

It was the following week before he realized that he still had not met many Haitian people. In general at the masses, he had noticed only a few black faces. On this day, however, one of them played the drum in the back of the church, adding a Caribbean flavor to the Mexican music. After Mass, as *Padre* Sanders stood at the front door talking to people, the drum player came up. He looked to be about twenty years old.

"*Bon jou, Padre*, I am Fanoly Dervil," he said, with a thick French accent.

"Fanoly. I heard about you."

"*Wi, Padre*." Fanoly combined the Haitian Creole word for "yes" and the Spanish word for Father, which he pronounced with the "r" under, rather than rolled.

"Do you speak much English?"

"*Tubitsi*." He motioned with his thumb and index finger. "A little bit. I'm getting better."

Richard was so interested in Fanoly that he forgot the thirteen families and godparents who waited inside for him to baptize their babies. Soon Sister Octavia came out to remind him. He asked Fanoly to visit him soon.

"*Wi, Padre*, I will."

Sunday afternoon *Padre* Pedro went back to his new job and Richard felt lonely again. On Monday he said the 7:00 a.m. daily Mass, and afterwards he spoke to the small gathering of mostly nuns.

"I'd like you to start doing the homilies at the daily Masses." They looked shocked as he continued, so he didn't add that he really wished they could be allowed to say the whole Mass. "I'm not really awake this early – it's just not part of my metabolism anymore, and that fact is depriving you of a good sermon that you deserve and need to inspire your work. It would be great if you could alternate, one day one of the Guadalupanas in Spanish, and the next, one of the Anglo sisters in English."

Later, he went to the hospital in Naples, visited a few people and stopped to see Corina and Maria. They could only spend a few minutes; they were keeping busy helping the farm workers.

"How is the new priest?"

They replied with little enthusiasm. "He's OK – but he's not you."

On Tuesday morning Sister Manuela came in and reminded him that he was supposed to be saying a funeral Mass. He walked quickly over to the church, where the family was already seated inside. The funeral director, John Brister, introduced himself.

John and the pall bearers had been waiting in the foyer of the church with the remains of *Señora* Rodriguez. The casket, covered with a pall, needed the priest's blessing before it could be brought inside. *Padre* Sanders blessed her and then processed in, accompanied by Casto who would serve at the altar. Sister Manuela led the mourners in the Twenty-third psalm. "*El Señor es mi pastor, nada me falta....*" The Lord is my Shepherd, I shall not want.

The pall bearers moved the casket slowly down the aisle toward the altar, feet first. It was an old custom, done so that if the deceased were to stand up, she would be facing the altar. John later explained something Richard did not know, that the only exception was for burials of priests. Priests went in head first, so if they stood up they would face the people.

Padre Sanders stood at the altar and looked intently from face to mourning face, sharing their grief. He had said only a few funeral masses in his life, but had a sad feeling that would change now. He believed that people entered heaven soon after they died so, in a way, he celebrated, but the grief of the families always saddened him. Afterwards, he rode to the cemetery in the hearse with John Brister, curious about the vocation of undertaker.

"I decided to open a funeral home when my father died in north Georgia," John explained. "He had gotten so thin that when I visited him I walked right past him and didn't recognize him. He was only forty-nine years old."

"I'm sorry." As always, Richard thought of his own father when he heard of another's death.

"Yeah, thanks." John shook his head. "The funeral home did such a good job and made him look so good, it made us all happy. So right then I decided I would like to do that kind of work."

"How did you end up in Immokalee?"

"My wife, Mary. Her family moved here from the Tampa area when she was young. Her father was a sawmill worker. Lots of cypress back then. She likes this business, too. I do the embalming and Mary does hair and makeup."

Richard wanted to ask more questions but they had arrived at the cemetery, about ten minutes away, he noted, an exception to the five-minute generalization. He said the standard grave-site prayers in Spanish, and then watched mourners approach the coffin and drop flowers and handfuls of dirt on top.

After *Padre* Sanders blessed the casket and was about to send the mourners home, a man stepped in front of him. He looked Mexican but was shorter than average, heavy set, maybe fifty years old. Richard assumed he was a family member who had arrived late.

The man straightened his shoulders up and back, hiked up his pants and thrust out his chest, then said comforting words and prayers for about five minutes. At the end he chanted slowly, with great emotion, "*La muerte llega, no sabemos cómo, no sabemos cuándo, y nomás los recuerdos llevamos.*" Death comes, we know not how, we know not when, and all we have left are memories. The man thanked everyone for coming and then raised his voice to a higher pitch, looking mournfully at the casket as he cried out loudly over the tops of the tall pines, "*Adíos, adíos, Irene!*"

When the mourners walked slowly away, *Padre* Sanders introduced himself to the last-minute speaker. His name was Juan Ramírez. Richard started to ask why he was there, but just then one of the sisters of the deceased came up and, by the time she finished talking, Ramírez had disappeared. Richard asked John Brister about him.

"He's been in town as long as I can remember. He does that at a lot of funerals; sometimes I give him a few dollars. Really, though, I know him from playing poker. He's the best poker player I've ever seen. He was a veteran of World War II, also, and so proud of his service to this country. But I've never seen anybody beat him at poker."

"Why do you think he does that, saying those prayers at the end of the funeral?"

John shrugged and shook his head. "The families seem to like it."

The next morning Sister Eileen came to visit. Richard greeted her and they sat together in the living room.

"How much time do you have?"

"I told my staff I would be back in an hour, but I don't have any appointments or anything specific, so my time is flexible."

"Good. I want to get to know you and discuss how we will work together."

Eileen nodded and they sat for a few minutes in silence. She seemed to be comfortable with not speaking. After a few minutes, he asked her about her order, the S.S.N.D.s.

"School Sisters of Notre Dame. Do you know us?"

"Teaching sisters, yes, from Germany? Tell me about them."

They had been founded in Bavaria after the Napoleonic Wars in which many men died and left poverty-stricken, illiterate widows and their children. The sisters educated the women so they could support themselves. They first came to the United States to help German people in Pennsylvania. S.S.N.D.s had been coming to Immokalee since 1970.

"There are seven of us here now," she continued. "The organization I manage is called, 'Our Lady of Guadalupe St. Vincent de Paul Society' because they send regular money to help support us. Basically, we do everything you can think of to help people in emergency situations: help pay for rent and utilities, give out bags of food, process immigration applications and provide cribs for mothers who don't have money to buy them. What I don't want to do is to have it become just another agency giving out material help, even though it often ends up that way. I want to help the people acquire respect and motivation to change their own lives."

He agreed completely. "What kind of staff do you have?"

"Just a secretary, but I have about twenty volunteers."

"I want us to figure out how to best use our skills to empower the people, exactly as you said. Let's also work on legislative issues related to farm workers."

She agreed, nodding, but he sensed some discomfort and made a suggestion. "Why don't you call your office and tell them you'll be here if they need you?"

After she made the call, he began asking questions and she told him her story. She was born in late August, 1946.

"I'm older by about ten years," he interjected. "And I feel, it, too!"

Originally from Baltimore, Eileen had been a teacher for many years, most recently teaching Religion at St. Petersburg Catholic High School in Florida. She had recently completed a Master's Degree in Theology with an emphasis on Spirituality, but had come to Immokalee as the Director of Immokalee Outreach. She had been in Immokalee for just over a year.

"I felt called to work with the poor," she said, simply. "Several sisters from my order were here in Immokalee. One of them, Veronica, invited me down for the Christmas holidays. I shadowed her as she went about her work, admiring everything she did and impressed with how much she was helping and also with the beauty of the people she served. She seemed so happy. When I was leaving, Veronica said, 'So when are you coming to stay?' I wasn't ready at that moment to make any type of commitment, but I went back to St. Pete, thought about it, talked to some people who knew me, and decided this was the right time to live among the poor."

Richard smiled as he thought about the different ways God called people.

"I contacted Father Jiménez and he said, 'Come on down, let's talk about it.' We discussed it with the Guadalupana sisters, talking about what needed to be done, and what I would do. The next day, Pedro and I worked out a job description."

"He gave me a copy," said Richard. "It's quite a job!"

Then Richard started telling Eileen about his life. Usually he kept his history to himself, but in this case he really wanted her to know him. He kept it brief, and suddenly realized he was hungry.

Rosa had oxtail soup all ready on the stove and sat with them as they ate. He raved about the soup. "Rosa, *muy rico!* Delicious!"

The housekeeper and the priest told Eileen how Rosa first heard of the *Padre* from her brother when he was up in Johns Island. It seemed a long time ago, but it was only four or five years ago that he first said masses on Johns Island.

"How did you end up here?" Eileen was curious.

Richard frowned and nodded toward his housekeeper. "Rosa wrote a letter to the bishop..." Rosa laughed and pushed him lightly on the shoulder and he pretended to be knocked off his seat.

After the meal, Richard suggested that he and Eileen move to the living room again to continue their discussion. "I thought we were done," she said hesitatingly, thinking again about her work.

"Eileen, you are in charge of everything I will not have time to do in the area of social justice. I'm going to be busy enough with the people on a religious basis, teaching them their faith, getting them more involved in the church and also the community. We may not get this kind of time again. I'm sure everything is going fine at your office. I really want to spend just a little more time with you today."

"OK, you're the boss," she smiled.

He told her about Yolanda, how she answered his ad and became his closest friend, companion and helper with the migrants, then about Yolanda's cancer and how much he feared losing her.

"I will pray for her, too," said the gentle sister. Then she changed the subject. "Do you miss the abbey?"

He smiled and nodded. "All the time. It was a beautiful life. I still go back though, for retreats, at least once a year."

"Don't you feel strange, going there now?"

"Why should I feel strange? I will always consider Mepkin home."

As they continued to talk, Richard had a sense that he had known Eileen for a long time. They would face many challenges together.

He visited the RCMA daycare on the property and spent some time playing with the children, happy they were close by. The center coordinator told him that all the staff members were former fieldworkers – that's why the workers trusted them with their children.

On Friday, Fanoly came to visit. The two men walked together around the church grounds, appreciating the warm spring day. *Padre* Sanders immediately liked this upbeat young man. Fanoly actually spoke English quite well and also some Spanish. His English was not perfect as he mixed up tenses and sentence structure and tended to run sentences together, but he was understandable.

"I leave Haiti in 1979. There were three of us and my daddy passed away and we don't have money. Actually, I was in the seminary to study to be a priest."

"Really?"

"*Wi, Padre.* I love to become a priest, but my mother didn't have enough to pay for her and my two little brothers to live, for food, rent and everything. So I said, let me come over here to the United States. My brother-in-law he get me a visa. After a couple months I apply for residence and they give it to me. After five years I become a citizen."

"Did you live in Miami first?"

"No, I came straight to Immokalee because my brother-in-law was here and he knew this place." He motioned across the street and to the right. "I live with my sister and him and their children in a little house on East Delaware."

"What about the priesthood? Are you still thinking of becoming a priest?"

Fanoly hesitated. "Well, no, *pa kuneya*, not right now, anyway."

"We could use you. We're going to need more services for Haitians."

"*Wi.* More will come."

"Do you think you could continue to hold prayer services, maybe at least until I learn Haitian Creole?"

Fanoly nodded.

"Good. We can even start saying a Mass. I will do the Eucharistic parts in English and read the Gospel, but I will need you to translate after me, give the sermon and lead the prayers in Creole."

"Sure, *Padre.* I love to do that."

They walked silently for a few minutes before Richard spoke again. He was already tired of living alone.

"How would you like to move into the rectory with me? There are two bedrooms in addition to mine. You could live there and teach me Creole."

Fanoly was surprised but interested in this offer. "I can have a nicer place to live, teach you Creole and teach you prayers and sermons in Creole."

"Good. Very good."

"*Bien,*" said Fanoly, beginning the lessons already. "*Très bien.*"

"Isn't that French?"

"*Wi, Padre,* but everybody in Haiti speaks a little bit of French. In Creole, though, you would say '*Bon. Bon anpil.*'"

"*Bon anpil,*" repeated the priest.

"If somebody speaks French as well, I mean really speaks it, you know they went to school because school there is all in French. Most of the people who come here to Immokalee only went to school a little bit, *tubitzi,* so Creole is what you have to learn."

A few days later, Fanoly moved his belongings into the third bedroom of the rectory. The second bedroom would remain the guest room, where *Padre* Pedro would stay on weekends.

One of the first words Fanoly taught him was "*Pe,*" pronounced like a soft, "pay," the Creole word for "Father." From that point on, Fanoly called him *Pe* Sanders. Richard began to write down every word Fanoly taught him and together they created a Haitian Creole dictionary.

On Sunday afternoons from then on, Fanoly helped *Pe* Sanders celebrate a Haitian service, including prayers and a sermon. Once a month, Father Wenski or *Pe* Darbouze came from Miami to say a full Haitian Creole Mass. Soon there were over one hundred Haitians coming on a regular basis.

To learn about the community, Richard started listening to the local Spanish radio station. It had a talk show hosted by a young man named Cuauhtémoc, the name of the last Aztec emperor.

He mentioned it to Rosa. "That Cuauhtémoc is really good!"

Rosa smiled. "Cuauhtémoc is Casto!"

Soon Richard asked Casto if he would like to move into the rectory, too. Casto looked surprised.

"I need to be speaking Spanish all the time," said Richard, "and having you here would help me do that." Richard didn't mention that he was also concerned about the young man, whom he knew suffered from diabetes and was unable to do field work.

"*Sí, Padre*, I would like that."

With Casto there, Richard hardly spoke English anymore. He enjoyed it when both his roommates were home and he moved from Haitian Creole to Spanish and back again.

His increasing fluency made him think of Sister Eileen, wondering if she could use some reinforcement in her language skills. She could definitely use time away from her office. Her work affected her emotionally as she let people not only into her office, but into her heart.

"Go to Cuernavaca," he suggested, "to the school I went to. They have a great language program, and also there's a lot of Liberation Theology floating around there that I'm sure you would enjoy."

She nodded and started to get up but he had another suggestion. "While you're there, take a bus to Guanajuato and see where a lot of our people come from."

In the late spring, two new sisters came to visit him at the rectory; Sister Marie and Sister Jane, both S.S.N.D.s, had come to research the needs of the community. They knew about Immokalee from Eileen and other sisters who worked here.

"I was here last year," said Marie, "and it was obvious there was great need, in spite of the efforts already in place."

Richard nodded; it was an understatement. "What are you thinking of doing?"

Sister Jane answered. "We're not sure, actually. We've noted the number of abused women. Perhaps a shelter and support programs that include training might be the most important need."

Richard had heard about battered women among his parishioners and agreed this was an important issue.

"We're hoping to take a year to study the area and the needs," said Marie. "I'll do that while Jane gets a job at one of the schools."

They all smiled, remembering pre-Vatican II days when sisters lived in convents and didn't have paying jobs.

"Just let me know when you're ready," he told them. "The parish will support you any way we can."

There were enough Haitians in town that *Pe* Sanders decided to have Holy Week services in three languages, Spanish, English and Haitian Creole, beginning with Palm Sunday and including Holy Thursday, Good Friday, the Saturday vigil and Easter Sunday. There would be one Mass each day, for all the people. They would have to hold them outside because so many would not fit inside the church that was too small for the congregations at the five regular masses.

The trilingual services went smoothly, although they were long. The music alternated between each of the languages and readings were repeated by different readers in three languages. *Padre* Sanders said his sermon in Spanish and English, keeping it brief. He even added a few words in rudimentary Creole.

"Mwen regret m'pa pale Creole pi bon. Mwen preske aprann." I am sorry I don't speak Creole better. Soon I will learn. Then he continued in Spanish. *"Todos somos Católicos.* We are all Catholics. We're all different people and different cultures but we're all Catholics. We are American and Mexican and Texan and Haitian and Salvadoran but our Catholic faith will keep us together as our many groups become one."

When it came time for the Our Father, he told the people to each pray out loud in their own language. Spanish, Haitian Creole and English joined together in a wondrous sound that rose up into the pines and glorified the Lord. The chanting of the monks of Mepkin returned in Psalm 137.

How shall we sing the songs of the Lord in a foreign land?

"Together," he thought peacefully. *"Juntos. Ansamn.* We shall sing them together."

CHAPTER TWENTY-EIGHT
– BUILDING A BASE COMMUNITY
– 1981

Easter this year signaled the beginning of the end of the growing season and immigration agents were showing up more and more frequently in town. Richard had some experience with this from Naples, and had learned some of the rules and regulations at Rural Life Bureau meetings.

One day Casto came in, flushed and out of breath. "*Padre*, immigration took a lot of our people, and you should have seen how badly they were treating this one Mexican!"

Padre Sanders frowned sharply.

"They pulled the guy with his arms behind his back real hard, really hurting him, then they pushed him on the ground and then threw him into the car like a really bad criminal."

"What? What did you do?"

It was the closest Casto had seen the *Padre* to being angry. Casto was a small, frail young man who stood about 5'4" and weighed 110 pounds. "What could I do?"

"At least did you get the name of the agent, or the badge number, or the license plate of the car?"

"No, *Padre*."

"I'm sorry. But you need to understand how serious this is. Sometimes people get really hurt."

Casto nodded, still shaken.

"But you don't accomplish anything if you don't say anything to stop them, or bring me information to find the people later. Come with me."

They drove to the spot where Casto saw the mistreatment but there was no sign of anything there. Then they went to the stockade just south of town. The *Padre* explained things on the way. "I want to see how many were taken, if they're OK, where they were from. Maybe some of them have families we have to advise. Some of them could qualify for asylum or stay here some other way. There's legislation coming, I hope, that's going to give them a chance, but if they get deported, they will have no chance at all."

Not wanting to officially involve the Church, he identified himself as a friend. They brought the men Casto had seen plus a number of others; fourteen all together, but the only one he could help had a pending family petition to stay in the United States. After several hours, that man was released.

From then on, *Padre* Sanders sent Casto to follow up when others reported that people had been taken by *la migra*. Casto functioned as a kind of middle man between the stockade and Father Sanders, getting him the information he needed. Richard also learned more about how immigration agents worked. There was a movie theatre on Main Street that showed films in Spanish. Periodically, immigration officers would drive up in empty busses and stand at the door exits of the theatre, checking documentation. If people didn't have their papers, they were taken to the stockade.

Padre Sanders started taking time during sermons to highlight the rules and the abuses, demonstrating what the agents were not permitted to do from in front of the altar. Putting his hands behind his back, he explained, "They can grab you this way and restrain your arms like this, enough to put handcuffs on, but they cannot pull your arms upwards or handle you roughly in any way."

He realized he had to get some of his congregation to classes. He called Pat Stockton at the Miami Archdiocese who told him about immigration training that was available in Orlando and he sent Casto and several others to weekend meetings. When they returned, Casto explained to *Padre* Sanders what took place there.

"There was a big platform and we role-played being questioned by immigration agents. The organizers of the sessions videotaped us and then gave feedback about how we behaved. Smiling and playing around was reprimanded; this was serious business. They said, 'You must present yourself as a mature young woman or man.'"

Soon Richard put Casto in charge of an informal organization to help the undocumented immigrants who were picked up. People paid into a fund so that there was money to get them out on bond. When the Guadalupano group members saw or heard "*la migra*," Immigration, was in town, they would call the *Padre* or Casto and one of them would announce it on the radio.

"*Hermanos y hermanas*, brothers and sisters, don't leave your houses. It's going to be a bad day."

"Is that against the law, for you to do that?" wondered one of the Guadalupana sisters.

"I don't know, but it's not against God's law."

One afternoon in late April, *Padre* Sanders was reading in his room when he got a call from John Brister. Richard liked John, but hated to get his calls.

"We have a stillborn baby who needs a funeral."

"Oh," said Richard, breathing out a long sigh. "That's one of the worst things –babies who never get to experience life at all, and mothers who carry a baby for so long only to lose it."

Stillborns were not uncommon in Immokalee because migrant women rarely went for prenatal care. There was no insurance for farm workers and most could not afford to pay for it. There was a local health clinic but the undocumented workers were often afraid to go. It was particularly dangerous for Hispanics, who had a higher risk for prenatal diabetes. If they got it, the baby could grow up to ten or twelve pounds in the womb, creating serious problems at delivery.

At the wake, before *Padre* Sanders began the rosary, he talked to the parents.

"His name is Juan," the father said, looking down at the tiny casket. It was the first one Richard had seen, made of shiny white plastic. It was quite pretty, actually.

Padre Sanders led the small group of mourners, relatives and a few friends, in the rosary. As the parents left they gave him ten dollars. He handed it back and said, "*No, no es necesario.*" It's not necessary. "I'll see you tomorrow."

After everyone left, he and John had coffee and talked for a while. "You know, Father, they didn't used to have a baby section at the cemetery. When they opened the cemetery in 1968 it was only for full-sized graves. People with stillborns or small babies had to pay for a whole grave, the same as for an adult. These people can't afford that. I finally got the County Commission to open a baby section."

"Good for you," said Richard. Then he felt a surge of sadness and grimaced as he asked, "How big are the baby graves?"

"Thirty-six inches long and eighteen inches wide."

Father Sanders was silent for a long time before he spoke again. "That's sad all by itself."

The next morning Richard said the funeral Mass for the baby who had never lived. He took his own car to Lake Trafford Cemetery and viewed the baby section for the first time. There were only eight graves, the new one making nine. They were small, as John had pointed out, decorated as if the children were still alive, with toys, angels and flowers. John was already there. He had brought the coffin in a limo rather than the hearse.

After *Padre* Sanders said his final prayers, Juan Ramirez appeared out of nowhere as he had at the last funeral. Richard took two steps back and stood next to John Brister as Ramirez went through the same motions as before, solemnly hiking up the waist of his pants, shoulders squared, back straight and chest out.

"*La muerte llega, no sabemos cómo, no sabemos cuándo, y nomás los recuerdos llevamos.*" Death comes, we know now how, we know not why, and all we have left are memories. Juan's final words echoed as they always did when he raised the pitch and volume of his voice. "*Adíos, adíos, Niño Juan!*"

After the family left, Richard watched a cemetery worker respectfully bury the tiny coffin and smooth out the dirt over it. Then he stayed for a while, studying the graves. It was a cool, breezy day and he felt peaceful. Wildflowers crept across a few of the graves and he noticed the scent of recently cut grass. On one, a toy Excalibur sword stuck in the ground next to plastic alligators and an Olympic-style medal that read "Winner" rested on the tiny headstone. The grave of a little boy had a sandy playground bordered by rounded half-bricks, with toy soldiers, little tanks and military jeeps. A grave marked with a dollhouse and a replica of a church said, "Unknown Baby."

When he got back to the rectory, he remembered that at least half of his parishioners would soon be leaving for the summer. The thought saddened him, but he would visit them in South Carolina and, while there, would spend a few days at Mepkin. Beginning that Sunday, he blessed each pickup truck that pulled in front of the church after Mass, sprinkling them with holy water and praying for safe and prosperous summers.

In mid-May, before leaving for South Carolina, he took the altar boys to a bowling alley in Naples. The boys laughed as the *Padre* bowled with them, stumbling and dropping the ball into the alley. Richard laughed as he realized they thought he made mistakes on purpose, to amuse them.

While at Mepkin, he reflected on how much he had learned about his Immokalee parish in a short time, but how much he still had to absorb and get used to. He spent most of his time in the church and walking by the river, observing his brothers in their habits and sometimes wishing he were staying with them. Immokalee was going to be more of a challenge than anything he had ever done.

When he returned, there were more people in Immokalee than he had expected because many had begun to settle down and get regular jobs. He was thrilled to see it, reminded of Corina's words, "No more migrants!"

Soon the rains came. Southwest Florida had the most magnificent summer storms Richard had ever seen; even better than South Carolina's. Sometimes the afternoon skies grew almost as dark as night, followed by spectacular lightning strikes and thunder that shook the rectory windows.

Sitting in his room that was temporarily darkened by the storm, he decided it was time to improve his Haitian Creole. Richard could never find focused time to work on it; there were too many interruptions. He found a three-week course at the University of Indiana that would be held later in the summer. He looked forward to it as something of a rest, too, because he had not been feeling well lately. He could hardly sleep at night, and was tired all day. He fell asleep more during the day now, too.

In July, he drove up to Indiana University. He planned to drive to Peru when the course was over to surprise his mother and old friends. Toward the end of the course, he was walking up the hill to the campus building and, too quickly, got out of breath. Slow down, he said to himself, and maybe one of these days you will stop smoking! He paused for a moment until it passed, then continued walking. Almost immediately he felt tightness in his chest, as if being squeezed from the side, and he could barely breathe. His whole body shuddered as he tried to remain still – the small breaths he could take made the pain worse. He fell to his knees and then onto his face, praying for it to leave him.

When it finally passed, he was still lying on the grass, grateful that no one had seen him. His watch told him that only a few minutes had gone by. Feeling dizzy, he struggled to his feet, made his way back to his car and drove to a local clinic. By this time he was feeling better and felt almost foolish for having gone there. It was probably just indigestion.

The doctor assured him he was wise to have come, however, and ordered several tests at a nearby hospital. The incident scared Richard enough that he had the tests done. The doctor spoke frankly.

"You had a heart attack."

"What?"

"We did a test for your 'ejection fraction,' that measures the ratio of how much blood the heart pumps each time it beats. It's very low. It means your heart is blocked and is working more than twice as hard as it should to get the right amount of blood circulating in your body."

Richard sat silently for a while, then asked, "Can you treat it?"

"Eventually you'll probably need surgery, but I would wait if you can. They're coming out with some promising new techniques."

He breathed a sigh of relief. He couldn't take time for an operation. He had already been gone several weeks.

"In the meantime," continued the doctor, "I can give you a prescription for something that will help. Do you smoke?"

Richard nodded.

"Stop it immediately. Exercise?"

Richard shook his head. "It's always been hard for me to do much, even when I was a kid. I have trouble breathing."

"I'm not surprised." The doctor continued to take notes as he asked about family history and Richard told him about his father's high blood pressure and stroke, and his mother's recent heart surgery and stroke.

"What about your diet?"

Thinking guiltily about his favorite foods, eggs and bacon, Richard said, "Not great, I guess."

"Clean that up, too, and you'll have a much better chance. Stress?"

He thought of the challenges that faced him in Immokalee, the thousands of people now in his care. "A little."

"Try and minimize that too. And definitely see your regular doctor when you get back to Florida."

Richard was so shaken by the experience that he did not finish the course in Creole nor visit his hometown, but drove directly back to Immokalee. By the time he got there, he was feeling normal again. He called Miguel who knew immediately something was wrong.

"*Cuénteme.*" Tell me.

Padre Sanders hesitated, then just blurted it out. "I had a heart attack."

"*Padre,* you are only forty-five years old! How can that be?"

"I don't know."

"I remember when your mother had a heart operation when you were still in Naples. Do you think you inherited her problem?"

"I always thought I got more of my father's genes, not my mother's. My brother used to say that he had my mother's heart and I had my father's."

"So what do you do for it?"

"Not a whole lot. Besides the medication, I have to stop smoking and start exercising. I even bought a pair of running shoes."

"Did you tell anyone else?"

"No, and I don't want anyone else to know, especially not the bishop. He might move me and I couldn't stand that. Besides, the people have enough to worry about."

When the *Padre* stopped smoking, Rosa, Fanoly and Casto were thrilled. They had never said anything to him about the cigarettes, but the house always smelled. He suffered withdrawal symptoms as he had when he entered

Mepkin, but got through it. Richard also tried to rest more, easier now in the summer when the migrants were "up the road."

His mother had sent a book by **Thomas Merton**, a pamphlet, really, published before Merton's death, called *What Is Contemplation?* Richard knew that contemplation would help his physical condition and even wondered how things would have gone, had he remained at the abbey. With the different diet and lifestyle, would he be having any problems at all? His plan to return seemed to elude him, but maybe someday he would go back. But not now. Part of the book described Richard so closely that it could have been written about him.

> There are many Christians who serve God with great purity of soul and perfect self-sacrifice in the active life. Their vocation does not allow them to find the solitude and silence and leisure in which... to lose themselves in God alone. They are too busy serving Him in His children on earth. ...their minds and temperaments do not fit them for a purely contemplative life: they would know no peace without exterior activity. ...They would vegetate, and their interior life would grow cold.

It was clear that his interior life would indeed grow cold if he were still in the abbey – his people were the source of his faith and peace now. Still, he made a plan to spend more time in contemplation, not with the intention of losing himself to God, but for greater strength so he could continue to serve the people he loved. All his prayers were focused on continuing good health.

"Please, God, don't take me away from my people!"

Sister Eileen returned from Cuernavaca the following week and came to the rectory to tell him about her trip. They both laughed as she described the hot, dusty, bumpy bus ride to Guanajuato. "It took twelve hours! Then when I got there, it took me two hours to find a place to stay. The people were nice, but the chickens on the bus were an experience! But I'll tell you, you were right. I can relate to our people in a whole different way now that I have been to the place many of them call home."

He smiled. "I'm glad you did it. In this environment, caring for the whole person doesn't just mean caring for the person who is in need now. It means getting to know the part of their lives they left behind, too."

Then he decided to tell her about the heart attack. As he explained the details, he became frightened again, but brushed it off. Everything would be fine if he just reduced the stress.

Later that week, Sister Octavia told him another Guadalupana was coming to replace Sister Manuela, who was moving to another migrant parish. Sister Aida was a beautiful singer and guitar player, and she attracted a larger group of singers than they ever had before, plus guitar, maracas and tambourine players who alternated playing at various Masses.

In late September, Richard read that President Reagan had issued an order to the Coast Guard to intercept ships on the high seas that were suspected to be carrying illegal immigrants from Haiti. Up to this point, they had only been stopped if they entered U.S. territorial waters. Haitians had been coming to the U.S. for the past ten years and absorbing them was becoming an issue, particularly for the city of Miami. American officials threatened that U.S. companies would take what business they had with Haiti to other Caribbean islands if Haiti did not stem the flow of its people coming to the United States illegally. Celestine Pierre, one of the Haitian men Richard was getting to know, came to see him at the rectory, asking to understand the U.S. government.

"*Pe* Sanders," he began. "How can this be right? They say the way to keep Haitian people from dying in the sea is to stop them from trying? Our people are dying down there! Why can't the answer be that they accept us, take us in here, like they take the Cubans?"

"I'm afraid the answer they would give is Communism. The United States is protective against Communism and Cuba is a Communist country. That's why our government accepts the Cuban people and not Haitians."

"But the Haitian people would never go to Communism. We would never look for that. Why wouldn't the U.S. want us?"

"Tell me what it was like there."

Celestine hesitated. Getting information from the Haitian people was difficult. There was too much fear where they were from, and bad things happened when people knew too much. As *Pe* Sanders sat quietly, however, Celestine seemed to grow more trusting.

"I'm from southern Haiti originally, near a city called Jacmel. When I was young, Haiti was a great place, a beautiful place. We didn't have much money, but we didn't need much either. And I never thought about the fact that it cost so much to go to school, because I didn't care if I went. But then it got harder and harder to get food to eat, so my father and mother and me and my five brothers and sisters moved up to Port-Au-Prince, the capital."

"Was it better there?"

"No. Much worse. My father was able to get work, but the city was dangerous, with Duvalier and more of the *Tontons Macoute*."

Richard's look asked him to explain.

"They're real bad men, Father. The name is kind of like your word for 'bogeyman' but it's real. They don't get paid; they just take whatever they want from the Haitian people. They can steal from you, beat you up, rape your wife, even kill you and get away with it because they protect the president."

Celestine turned around to see who else was in the office with them, reliving the fear he had felt constantly in Haiti. *Macoutes* and their informers were always listening.

"François Duvalier, the one they called 'Papa Doc,' made a deal with them that they could do what they wanted as long as they protected him from anyone he thought might be a threat, but mostly from the Haitian military."

Richard looked confused and Celestine tried to explain sixty years of Haitian history in a brief conversation.

"*Wi*. Before François, the military decided who the president was and how long he would stay in office. If they liked him, he stayed. If they didn't, they killed him. The U.S. helped Duvalier become president and then he developed the *Macoutes* to protect him. Pretty soon, Duvalier made himself 'president-for-life.' When he died in 1971, his son Jean-Claude took over and the *Macoutes* protected him too. But things for the people got worse because Jean-Claude is weak, not strong like his father, so the *Macoutes* got stronger and hurt the Haitian people more. That's why so many of us come here now."

Not long after, he noticed that there were Haitian children attending the RCMA daycare on the church grounds. Rachel, a young woman from the parish, had taken over as center coordinator, and a Haitian woman named Emma worked with her and took care of twelve Haitian children. Father Sanders now had additional opportunities to practice his Haitian Creole as he would stop over to see Emma and help her teach the children. Emma invited Father Sanders to the first meeting with their parents, and he helped her explain the rules of the center and the way the children were supposed to behave. They had a curriculum to follow. This was not just childcare – few migrant children ever completed eighth grade, never mind high school, and RCMA was preparing the children to succeed in school.

One day he stopped over to play with the children and noticed that Rachel, the center coordinator, did not seem to be doing well. She sat on the floor as the children napped, looking sad and stressed. Richard sat next to her, on one of the little children's chairs.

"*Cuenteme*," he said softly. "What's wrong?"

She looked up at him with such sadness that he thought his heart would break.

251

"It's my family, Father. I don't know what to do."

He waited patiently for her to continue.

"My father, he's seeing another woman, and my mother is so hurt and she doesn't know what to do. I want to help her and I don't know how. I can't believe he's doing this to her. I can't even talk to him I'm so upset about it."

Richard paused. How could he explain such a complicated situation to a young woman? Her family thought she might become a nun, and such a betrayal was of course a tragedy to her. He wished he could explain how sins of the flesh were the ones emphasized so strongly by people, while the greater sins were the living conditions of the poor, their inability to buy food, the terrible housing and the lack of medical care. Still, he did not discount the pain this caused the family. He hesitated, and gently put his hand on her head.

"Rachel, you cannot even begin to understand what your mother is going through. You can just support her, but don't just put your father aside, like he doesn't exist. He is part of your life and he is going to be there for you for a long time. Your parents have an issue that they have to go through, but it really isn't on your shoulders."

She looked up at him. "I thought I had to get them back together, get him to stop, like it was my responsibility. I've made decisions in the family since I was very young. Are you sure this isn't something I have to fix?"

"No," he smiled, and said softly. "It's not your job. Now, try to feel better or your mood will affect the children. Remember how important it is – these children have hope for a better future because of the work you do here."

Chapter Twenty-Nine – Learning Our Faith – 1981

In October, after a month of planning, *Padre* Sanders began the religious training that he had originally wanted to do in Naples. Our Lady of Guadalupe's parishioners would become one of the "base communities" he had learned about in Liberation Theology. He reread the documents from the Third General Conference of the Latin American Episcopate at Puebla, Mexico in 1979 that called for a "personal conversion and social transformation." It meant that not just the priests but the entire community was responsible for evangelization and liberation.

The people needed to experience the church as a place of participation and communion, but first they needed to be educated in their faith. Richard came up with an overall structure and then called the Guadalupanas to help work out the details. Workshops would be held one intensive week each month in October, November, January, February and March, weekday evenings for four hours. The people would study the sacraments, the Church, Christ and the Bible.

"Twenty hours in one week? That's a lot of time!" said Sister Octavia.

"*Sí, hermana*, but we will feed them and watch their children so they can participate. It will build their faith and the community at the same time."

More than one hundred attended on a regular basis. The format was structured, yet the meetings were fun for the people and their priest. Richard set specific topics, basing them largely on the teachings of the historical Jesus and viewing the Gospels in light of today's world.

He assigned New Testament readings to different people in advance, usually about how to live better as a family and community and how the Gospel readings could help them do that. At each meeting, one person read the scripture, then another gave an introductory talk about the subject and, after that, *Padre* Sanders gave them a few questions to answer at their tables. The people then broke into small groups, took food from a buffet table and talked as they ate. One person was chosen to present their findings to the whole group. The idea was to get discussion going that would lead to a consensus of what the scriptures meant in their lives. Often the evenings were filled with laughter, and Richard realized how much he was beginning to love these people. And in the meetings, particularly, he could see how much they loved each other.

In early November he assigned a portion of the Sermon on the Mount, Matthew 5: 38 – 42.

> You have heard that it was said, 'An eye for an eye,' and 'A tooth
> for a tooth.' But I say to you not to resist the evildoer; on the

contrary, if someone strikes thee on the right cheek, turn to him the other also. And if anyone would go to law with thee and take thy tunic, let him take thy cloak as well: and whoever forces thee to go for one mile, go with him two.

"This is a tough one," said the man who was assigned the talk. "I'm an eye for an eye guy myself, and that's in the Bible, too."

One of the women spoke up. "Yes, but it's not what Jesus believed. Jesus came to teach a new way, and sometimes things he said are different from the rest of the Bible, aren't they?"

After they ate and discussed the topic among themselves, group leaders started giving opinions. They agreed generally that Jesus had brought a new way, and that because they were Catholic, they were supposed to follow Jesus. Richard smiled, pleased with their progress.

Several tables later, Willow, one of the men Richard enjoyed most, stood up with a piece of paper to read the thoughts of his group. He spoke directly to *Padre* Sanders.

"*Hola, Padrecito. Buenas tardes, Padrecito. Buenas noches.*" Hello Little Father. Good afternoon Little Father. Good evening.

He continued in an exaggerated monologue with a straight face. "My name is Miguel Alejandro Carlos Óscar Jesús Maria Martínez Angélico Pedro José Manuel Elías Francisco de la Luz..." He paused for emphasis. "But they call me Willow."

Padre Sanders and the whole group burst into laughter. Willow frowned and looked sternly at the priest.

"Look, *Padrecito*, this is nothing to laugh about." He wagged his finger and frowned again. "Don't be laughing at me."

This made them all laugh even harder.

"OK, we were at that table over there." Willow gestured. "Those people over there. We were discussing this stuff and they choose me. I don't know why. Anyway I'm gonna say whatever they were saying and I'm gonna read a little bit of what they were writing."

He looked down at the paper but then looked at the priest again with a mournful frown.

"But *Padrecito*, I can't read!"

After they settled down from laughter again, the meeting continued. Richard enjoyed these sessions more than anything he did, except maybe playing with the children. He loved watching the faith and confidence of the people grow. At the end they sang the song that reaffirmed that they were becoming a base community of believers. *Padre* Sanders joined them, singing for the first time in many years.

Somos un pueblo que camina, y juntos caminando...
We are a people moving forward, and traveling together,

In the end of October, the Haitian community was saddened when an old thirty-foot boat holding sixty-six Haitian people capsized less than a mile from Miami. Thirty-three of them drowned and the rest were taken to Krome, the Federal Detention Center, where they would remain incarcerated for months until their asylum cases were heard. Governor Bob Graham called the accident "a human tragedy which has been waiting to happen," and urged the federal government to step up efforts to stop illegal immigration from Haiti. *Pe* Sanders and Fanoly led the people in prayer at an all-night vigil for the dead.

Richard was grateful for the happy times that offset the sad. One Sunday in early November after the first Spanish Mass, he stood at the door of the church and a young man passed by, smiling.

"*Buenos dias*," said the *Padre* warmly. "*¿Como se llama?*"

"Lolo – Lolo Duarte."

"You are new here?"

"I just came this week from Mexico."

Whenever Richard saw a new person he made it a point to get them involved in the parish, particularly those who came to church alone. It often meant they didn't know anyone at all. After finishing his greetings, with his vestments still on because he would say the English Mass next, Richard chatted with Lolo at the grotto.

"*¿De qué parte de Méjico eres?*" What part of Mexico are you from?

"Querétaro, about 250 miles northwest of Mexico City."

"I don't know that place. *Cuéntame.*" Tell me.

"It's in the northwest part of Mexico. It's beautiful. There are tall hills and underground caverns, lots of old buildings from the time of the Spanish. In the capital city there is a Convent of the Cross. They have a tree that has thorns in the shape of crosses. Our family lives about an hour away from there, in a little town, but there is no work there. "

"How old are you?

Lolo was usually shy around white people because he did not speak English and had crossed the border illegally, but he felt comfortable with this gringo priest who was speaking Spanish. He was twenty-five.

"That's a perfect age for a group we have here that you should join," said the *Padre*. "It's called *Grupo Guadalupano*. It's a social group but we also do serious work in the community. It would be a good way for you to get to know people, and you could be helpful to us."

"*Sí, Padre, me gustaría.*" I would like that.

"They meet on Tuesday nights in that building over there." He pointed to the CCD building. "Look for *las hermanas*, sisters from Mexico called Guadalupanas, and tell them I suggested you attend."

Lolo came back to the church grounds on Tuesday as *Padre* Sanders had suggested. First he went into the room of a group for young people that were speaking in English, but Cynthia Garcia, the leader, showed him to the room where the Spanish-speaking group was gathered. Sister Carmen introduced Lolo to the four women and three men, all about Lolo's age. They prayed, sang songs and ate food the sisters had made for them. Then *Padre* Sanders came in, said a prayer with the group and began the discussion.

"I need to know more about things that are happening related to immigration. I hear about raids and people being taken back to their countries but I don't know enough details." He knew several of this group were undocumented. "What are you seeing out there?"

"It's getting worse," said one of the young men. "We see it all the time now, *la migra*, Immigration, waiting outside the theatre and arresting everyone who comes out, or stopping buses on the way to the fields and checking papers. Who takes their papers to the fields? Sometimes they treat the people roughly and we are afraid for ourselves."

"*Sí*, and sometimes they just bust into the houses without knocking and drag the people out of there with no questions, no explanations, nothing."

"Sometimes they hurt the people they take, if they resist at all. Sometimes the kids don't even know the parents are gone."

"A lot of times they don't have any money. They get paid at the end of the week and can't even go get their paycheck and the farmer or the crew bosses keep the money."

"They just take anyone who looks suspicious to them, even if they don't know for sure, they will still take them to the stockade. But what can we do?"

The *Padre* sighed. "Start writing down the number of the tag from the car, write the names on the agents' badges, and write down what happened. If you have your papers, you don't have to be afraid; it's OK to let them know you are watching. They should not be mistreating anyone. If you want peace, you have to work for justice, and that is what we will do."

Sister Carmen took over from there. "The last week of the month, this meeting will become an update on immigration and we'll make a report for the *Padre*. The rest of the meetings will be about prayer, taking care of ourselves, keeping ourselves and our mind pure and focused on God, how to respect ourselves and others. All the things Jesus taught."

The next morning Richard went to breakfast at a local restaurant where white farmers and ranchers ate. They made the best American-style breakfasts in town. He overheard a group of farmers who were also complaining about the recent activities of immigration agents.

"You'd think they could wait until after the growing season," said one.

"Yeah, I know," said another. "Sometimes now it gets worse during the season. Who do they think is going to harvest these fields if they take the workers? We're not gonna get Americans to pick tomatoes."

"Most of the white people who will do fieldwork are winos, anyway, and you can't rely on them to even show up two days in a row. And if they do, they don't work as hard, or as fast."

"I've invested tens of thousands of dollars to put crops into the ground and we're not gonna have with enough workers to harvest them. It's just not fair."

Richard thought with interest about the economic side of illegal immigration; the farmers had a point. So why didn't the U.S. Government do something about it? President Reagan had asked Congress to come up with a bill to deal with it. Reagan wanted employer sanctions for hiring undocumented immigrants, but also sought a way for those workers who had been here for some time, to get their papers. After all, they had contributed to the American economy. Richard, with so many undocumented workers in his parish, wondered why these things took so long. His people were being deported while Congress debated issues.

Later that week, Yolanda called from Miami. She was sick again, and was going to have her gallbladder removed. He had never heard of such a thing.

"I never heard of it either," said his friend. "I guess it's new. But they think it will help. I can hardly eat without feeling sick."

"You are still on chemo, aren't you?"

"*Sí*, but I was never this sick from it before."

"I'll come over the night before the surgery."

Wearily, he walked over the grotto, knelt and prayed once again for his friend. Yolanda was strong in the face of all her problems. He asked Our Lady of Guadalupe to continue to protect her.

A few days later, Corina's daughter Maria came out to help him catch up with paperwork. She brought a copy of the December issue of "Naples Now" that contained an article called "Children of Despair" by Ellie Springer, about the educational plight of migrant children. It said that the drop-out rate for migrant children in Florida was 68 percent. By the time they got to age sixteen, their families needed the money they could earn in the fields, and their future was one of field work anyway. So why did they need an education? Richard shook his head and thought back to Sawny, who had embraced education to avoid a life of shucking oysters or picking crab.

On December 12, *Padre* Sanders celebrated his first "*Doce de Deciembre*" in Immokalee. The base community that was forming built the outside platform, moved the altar on top of it and set up hundreds of folding chairs on the church grounds. They also moved the painting of Our Lady to a pine tree over the outdoor altar.

Well before dawn, the Guadalupana Sisters knocked on Richard's window. When he got outside, still groggy, he could not believe what he saw and was even more amazed that the singing had not awakened him. The seats were completely filled and many more people stood behind and beside the chairs. He could hardly see the platform-altar because of the number of flowers that covered it. He was moved as he watched his people singing *Mañanitas*, "little dawn songs" for Our Lady of Guadalupe.

> *Oh Virgen, la más hermosa del Valle del Anáhuac,*
> *Tus hijos muy de mañana te vienen a saludar...*

Oh Virgin, the most beautiful in the valley of Anahuac
Your children come in the morning to greet you.
Wake up, mother wake up, look the dawn is already here
Look at the flowers I bring for you.

The singing and prayers went on for two hours. Afterwards, Aztec dancers marched down 9th street and danced in the field on the other side of the church. Richard was fascinated. The *Caballeros de Colón*, Knights of Columbus, and their wives served hot chocolate, coffee and *pan dulce*. At 5:30 a.m., though it was still dark, the celebration ended and workers left for the fields. The Mass to honor Our Lady of Guadalupe would be held that evening but the singing of the *Mañanitas* was complete.

The third week in Advent, Sister Octavia reminded Richard about *las posadas*. He had learned about them in Mexico but did not know they had them in Immokalee. "We have them every year," she explained. "They are like a religious play where we all accompany Joseph and Mary to find a place where Mary can have the baby. We walk in the streets with lighted candles and sing and pray. We knock on several doors where the people tell us to go away because there is no room. Then finally there is one home that invites us in. We finish there with prayers, hot chocolate, punch and cookies. It's beautiful!"

It was cold the night of the *las posadas* and *Padre* Sanders brought extra sweaters and jackets for others to wear. He knew that feeling cold was the least of their problems, however. If it froze that night, the crops would freeze and there would be no work except for cleaning up the fields, and nothing after that. He noticed that several of the church regulars were missing and learned later that they had been called in to work, covering plants to protect them. In addition to prayers for the Christ child, *Padre* Sanders said prayers for the weather.

The next morning, the frost on the mean grass around the rectory told him the news was bad. He had been up until about 2:00 in the morning when his outdoor thermometer showed forty degrees, but it had obviously dropped below freezing later on. The effects of the freeze would be seen for weeks afterwards as damaged plants led to damaged lives. Any work now would be short-lived, and farm workers who lived day-to-day would not be able to buy food or pay their rent.

Richard also knew that Christmas would see many disappointed children because the workers counted on current work to buy presents. Their children didn't usually get much anyway, not only because of lack of money but also because there was no place for toys. Most of the migrants shared trailers where there was barely room for them to live. When they went up the road, children were usually given a box that they filled with things they wanted to take with them, and anything else was left behind.

Richard planned his Christmas Eve sermon to focus heavily on the religious aspects of Christmas and downplay the material and commercial nature of the holiday, but could not help but think about disappointed children. He gave the Guadalupanas money to buy candy canes and small stuffed animals that they would pass out in church.

Later at the rectory, he thought back over this, his first year in Immokalee and to his first impression about how far it was from Naples. It truly was a different world, and seemed even more so, the longer he stayed. He entered recent marriages, baptisms and funerals in the register, something he rarely did, but the entries were backing up.

Flipping through the funeral list, he noticed how many he had buried in just this short time. In May and June there had been seven deaths, mostly from unusual causes and almost all Mexican-Americans or Mexicans. A three-month old baby died for no determined reason, but her mother blamed herself because she had laid her baby on a blanket between rows while she worked. Many families did this, but he had not been able to console her nor relieve her guilt. Not long after, a twenty-two-year old man was killed in a fight, then a young man was found drowned in his car in a canal and less than a month after that, a twenty-eight-year old was killed in an accident and a twenty-six-year old was crushed to death by a moving device on a tractor.

Death had apparently gone north with the migrants in the spring but returned with them in the fall. In October, a man was shot in the chest; Richard remembered hearing the shots. Shortly after, a thirty-three-year old indigent white woman was found dead in the street from pneumonia. The only mourners at her funeral were John Brister, *Padre* Sanders, one of the Guadalupana sisters and Juan Ramirez, who chanted mournfully, "*Adíos, adíos, Paulette.*" Richard prayed once more for the souls of all of them and for the living who mourned yet woke to face each new day in the hope and light of Christ.

He walked outside so he could hear the choir practicing Christmas carols, singing the Spanish version of "Silent Night."

Noche de paz, noche de amor
Night of peace, night of love

He thought about the past year and other travelers looking for a place to stay – the seemingly endless stream of poor immigrants who had come to this place to find work and peace. How many of them might be Joseph and Mary, or Jesus Himself, walking on earth?

CHAPTER THIRTY – YOU CAN DO IT – 1982

More than just New Year's Day, January 1 was also Haiti's Independence Day. The growing Haitian congregation at Our Lady of Guadalupe decorated the church and parish hall where they would have a *fet*, celebration, after the Mass. Richard worked with Fanoly and the Guadalupana sisters to make sure it was not just a Haitian celebration, but included other members of the parish. In three languages, the church bulletin read, "We join our Haitian brothers and sisters in this celebration. After the Solemn Mass in Creole at 10:15, there will follow a cultural feast."

Father Wenski came from Miami to celebrate the Mass. Not as many Latinos or Anglos came as Richard had hoped, but the Haitians were thrilled to have one of their biggest national holidays celebrated in their church. They were dressed as if going to a wedding.

As he sat in the back pew watching, though, Richard noticed sadness among them as they celebrated their country, the first Black Republic in the western hemisphere. For many of them, this was the first Independence Day away from their home. He understood how much they loved Haiti but could not live there; the poverty and the violence were unbearable. Still, he thought, the strength and beauty of their faith was remarkable, particularly on this day, singing this song, "*Mesi Papa, Jodia, e pou tou ton.*" Thank you, God, for today and for all time.

The feast afterwards was rich and delicious, typical Haitian dishes with fish, chicken, vegetables and rice, plus the traditional New Year's Haitian pumpkin soup. Richard had not had anything like it before, and he loved it. It was made from fresh Haitian pumpkin, available at the recently-opened Caribbean Market, plus vegetables, chunks of beef and several different kinds of pasta. While they ate, a Haitian band played in the background. He looked around and realized they could have been in Haiti.

A few days later, Corina called, excited to say she had been asked to be the director of the RCMA-sponsored day care center on the A. Duda farm in Naples. "Olga asked me, from RCMA in Immokalee."

Padre Sanders knew. He had suggested it to Olga. "Are you going to do it?"

"I don't know. I told Olga, 'No, I never work in this kind of office. I work in the fields but not here. I can't do it.'"

Richard smiled; some things never changed. "What did Olga say?"

"She sounded like you! She said, 'Yes, you can do it, Corina.' And I said no, I can't because I never had no education and I went to school to learn English but I still am not good. And I said, but I never did nothing like this before."

Richard was smiling broadly now, listening to Corina's rendition of the exchange. "And what did she say?"

"She said 'You can do it. Because you got so many kids you can do it!'"

"So you're going to do it?" asked the priest, almost laughing at the other end of the phone.

"*Sí*," sighed Corina. "I'm gonna do it."

Above, Corina Hernandez, middle, is director of the RCMA-sponsored day care center at Naples. Standing beside her are Mariano Vasquez and Farm Manager Jim Malcolm. Right, teachers Norma Olivera and Irene Anguiano cut out paper hearts for a Valentine's display while the children take an afternoon nap.

Photo thanks to A. Duda Farms' publication, "Growing"

Not long after, in January of 1982, there was another freeze. Richard sighed. What was God doing to His people? Then he caught himself and said a quick prayer for forgiveness for his doubts. Still, it was devastating. Just a few weeks had passed since the last freeze.

On weeknights and weekends he gave out food and clothing at the rectory and noted the that the line of people waiting to see Sister Eileen stretched almost out to the grotto. He decided to go and see her, glad they had relocated her office to a trailer behind the parish hall. He also remembered her complaining that the trailer was cold, and wanted to be sure she had purchased a space heater for under her desk. He zipped up his jacket, sheltering his hands in his pockets.

He spoke to everyone on the line of shivering people outside the trailer and more in the small waiting room inside where it wasn't much warmer. When he stuck his head into her office and said hello, she introduced him to the young man who was in her office. He was about sixteen years old.

"Oscar was just telling me about how hard it is for him and his mother to support their family."

"My father is dead, *Padre*," said the young man. Richard felt a pang of sadness, remembering how it felt. "Me and my mother work in the packinghouse to support my little brothers and sisters, except now, with the freeze, the packinghouse is closed, so we've been working in the orange groves. We don't know oranges, so we only make twelve to fourteen dollars a day, each. The other children are too young to work. I have an uncle in

Arkansas who said he can give me a mechanic's job. If I could get there, I could send money back here to my mother."

"I think we can give you enough for a bus ticket," said Sister Eileen.

Richard opened his wallet and gave him twenty dollars, all the money he had. "Take this for food."

He walked back to the rectory, reflecting on how much more difficult Eileen's job was than his, emotionally. For the most part, she saw only the suffering. At least his job had highs as well as lows, happy events like weddings and baptisms in addition to funerals.

That Sunday, he listened to the choir at Mass, with the new guitarists who followed Sister Aida as she played, and noticed how beautiful Aida sounded – she was a better singer and player than any of them. After Mass he talked with her.

"Sister, I'd rather you didn't take such a leading role in the choir. Help them – teach them how to play and sing together. But when they are performing the music ministry, please don't take over."

"But *Padre,* what about the quality of the music for the people in the congregation? Doesn't it make the worship better if the music is good?"

"Maybe in most places but not here, not with our people. Teach them, and give them confidence. If they don't do it well at first, it doesn't matter. Instead of being focused on perfection, focus on empowering them."

Later, in the parish hall, *Padre* Sanders announced an idea to the people who gave in service to the church: parish workers, religious education teachers, Eucharistic Ministers, lectors, altar boys, choir members, English youth group and *Grupo guadalupanos.*

"I want to have a passion play here in Immokalee."

Lucy Ortiz rolled her eyes and raised her eyebrows as she whispered to her husband, "*Pasión?* Passion? Doesn't that mean sex?"

A few others had the same reaction and soon they were all giggling like children. *Padre* Sanders laughed along with them at the confusion, and then explained.

"Passion play is *pasión* with a different meaning. It's about the suffering of Christ. People act out the last days of Jesus' life, the way they are told in the Gospels. It's a play for Holy Week. I want you all to be in it."

He sensed their nervousness. It sounded exciting, but he knew none of them thought they could act. Most of them were farm workers or previous farm workers with little education. They had never done anything like acting.

"Don't worry," he reassured them. "First we're just going to go and see one. I'm going to get tickets for all of us to see one of the best passion plays in the world, at Lake Wales, Florida. Then we'll come back and have our own, here in Immokalee."

The next day Richard was reading in the living room when Fanoly came in and voiced a concern he had heard from several of the people. "They have meetings at the schools but none of the Haitians can understand them because they talk only in English, and very fast."

Casto, overhearing them from the kitchen, said he had heard the same thing from the Hispanics. "The Latinos go to the meetings, too, but they have no idea what's going on."

Padre Sanders sighed. "Casto, do you announce these meetings on the radio?"

Casto nodded.

"OK, then will you please let me know when they are going to be held? I'll start going, and Fanoly, you come too. We'll translate for the parents."

From that point on, when Father Sanders walked in to the meetings, school officials sighed audibly, knowing his presence there would double or triple the length of the meetings. Richard bristled at some of the comments and questions.

"These parents should learn English, Father. Why do we have to cater to them with translating?"

He answered them with questions. "Is that what these meetings are about? The parents' education? No. It's that the parents understand decisions that will affect the futures of their children."

At the end of the month, *Padre* Sanders held the funeral for a young farm worker who had been shot in front of *El Lucero* Bar. Tempers were short because of the freeze and the lack of work, and there had been more problems lately than usual. John said this young man's family wanted his body sent home to Mexico.

"How does that work?" Richard was curious.

"I have a contract with a Mexican hearse company that will take bodies to anywhere in Mexico for two hundred dollars, but the Mexican government requires that bodies arrive in a sealed casket. We use cheap ones that meet requirements, but every once in a while the families will send them home in a better casket, and customs at the airport will hold them for bribes. Can you imagine doing that to a family?"

Richard shook his head, saddened, but fascinated. So many things happened in this world that most people knew nothing about.

The group of future passion play actors boarded a bus provided and driven by one of the crew bosses, and headed to the Black Hills Passion Play in Lake Wales. It took about three hours to get there but the drive was beautiful – thousands of acres of land used for cattle grazing, horse farms and orange groves. As they got closer to Lake Okeechobee they saw more and more sugar cane. When they reached the lake, they stopped, because some of them had not seen it before; it was so big they couldn't see across to the other side. Fanoly said it reminded him of the Gulf of Mexico, but a little calmer.

The performance was in a huge amphitheater with a stage as long as a city block. *Padre* Sanders asked the bilingual people to position themselves among the non-English speakers to translate during the play.

On the way back, he moved around the bus talking to different individuals about playing parts. "Lolo, you are a good person to play *Cristo*."

The young man laughed nervously. "*Padre*, I don't have the memory to play Christ. I could never learn all that."

"You can do it. Don't worry." But then he noticed the fear in the young man's eyes and thought better of putting too much pressure on him. "Maybe we'll have you do two roles that together don't have as many lines. How about if you play a double role – Judas and St. Peter?"

"*Vamos a ver,*" said Lolo, hesitantly. We'll see.

Richard was saddened when Rachel, the center coordinator for the RCMA daycare, came to tell him that they were going to move to a new building they had purchased from the Baptist Church, on Main Street. It was not far away, but more than a few steps from the rectory, and Richard would miss seeing the children's happy faces every day. But he looked forward to Wendell Rollason's dream of a tile mural that would one day beautify Immokalee's dreary Main Street. "But not one penny of children services money will be spent for it," Wendell had said. "Instead we will have to find special art money or donors who want to help make it happen."

Late the next afternoon Richard spotted Sister Eileen praying at the grotto and walked over to join her. For a few minutes they prayed silently and then he spoke. "Can you take a minute? How was your day?"

"It was long and it's not over yet." She seemed tired. "I'm finished in the office, but I have to take some rice to Patty on the way home. She has a family of seven and she left word that they have no food. There was one family today that particularly moved me. Lorenzo, his wife and three children just moved into a house in ill repair, needing furniture. He has been fortunate, considering the freeze, to be able to find three days of work a week in the fields that just about pays for their rent and food. When I visited them, I saw their empty bedroom and the concrete floor where they were sleeping. We were able to help them with beds donated by people in Bonita Springs."

As they walked toward her car, she told him about others who came to her. "Every day there are new faces, filled with worry and years of suffering. Sometimes I get so drained."

Just after he got back to the rectory, the phone rang. It was Yolanda. He worried each time he heard her voice, but this time it was a happy call. Her cancer was in remission! Richard ran joyfully to the grotto to give thanks for this miracle, feeling like a twenty-year old monk.

"My sweet Lady of Guadalupe, thank you for saving the life of my friend! I am sorry I doubted you. In the future I will listen more carefully to your words. I know you are here, my mother, and... thank you, thank you!"

Soon, Yolanda was able to come and visit, and Richard cherished the time they spent together. He even asked her to help him train *Misioneros Católicos*. Catholic ministers. She looked at him questioningly.

"Don't you have Eucharistic Ministers here already?"

"*Sí, amiga*, we have them here, but this training will be more and there will be more people trained. We're going to prepare the people to assist in all ways at Masses, be ushers, do readings, etc. I want the people to be able to take part when they go up the road. Remember how hesitant they always were to go to white churches? I want to give them a certificate they can take to pastors along the way, showing their qualifications. If they have this, they'll feel more confident."

"Are you doing this on your own?"

"No. I talked to Pat Stockton from the Rural Life Bureau at the diocese. She'll organize it for us."

Yolanda was excited about taking part as a teacher. She would come one weekend per month and Casto would spend a couple of nights with his friends so she could stay in the third bedroom. Yolanda awoke and helped her old friend when people knocked on the door in the middle of the night, heating soup as he fed them sandwiches, feeling as if they had never been apart. *Padre* Sanders was delighted to have his friend and companion back and was thrilled she would come on a regular basis to help with the training.

As the weather warmed, Richard looked forward to *Semana Santa*, Holy Week, the tri-lingual Easter celebration, and Immokalee's first passion play. He also had decided to expand the Friday evening Stations of the Cross beyond the church grounds and into the streets, like they did in Mexico.

They had practiced for weeks for the passion play. The role of Christ would be played by Ramón, one of the members of the *Grupo Guadalupano*. Lolo finally had agreed to be Judas and Peter and Richard had talked Santos Ramírez into playing Mary. She was one of the fieldworker women Richard was just getting to know, who had a gentleness combined with inner strength that he thought would make a perfect Mary.

Richard told them to make the play seem real, so the congregation could feel the suffering of Jesus and his followers.

He coached Santos. "Since you are playing Mary, you need to really cry."

"I can't do that."

"Yes you can. You can do it. Just think of something really sad, like how Mary must have felt. You're a mother. Can you imagine how terrible it would be to have one of your sons suffer like that?"

"*Padre*, I can't think of that! But I've seen that Jesus of Nazareth movie and I cried a lot then. I'll just remember the movie. But don't expect a lot."

After the tri-lingual Palm Sunday Mass, the people stayed to see the passion play. The cast wore costumes made by the Guadalupana sisters, including long, brightly colored satin tunics with contrasting shoulder sashes. Ramón was a perfect Jesus, gentle and quiet yet powerful. Santos was the most emotional Mary *Padre* Sanders had ever seen. He was close to tears himself as he watched her sobbing on stage, "*¡Mi hijo! ¡Mi hijo!*" My son! My son!

Richard video-taped the play with a movie camera his mother had sent him. Later the group of actors watched the filmed version, applauded each others' performances and agreed to do it again next year.

On Friday, he excitedly anticipated the first Stations of the Cross in the streets of Immokalee. Prompted by Richard, Sister Octavia had found fourteen homes that agreed to set up a Station in each of their front yards. The Knights of Columbus brought a flatbed truck from the fields on which they placed container palms and life-sized wooden crosses, and three people dressed in purple rode on the truck, representing the Virgin Mary, Mary Magdalene and James.

About two hundred people from Our Lady of Guadalupe Church followed the beautifully-decorated truck through the streets of the south side, singing as they walked and praying at each Station, in Spanish, English and then Haitian Creole. The stations in the yards were perfect. One home brought out a dresser and set it near the road, decorated with a crucifix and picture of Jesus. Another had a statue of Our Lady of Guadalupe adorned with helium-filled balloons. A few were quite elaborate, with sheets spread over frames as backgrounds for candle-lit scenes of crucifixes, statues and pictures of Jesus. Hearing the procession pass by, people came out of their homes and out of bars and taverns, some setting down their beers to watch and pray.

On Sunday morning, Mass in three languages began the joyous Easter Season. *Padre* Sanders looked forward to the coming weeks that would celebrate the Risen Christ.

With Holy Week over, he would have time to spend with some of his people, including Lolo Duarte, who was quiet but always smiling. The *Padre* made an impromptu visit one Saturday, recognizing the motel-like building by the large cactus that grew in front – Lolo had told him the renters planted it there, to remind them of home.

When Richard knocked, he heard Spanish television and several male voices yelling to each other to get the door. A young Mexican man he did not know opened it, wearing only a pair of pants. Lolo appeared behind him.

"*Padre!*" said Lolo. He pulled the other man out of the way and said firmly, "Put on a shirt, Julio! This is a priest!"

The young man hurriedly retreated into the living area. Lolo seemed flustered, treating the *Padre* like an honored person and embarrassed by their poor home. "Come in *Padre*, sit down, let me bring you something. I think I have a soda." He looked in the refrigerator and Richard saw that the soda was one of the few items in it.

"Just a glass of water."

Lolo introduced him to his five roommates and *Padre* Sanders nodded to each of them.

It was a small dwelling with a living area, kitchen and bathroom. Mattresses on the living room floor were beds that doubled as couches, from which they watched the small black and white television. In the kitchen area was a wooden table and four chairs. Richard and Lolo sat at the table and his roommates relaxed back into their mattresses.

Lolo was excited. "I can't believe you came here to this rundown place. Wait until I tell my mother that our priest visited me in my home!"

"How often do you talk to her?"

"Only sometimes. There is a phone service near their house and somebody runs to get them if I call, but usually we write letters because the phone is expensive. Sometimes I think I'm gonna use up my whole paycheck on the call."

"You should write more often." Then he thought of his own mother and reminded himself to do the same thing. "And is there a girlfriend?"

The young men in the living room snickered, "Not in Mexico!"

Lolo blushed and turned to Father Sanders. "There is one here in Immokalee, but she's not really a girlfriend – yet. She's smart, *Padre*. She's a tutor at the school and she just does fieldwork to make extra money. One weekend we were both working for my cousin, picking tomatoes. My cousin told me she said I was 'cute.'"

The other guys were laughing now but Lolo tried to ignore them. "Then later I met her again, at the church."

"Who is it? Do I know her?"

"Her name is Esmeralda."

Richard remembered her and nodded. "I like the way she smiles."

"*Sí, Padre*," said one of the other men, and they all started giggling again. "Lolo likes the way she smiles, too."

"Do you sing, Lolo?"

Lolo shrugged, wondering where the question came from.

"I bet you do. Esmeralda is in the choir. Maybe you want to join?"

The other young men started laughing again. Lolo shot them an embarrassed yet irritated look and changed the subject to immigration.

"*Padre*, is anything happening lately? I haven't been to *Grupo Guadalupanos* because I've been working all the time."

"*Nada diferente*, nothing different, at least not today. But if I hear of anything I'll come and tell you. You do the same, of course."

Lolo nodded and walked the *Padre* out to his car. As soon as they were out of earshot of his roommates, he asked about the choir.

Richard grinned. "Go see Sister Aida. She will be happy to have you."

Soon, however, Lolo would head up the road along with more than half of Our Lady of Guadalupe's parishioners. His hopes for Esmeralda would wait for the fall.

Chapter Thirty-One – Expanding Social Justice – 1982

As his people packed up to leave for the summer, *Padre* Sanders sprinkled hundreds of pickup trucks and vans with holy water and blessed them for a safe journey. Not long after, he followed them, first going to Blessed Sacrament Church to spend some time with his old friend, Father Bobby. He was doing well. Bobby had taken over Father Sanders' migrant ministry, but was still struggling with Spanish.

"Thank God a lot of them speak English," Bobby said with relief. "How's your Spanish now?"

"I speak it all the time, so it's improved a lot. It took a long time, though."

"I notice you're not smoking. Can that be true?"

Richard nodded but did not mention the heart attack. "Yeah. I just wanted to get a little healthier. What about you?"

"I quit last year."

"Do you miss it?"

"All the time."

"Yeah," said Richard. "Me too. I wonder if the urge ever goes away. It did when I was in Mepkin, but it sure started up again as soon as I got out."

The next afternoon he drove down to a camp on Johns Island and waited for the workers. While there, he talked to mothers who stayed in the camp while their husbands worked, and played with their children. After about an hour, buses started to pull in and he saw Santos from Immokalee step out of one of them. She looked tired, walking with her husband and six children toward the *barracas*.

She laughed when she saw him. "*Padre!*"

Richard smiled broadly. She was dirty from working, but looked happy and healthy. He shook the hands of the older boys and her husband, then hugged the smaller children. The three-year old giggled as he picked her up and said, "So, you go to work, too?"

"*Sí, Padre*," said Santos. "My children are always with me; there's no daycare around here. They play around the rows near us while we're picking, or take a nap on a blanket I lay down for them."

Richard hesitated, remembering the woman who blamed herself for her child's death because she took her to the fields, but he said nothing.

"*Venga conmigo,*" she said. "Come to our house here so we can clean up and talk."

She brought him a glass of water and they sat on the steps of the house. Richard asked where they would go next.

"We pile everyone in our van and go down to Michigan."

He smiled to himself, finding it interesting how most of the migrants referred to going "down" to the north, or "over" to the south. He also loved talking to Santos. She was always happy and smiling, no matter what was going on.

"We have a farmer in Michigan we work for. We go to Pinconning, MI, the capital of the cheese in Michigan. They're nice, Polish people. They let us stay in their hunting trailer. It's good, well kept and we go there every summer and sharecrop. We stay for the whole season, picking pickles."

"You mean cucumbers?"

She smiled again. "No, not cucumbers. Pickles and cucumbers are different, but most people don't know that. Even the plants, the way they grow, they are different. The pickles, when they grow, turn into balls, and the cucumbers turn into, like, big ol' long watermelons."

"What did you mean, sharecrop?" He knew the term but had not heard it from migrants.

"The farmer plants the fields and each family gets their own acres, so we get three or four acres for just me and my family. We pick so many rows every other day, and those acres are ours until the end of the season."

"How do they pay you?"

"If we pick over two thousand dollars worth, it's one thousand for the farmer and a thousand for us. He weighs them and pays us by the pound, and every week he cuts a check. He doesn't charge us for the housing, and he fertilizes the plants. Whenever he's going to water it, my husband goes out there to make sure the spots are well-watered where we need it. Also we go and look at our vines and make sure they are not growing into each other, because they can tangle up and then we'll have problems trying to lift up the plants to pick the pickles."

"Is it hard to pick pickles?" He stuttered over the words and they both laughed as he told her the childhood rhyme that Santos had never heard. "Peter Piper picked a peck of pickled peppers."

She laughed again and then explained. "Well, it's a bending job or a kneeling-down job so it's hard, especially around July. In Michigan it gets really hot and humid. We pick by sizes. First we have to pick the baby pickles, then medium pickles."

He nodded, always fascinated with stories of different kinds of farm work. He asked what they did after the pickle picking.

"We usually finish around August or the beginning of September and then we stay for apples. We come down to an area near Grand Rapids, there's like a valley there and a little township called Conklin – it's just a general store and a gas pump. They have housing, really nice cottages, and it's warm when we start picking."

"Apples are a lot different from pickles or tomatoes, aren't they?" He knew the workers usually had crop specialties.

"Yes, but it's not like picking oranges. In Texas I used to pick oranges but in Florida I don't like oranges much, because it's so hot. Over there in Michigan with the apples it's kind of cool, and there are no thorns. The orange trees have big ol' thorns that poke you, but the apples don't. Once we finish with the first and second picking, then we come home because then it starts freezing and flaking up there."

He smiled at her reference to snow. Flaking.

"Then we plant tomatoes in Immokalee and it starts all over again."

Richard heard Santos' husband clearing his throat inside the house, and saw the children looking at her, wondering about dinner.

"Well, I better get cooking. Why don't you stay and eat with us?

"*Gracias, pero no*. I can't. I'm going to visit my old monastery and I want to get up there before dark. But I am really happy that I got to see you!"

"Me too, *Padre*. See you at home in the fall!"

"*Sí*, Santos." He waved as he walked back toward his car, and then murmured meaningfully to himself, "See you at home."

He went to Mepkin Abbey and spent four days in silent retreat. He needed the rest and what he had come to think of as recharging his soul. Richard noted changes, as each year something was modernized or updated. He spent time with the previous abbot who was still filled with great peace and wisdom. They talked about the many people who were drawn to leave contemplative life yet missed it after they were gone. St. Augustine felt it often, and Thomas Merton talked about the only way people could manage to combine the two lives of active service and contemplation.

"It had to do with how much you loved the thing that drew you from the abbey."

In that reference, Merton was actually talking about Saint Thomas, who saw three variations of religious life: active, contemplative and a combination of the two.

> The 'mixed life' is to be rated above that of the pure
> contemplatives only on the supposition that their love is so much
> more vehement... that it has to pour itself out in teaching and
> preaching.

Remembering the quote gave Richard pause. "I never thought my love for anyone besides God could be strong enough to help me fit into a mixed life, but I was wrong."

"So you feel that great love for the people you serve?"

"I do," smiled *Padre* Sanders. "I do."

He returned to Immokalee in mid-June, wishing he had the freedom to follow his people on the rest of their summer journeys, but he had a church to run. With the migrants gone, though, his congregation was cut in half and he had more time to read. He had gotten a copy of an English translation of a book by Plácido Erdozain called *Archbishop Romero, Martyr of Salvador.* He remembered when Romero died. It wasn't long ago – Richard was in Naples at the time.

Romero was originally a conservative on the side of the Salvadoran government. Six priests and hundreds of lay people had been killed but still he did not believe Catholics should be involved in political activities. Romero switched sides when a priest friend was killed for helping the poor, in 1977, and began to listen to the claims of Liberation Theology. The priests in his diocese had developed base communities that held discussion groups on improving conditions of the poor and oppressed. Inspired by Gutierrez' assertion that the Church has "not only a right but a duty to condemn unjust practices....as clear indications of sin and evil," Archbishop Romero took up the cause and led his people. In 1980, after three years of speaking out against the Salvadoran government, he was shot to death while celebrating the Holy Eucharist.

Padre Sanders was moved by Romero's conviction and courage. He would never be able to work in an environment that dangerous. Or would he? He had stood firm with Father Duffy, facing tanks and guns in Charleston. Perhaps, had he been drawn to a Latin American country instead of to the migrants in the U.S., he might have stood with Romero. He re-read the Foreword to the book that said, "Together with thousands of Salvadorans I have seen Jesus. This time his name was Óscar Arnulfo Romero."

The assertion that people had seen Jesus in Archbishop Romero led Richard to meditate on how important it was to die for a cause, yet he wondered if it were necessary to go that far. He thought of the base community he was developing. Some of us, he reasoned, serve in smaller ways, but we can still all be Jesus' active presence on the earth.

The next day Sisters Jane and Marie came to see him. They had completed their research over the course of the past year and had learned that, while the needs of battered women were great, there was something more primary: people were hungry. They wanted to open a soup kitchen.

Richard agreed wholeheartedly. Sister Eileen's group gave out bags of food that could be cooked at home, but a soup kitchen would serve hot food every weekday at noon. They discussed bringing the organization under the parish, as Eileen's was, but the Archdiocese of Miami was in the process of spinning off a separate diocese in Southwest Florida, so they decided it was probably easier to become a separate organization. Richard breathed a sigh of relief that he wouldn't have to deal with the paperwork. To emphasize the connection with the church, however, they would call it Guadalupe Center. He supported the sisters and offered them the use of the parish hall, which was used infrequently now. He would charge them one dollar per month.

Neither of them had any experience in cooking or feeding the poor, so they observed other soup kitchens and determined what they had to do, keeping Richard updated on their progress. The *Padre* was amazed and grateful when funds came. The center also received contributions of building materials, labor and other items at suppliers' costs. Foundations and private donors gave generously to support the effort. Many volunteers spent that summer remaking the building into a cooking and eating facility. In the meantime, Sister Marie went to Mexico to improve her Spanish.

Sister Eileen's monthly letter arrived later in the month. Richard never ceased to be amazed at her compassion and at the dire condition of many of the people in Immokalee that her letters showed him. He glanced at the first of nine personal stories of people she'd helped recently.

> Maria's husband left her when she was 7 months pregnant. She had two small boys, ages 3 and 4 and is now unable to support them. She is undocumented and so cannot receive welfare or food stamps. We've helped as much as we could with food, clothes and rent.

Richard thought again about the concept of ordinary people as Jesus. He wondered if Eileen knew that she herself was Him, every day she worked in Immokalee. He wondered if all the sisters knew.

In the end of June, the parish celebrated the Feast of *Perpetual Secours,* Our Lady of Perpetual Help, the Patroness of Haiti. Father Darbouze came from Miami to say the Mass and stayed for the picnic celebration afterwards. Richard talked with *Pe* Darbouze and Fanoly about this manifestation of Mary.

"She is the Patroness of Haiti," began Fanoly, "but we who are the *dyas*, the Diaspora, along with our brothers and sisters in Haiti, are united to celebrate the *Perpetual Secours*."

There was no mention of a vision, yet the painting that was found on a ship was believed to have been responsible for many miracles. The Haitians celebrated her Feast Day every June 27, or the closest Sunday to it.

"*Di mwen plis,*" said *Pe* Sanders. Tell me more.

"In the year 1882, the people in Haiti suffered from a contagious illness, *malad*, I think it was smallpox, in a place in the capital called Bel Air. The bishop carried the image, the icon of *Perpetual Secours* through the streets, the people prayed a novena, and the people were cured. It was a miracle. Since then, the Haitian people are consecrated to the Virgin Mary, mother of Perpetual Help."

"Fascinating. It reminds me that I need to study more Creole and also Haitian culture. More Haitians come to Immokalee every day now, it seems."

Father Darbouze suggested that Richard study at the Haitian Catholic Center in Miami where he and Father Wenski worked. Not long after, Richard took him up on the suggestion. He studied for a month there, driving over on Mondays and returning one or two evenings and on Fridays.

In addition to Haitian Creole, he also learned more about Our Lady of Perpetual Help. The interpretation was that the painter made her lips small to show that Mary spoke rarely, but when she did, it was wisely and kindly. The four Greek letters at the top of the painting meant Mother of God, and the Greek letters over the child meant Jesus Christ. The two angels in the painting were the Archangels Michael and Gabriel. Gabriel held a cross and nails, and the baby was so frightened at the sight of them that he kicked out his right foot, causing his sandal to slip off. The child grasped Mary's hand, as if telling the people to cling to her if they ever needed help.

Through the summer, Richard tried to relax a little and organized a picnic at Vanderbilt Beach with the Guadalupana sisters and several parishioners. Some of the people went swimming in the gulf. He thought about it but was vain enough that he did not want anyone to see him as out of shape as he was. Also, though the gulf waters were calm, he didn't really have the energy to swim.

The next day Richard took some time to analyze what he had been doing and tried to organize his thoughts about the greatest needs. The issues he saw were closely related: housing, wages, healthcare, immigration status, education, food and clothing. It was pretty much everything. The people needed to get more involved in not only the community but the county, state and federal governments. Voting was going to be an important part of that. Fortunately, the Voting Rights Act of 1965, amended in 1975 and 1982, now protected against discrimination of people in language minorities and even had a provision for language assistance. Later he called Eileen to talk about getting the people registered.

"Good idea," she said. "We can start by putting something in the church bulletin," she suggested. "We'll keep registration forms over at my office, and tell people to go there to fill them out."

Then Richard thought about how they did it in Union Heights. "When election time comes, we should probably also get a van and take people to the polls."

The following Sunday and every Sunday until November, the bulletin read: "Migrant workers can register to vote if you consider Immokalee to be your home. Register Monday through Friday at the Guadalupe Social Services trailer."

On the morning of July 29, Richard went out to visit a sick parishioner in her home and, as usual, lost track of time as they talked. When he returned to the rectory he noted several familiar cars parked outside including that of Corina Hernandez. He said a quick prayer that it did not mean a tragedy. When he opened the front door it was dead-quiet, and he warily walked toward the kitchen. Suddenly he heard the words "Surprise!" and saw Fanoly, Rosa, Sister Eileen, Casto, Miguel, Corina, Maria, and Sisters Jane and Marie. He had completely forgotten about his birthday. He feigned passing out from the surprise, then laughed and was delighted. They had all brought presents, and he stared at the small pile on the table.

"No *Padre*, not yet," smiled Rosa. "First, we eat. Then we blow out candles and serve cake. Then you can open the presents."

After they ate, Rosa brought out a sheet cake she had made, with more candles on it than he had ever seen.

"Am I really that old?" he said, shocked. Forty-five candles were a lot to blow out. "Be careful – that flame is going to burn down the rectory!"

Then he opened his presents. Two were new guayaberas, his favorite shirt, and a beautifully cut metal sculpture of the Virgin Mary holding the baby Jesus, mounted on wood. "It's from Jerusalem," said Rosa. Miguel had brought him a book of Abraham Lincoln's jokes and his mother sent another book by Thomas Merton. Looking at its cover gave him a fleeting feeling of sadness; the monastery was still part of his being, there was no doubt about that. Betty had sent a card too, in which she expressed as always that she wished she could make him an angel food cake.

Richard was moved by the love he felt around him and led the group in a prayer. "Dear Lord and God of all our people, thank you for these beautiful friends. Keep us all filled with your light, and may we always be as happy as we are right now. Amen."

In spite of his prayer, the next day life in Immokalee got back to its normal ups and downs. Richard alternated between warm, happy experiences with the people he loved, and sadness and anger as he shared their lives in an all too real way.

Later that week one of the women from the parish, Maria Luisa, came in to see him. She attended Mass regularly and took part in many of the parish programs, but always alone. What he did not know was that she surrounded herself with the church in order to survive her life at home. On this day, Richard was sitting in the living room and Rosa was in the kitchen. Maria Luisa whispered to him, nodding her head in Rosa's direction.

"I got a problem, *Padre*, a big problem. Can we go someplace private?"

"*Claro*," he said. Of course. He brought her into his office/bedroom, closed the door and sat with her on the couch. She moved slowly, as if she were in physical pain.

"*Cuéntame*," he said softly. Tell me.

"Well, this morning my husband was real irritable and we got into a fight. It was about nothing, a little thing...."

Padre Sanders listened intently as she started to cry.

"Suddenly, out of nowhere, he grabbed me and dragged me down the hall by my hair." She was sobbing now. "He punched me over and over in my head, breasts and ribs!"

"Maria, *qué lástima!*" How terrible!

She described it so painfully that he felt as if he had been punched, too. "Has this happened before?"

"Yes, a few times. I feel confused, *Padre*, and I still hurt so much. But the Bible says to forgive so I keep forgiving. What should I do?"

Richard sighed and shook his head; he heard these stories too often. He was happy that Sisters Jane and Marie were opening the soup kitchen, but wished someone would do something for the victims of domestic violence.

"Are you sure you are OK, physically? Should I drive you to the clinic?"

"No, I don't think anything is seriously injured. It just hurts all over. I want to go home but I don't know what to do!"

"Maria, it is one thing to forgive, but you do not have to live with him. God does not believe that, and the Church does not say it. Relationships should never be violent. Does he drink?"

She nodded. "That's when it usually happens. Or when he has a hangover, like he did today."

"That's not a real marriage, Maria. A real marriage involves communication and mutual respect, not pain."

"But I thought if you are married in the Church, you're not allowed to leave."

"That is not true, at least not in this church, and certainly not with me. You may not have been compatible to begin with. I know your husband doesn't share your commitment to the church or the community – otherwise I would see him here and I never do."

A week later, *Padre* Sanders called Maria who told him her husband, Manuel, had calmed down. Later that day, knowing Maria would not be home, Richard stopped over at their house, pretending he had come to see her, but then sat down to chat with her husband. With his quiet way of asking questions, he befriended Manuel, and after a few weeks, Manuel even started showing up at Mass. Then Richard asked him if he would like to go to a *Cursillo de Cristiandad*, meaning 'short course in Christianity.'

"It's a Catholic program that starts with a three-day weekend in Miami. The first weekend is just for men. The women go separately later. I haven't been yet, but *Padre* Pedro told me that when we go there, the Holy Spirit teaches us to live like Christ and bring His light to others. The idea is that you go in, get away from the world, and live in community with other people just for this week-end. A lot of the guys from the parish have been. Why don't you come?"

Manuel consented, reluctantly, but during the prayerful weekend, he seemed fairly comfortable. Though still traditional in his prayer activities, Richard enjoyed the experience, too. Most important to him personally was that, after the *cursillo*, Manuel's attitude seemed to change. He was gentler and nicer to people, began to attend Mass once in a while, and never hit his wife again.

CHAPTER THIRTY-TWO – TOGETHER AS ONE –1982

In September, as people started returning from the north, *Padre* Sanders noticed the number of people standing in the aisles at the crowded Masses. He knew they were in violation of fire codes, and it was still early. By the time all the workers returned, half of them would be listening to the Mass in the parking lot. Richard talked to the Guadalupana sisters about ways to raise money for a new church.

"What, *Padre*? A new church? We can't afford that!"

"We can, actually. The church I used to be with in Naples was built with money raised by the community. I knew another one, too, in South Carolina. It took a long time, but we got it done. I checked with the diocese. At first, we just have to start raising money. We can take a special collection once a month for a building fund. We can also expand the carnival and use part of that money for the new church."

The carnival had been held for many years, but was mostly small rides and some small *puestos*, or booths. The sisters brightened as he continued.

"Maybe we'll get more people to come to the carnival if they know the money will be for a new church. We'll add big rides – lots of them. In November, we will sell advance tickets for rides after each Mass, ending one week before the carnival. The advance tickets will be cheaper than the tickets purchased at the carnival itself, and all the money from them will go to the building fund. One of you needs to coordinate the people, who will manage food booths. We can make a lot more money selling food if there are more rides, because more people will come. Let's have lots of different colors, bright primitive colors like they use in Mexico and Haiti in the booths. I want decorations everywhere that say who we are – a people of many different countries, all together as one."

As Richard added carnival expansion to its list of objectives, Sisters Jane and Marie continued work on the soup kitchen. On October 4, 1982, on the Feast day of St. Francis, its doors opened for the first time. Their mission statement read, "Guadalupe Center believes in the dignity of each person as created and loved by God, and is therefore committed to serve the disadvantaged poor of Immokalee with interim help and long term programs that promote self-sufficiency and social change."

Richard was pleased to see the Center's commitment to dignity evidenced by the volunteers. Poor people would come, sit at tables, and be served. If they wanted more food it was brought to them. For many, it was the first time they had been served in their lives.

Once it was operating smoothly, Richard walked over to talk to Sisters Jane and Marie about another idea. "I've been talking to a black woman named Mary Evans who lives here on the south side and makes food for the hungry. She even had a shelf put into her kitchen window to serve food to poor people. She also used to feed homeless people at the park at Thanksgiving. Maybe we could do a larger version, here, as a thank you to the farm workers?"

Jane sat down heavily, exhausted from cooking, serving and cleaning up that day. Marie smiled. "That's a great idea, Richard, but we can't have it here. The soup kitchen doesn't hold enough people at one time."

"What about if we set it up so they could eat on the church grounds?"

Jane shook her head. "Not enough tables. But there is the park. It's really set up perfectly for it."

Richard thought for a moment. The park Mary used, on Highway 29, had a building designed for serving large crowds, and plenty of cleared space and picnic tables.

"Let's do it," he said. "We can get volunteers to cook and serve. There are a lot of people who feel good about helping the poor, especially on holidays. It would be good for the workers and good for the people providing the food, too."

During the middle of the month, about an hour after the last Mass, the people who had attended *cursillo* got together at the home of Lucy and Talí Ortiz. Part of the *cursillo* message was to continue learning, reading and helping new people, so they had a social afternoon that would include a discussion about what they might do together in the future. About thirty people came; each person brought a covered dish plus some kind of raw meat. While the women set out the plates and arranged the covered dishes, Lucy's husband started the barbeque.

Padre Sanders arrived late as usual, but after he said the blessing, they all ate hungrily.

"Why don't we have the meeting every month?" suggested Lucy. "It will be a meeting of the *cursillistas!*"

Padre Sanders, however, expressed concern that this might become an elite group whose members felt superior because they had attended a *cursillo*.

"You can have a meeting," he told the group, "but if you're going to have this kind of social gathering, you cannot make it exclusive to *cursillistas*. You have to allow everybody to come."

They started discussing whether it was right to include people who had not done a *cursillo*. Were they being true to the movement if they did?

Slowly, *Padre* Sanders stood up and spoke in his firm voice that showed this was not a debatable issue.

"Either you will allow everyone to come, or you will have no meetings."

The monthly social gatherings from then on were announced in the church bulletin, and everyone was welcome.

The next Sunday he spotted Santos coming out of the church after Mass. "You're back!"

She smiled. "Yesterday. I had to get the kids in school."

"So was everything OK up north? How was the pickle picking?"

"Good *Padre*, but I'm really tired of field work. I feel like every year I turn into more of a prune!"

"Why don't you do something else?"

"Ah, my husband likes this work, and we make enough money to survive pretty well. I don't know what else I could do anyway. I don't know anything else."

"You could do a lot of things, but we'll talk more about that some other time. I wanted to mention to you that a few people are going over to Miami to a Charismatic Evangelization meeting next weekend. You might like it. Talk to Casto if you want to go."

After he changed into his *guayabera* and a pair of slacks, *Padre* Sanders walked back toward the church and saw some of the altar boys near the soup kitchen, running in a circle, playing a version of tag. The *Padre* ran with them for a minute but quickly got out of breath and had to stop. He thought to himself that Jesus probably played with the children in the towns he visited, but then He was younger, and undoubtedly in better shape.

"Tell us a story, *Padre*."

He smiled and nodded, walking with the boys to the grotto of Our Lady of Guadalupe. He sat on the stoop with his back to the statue and they sat down on the cement ground, facing him. He told them how Jesus said people had to be like children in order to get into heaven. Their bright smiling faces showed that they wanted to know more.

"One day after Jesus had become really popular and he had all sorts of followers, some people brought their children up to see Him, but His disciples told them to take the children away."

"Take them away? Why?"

"That's exactly what Jesus thought. The scripture says, 'But when Jesus saw them, he was indignant and said to them, 'Let the little children come to me, and do not hinder them, for of such is the kingdom of God.'"

"*Padre,* what's indignant?"

"It means annoyed or a little angry at something that isn't right. He felt it wasn't right to keep the children away. Then Jesus explained to them how important the children were: 'Amen I say to you, whoever does not accept the kingdom of God as a little child will not enter into it.' Then he put his arms around all the children and blessed them. That's how much the Lamb of God loved the children."

"*Padre,* what does it mean, 'Lamb of God'?"

"It comes from the old days when the people used to sacrifice a lamb as an offering to God. They would put the lamb on an altar and kill it, to please God."

"Oh, the poor lamb!" The boys did not understand this at all and the *Padre* agreed it was sad to kill a lamb. "But when Jesus came, they stopped doing that, and when He died on the cross, the people realized that Jesus was God's sacrifice of his own Son, for His people, to save all of us so we can be with Him in heaven."

The boys were silent for a minute, and Jose Dimas stared at him intently. "*Padre,* maybe you're the Lamb of God and we're your flock." The other children nodded.

Richard smiled, leaning forward. "I don't know if I'm good enough to be the Lamb of God, Jose, but *you* could be!"

The children smiled happily and *Padre* Sanders got up to go. Afterwards, one of their parents walked with him back to the rectory.

"I'm curious about how you explain complicated Bible stories to the children. Some of those stories are hard enough for us to understand."

He thought for a moment before answering.

"You know, for me it's easier to explain to the children than to adults, because the children believe. They are pushed by love, like the way they believe in their mother. They don't know why, but they trust their mother because they love her, and their love is stronger than the mind that takes over when you become an adult. That's why Jesus said, 'If you don't become like children, you can't understand me.' The children have the capacity... not really to understand, but to accept. That's why he said, 'Let the children come to me,' because the kingdom of God belongs to them."

A couple of weeks later he saw Santos and asked how she liked the Charismatic meeting in Miami.

"Have you come back waving your hands in the air shouting 'Praise Jesus'?"

"No, *Padre*," she laughed. "But it was a really moving experience. You know, I feel like I have been a 'sleeping Catholic' for all these years, and now I'm finally open. I swear I felt like a gush of water just washed over me!" She laughed again. "I called my father and mother and told them about it. My father said, "What, are you turning Protestant now?" And my brothers have started calling me '*hermana* Santos!'" Sister Santos!

Then Richard changed the subject. He had discussed something with Pat Stockton who thought it was a great idea, and he wanted Santos involved.

"So many of our people are here without papers, and I'd like to get a few people from the parish educated about immigration laws and maybe open an office here at the church to help the undocumented find ways to apply. We just need to learn more about how to do it."

"That's a great idea, *Padre*. Who would you send?"

"I'm not sure, but I'll let you know. You, of course, would be one."

"But, why not lawyers?"

"We'll have lawyers tell us what to do, but I want the people to help each other with this. I want to empower the people to do it."

Santos agreed and *Padre* Sanders lined up a few others to go to a meeting in West Palm Beach about immigration application procedures. Lucy Ortiz and Rosa would go too.

Unfortunately, what they learned would not help many of the undocumented immigrants in Immokalee as there was no way for most poor people to come legally. Richard sadly thought how ironic it was that the words on the Statue of Liberty, "Give me your tired, your poor," did not reflect the country's immigration policies at all. There was hope, however. A bill had been proposed by Congressman Mazzoli and Senator Simpson that would give some of the immigrants who had come illegally a chance to gain legal residency. Richard prayed that the bill would be successful and give many of his people a chance to remain in the United States without living in constant fear.

Early in November, 1982, he read Sister Eileen's monthly letter that always kept him in touch with the reality of Immokalee. This time she focused on the relationship between the weather, the crops and the workers. The freezes of the last two winters had set the farmers back financially, so many of them had planted smaller fall and winter crops this year, counting on a larger crop in the spring of 1983. That worked for them, but was disastrous for the workers who lived day to day on their wages.

Richard thought to himself that people often thought only about the economic implications of bad weather and did not understand the human costs. Workers had already returned from the north, expecting normal crops and the usual amount of work, but now many of them had no way to make money. What could he do to get Eileen more funding and volunteers, and more support for Jane and Marie in the soup kitchen? He prayed for ideas, but none came. Sadly, he realized he could not fix this situation; God, the sisters, volunteers and donors would have to take care of it.

One day one of the women who taught Catechism came to the rectory to see him about a completely different topic. She was concerned about the indigent people on the church grounds. Her husband taught Catechism too, and he was a member of the *Caballeros de Colón*, Knights of Columbus. Not wanting to criticize the *Padre*, she carefully broached the subject.

"People are talking, Father. They're talking about the fact that we have a whole bunch of drunken people and crazy people on the church grounds all the time."

He remained silent, looking at her gently, but with concern. He struggled himself with the alcoholics and prayed for the strength to love them, but still, he did not have the heart to send them away from the church grounds. And then there were the homeless who did not have substance-abuse problems. They were easy to care about. Where would they live? At least here they could feel a little safe. Maybe one day God would touch the alcoholics, too, and help them with their disease. At the same time, the woman made a good point as she continued.

"I'm concerned about the children. People say they don't dare take their kids to Catechism because there are all those drunken people around. They drink without worrying about anything because they know they can sleep here, on top of the picnic tables, everywhere."

"I'll try to think about how to deal with it," he said, with a weak smile. Parents could not be afraid for their children to be on the church grounds. "Thank you for telling me."

He did nothing at first, not having the heart to turn desperate people away. He would talk to some of the sisters to see if they had any thoughts. At a minimum, he thought, we need a homeless shelter in town where people could stay, at least for a little while. Finally, he hired a guard who would keep an eye on the people coming for activities and tell the homeless they had to find another place to sleep. He prayed they would find somewhere safe.

The religious training continued five evenings, one week per month as it had the previous year. These were happy times, filled with laughter and Richard's joy at the people's growing understanding of their faith. On the evening of the parable of the vineyard, Lucy Ortiz read the scripture about a man who hired workers at several different times during the day, paying them all the same. When the earlier workers complained, the man said, "Didst thou not agree with me for a denarius? Have I not a right to do as I choose?"

Chanito Urbina gave the introductory discussion, pointing out simply that he did not understand it.

"If I worked all day and then the grower gave somebody who worked a few hours the same pay, I wouldn't be too happy either. But then," he pointed out, smiling, "we get paid by the bucket so there's no way that could happen. Maybe they should have switched to piece-rates!"

Richard laughed and got them back to the point. "Here's what I want you to discuss. What did Jesus mean when the farmer in his story said, 'Didst though not agree with me for a denarius? Have I not a right to do as I choose?'"

"This is a hard one," said Lucy, who agreed with Chanito. "It doesn't seem fair."

"Think about it this way," suggested the *Padre*. "What if you were the ones who came late? You were waiting in the square for someone to hire you, but no one came until the afternoon to get you?"

One of the men shook his head. "I don't think it would be right for me to make more than the ones who worked all day, especially because the earlier workers were in the hot sun all day, and the late guys came in the afternoon when it was getting cooler."

The people broke into groups at the round tables, five or six to a table, discussing the meaning of this difficult parable. After they ate and talked, one person was selected by each table as a spokesperson.

Maricela, a Mexican woman just under five feet tall, stood up to give her group's answers. "When I was little..." she began.

Talí Ortiz leaned over to his wife and whispered loudly, "She still is!"

Everyone in the room started laughing. After a few minutes, Maricela finally was able to finish her group's consensus.

"We think that it's OK if God chooses to treat some people different from others. We just don't think it is right for the growers to do it!"

The group laughed again, and Richard suspected that the selection of this parable for a group of farm workers might have been a mistake. Most of them still had a problem with the late workers getting paid the same, and Richard realized that in today's world, he would agree with them. Frustrated, he blurted out, "Maybe the parable means God can do whatever He wants!"

That got their attention again, and he continued.

"What if, instead of a farmer it was God? God can do whatever He wants, and people can't always tell what's fair and what's not. Now, think of the workers as sinners and the money as heaven, wouldn't you think God should let someone into heaven if they had only been good for five years even if you had been good for fifty years?"

"*Sí, Padre*," they all murmured similar agreement.

"What about one year?"

The answers came more slowly. "I guess."

"What about five minutes?"

"Well, I don't know about five minutes," said one of the men. "I mean, anybody can do that when they're dying – be good for five minutes."

The *Padre* smiled and said again, "God can do whatever He wants. He'll decide."

Then Cristina spoke up. "Are all the parables going to be this hard?"

"No," Richard smiled again. "Although there are a few more that will take some figuring out."

Willow, the jokester in the group whom *Padre* Sanders particularly enjoyed, stood up.

"Maybe, *Padrecito*, we could leave those for the late spring, after I go up the road!"

In November, *Padre* Sanders buried an abused woman who was not as lucky as the others he had counseled. She was twenty-seven years old, killed by her husband with a gunshot to the head. Domestic violence was bad enough by itself, but far too often it led to death.

He started requiring extensive counseling sessions before he would agree to marry anyone and requested compatibility tests from the diocese. The first part asked about dates of sacraments, previous marriages, church attendance, emotional disorders, drug use and demographics. It even included a question about giving each other "the normal rights necessary to have children."

The couples came in together and then separately, and what he learned in the separate sessions often caused him the greatest concern. He went over questions on a second scored test about personal adjustment, interests, sexuality and activities, and then asked a few questions of his own, making notes as he listened.

- Don't respect other's wishes to pursue personal goals
- Do not share friends.
- Fiancé changes when he is drinking.
- Do anything to avoid an argument.

Saddened after several of these meetings, Richard discussed the situation with Miguel, who still visited often. "Miguel, they didn't even know each other. It almost makes me wish some of them would live together first. I bet half of them would never marry if they knew what they were getting into."

Miguel raised his eyebrows. "You sure do have some different ideas, for a priest!"

Richard sighed. "Yes, I know. I wouldn't say it to the people though. I just think it sometimes."

On Thanksgiving Day, 1982, the first "Thanksgiving-in-the-Park" was held to thank the farm workers for their labor. Five hundred dinners were served, including turkey, potatoes, corn, stuffing and gravy. *Padre* Sanders gave the blessing and happily walked among the people with their families, chatting with them as they ate.

"What is this, *Padre?*" They were asking about stuffing, which Richard tried to explain.

"What do we do with this gravy?"

"Do they have any salsa?"

Padre Sanders smiled. "I'll ask them to bring salsa next year."

"Oh, no, *Padre*. They have done so much already. Tell them that next year we'll bring the salsa."

Back at the church grounds, the people were making final preparations for the first night of the expanded carnival. Richard had contracted with a larger carnival company than previous years, so they would have more, larger and faster rides. Earlier that week, the *Padre* and the people had built food booths, laughing together as they worked. He bought paint in primary colors and helped paint the stalls bright red, blue and green. People brought serapes and shawls from their countries and hung them as decorations, too.

Suddenly Richard realized that he had been so excited about the new church that he was overly focused on making money. The carnival had to be fun for everyone, and there were many people in Immokalee who had no money for rides, games or even carnival food. They had to have *puestos*, small booths that were free for the children, including face painting and other low-cost activities. Richard ordered little plastic toys and set up a booth with a free fishing game. When the children dropped their line behind a board at the stall, a hidden worker would hook a small toy onto the line.

That evening, the *Padre* stood at the entrance, thinking about the new church while looking at the lights and the people smiling as they watched their children. He wanted to go on some of the rides but didn't want to do it alone.

Then he saw Sister Eileen.

"Will you go on the Ferris wheel with me?"

She shook her head, smiling. "Richard, you sound like a little child!"

He grinned and pleaded, "Please?"

"OK."

During the evening he talked to people he knew and laughed with the children as they waved to him from the kiddie rides. Then he noticed a familiar face.

"Adán! Adán Hernandez! What are you doing here? Where have you been?"

Richard had not seen Adán since Johns Island several years before. The two men shook hands warmly.

"I've been in South Carolina, *Padre*. I bought a farm up there. I just came down here to visit my family for Thanksgiving. I was gonna come and see you tomorrow."

Padre Sanders was surprised. "You bought a farm? How wonderful! How did you get the money for that?"

"I stole the money. I stole $250,000."

Padre Sanders frowned skeptically. "*¿Qué?*"

"I stole it from my family. Instead of buying things for them, I saved it. Sometimes when they needed new clothes or shoes, and I said, 'No, we don't have the money,' so I really did steal it from them. So I saved it all and now I have a farm up there on Johns Island."

Richard was relieved that the theft was a metaphor. "So is your family OK now that you are a big farmer?"

"*Sí, Padre*. They're fine. It's going well and someday I'm gonna buy them everything they want."

Then they talked about the carnival. "It looks good," said Adán.

"*Sí*, and hopefully soon we'll have enough money for a new church."

"A new church? You're serious?"

"I'm serious. We have already outgrown our church. We need more land, though. Do you know who owns that land over there?" He gestured to the south.

"Actually, I do. It's a guy who used to be a crew leader around here. He's up in South Carolina now, too. I'll talk to him if you want."

"*Sí*, Adán. Find out if he would sell it and how much he wants."

"But where are you gonna get the money?"

"It looks like we'll make about $10,000 from this carnival. That's a start. We can probably get some money from the diocese, and from donations."

"That's good money for the carnival – I'm surprised. You know, you could also use that land to have a bigger carnival. This one is too crowded. The streets are almost blocked off because of people parking all over the place, and a lot of them are charging to park at their houses. If you had the land you could have a bigger carnival and charge for parking too, and the money would go for the new church."

The following week, Richard sat in his office tallying up the proceeds, feeling good about the financial results. Later that evening Adán called. He had talked to the man who owned the property adjacent to the church grounds that Richard wanted for a new church.

"He said he needs $24,000."

Richard let out a quick breath. "That's a lot. Well, he'll probably take a little bit less, but I better start talking about it in the diocese."

Not long after, he requested a meeting with the bishop to ask him to approve the purchase of the property. He was thrilled when the answer was 'yes,' but there was a great deal more money to be raised. Trying to be optimistic, Richard thought that at least next year they would have the land and therefore expanded space for the carnival, for rides, food booths and parking. He prayed that the monthly building fund would help, too.

CHAPTER THIRTY-THREE — THEY MIGHT BE LONELY, OR SAD — 1983

Just after the New Year, 1983, Richard and Eileen had to go to a meeting at the Miami Archdiocese about social services for migrants. He had piles of mail that had not been opened in months, and asked to sit in the back so he could go through it while she drove. Besides, he got more tired these days and they would be coming back in the dark, so it was safer to have Eileen at the wheel.

As they drove, he chatted with her about the things he was opening.

"Uh oh, here's a Christmas card from one of my old parishioners in Columbia. It says, 'Dear Dick, We wondered if you received the check we sent to support your ministry in Immokalee. We sent it three months ago and it still hasn't cleared.'" He started shuffling through the piles of unopened envelopes. "I bet it's in here somewhere."

Eileen glanced back at him and raised her eyebrows, smiling.

"I think it's time you got a secretary."

She recommended Cristina Vazquez, one of the people Richard had been getting to know. Cristina and her husband Cande were involved in many parish activities. Eileen knew her from a year ago when Cristina was taking a class at a vocational-technical school in Naples.

"She was looking for someone to ride with because she only had an old car, and I was looking for someone to drive a van and take a number of others to the school, so I told her if she got a chauffeur's license she could use the van and take the other people too. She's responsible, hard working and nice to be around."

Richard thought about it and decided to talk with Cristina. Then he picked up another paper from one of the piles, Eileen's January letter, reading it aloud to her.

> One of my most memorable moments this Christmas occurred when we took toys to a family living in a shack. There was such a sparkle in Dianna's eye as she said, 'Did Santa really leave these for us?' The Lord has his ways of sending His love.

He remembered the smiles on the faces of children in Union Heights when they received toys, years ago. "You know what we need, Eileen?"

Eileen smiled, "More help and more money!"

"*Sí*, but we need a toy program that will reach many more people. We should be getting more toys from people in Naples, Bonita and Ft. Myers, and distributing them at the parish hall before Christmas. We did it in another place where I worked. Here, though, maybe parents could register ahead of time and select one or two toys for each child."

The following Sunday *Padre* Sanders remembered Eileen's suggestion that he get a secretary. He stopped Cristina Vazquez after Mass. "Cristina, Rosa told me you used to work in the rectory."

"I was the housekeeper for Father Henderson and Father Singleton when they lived in a trailer behind the church. Then I went to school. Right now I'm studying to be a Certified Nursing Assistant."

Richard was disappointed. "Are you going to work at a hospital?"

"No, I just want to maybe work in a doctor's office, weigh people and take blood pressures. I'm not strong enough to work with really sick people. I'm too sentimental. If I see them suffering I might start crying and scare them."

Richard laughed. "I have a different idea, and you won't scare anybody. Why don't you come to work as my secretary?"

Cristina frowned. "*Padre*, I don't have skills for that."

"No problem," he assured her. "We'll learn it together. Sister Eileen recommended you. She thought you would do a great job."

"OK, *Padre*, I guess I could try it."

At that moment her husband came up behind them and the *Padre* smiled.

"I think it's good," said Cande, surprised. He thought for a minute about the extra money and also that his wife did not have to drive to Naples anymore. "Actually, that would be great."

Cristina would have a desk in the front room of the rectory, just as people walked in the door. She picked up the job quickly.

Her daughter came every day after Kindergarten, one of the brightest spots in *Padre* Sanders' days. Lupita was a sweet little girl who seemed unaware of how beautiful she was as she smiled and followed him around, laughing. He loved having her in the office. She brought drawings and little projects she had done at school, which the *Padre* inspected and admired. Then he and Lupita would sneak over to her mother's desk and arrange them there while Cristina pretended to be engrossed in her typing. After they slunk quietly away, Cristina would look up and express surprise at the things her daughter had made.

Lupita also sat at the kitchen table and helped Rosa make ham and cheese sandwiches with mayonnaise for the *Padre* to give out when the soup kitchen was closed.

One day he asked, with a twinkle in his eye, "Lupita, did you ever work in the fields?"

The little girl nodded confidently. "*Sí, Padre.*"

Cristina overheard and laughed. "We used to take her but she spent most of her time hiding under the truck!"

One day Richard stopped over to see Rob Williams, an attorney with Florida Rural Legal Services, something he had been neglecting. He had not learned much about farm worker organizing because he was so focused on pastoral activities with his people, but he knew he needed to get involved with it. Rob explained what had happened in the past with attempts to organize the workers.

"There was someone here in 1977, named Juan Velazquez, from Chicago. He was a great guy and there were beginnings of meetings and discussions about what to do. It never got very far, though. Really one of the most helpful things came about not because of organizers, but from the workers themselves, people who never went to a meeting, who just did their jobs."

"*Cuéntame.*" Tell me.

"Back in January, 1977, there was a crew of workers that included Cande and Cristina Vazquez and their extended family. These were the bedrock, people who didn't complain, that were not whiners, that had the respect of everybody. They were working for some really despicable growers out by Devil's Garden, picking bell peppers. The growers did this deal where they adjusted the piece rate up or down depending on how the picking was going, so the workers could never get ahead. So the crew decided one day that they weren't going to take it and they sat down and refused to work; there were about thirty-five of them. The grower ordered them out of the field and they came to our offices and got one of the attorneys here to go with them, and went back to the field to negotiate. That's when the grower and his guys pulled out guns, held them all hostage and then had them arrested."

"Arrested? For not working?"

"No. For trespassing. I'll tell you, their arrest really sent a ripple through the town. Like I said, they were a stand-up crew that worked hard and never complained. It had such a big impact because the other workers said, 'If *that* crew got arrested, anyone can get arrested.'"

Richard nodded. He had no idea Cristina and Cande had this kind of strength.

"It quickly built into a general strike in Immokalee. It only lasted a week because there was a disastrous freeze that destroyed everything. It couldn't have been sustained anyway because it wasn't organized. There was no planning, no support. It was just an impromptu, wildcat kind of strike. The freeze gave the farm workers a way out and the growers lost a lot of money."

"Did it end up helping the cause of the workers?"

"It did. The next year the growers raised the piece work rate. Little reverberations from that '77 thing are still going on."

"Well, we ought to get something like that going again. Maybe I can help."

The next day he talked to his secretary. "One of these days soon, Cristina, I would like to get Cande involved with labor organizing. We should be doing something here at the church."

Cristina thought for a moment. The *Padre* told her where he got the idea.

"I heard about the strike you were in, in 1977."

She nodded her head seriously. "Cande would be good at organizing."

When he discussed the idea with Cande, however, he was resistant. "I can't do it, *Padre*. I don't have the time and I'm not educated enough or anything to do that. I don't even speak English good enough."

Richard tried arguing that he would get him a secretary but Cande had a busy job that he really liked, and a family to support. He was adamant that he couldn't add a thing to his responsibilities, though it pained him to refuse the *Padre*. Richard understood. He and Cande were becoming good friends and he didn't want to pressure him. Labor Organizing would be added to the ever-growing list of things he wanted to get started.

Each Sunday *Padre* Sanders noted more new people in the parish, from different countries, and the stress on their weary faces. He prayed about ways to make them feel welcome, and one Sunday he offered a suggestion at Mass.

"At the Sign of Peace, greet everyone around you, not just those next to you. Who knows, they might be lonely, or sad."

He walked around and shook the hand of everyone, too, especially people he had not seen before. Beginning at the front of the altar, he went up one side, down the middle, then up the other side and down the middle again. The people followed his example, greeting everyone. Because it took a long time, the choir would sing two or three songs. It gave the *Padre* an even greater sense of belonging and he really felt it was important to have all his people wishing each other, "*La Paz del Señor esté con ustedes.*" The peace of Christ be with you.

After Mass, Santos Ramirez waited for him. He saw her rarely now, only on Sundays and occasionally for meetings.

"I want to tell you, *Padre*," she began. "That was *una idea buena*, to give the kiss of peace to everyone. *Creo que les gustaría.* I saw some new people *sonriendo.*"

He laughed at how Santos, like many others in Immokalee, spoke two languages at the same time. "I was wondering about your kids, when you migrate. How do you make up for the education they miss?"

"Oh, I never take them until school is out. The places we work we have already built relationships with the farmers, so we don't have to take the kids until school is done."

"But in the fall, you're not done with the apples in time for school, are you?"

"No. When we're gonna come late, now that the boys are older, we send them back ahead of us. But I'm not gonna let the girls come down alone. When they get old enough, I won't go anymore. I will not let my girls be by themselves over here, with all these two-legged alligators around!"

The comment caught Richard off guard and he laughed out loud. "I couldn't agree more!"

There were many other children, however, whose parents were not willing or able to do what Santos did, and those children suffered in school. Richard remembered the drop-out rate of 68 percent that he had read not long ago. That summer he talked with Sisters Jane and Marie about adding tutoring to Guadalupe Center's services. They would put something in place soon.

Cristina Vazquez learned her job well as parish secretary and *Padre* Sanders was pleased. She answered the phone, sold Mass cards and entered sacraments into the records. Her typing was slow but passable, not too important because Father Sanders rarely wrote letters or reports. He did not make appointments, either, so when people called, Cristina would just tell them to come over. Whenever anyone came, he would see them.

One day she told him that Cande had asked her about the *Padre*'s habits and hobbies.

Richard smiled. "What did you tell him?"

"I said I think your hobby is people, because that's what you do most of the time. A lot of times if nobody comes to the rectory for a while, you go to visit somebody."

The *Padre* laughed. "I think you're right. Maybe I should go visit someone right now. No, wait. Lupita will be here soon from school. I would rather see her than anyone!"

Party at the home of Cande and Cristina Vasquez

Later that afternoon, one of the men came in to tell him he had just learned there were Guatemalans living out in *El Jardin de Diablo*, Devil's Garden, about forty-five minutes east of Immokalee. Richard had been reading about the increasing violence in Guatemala's Northwest Highlands and was not surprised that some of the Mayan people ended up in Southwest Florida. He asked Rob Williams about it.

"In January," Rob explained, "a farm worker organizer named Fernando Rangel told me there were some Guatemalans living out there, in a labor camp in an orange grove. He said they were scared and wanted to talk to a lawyer. There are about thirty-five of them. At almost exactly the same time that I got to know them, another one of our attorneys found fifty more over by Indiantown."

"Are they here legally?"

"No. That's why they're scared."

He explained that they came from the northwest highlands in Guatemala where the government was persecuting Mayan Indians. A group of rebels fighting the government had evolved over the years, but most of the indigenous people were just caught in the middle. Thousands were being killed, "disappeared" or displaced from their homes. The government was constantly accusing the Mayas of working with the guerillas and created impossible rules for the villages: the people could only be outside their homes at certain times, they were limited on how much they could work and even how much food they could carry with them. The guerillas were sometimes just as bad. They would come and try to get the Mayas to join them, and when the people refused, the guerillas assumed they are working with the government. Many of them escaped to Mexico, worked there for a while, and then heard about the need for labor in the United States.

"So I said, these guys are refugees obviously," continued Rob. "They ought to apply for political asylum. But nobody was helping them."

"Do they speak Spanish?"

Rob explained that they picked up some Spanish coming through Mexico, but among themselves they spoke their Mayan language, Kanjobal. There were different dialects in the areas where they live in Guatemala. The general area was named Huehuetenengo but they referred to it as 'Huehue,' pronounced "way-way."

"We were fortunate in finding an anthropologist who knew of a guy named Geronimo Campeseco who was from Jacaltenango which is right next door to where these people were from, and he spoke a similar language."

Richard located Geronimo who was able to take him to Devil's Garden the next afternoon. They drove through some of the most beautiful yet isolated agricultural lands he had seen. When they arrived at the labor camp, Richard looked around. It was exactly as Rob had described it: a bunch of wooden shacks in an orange grove, next to a polluted canal.

After about an hour the Guatemalans appeared, walking through a group of trees that separated the camp from the gladiola fields. Richard noted how they looked different from the Mexicans in the parish. They were smaller than most of the Mexican people and had straight thick black hair. Geronimo introduced him to Pedro Lopez and Francisco Jose. Pedro's wife stood behind him without speaking, but Francisco's wife, Enriquetta, stood and talked with them; she spoke Spanish because she was from Mexico. Francisco had met her there after he left Guatemala.

Richard asked how they were treated. Not well, it turned out. They told him the big boss man lived in Ft. Myers. He had his own big plane and was a good boss.

"The supervisor who lives here is a real problem, though. He makes us work ten hours a day every day, even if it's raining. But we do much better here than at home. We make $3.25 an hour here. In Guatemala we made $.25 each day."

Then *Padre* Sanders asked about their faith. They were Catholic, but were not practicing their faith except personally. They had no transportation and were afraid to go into Immokalee in any case, because they had no papers. Richard said he would get a bus if Geronimo would pick them up once a week and bring them in for Mass. Geronimo said yes and also suggested they take them to the grocery store at the same time. When Geronimo explained in their Mayan language, the group of isolated people nodded gratefully. The women had tears in their eyes, moved by the fact that someone would care that much about them. They would be ready.

Geronimo suggested a book that had just been released in Spanish that the *Padre* should read if he wanted to understand these people and what they had lived through. It was called *Me Llamo Rigoberta Menchú Y Así Me Nació La Concienca. My Name is Rigoberta Menchu and This is how my Conscience was Born.* Richard ordered a copy through a bookstore in Naples and when it arrived, read it eagerly. It was simply and beautifully written by an anthropologist who interviewed Rigoberta. The first part of the book gave a clear picture of the prejudice and oppression the Mayan people had lived under for centuries since the Spanish conquest, and the intense poverty of their lives. The book then described the recent horrors that the people in Devil's Garden had experienced. Soldiers, looking for guerilla fighters, came to villages, stole or destroyed all the Mayas' food and crops and burned homes. The men were kidnapped, tortured and left for dead. Sometimes the men left the villages before the troops came, thinking the soldiers would not harm the women, but the women then took the beatings. Most of the time, the villagers were not involved with the guerillas in the first place. They were caught in the middle of a deadly political game.

As Richard got to know them, he found the Mayas to be gentle, peaceful people. Pedro, Andres and Francisco shared stories of the fear they had lived through and the sadness they felt when they left their families. They, like the thousands of immigrants who had come to the United States, only wanted to work and live in peace.

He thought about learning Kanjobal but it was very different from any languages he knew, and he found some of the sounds impossible to pronounce. They could follow the Mass in Spanish, and when they came to confession he let them speak in Kanjobal even though he didn't understand it. It was God who was listening, after all, wasn't it?

The following week was cold, and Richard again noticed many people in the streets, shivering in tee-shirts or light cotton shirts. He brought it up at a staff meeting, focused on Sister Eileen.

"People need warm clothes. I'm wondering if that's something you could add to your services, Eileen."

Her look told him it was not a good idea. "Richard, we're barely handling the work we have. If we add another service like that, it could overwhelm us. Besides, there's no room. I don't have space for the people who come now."

"Maybe Jane and Marie could take it on."

Soon, Guadalupe Center added a clothing distribution service. A volunteer named Martha Beckman took charge of the "Immokalee Boutique," working in an old trailer that was brought onto the property where she collected, sorted and distributed donated clothing. The clothing room was open on Mondays, Wednesdays and Fridays. On the days it was closed, people who donated would leave bags of clothes at the rectory/office. *Padre* Sanders kept some of the clothes there all the time, for people who came when the clothing room was not open. He would talk with the people while Cristina looked for things that would fit them.

In late March, Richard wrote a letter asking for building funds for more space to help the poor. It was still "season" in Naples, with many wealthy part-time northern residents there who stayed until April 15th. Hopefully, his plea would help bring in funds for more space for the clothing room and soup kitchen, and more office space for Eileen's organization for offices and meeting rooms.

Late that night he had just fallen asleep when Fanoly woke him. "There's a Mexican guy knocking on my window, looking for you."

"OK, tell him to come around," Richard said, sleepily.

Then the man knocked on his window. "*¡Padre, levántete por favor!*" Get up, please!

"*Sí, sí, vayas a la puerta de enfrente. Yo vengo ahorita.*" Go around to the front. I'm coming right away.

Richard put on his robe and opened the door. He recognized the man from church but did not know his name.

"*Padre*, I got a problem at home. It's a big problem. I need you to come to talk with me and my wife. Well, she's not really my wife, but the mother of my children, and I love her."

Richard got dressed and left. He followed Pablo to a small rundown trailer not far away and found his partner, Maria, sitting at a table. Four children lay on a mattress on the other side of the room. Pablo turned to him, helpless.

"*Padre*, she says she's leaving in the morning. She's gonna take the kids and go back to Mexico!"

"I will and you can't stop me." The woman seemed frightened, yet determined.

"*Cálmate*," said Richard softly to all of them. Be calm. "Let's just talk about this."

"*Padre*," said Maria, "He has a green card but I do not, and neither do the two older children." She motioned to a boy and girl about nine or ten years old. "We brought them with us when I came, across the border, across the desert. We were happy here, my husband working very hard, but now *la migra*, Immigration, I keep hearing about the raids. I'm afraid they will come and take me and the older children but the younger kids will stay here. I can't lose my children! I'm going home to Mexico where I don't have nothing but at least I don't have to be afraid."

"I don't want to lose my children, either, *mi amor*," pleaded Pablo.

"Then you come with me," she said, stubbornly.

Pablo looked desperately at the priest. "*Padre*, I can't make any money in Mexico. The kids won't be able to go to school there, nothing."

"*Sí*, but I can't do nothing here," said Maria, suddenly sounding panicked. Richard was confused and looked at Pablo again.

"Why don't you just get married? Then you could apply for her as your wife."

"Well, that's not possible."

The woman glared at the father of her children as he explained.

"I was married before in Mexico and I already applied for that woman to come here.... before I met Maria, *Padre, verdad*, really."

This was more complicated than Richard had first imagined. They spent the entire night talking through options but came up with no answers. Finally the *Padre* convinced Maria to stay in the United States, at least for a little while.

"I know it's hard, but it's the best thing for your children. Here at least they will have decent food and a place to sleep, and they can go to school. I am working on some things at the parish that maybe will be able help you. I promise we will figure out something."

As he drove home he wondered if what he told her might ever come true. There had to be a change in the immigration rules of the country, especially since the workers were needed here. Tomorrow he would talk to an immigration attorney for her. Then he realized it was already tomorrow. Fanoly and Casto were up and getting ready for the day.

"You just getting back from that guy last night?" asked Fanoly, incredulously.

"*Wi, Fanoly. Li te-gen gwo problém.*" He had a big problem. "We worked through it, though."

"You have to say Mass in a little while."

"I know," Richard said wearily. "Can you wake me in a half hour? I just need to rest a little."

Later that day he lay on the couch and listened to the Spanish television's news coverage of Pope John Paul II's recent visit to Central America. The pope's stated purpose for the trip was to consolidate a strong church that was guided by the Gospel message "as traditionally understood." Richard remembered the words of another pope who started the Second Vatican Council and gave the Church back to the people, words that spoke to Brother Robert so many years ago. "It is not the Gospel that changes; it is we who are beginning to understand it better."

The current pope also said he was deeply concerned over "new church movements" in Central America, especially the base communities that led people to take part in political movements. He repeatedly warned against the dangers of what he called the "popular church."

Richard shook his head. He wouldn't change anything he was doing in Immokalee. There was too much need and his people were just becoming empowered to help themselves.

He cheered up when Cristina announced that she was pregnant with her third child. *Padre* Sanders was as happy as she was

"We're hoping for a boy and we're gonna name him Candelario, Jr. He'll be Cande, too."

Richard grinned, thinking of the diminutive form of Cande.

"I bet he'll be 'Candito' for quite some time!"

The next day he worked up a letter he would soon give to his people who migrated, listing several people along the migrant stream whom they could call if they needed help. It included Father Frank Hanley in Charleston, Sister Ellen Robertson at Camp St. Mary's, and a priest he knew in Michigan, Father Dick Notter. That should at cover some of the places they go, he thought, satisfied.

Unfortunately, his mood would not last long. Though he was used to the ups and downs of this life, there were times when the good could not outweigh the bad.

CHAPTER THIRTY-FOUR –
SAVE US, FOR WE ARE LOST – 1983

"*Padre*! Immigration took some of our people! *La migra*, Immigration agents, went right into the tomato fields close to town."

"How many?"

"A couple of busloads."

Richard was confused. Immigration was supposedly not allowed on private property. "You're sure?"

"*Claro*, sure. I checked it out, like you taught us."

"Go and get on the radio and tell the people to stay in their homes. I'll go to the stockade."

When he got there, one of the crew bosses told him that thirty of his parishioners had been taken. Richard went in but learned there was nothing he could do for any of them. He gave some money to a few that he knew, but didn't have enough for all of them. Dejected, he returned to the rectory and a woman called to tell him about the raid.

"I know," he said. "How did you get away?"

"Somebody told our crew boss that *la migra* was here so he took us all home on a back road. I came into the house and stayed here."

"Good," said the priest.

"*Sí Padre,* but then my friend told me they took my sister. They went with her to the school and picked up her two kids, too. What's gonna happen?"

"They'll take them to Krome, the detention station over by Miami, and then back to Mexico. I gave your sister a little money for food for the children."

"Can I even go see her to say goodbye?"

"No, it's too dangerous. They'll get you, too."

The woman came to the rectory a few days later. "My sister called. After Krome, they took them in a bus and just dropped them off at the border. *Padre*, our family lives far to the south, and my sister had no money except for what you gave her. *Gracias a Dios* another family on the bus gave her enough to get home."

"*Sí, gracias a Dios.*"

A few days later he sat quietly in his office, reading. It had been a tough two weeks, with the raid and then the death of a one-year-old crushed by a dresser he tried to climb. Then a baby boy died in a fire caused by faulty electricity, in one of Immokalee's many rundown trailers.

We have to do something about housing, he thought, sadly. He was grateful that Habitat for Humanity had come to Immokalee and had built several houses already, but the only decent rental housing was nearby Farmworker Village. Much more was needed.

"I need to hire someone to work on housing," he thought, shaking his head. "There's got to be a way to get funds for it." Soon he would forget about housing, however.

Cristina tapped on the door and peered in. "There is someone to see you."

José Luis, one of the men he recognized but did not know well, came in behind her, staring down at the floor as he turned his cowboy hat nervously in his hands.

"There has been a fight," he said, breathing heavily. "In the fields."

Padre Sanders looked at him blankly. "There are lots of fights in the fields. Why are you telling me this?"

"One of them was a Haitian. I think his name is Toussaint," said José Luis, pronouncing the name badly. "A young guy, like twenty-two or something. From this church. He just came from Haiti."

Richard stroked his beard and frowned as he listened.

Jose Luis spoke rapidly. "We were picking tomatoes out at Keri Farms late this afternoon. You know how we're assigned rows, and there's someone on the other side of the row opposite us, and we're both picking and supposed to only pick on our side? The Haitian was on one side of the row and the Mexican was on the other."

Padre Sanders could visualize it.

"Well, this Mexican guy was picking through and taking the tomatoes from the side of the Haitian guy – you know how we do that sometimes, especially when there's somebody new who doesn't know the tricks, right? I mean, the Haitian guy couldn't make any money like that because this Mexican guy took all the tomatoes that were his to pick." Juan Luis hesitated, more nervous every minute.

"Go on," said the priest, still puzzled and beginning to feel concerned.

"Well with Mexicans once they figure it out they say 'fuck you' – oh, excuse me *Padre*, I'm sorry – but something like that, right? And then you just keep working and everything is OK."

"Right," said Richard, warily.

"But you know sometimes the Haitians take all that so seriously, standing up for themselves like they do, right?"

"*Sí*," said the priest, losing patience. He understood why Toussaint would feel he had to do something. In Haiti, if they didn't stand up for themselves, they could lose everything. "*¡Cuéntame!*" he said, firmly. "Tell me what happened!"

"OK, so *Padre*, the Haitian guy pulled up a tomato stake and started hitting the Mexican with it. Then somebody said, '*¡Defiéndete!* Defend yourself!' So the Mexican guy pulled out his knife, you know how we carry knives in our belts, so he took it out and was stabbing the Haitian. The Mexican was bleeding so bad he went to the hospital. But *Padre* – the Haitian guy... the Haitian guy is dead!"

Richard's jaw dropped. "Dead? Dead! Why didn't somebody take the stake out of his hands? Why didn't somebody stop the guy with the knife? Why didn't somebody stop them both?"

His eyes were fiery yet filled with sadness, and his voice was agitated. He made a fist with his right hand, brought it to his lips and then set it back down on the desk, sighing heavily.

"You have to do something! You have to do something and not just watch – not just wait for the worst thing to happen!"

He turned and looked out the window and Juan Luis hastily left, closing the door behind him. Brother Robert knelt and prayed, hearing the voices of the monks at Mepkin.

We Cry Out to You, Oh, Lord. Save us, for we are lost.

Each day he slipped more into a serious depression, feeling worse than he had during his last year at the abbey. He knew the heart pills he was taking had depressive side effects and, without consulting his doctor, discontinued them. He had not had any problems since that one heart attack in Indiana and he had too much happening right now to risk being depressed again.

A few days later he drove to St. Margaret's in Clewiston to a meeting of the Rural Life Bureau. He looked forward to being in the company of priests, sisters and laypeople who worked in parishes similar to his own. He would not share details of his grief with them, but he would feel comforted just being with others who struggled with similar challenges. It was a three-hour drive, and he worked at lightening his mood as he looked at the scenery.

He tried to think back to his joy on Easter, the celebration of the reality of the resurrected Christ, the redemption of all people. In the meantime, however, so much had happened. Then he thought about the upcoming *Cinco de Mayo* celebration and his discussion with Cristina.

"But Cristina," he had said when she first brought up the idea, "I've always been told that's more of an American holiday than it is in Mexico."

"Not where I'm from," she had assured him. "Where I come from it's a big *fiesta*. There's an arena in the town of Chamaquaro, Guanajuato, where my mom grew up. They start on May 3rd until the 5th of May and they have big processions, dancing, food, everything! The sad thing, though, is that the people who migrate only go back to Mexico for a while, and they leave after that celebration. For a little while the town survives on the money they brought with them but when they go back to the U.S., the town goes dark and it's sad again."

"Well, let's celebrate it here in Immokalee, and we won't be sad. You sing, *sí?*"

"I sing in a band and they could play for us. Lupita dances. We have a beautiful costume for her."

He was feeling happier now, just thinking about it. "OK," he had told Cristina. "We'll make a big party for *Cinco de Mayo*. We can set up a stage outside at the back of the church. We'll put up decorations and have a *piñata* and music and *comidas auténticas de Méjico*." Authentic Mexican food.

He smiled, looking forward to it as he pulled into Clewiston, a sugar town on the southwest side of Lake Okeechobee. A railroad ran through the town to transport raw sugar cane, loaded by huge crane-like machines that straddled the tracks. Richard wished he had the time to wait for the next load so he could see it work.

The talk at the meeting was about the training of catechumens, people of other faiths wishing to convert to Catholicism, but Richard had trouble paying attention. He wished today's topic had more to do with how to deal with social challenges faced by the priests in migrant parishes. Still, being in the company of others who worked in environments similar to his own made him feel better. By the time he headed home he was more peaceful than he had been on the way over, and thanked God for the spectacular setting sun that blinded yet mesmerized him with its beauty. He drove into it all the way to Labelle, watching it sink into the horizon just as he turned south toward Immokalee.

That afternoon he remembered that the funeral of the young Haitian man would take place Monday. As Richard thought again about the tragedy of this death, the happiness he had regained slipped away. Since the killing, *Pe* Sanders had learned more about the young man. Toussaint had come here recently to join his parents and knew nothing about how things were done in the fields. Richard began to feel responsible, thinking that he should organize some training to explain to new people how things worked. Fanoly might have a suggestion.

At Sunday Mass the following morning, *Padre* Sanders spoke softly, but his grief over the incident was still evident. Most of the people had heard what was upsetting him.

"We all come here for the same reason," he began, softly. "Here in Immokalee we have Americans, we have Haitians, we have Mexicans, we have Guatemalans, we have Whites, and we have Blacks, everyone together. All everyone wants when they come here is peace and a place to work and make a better life."

He paused, feeling desperate again. How could he get this message across?

"We have to love each other. It is difficult sometimes, but we have to try. Remember Zacharia, 7:10, 'Let none of you imagine evil against his brother in your heart.' Never forget it." Then he repeated the words for emphasis. "Never imagine evil against your brothers or sisters. But there's more to it than that. We also have to help each other when there is anger, or violence. When you see something happening, you have to stop people who are hurting each other."

His emotions started to overwhelm him and his voice trailed off as he looked out at the people he loved, so moved he was unable to finish. Sister Octavia took over as he sank heavily into the chair behind the altar.

"We believe in one God, the Father Almighty....."

Gerald Darbouze was in town that weekend and could stay an extra day for the funeral. *Pe* Sanders was relieved. This family deserved genuine sentiment in their own language and, although Richard could speak Haitian Creole, he could not have conveyed what he truly felt, in their language.

He was surprised at how loudly the family and friends grieved at the funeral Mass. They wailed and sobbed until they could barely stand up, then rested briefly and started all over again. *Padre* Sanders prayed for the soul of Toussaint and for the life of the Mexican man who was in jail, charged with second-degree murder. Both had come here with dreams for a bright future in which they could live and work in peace. It would take weeks for Richard to recover from his grief.

He felt a little better by *Cinco de Mayo*, when parishioners from many countries all came to the celebration at the church. The *Padre* was as delighted as his people were, watching Lupita dance and Cristina sing with the band, dressed in Mexican costumes with black, beaded sombreros.

Still somewhat shaken by the fight in the fields, he decided to make a retreat to Mepkin. He would not visit anyone this trip; just the thought of being at Mepkin was so welcoming that he sped up in his hurry to get there. He got there in mid-May. His previous brothers, noting his obvious unhappiness, welcomed him as if he had never been gone and he spent five days with them in silence. For a brief time it was as if he had never left. He prayed about something he had not considered in a long time – his decision to leave the abbey. He knew the stress from his work could not be good for his heart, and thought perhaps it was time to recede into the peace and obscurity he often missed. Maybe it was time to come back.

Remembering Martin Luther King, he decided to write his own eulogy to help sort out his thinking, but found he could not write about a monk who went into the world to help and then returned to finish his life in the monastery. He could only see himself as a priest who worked with, lived among and loved the migrants. He could only imagine being remembered through their eyes, as he wrote in his spiritual diary.

> I would like my people to remember me as their priest... who was
> a real part of the parish, who helped the people to come alive and
> grow in their lives, to develop in their ministries within the Church,
> to feel God's presence with them.

Almost immediately after he wrote the words, the questioning stopped and he settled back into being on retreat again. The week at Mepkin rejuvenated his spirit and his body. It was good that he went; he would need the strength, to deal with coming events.

Back in Immokalee, in early June, Richard was talking with Fanoly in his room when Cristina interrupted him.

"*Padre!* There are people here to see you – a lot of people. They're upset. More are lining up outside and I see more coming, out in the street."

He got up immediately and saw several people in her office. One of the men stepped forward. "*Padre*, you know how we keep our money at Fred's Barn?"

"*Sí*," said the priest, warily.

Fred's Barn had been functioning like a bank on behalf of the farm workers who could not get to banks during regular hours. Before Fred's Barn offered the service, the workers often carried hundreds of dollars in cash until they paid their rent, water and electric bills, and then got wire transfers to send money to their families at home. The store was strategically located where the buses picked up and dropped off the workers, opening early and closing late to accommodate their schedules. The workers did not earn interest on the deposits there, but it was safer than carrying cash around. Fred's Barn also acted as a post office. That way, the workers would spend their money in the store, deposit their money and pick up their mail. They had even added a teller window, like a bank's. Richard had always viewed it as a useful service.

"*Padre*, I went to get some money out and they said they don't have our money! *Padre*, I have to go north in a few days, but all our money was in that store. I can't even pay for gas to get to South Carolina!"

Richard told those who were waiting outside the rectory that he would be back, and drove over there. A huge crowd had gathered outside the store.

"*Padre! Pe!* They took our money! All our money is there and they locked the doors and we can't get in!"

Rob Williams and a new volunteer attorney named Sister Maureen Kelleher watched as the crowd grew more agitated, and soon the Sheriff's Deputies were called to keep order. The people clamored around, telling them how much money they had at that store, showing their receipts for it. The Naples Daily News would report the following week that the field workers lost a total of $300,000. When the store closed that day, it had $1,000 in cash on hand. The owners were later charged and convicted of money laundering.

When he got back to the rectory, Cristina told *Padre* Sanders that she had just talked to her husband.

"I didn't even know," she said sadly. "I was just calling Cande about what happened and he said 'Yeah, Cristina, I know. I have to tell you something – I had four hundred dollars in there.'" Cristina looked at the *Padre* with exasperation. "Four hundred dollars! Every day after he got paid he would put ten, fifteen dollars, whatever, in there, maybe just put in five, but always something. What some other man would spend on beer, Cande saved, to take us to Mexico. Now it's gone."

Just then the phone rang; it was a reporter from the Miami Herald, wanting to do a story. They would be over in two hours. Richard hung up the phone and asked Eileen to come and join him for the interview. Before they arrived, they discussed the possibilities.

"If this gets in the paper, maybe people will be moved to send money to help replace what was lost," he suggested.

"You're right. But we should think about the name of our organization. It would probably confuse people if we ask checks to be sent to 'Our Lady of Guadalupe St. Vincent de Paul Society.'"

"How about Guadalupe Social Services?"

"Done," said Eileen. "I'll get the legal and accounting changes started."

The story in the Miami Herald was picked up by major newspapers all over the country. A few days later Eileen called the rectory. "You need to come over and see this."

She showed him the bag of mail that had come in – hundreds of letters containing donations. People touched by the story sent money, and Sister Eileen's newly-named organization coordinated replacing some of the lost money. Every day more letters came and the newspapers continued to cover the story. About a week later, Dan Rather, who had done a documentary on Florida farm workers in 1970, sent a representative who interviewed Eileen for the CBS News. They held the interview in the soup kitchen, with 2,500 letters piled on the table in front of her. It was not enough to replace all the workers' savings, but they each got at least part of their money back. The total was over $95,000.

Richard studied more about the Guatemalans, feeling guilty that he had not incorporated them more into the parish. He stopped over to see Rob Williams but was greeted instead by Sister Maureen Kelleher. They had met a few times at church, meetings or parties but had not talked much. Maureen had gotten involved with the Guatemalans in Devil's Garden, and she told him what she knew.

"I first met them after Rob and his wife were already working with them. They are living in terrible conditions, with really bad diets. Did you notice Francisco's hair? It's long, reddish black, but it's not supposed to have red in it. I think it's from poor nutrition."

She told him that their baby, Marta, had been sick in the hospital for weeks. Sister Maureen was certain it was caused by the conditions at the camp. "We have to get them into town, into better places to live." It reminded Richard that he still needed to hire someone to address housing needs.

He asked Maureen how much she knew about what was happening in Guatemala. "Some. I was in law school in Washington D.C. and went to a U.S. Catholic Mission group meeting about it. Rigoberta Menchú was there."

"Really? I just read her book."

"She told us about such unbelievable atrocities, yet she was so soft-spoken that listening to her was like a sacred moment. Then I did a project in which I gathered documentation on the Guatemalan death squads and massacres, to help those filing for political asylum."

"So what do you do here, now?"

"I'm here as a volunteer this summer but I'm quite sure I'll be back. I've spent most of the time putting in long hours, trying to keep up with Rob, preparing political asylum applications. The people have told me about the Guatemalan army's machine gun strafing and aerial bombings of Mayan villages, and killings by not only the government but the guerillas. The Mayas are getting hit from both sides, as you know."

Richard nodded. He would have kept talking but the tone of her voice told him she was getting anxious to get back to work. He had just one final question.

"Did you ever think of working in Guatemala?"

She smiled. "I thought about it, but when I heard about the nuns who were killed in El Salvador, I decided I'm not ready to die." Then she paused thoughtfully. "I guess I'm too much of a coward."

Richard smiled with her. "Me too. We can help them here, though."

"Right on," said Maureen. She flashed him a peace sign with her index and middle fingers. He returned it, then drove back to the rectory.

CHAPTER THIRTY-FIVE –
LOVE ONE ANOTHER – 1983

In spite of the recent, mostly sad events, Richard started to feel better and could focus again on joyful experiences. In late July, Cristina reminded him that his birthday was coming up.

"Will you come to our house for your party?"

He frowned, realizing that he would turn forty-six, but then smiled, thinking of how Cristina's house was so warm and happy, always filled with people. "*Sí*, Cristina, I would like that."

That Friday, he arrived late as usual. It was hot and muggy and they sat outside on the steps after dinner. Slowly and with great ceremony, little Lupita presented him with a present. He gave her a big hug and then effusively admired the wrapping.

"*¡Qué bonita!*" he exclaimed, to her delight. How beautiful!

As he opened it he continued to make excited sounds and Lupita laughed and helped with the unwrapping. The present was a light blue guayabera with white stitching.

"Oh, *perfecto*," he said, smiling broadly at Lupita, who was beaming. "I love it!"

Richard prayed a short, silent prayer in gratitude for the warm and caring people who had become his friends.

Sister Eileen's July 30th letter contained bad news about large numbers of their people who had gone north but come back sooner than expected because of mistreatment. One family lost most of the money they made, working for an unscrupulous crew leader. Others returned from North Carolina because their whole families were making only eight dollars a day picking lemons. Haitians came back after being made to sleep in barns and fed nothing more than a steady diet of beans; the farmer who hired them beat them when they didn't work fast enough. Why wasn't anyone policing these farmers? Richard wondered. He knew the growers weren't all like that, but also knew that someone ought to be protecting the workers from the bad ones.

In the end of July *Padre* Sanders celebrated seven baptisms, including the first Guatemalan to be baptized at Our Lady of Guadalupe. He was from one of the families that lived out in Devil's Garden.

That week, Sister Jane came over from the soup kitchen to discuss something they had talked about briefly a few months back; helping the migrant students with tutoring.

"We figure we can use high school students as tutors," she said, "and maybe get some scholarship monies to give them in return."

"Great idea," smiled Richard. He was impressed with the work of all the sisters in the parish, and how willing they were to step up to new programs.

In late August he organized a trip to Busch Gardens. Everyone had been working too hard, and they all deserved a vacation day. The sisters, altar boys and Lucy Ortiz went with him. He told the Guadalupana sisters to wear regular clothes instead of their habits.

Busch Gardens was one of Richard's favorite places. He rode on the roller coasters with the older altar boys, and then insisted that they all get his favorite water ride, a train of logs that led to a water slide.

"OK," he directed. "Two people get in front and two in back of each log."

"But we'll get soaking wet!" protested the sisters.

"That's why I told you not to wear your habits. We'll get wet! It's a hot day and we'll dry soon enough. I don't want the adults just sitting here while the kids have all the fun. I want us to play together!"

Reluctantly, they all went on the ride. *Padre* Sanders got on the front of the first log with Sister Octavia and Lucy and one of the altar boys straddled the back. Richard couldn't stop laughing the whole time.

Later, though, he got so tired that he had to rest. He sat on a bench and told the others to go on. "Come back for me in a half hour, OK?"

It seemed he had just closed his eyes when a hand gently shook his shoulder. "*Padre,* we're back."

He looked up groggily, still sitting up, and shook himself awake. "OK, what ride do we go on next?"

The following Monday morning, Sister Eileen came to discuss his request for additional staff. She had drafted a letter requesting two part-time and a few full-time volunteers who could live and work in Immokalee. Guadalupe Social Services would support them with four hundred dollars per month for room and board. Those volunteers would help with interviews, administration, home visits, meetings, working with other agencies and fund raising. Another would work on issues in the community. She and Richard had already discussed the duties, and he liked her summary of the goals: better and cheaper housing, a way to address spousal abuse, public transportation, adult education, protection for school children and increased jobs.

"Yes," he nodded. "And let's do something to clean up all these empty overgrown lots. They're full of refuse and rats, and are perfect lairs for muggers who attack people walking by. We really need someone who can get the people involved in solving the problems."

Eileen smiled. That was in the next document – someone to do community organizing to help people learn how to help themselves and each other. This would involve things like organizing co-ops, especially food co-ops, neighborhood watch, voter registration, developing community and civic leadership, pride and involvement.

"It should be a necessary part of charity and justice," said Eileen.

"Amen," said Richard.

On September 28, *Padre* Sanders held Our Lady of Guadalupe's first Feast Day of Saint Michael the Archangel for the Guatemalans. A priest came over from Indiantown to celebrate the Mass in Kanjobal. The Guatemalans were overwhelmed with emotion that this church, in a country they did not know, would celebrate the feast day of their beloved saint. Richard sat watching them, feeling the same way and noting the beautiful job they had done, decorating the church with multi-colored cloths, the patterns of which were specific to their town. The *Padre* and the Guadalupana sisters had organized a party for after the Mass, in front of the soup kitchen, where they served soft drinks and *tamales*. All the Mayas from the Devil's Garden camps attended and contributed what little money they could, for the *fiesta*.

After the Mass, Richard talked to the priest from Indiantown. "So St. Michael was the patron of Guatemala?"

"No, although that's a natural assumption," replied the Kanjobal-speaking priest. "In the Highland areas, each town celebrates the feast day of the saint after which it was named. Most of the Guatemalans here in Immokalee came from *San Miguel Acatán*. That's why they celebrate St. Michael."

Richard was happy that the Mayas finally seemed to feel like they were a regular part of Our Lady of Guadalupe Church. He sat back, smiling, listening to the marimba music and watching the people.

On Friday, Cristina reminded him that she might not be there on Monday. "The doctor said the baby could come any time."

Padre Sanders had figured he would be hearing these words soon, based on Cristina's appearance. He told her to not even think about work, just focus on the beautiful child she would bring into the world.

Sunday night, Cande called. "*Padre!* Candelario Vazquez, Jr. has been born!"

That afternoon, after the Sunday masses, Richard drove to Naples Hospital to see them. The baby was beautiful and the delivery had gone smoothly. She and Cande beamed at their son.

"*Demos gracias a Dios*, let us give thanks to God," prayed Father Sanders as he blessed the baby. "*En el nombre del Padre y del Hijo y del Espíritu Santo. Amén.*"

When Cristina offered the baby up to him to hold, he backed away and shook his head. "No, I don't think so. He's a little small for me just yet!"

Two weeks later, Cristina came to the office and gasped when she saw the papers piled up all over her desk. *Padre* Sanders laughed, embarrassed, when he saw her reaction.

"We really miss you."

She smiled with a mock exasperated look. "OK, I am ready to come back to work but first I have to find someone I can trust to take care of my baby."

"No, no, no," said the *Padre*. He had still been feeling depressed and wanted her back as soon as possible, and he knew the presence of the baby would make him happy.

"You're going to keep a playpen here and bring him to work with you. Candito is going to bring us life!"

A month later, Richard could tell by the attendance at Mass that most of the migrants were back. Now there were so many that his prediction about overcrowding had come true. Many of them stood or kneeled out in the parking lot, listening to the masses through the speakers. He thought about adding a sixth weekend Mass, but did not think he would have the energy to say one more plus the increasing numbers of sacraments and people coming to him for help. We really need the new church, he thought to himself, trying to come up with additional ways to raise money.

The religious training continued, five nights per week, one week per month. One evening, the discussion centered on the story of the Good Samaritan. *Padre* Sanders explained the scripture.

"A man was going down from Jerusalem to Jericho and he fell into the hands of thieves, and they left him half dead, lying there. Three men passed by. One was a priest who saw the man but didn't do anything. He just kept walking. He saw the reality, but he didn't change it. And then a Levite passed by, someone who followed all the rules of the church, but he didn't do anything either. In the end it was the Samaritan, a sinner, who helped the man."

Later *Padre* Sanders prayed in his room, remembering his own words about the parable of the Good Samaritan. "He saw the reality but he didn't change it." How often did he do that himself, right now, today, here in Immokalee? How many things did he see that were wrong, unjust, unfair?

How many people lived in rundown housing where fires killed little children and people were abused and cheated out of their money, or where they had no water or electricity because they could not pay their bills? Far too often, he realized, he, like the priest and the Levite, accepted the reality and did nothing to change it. He prayed into the night about how to get more accomplished and he was unable to sleep. His pulse raced and his heart, he knew, was beating way too fast.

But as the year drew to a close, he brightened. There had been progress since he'd arrived, he reminded himself, and more was in the works. He moved with hope into another holiday season and a successful carnival that would help build the new church.

The peace he felt would not last, however. In early December a fire raged through the Immokalee Apartments. Richard was not surprised when the fire department later determined it was caused by faulty wiring. Sister Eileen's office was now crowded with seventy-four people who were homeless. The Red Cross helped them with temporary housing, but they had lost all their belongings. Eileen told him about one of the men whose family of six was burned out.

"He said, 'I'm sad, but not too sad. We lost everything. Things aren't important. I worked hard, sweated, and bought most of our things new. But we can get more things. Things are not important. We know that all we really need is Jesus.'"

Richard's faith in the compassionate Jesus grew, just by living among these people.

To add to the problems of the people left homeless, other housing options in town, trailers, apartments and labor camps of small single-room buildings, suddenly became more expensive. Richard went to talk to one of the owners, feigning understanding as he struggled to comprehend how anyone could exploit the poor that way.

He spoke as if they were on the same side. "Father, you know how it is. These people come here and I rent them one apartment for a family of five. Then, I go to check on things and they have two or three families living there. They fill up the sewers and make a mess of the inside. They don't know how to use the stoves and they leave food out that rots and ruins the counters. So I started charging by the head. And rents go up all the time. That's part of life."

He tried to appeal to the man by explaining how little they earned. "Maybe if you lowered the rents a little, they could afford to live there by themselves."

"Forget it. If I lowered the rents they'd move even more people in."

Richard shook his head and left, thinking of Jesus' instructions to his disciples to shake the dust from their feet. Someday he would figure out a way to get more decent and affordable housing built.

On Christmas night, temperatures dipped to 27 degrees for over six hours, killing the vegetable crops and even the citrus. Thousands of people were now out of work and, except for a lucky few involved in cleanup, would remain that way until the spring crop. Most of them would stay in Immokalee. There was no work anywhere else, either.

"We need to get working on job programs for times when there is no work in the fields," he told his staff in their biweekly meeting. "They're poor but not ignorant or incapable of learning. We need to put something together to empower them to help themselves."

"There is a guy," said one of the sisters. "He comes to the church grounds looking for men who are looking for work."

"Tell him I'd like to meet him," said the *Padre*.

Not long after Cristina came in and told him that the man who hired people was over at the grotto, talking to a bunch of guys, so Richard walked over. As he approached, he noted that the man was reading aloud from a clipboard, describing jobs.

"We need five guys for landscaping, three to do construction labor and someone to work in an office. You have to have secretarial skills for that one." The man looked around at the group of men gathered there and went back to discussing the landscaping and construction jobs.

Richard introduced himself and congratulated him on his work.

"*Gracias, Padre*," said the heavy-set man. "I feel lucky to be able to do work to help the people."

"So do you find the jobs, too?"

"Our office does. One person works with the employers and I get the workers. If there are jobs available I offer them and make sure they get the training they need. Sometimes we even arrange transportation."

Richard smiled as he thought of Stanford Williams who used to do the same thing for the people of Union Heights. He knew there should be much more of this type of coordination, and that the church should involved, but he couldn't do everything.

"Blessings on your work," he said. "Call me if you need help; I'll support you any way I can."

He walked back to the rectory, looking forward to a Christmas visit to Staten Island with his family. Once again, he needed the rest.

When he returned from Staten Island, his people were still trying to recover from the Christmas freeze. One of its results was that the lack of work made men feel inadequate to take care of their families, and the women felt angry about their positions in life. Some of the men just took off and did not return; others took their frustrations out in violence toward their wives.

Cristina told him that, while he was gone, one of their parishioners had been killed by her husband. The woman had gone to a shelter in Ft. Myers but left her children behind because he had never hurt the children, and a neighbor said she would look in on them. When the woman went back, apparently thinking he would be reasonable, he was more insane than the last time they fought. Outside, her mother and sisters heard yelling, and then there was a shotgun blast. She staggered out the door, holding her stomach with her hands, and fell to the ground. As the mother and sister screamed, the husband came out, fired at his wife again and hit one of her sisters. Then he stood over his wife and shot her twice more.

As Richard tried to come up with the words he would use to console the family of this woman at her funeral, he found himself short of breath and weak. He lay down on his bed for a few minutes, trying to regain his strength.

"Stress," he sighed, remembering his father's high blood pressure and his own doctor's advice. He would rest more, starting right now. He could work on the funeral sermon in the morning. Soon, however, a knock at the door woke him and he got up to talk to yet another farm worker who had come to him for help.

Later that week, Sister Eileen came over to the rectory to visit. She looked tired.

"Eileen, I see the line of people all the way outside your office and around the corner of the building now. This freeze is hitting everyone so hard. How are you holding up?"

"Fine, but we both know these short-term 'fixes' are not the solution. Rather than providing food and shelter, or maybe in addition to... we really have start focusing on training, education, and better laws and wages."

"Of course," he nodded. "Hopefully the job program will help some. Do you have any ideas about how to approach lobbying?"

She sighed. "I'm afraid the task is more difficult than the theory."

"*Sí, hermana*," he said. "But I agree our compassion should go in that direction. Have you gotten the money that was promised by the state?"

"No, not yet." She shook her head. "The bureaucracy continues to amaze me. There are real people out here with real needs. It doesn't help someone who is hungry to know that money that could help them is tied up in paperwork."

Richard could tell she needed to talk.

"We have so many families whose utilities have been cut off, too. Talk about the poor being penalized for being poor! There is a $25 fee to reconnect electricity, and if it's cut off too many times, the electric company charges an additional $80 deposit. Water reconnection costs $5 the first time, $7.50 if it happens twice, $10 the third time, etc. The people never get a chance to break out of the constant fee cycle."

"Go back to your earlier thought, Eileen. Let's you and I both figure out a way to provide training, education, legislation and organization for better wages. That would eliminate many of these problems in the first place, because the people would be able to save money to tide them over from problems like the freezes. We need paid staff, not volunteers. We'll figure out a way to get the money for their salaries."

Later that day Cynthia Garcia, the volunteer teacher of the English-speaking Youth Group, came to the rectory with a different problem. She was apprehensive about telling him.

"Father Sanders, I want to quit. If there is an outing or some fun event, we have thirty or forty kids. But for our weekly meeting, it takes me a lot of time to prepare, and sometimes only three or four show up."

"Cynthia, please reconsider. The kids have to know they have a place that they belong to. If only one comes, be happy that that one showed up. They have to have a place where they can go, where they know someone will be there for them."

He closed his eyes for a moment, understanding her position and hoping she understood his. When he opened them again Cynthia was staring at him intently, as if she had seen a ghost.

"What is it?"

"*Padre*, for a minute there I felt like I was in the presence of Jesus. Instead of you, Jesus was there, calming me with His peace and serenity."

"Hmmm," he smiled softly, remembering a similar incident with Yolanda. "Well, Jesus is around here all the time, so I wouldn't be surprised if you saw Him. You probably brought Him in here, in your beautiful soul."

Cynthia smiled, sighed and shook her head.

"OK, I'll keep teaching them."

Chapter Thirty-Six – Night of Peace – 1984

One morning just after New Years, Eileen came over with a proposal to staff a "Social Issues Advocate Department." She sat patiently as he read the objectives they had discussed.

> Housing – monitor and report landlord/tenant abuses... organize
> community workshops, working with Florida Rural Legal
> Services, to educate the community about landlord/tenant rights.
> Voting – develop workshops to educate citizens about issues
> to be voted upon, and offer registration at convenient times and
> places.
> Jobs – Assemble a clearing house for jobs available in
> surrounding communities.

The description also included "keeping informed on issues, monitoring local community boards, getting to know legislators and their positions, bringing issues to the attention of the public and working with other advocates."

"It sounds good," he said, handing the paper back. Then she showed him something else she had prepared, "An Introduction to Immokalee," that would be sent to people interested in the positions she had described. In it she talked about Immokalee's 25 packing houses and the main crops of tomatoes, cucumbers, bell peppers and watermelons. The population was now 14,000 full-time residents and 27,000 in the winter growing season, including about 4,200 Haitians. Then Richard read a statistic he had not seen: "The life expectancy of the farm worker is 49 years."

"We just got that number," said Eileen. She read aloud from the document: 'By the time they reach that age they suffer from arthritis, bronchitis, asthma or tuberculosis. The average farm worker is more than three times as likely to die from pneumonia and flu, and four times more likely to die from tuberculosis than the average American. Alcoholism and mental illness plague this population and many suffer from pesticide poisoning.'"

Richard didn't have to hear more. "Get someone to fill the jobs. We'll find the money."

"I have someone in mind, a sister from my order named Barbara Pfarr. I know her. I talked to her a few weeks back and she's interested. She also found two other people from Milwaukee that she recommends, a man and wife, John Witchger and his wife Maria Teresa Gaston. John would be the Social Issues Advocate and Maria Teresa the Bookkeeper. They speak Spanish and she has worked as a Hispanic Youth Ministry Coordinator. John also has done investigative journalism."

"That could come in handy," said Richard, thinking of the many areas of exploitation that could use publicity.

"They're all interested but have to finish up things they're doing now." She handed him three resumes. "They'll be here in May for an interview."

"Good," nodded Richard. "The interview isn't necessary if you think they're right for the job, but I'll look forward to meeting them."

Richard was excited about these positions being filled. Many more of the things he had wanted to get done would be possible with additional staff.

Not long after, Archbishop McCarthy came to lay his hands on the newly-graduated *Misioneros Católicos* in a Mass of Sending Forth. Sixty-one had been trained, more than any other parish in the entire archdiocese. It was thanks to the efforts of *"las maestras,"* six teachers, including Richard's old friend Yolanda Wohl, Pat Stockton from the Rural Life Bureau and Lucy Ortiz. They were presented with flowers at the ceremony. Lucy would be the contact person in Immokalee when the migrants were up the road.

It was a beautiful ceremony in three languages with hundreds of people present. *Padre* Sanders assisted as the bishop offered the Mass, joyful for the people who would receive this certification. Fanoly, one of the recipients, accompanied the choir on a tambour drum. At the presentation of the gifts, the Haitians approached the altar dancing to the rhythms of their country, bearing all good things the land had yielded: vegetables and fruits from the fields around Immokalee.

After the Gospel reading, *Padre* Sanders addressed the people. "*Hace dos años...* Two years ago a group of brothers and sisters from our parish community expressed publicly their desire to form themselves to prepare to better serve God and the community... Today I feel very happy to present this group of men and women that want to respond to the Lord and make a commitment within their church to be *Misioneros Católicos.*"

He called the names of the candidates who came forward to stand in a circle around the archbishop who spoke to the congregation.

"*El Señor Jesús nos envió...* The Lord Jesus has sent us to be His witness in all the world. I feel great joy to see so many members of this community saying 'yes' to the Lord."

He then asked questions about the people's readiness to proclaim God's word wherever they found themselves, to which the group responded, "*¡Sí, estamos!*" Yes, we are!

The archbishop laid his hands on each head and presented them all with a certificate and a signature card to identify them as *Misioneros Católicos* of the Archdiocese of Miami.

"Now," said *Padre* Sanders after the ceremony, "whenever you are on the migrant stream, you can present your credentials and offer to help at local Masses." At the end of the service, the people sang *Somos un Pueblo que Camina.* We are a People Moving Forward.

A Hispanic Catholic publication called *La Voz* carried an article about the ceremony and *Padre* Sanders brought it to the group. It quoted one of the group members as saying that as the Archbishop laid his hands on her head, she forgot everything else that happened in the Mass.

"For me to be a *Misionera Católica* is like a great present from God, something which I would never have dreamed of...It is not a celebration to dress up like in my best clothes, but rather a celebration of my spirit."

Santos was excited that she was quoted, too. "Because we migrate every year, I always felt insecure, like I walked on shaky ground. Now with the card of the *Misioneras* I'm walking on firm ground."

Padre Sanders loved the way Santos used metaphors, probably without even knowing she did it. The group was thrilled with the article and they understood the value of the certification.

Soon work started up again in the fields around Immokalee. Relieved, the *Padre* said prayers of thanks and Cristina was elated that her husband was taking his crews back into the fields. Sister Eileen reported that, within days, the number of people who needed her help was cut in half.

On Palm Sunday they again held the annual passion play. This year, Lolo's now-girlfriend Esmeralda helped in the background, creating flats for scenery and costumes for the players. Richard enjoyed seeing how happy they were together. The play was again beautiful and moving. Richard was sure this was something they would continue, year after year.

Watching the congregation's emotional response to the play gave him an idea for another performance that would involve the people in the reality of Christ's life and passion. He decided to try it privately with a small group. If it went as well as he hoped, they would do it for the whole congregation next year.

The next day, Monday, he contacted several people who worked closely with the parish who had not been involved with the passion play. The group of adults included Olivia and Chanito Urbina and their son, Javier, Rosa, Fanoly, Casto and a few others. They came in the early evening for a meeting.

"This year, before the traditional Holy Thursday washing of the feet we will have a Seder, so you can actually envision Jesus in his last hours with his Disciples and understand how the Eucharist began. This will not be a play for the whole parish, but rather an experiment with only thirteen people. We'll start at 5:00 p.m. Afterwards, we will all go over to the church for the Holy Thursday Mass."

"But *Padre*, what about supper?"

"This celebration *is* supper. It is a Jewish Seder, a custom the Jewish people still observe."

They looked confused, until he reminded them that Jesus was a Jew. They looked around at each other, intrigued with this idea.

"We'll need a few volunteers to make the food for the Seder, according to the Jewish customs." He went over a list of items.

Sisters Octavia and Aida offered to bring brisket cooked with horse radish. Rosa said she would bring baked fish, parsley, celery and salt water, and one of the other women agreed to make the potato and vegetable kugel. Olivia offered to make matzah bread.

When she scanned the recipe, she looked up, surprised. "It's like a taco!"

Father Sanders laughed at the comparison. "*Sí*, Olivia, I had not thought of that. It is like a taco – no yeast!"

On Holy Thursday at noon, Father Sanders skipped the Bishop's luncheon for the priests and instead took his own staff out to a restaurant in Immokalee.

Holy Thursday lunch in Immokalee

As they chatted before the meal was served, Lucy asked a question. "*Padre,* I think we used to call this 'Maundy Thursday.' What does it mean, 'Maundy'?"

"Maundy comes from the Latin word '*Mandatum.*' It is the first of the most important words Jesus ever spoke, from the Gospel of John: '*Mandatum novum do vobis.*' A new commandment I give unto you, that you love one another as I have loved you.'"

He paused and looked intently at each one in turn, as if realizing for the first time how much they meant to him. He felt immense love, but also sadness. Noticing a change in him, no one spoke for a few minutes. Then the *Padre* said grace, ending enthusiastically with, "*Vamonos a comer!* Let's eat!"

Later that afternoon, he met with a few people who came to the rectory, took a short nap and he went to the soup kitchen. The people who were taking part had arrived early to decorate and were dressed up as if they were going out to dinner. As he watched them hang green paper on the walls and cover the table with a white tablecloth, he started to explain the Last Supper.

"But *Padre,*" asked Olivia's son. "Didn't the Jews kill Jesus?" Several of the adults seemed to have the same question.

"No," said *Padre* Sanders, shaking his head. "Many people think that, and it has brought terrible persecution to the Jews. Really, though, almost all the people were Jews then – Jews or Romans. Jesus died, not because of the Jews, but to fulfill His destiny and the scriptures. The pope even made a proclamation about twenty years ago that the Jews are not to be blamed."

"So now tell us more about Jesus' Seder."

"It started out like other Seders, symbolizing the story of the Jews when they were driven out of Egypt and went with Moses as their leader into the desert. Did any of you ever see the movie, The Ten Commandments?"

Most of them had.

"That's why the Jewish people have a Passover ceremony – so they remember the journey out of Egypt and how they suffered. In Seders today the Jewish people also remember the holocaust, when millions of their people were killed by Nazis."

"Is that really true, *Padre*?"

"*Sí*, it's true," said Richard, sadly. Then he got back to the Seder.

"The food we will eat represents different parts of what the Jews experienced coming out of Egypt." He looked specifically at Olivia. "The matzah is made without yeast to commemorate the hasty departure of the Jews from Egypt. The Seder is a remembrance of the exodus, bondage, struggle and freedom of the Jewish people, reenacted through this meal. Jesus did exactly what the Jews did, but it wasn't the remembrance of the Jewish event. Our Mass reenacts the Christ event and is the remembrance of Jesus' life, death and resurrection.

When everything was ready, Richard passed out cards with written prayers. They would celebrate the Passover Seder the way Jesus had done with his disciples – the Seder that became Jesus' Last Supper.

Padre Sanders was pleased with the enthusiasm of the participants and how their understanding of Jesus' sacrifice seemed to grow in the process. Next year they would have this ceremony in front of the people, the way they did the passion play.

On Easter Sunday, *Padre* Sanders felt redeemed through the resurrected Christ, and his hopeful mood was restored. The following week, however, John Brister called. They had their first Guatemalan death, a man killed in a farm accident. It was not one of the people Richard knew but he was aware that other Guatemalans had been coming to Immokalee.

"We contacted the family in Guatemala and they want the body sent home. We're going to have to find some money for that, Father. Guatemala is a lot farther away than Mexico. I called the funeral director over in Indiantown and he told me that these people live way up in the mountains where sometimes a car can't get through. With the funeral he performed, a vehicle carried the coffin as far as it could go and the people met them and carried the body the rest of the way."

Richard felt for the parents who would be waiting in their mountain village in Guatemala. The Guatemalans came to this country to escape violence and death, yet this man met his death here, through a tragic accident.

In the area of staffing, however, they were making progress. The three people Eileen had found to fill the jobs she and Richard had created to empower the people came to Immokalee in May. They spent two days, mostly with Eileen. Sister Barbara Pfarr, John Witchger and Maria Teresa Gaston were perfect for the positions. They shared Richard's and Eileen's ideas and had great energy. He also liked them personally, and looked forward to having them as friends.

They would start in August and focus entirely on training and empowering the people to take control and improve their own living and working conditions. Their positions also included getting government funding to improve the available housing.

He asked Eileen, "You got the grants for their salaries?"

"I'm afraid not," said Eileen.

"How are we going to pay them?"

"We're taking a giant leap of faith. I'm sending out a letter to our donors to explain the situation, and hopefully they, or their churches, will help us come up with the money."

The following weekend was Memorial Day and Richard was excited because Yolanda was coming over with her husband and children to spend the weekend. Richard looked forward to spending time with them at the beach. He rarely got there anymore. By the time Saturday came, however, it was pouring rain. He was so disappointed that Yolanda insisted they go to the beach anyway, and by the time they got to Vanderbilt Beach, the rain had stopped. Again, Richard was too embarrassed by his appearance and too tired to swim, but he enjoyed watching them in the Gulf of Mexico.

At Vanderbilt Beach with Yolanda and Ron Wohl and family

A week later, he drove up to South Carolina to check on his people working at Johns Island. He found Santos and asked how his reference letters had worked out.

"Perfect, *Padre*. We worked down there at Beaufort for a couple of weeks. In the *barracas*, there were not enough mattresses and sheets and pillows, so we looked at the letter you gave us and called Sister Ellen. She helped us, loaned us some beds and bedding."

He wished he had time to stop and see Ellen but he was anxious to get to Mepkin. He spent four full days there, needing the rest, both physically and emotionally. In his meditations, he realized he had never been happier, or sadder, at any time in his life, than he was in Immokalee. The ups and downs of it led to deep depressions and great joy, yet too much of it was stressful. This time he realized how tired he was and how much he missed the peace of the contemplative life. But when he lay down to sleep, Our Lady of Guadalupe and his people called him back.

In early July, Father Mike Murphy called to tell him that the long-rumored Archdiocesan split had finally taken place. Immokalee would now belong to a new diocese, the Diocese of Venice, and Bishop John Nevins would lead it.

Late that summer, the three people Richard and Eileen had waited for came with a vision to challenge unjust structures and empower people to help themselves. Guadalupe Social Services became more involved in the "politics of social conscience." Their vision was that of Sister Eileen and *Padre* Sanders, to challenge unjust structures, identify concerns of people in the community and to support and empower them to solve the problems themselves.

Sister Barbara Pfarr, John Witchger and Maria Teresa Gaston met with Father Sanders to discuss the greatest needs of the community. It had been a long day but he filled them in on one of the needs that bothered him most – housing.

"One of the things I want you to do, John, is relate to the county government and cover county meetings, especially those about housing. I get so tired of hearing about our people taking their little savings and buying mobile homes. The ones they buy are old to begin with, so they devalue every year. We have to get more decent yet affordable homes and apartments built."

Several weeks later, Richard walked over to the trailer where they worked with Sister Eileen. He had just heard about a Community Development Block Grant meeting in Naples and wanted John to attend to see if some of the money could be allocated to Immokalee.

"We could use it for housing for low-income workers," Richard explained, handing John the keys to the church van. "I don't know if anyone from Immokalee has ever gone before the committee that decides how those funds will be spent, and I'd like you to go tonight."

"Sure, I'll go."

"Not just you. I've lined up some from the Haitian community who will meet you in front of the church tonight at 6:00. Two of them speak English pretty well. Take them to the meeting and let them do the talking."

At the Collier County Commissioners' meeting, John listened, impressed, as Celestine Pierre translated the proceedings for the other Haitians. Near the end of the meeting, Celestine raised his hand and stood to explain the crowded conditions and expensive and substandard housing they were living in.

"We need housing. We live in places that don't even have plumbing," he told the committee. John was impressed when Celestine quoted numbers from the 1980 census. "Twenty percent of the apartments and trailers on the south side don't even have running water."

Committee members politely nodded, but said there was nothing they could do. "You already have Farm Worker Village, and this new grant has already been allocated in other areas of the county. Come back next year and try again."

Two from the committee, Ed Oates and Denise Coleman, however, were sympathetic. After the meeting, they came over to talk to the Immokalee group and explained that the money went only to nonprofit entities and organizations that had strict accounting procedures.

"Look, form a corporation and we'll give you some of the money next year, as long as you have the capability of building the housing."

Their disappointment made the hour-long trip back to Immokalee seem twice as long as usual. John dropped the Haitians off at their trailers and one-room apartments and went to the rectory. Richard shook his head, exasperated, as he heard what had happened.

"Don't they know the conditions so many of our people are living in? John, you're going to have to start going to the County Commission meetings regularly. Figure out who the players are and how to bring the county to some accountability for the living conditions out here."

On weekends, Richard looked out at the throngs of people attending masses and noticed that the church was looking as old and tired as he was. He talked to a group of men from the parish and they spent the following Friday and Saturday painting the interior. Richard, one of the tallest, painted the ceiling from the top of a stepladder. When it was done, he looked around happily. "The house of God has been made beautiful again. The next time we paint, may it be in the new church."

Photo courtesy of John Witchger

Barbara and John started addressing in other issues Richard had had on a list for a long time, plus more. They organized voter education groups, took vanloads of farm workers to Washington DC to advocate for national field sanitation laws and drove to Tallahassee to push to include field workers under benefit laws.

"Those laws protect other kinds of workers," Richard had explained. "They just don't apply to farm workers."

Sister Barbara also got involved in trying to find people jobs that would be alternatives to field work. As far as Richard knew, there was only that one man who coordinated workers and people looking for workers, so he encouraged her. But Barbara did not have hopeful news about the likelihood of many of them leaving the fields.

"I got some funding not long ago to train a promising young guy to learn telephone cable work. He had a wife and several children, and it was a great opportunity. Still, he could not move out of the farm worker culture. His whole extended family was in it, everyone he knew. He couldn't handle the change and feeling so different from them, so he ended up going back to the fields."

Disappointed in that story's ending, Richard sighed, "Well, keep trying."

He saw Lucy Ortiz that weekend and asked how things went over the summer for the *Misioneros Católicos*.

"You know I never heard from anyone over the summer, but the people say they were not well received at churches up north. No pastor allowed them to serve in any manner, only to attend the Mass."

Padre Sanders was deeply disappointed. He had high hopes for that training.

"I think the biggest problem might be the language, as most of the masses up north are in English, of course" explained Lucy. "I think maybe our people still have self-esteem issues related to their ethnicity and language skills. They probably just said 'OK' when the pastors turn them down."

Richard nodded, remembering the prejudice he saw in white churches in South Carolina. Apparently, things hadn't changed.

That Thanksgiving weekend, *Padre* Sanders walked around the carnival and parishioners came up to say hello. He ran into Cynthia, who still ran the English youth group, and Santos. Richard talked them into going on several of the more exciting rides, laughing with them at the exhilaration. Then he told them excitedly about the new church.

"I'm getting some plans from the diocese, from the architects, on Monday," he told them. "Wait until you see them!"

He showed them where the new church would be built and how big it would be. "I can't wait to see the design. I asked that it be built in a circle, so the people are all around the altar. That way everyone can see the Host and be part of the Mass, plus they can see each other. It will be perfect for making the Mass a celebration of all of us."

Cynthia laughed nervously. "That's gonna be too expensive. We don't supply enough money for that!"

"Oh, ye of little faith," he teased. "We need a new church and God will provide it. We already have the land and we'll continue to raise money, including the proceeds of this carnival and the monthly building fund collection."

On December 7, 1984, Richard sat in the living room reading the Diocese of Venice's newspaper. The article, by Jo Opitz, headlined "Immokalee Parish Reaches Out to Needy." He was quoted in it.

> (Father Sanders) said that the migrants are "on the move more
> or less all of the time, and suffer the hardships of inadequate
> housing, poor living conditions and unsteady work. They
> are poorly paid and have little or no legal protection or fringe
> benefits."

The article talked about Guadalupe Social Services and the Guadalupe Center soup kitchen that was serving at least 250 people every day, plus the hundreds of boxes of food distributed before Thanksgiving and Christmas. It also mentioned leadership forums related to community activities, educational opportunities and the work Richard and his staff had started to get a Vocational-Technical Center in Immokalee that would be part of the Collier County Public School system. The end of the article included a plea for contributions of food, clothing, blankets and toys. It also had a photo of *Padre* Sanders in front of the church and another with Sisters Jane and Marie and two of Eileen's volunteers. Overall, Richard was pleased with it. Anything that brought attention to the parish and the needs of the people was always welcomed.

Just five days before Christmas, 1984, as he was enjoying the pre-Christmas celebrations, he heard sirens and smelled smoke. He grabbed his keys and followed the smoke to one of the worst apartment complexes in Immokalee. The fire was so bad that three fire trucks had been called, but they were too late. A large group of people, mostly Haitian, stood outside, staring in grief and shock. Another December fire – there had been one just a year ago.

"*Eske gen moun ki blese?*" he asked. Is anyone hurt?

"*No, mési Bon Dye.*" No, thank God.

Ten apartments were completely destroyed, meaning that thirty-nine Haitians lost their homes and everything they owned. As *Pe* Sanders and Sister Eileen helped them find new places to live, they realized that two of the local landlords had jacked up their rents again, as they had with the last fire, because they knew the Haitians were looking for new dwellings. One family was charged five hundred dollars a month for a small old trailer with no kitchen.

Padre Sanders was so upset that he again went and visited some of the owners. He thought that, because it was so close to Christmas, there was a chance he could get through to them this time, but he got nowhere. One day, he thought, we will put these slumlords out of business.

On December 24, Richard dressed for Christmas Eve Mass, called *Misa de Gallo* in Spanish. Mass of the Rooster. He studied himself in the mirror, noting the deep wrinkles on his face and the gray color of his skin. "Well, at least it matches my hair," he thought to himself, wryly. He knew he looked older than his forty-seven years and felt it, too. He had less strength and energy all the time, yet his people needed him more and more. Then he reprimanded himself as he thought of how many men and women his age and older felt the same way, or even worse, yet they had to work in the fields every day.

He was also looking forward to the week after, which he would spend with his mother and brother in Staten Island. He walked slowly over to the church, stopped at the grotto and said a prayer to Our Lady of Guadalupe and to Jesus, her Son who was born this night.

Sister Octavia had outdone herself with decorations. It seemed everywhere he looked there were flowers, including poinsettias, called in Spanish *flores de Navidad*, flowers of Christmas. Sister Aida tuned her guitar as the choir assembled at the left side of the altar and he could hear the altar boys in the sanctuary, dressing excitedly in their Christmas robes.

The choir sang the entrance song as he waited for the people to stand. "*Noche de paz, noche de amor.*" Night of peace, night of love.

He stepped up on the altar and began Mass. "*Alegrémonos todos en el Señor...* Let us all rejoice in the Lord, for our Savior is born to the world. True peace has descended from heaven."

In his sermon, he spoke as usual in slow, clear Spanish.

> *Sabemos, hermanos y hermanas....* We know, my brothers and sisters, that in the beginning God created the world, created everything good and beautiful. Then the world began to sin and all began to fall. It is so well known, the long history of centuries and centuries, thousands and thousands of years, that the world was waiting for something or somebody to do something, to fill all that was empty, to take on fights, wars, battles, injustices -- the world was waiting, suffering.
>
> Over thousands of years, God made people understand that God was going to save us in a very special way. Little by little as we go through the sacred history of the Old Testament, we see stronger promises from the Lord. Then what we are celebrating tonight happened: what we read in the beginning of Isaiah, the promise of a light that was going to shine in the darkness.
>
> What happened tonight was the birth of that Savior, the baby boy, born to the Virgin Mary, to whom they gave the name Jesus.

Then, as now, we listen not only with hope but also with
firm faith in Jesus, the God that was born, the God who became
present among us, the God that became man 2,000 years ago
and the God that is very near, present here with us every day.

We see in the birth of this baby that the Lord's promise
was fulfilled. That God is with us, always working in our world,
our lives, our hearts, to make us God's people – new people –
renewed people – united people.

The Lord is with us. Let us celebrate this evening with joy.
Let us celebrate with confidence and hope.

The next morning two of the men from the parish knocked on the door
of the rectory at 7:00 a.m. and *Padre* Sanders came out with his suitcase.

"*Listo, Padre?*" Ready?

"*Sí, listo*," replied the priest, sleepily. "After you drop us off at the airport,
you guys are headed to the beach, as usual?"

"*Sí*," they replied happily. They loved the beach and it was not often that
they got the chance to go. It had become a tradition for them at Christmas,
one of the few days when there was no work in the fields.

Sister Barbara was waiting outside her home with her suitcase. She was
going home, also, and their flights left at about the same time. They put her
suitcase in the trunk and she got into the back seat with the *Padre*.

"Richard, you look tired," she said.

"I've heard that a lot lately," he sighed, then smiled. "God's work can be
tiring, Barbara. You know that better than I do. But always happy, yes?"

"*Sí*," she smiled. "Always happy."

Christmas was a welcome rest. His mother was feeling better than she
had in a while, happy to have her family around her.

When Richard got back to Immokalee, the stress began again with a
freeze that lasted two nights and destroyed 90 percent of the vegetable crop.
Eileen confirmed that this was the fourth freeze in five years.

"I thought you asked your supporters to pray that there would be no
more," he said, making a weak joke.

"I did," she sighed, "but I guess our prayers can't always control the
weather, just the way we deal with it. Helping the people recover is starting
to feel like a painful ritual."

He nodded in agreement, thinking about the workers. For the next
ten days they would work cleanup. In late February, some farmers would
begin to plant the spring crop, but that took only a one-fifth the number of
workers that harvesting did. *Padre* Sanders shuddered, knowing there were
more difficult times to come.

VII

COMPLINE

1985

CHAPTER THIRTY-SEVEN – TELL EVERYONE TO GO AND PRAY – 1985

At the first staff meeting of 1985, *Padre* Sanders continued the ongoing discussion about improvements that were needed in Immokalee.

"There are so many that it's hard to even know where to start," said Sister Barbara.

Richard nodded thoughtfully, confirming something he had thought about over Christmas.

"I think we have to get better at empowering the people to identify and fix problems," he said. "Let's develop a survey form and go from house to house and ask the people what they think the priorities should be for this new year."

Late that afternoon, he called Maria Marquez.

"Maria, *lo siento* but I'm going to miss your birthday dinner. Someone came in a few minutes ago with a problem and I have to help him. Save me some cake."

It was 7:30 before he finished talking with a man who had no money to feed his family. *Padre* Sanders gave him ten dollars and a few sandwiches and prayed with him. As they walked out of the rectory, he heard singing in the church. Choir practice. He stood quietly, listening, and then decided to stop over for a minute.

"Come in," welcomed Sister Aida, always happy when he came to their practice. The *Padre* sat peacefully with his eyes closed. An hour and a half later, she woke him.

"*Padre*," she said, as she shook him gently. "We are finished. And you are late for Maria's birthday party."

He smiled up at her. "*Gracias, hermana*. I don't want to miss the cake!"

Maria was happy to see him.

"*Feliz Cumpleaños*, Maria, Happy Birthday!" He gave her a birthday hug and said hello to Rubén and the rest of their family.

"*Sientase, Padre*. Sit down. You don't look so good."

"I am a little tired, but your birthday cake will revive me, I'm sure."

They laughed and talked as he ate the leftover food Maria had kept warm for him. Then he had his cake.

"You look a little pale, *Padre*, too. Are you getting enough rest?"

"Maybe I need to spend more time at the beach, huh Rubén?"

"Great idea. Let's all spend more time at the beach!"

He finished his last bite of cake and then said, "I have to go. Tomorrow morning, Lolo and Esmeralda are coming to start their pre-marital counseling." He beamed as he said it. "I think their marriage will be blessed and I am very happy for them."

On his way back to the rectory, his heart started racing. He had been feeling weak and short of breath all day and had experienced some mild chest pain, but it had passed. I just need some sleep, he thought. He thought of other things he needed to do. He had meant to start exercising, but never seemed to find the time. I'll start tomorrow, and lose a few pounds. The shortness of breath continued and he decided it might be allergies. He had been told that the longer people lived in Southwest Florida the more sensitive they got. He pulled up in front of the rectory, went inside and lay down to sleep, praying as always the words he had said since his first day at Mepkin Abbey, "May the almighty and merciful Lord grant us a restful night. And a peaceful death."

He slept restfully for a while, then awakened with tightness in his chest that he recognized from his first heart attack. The chest pains he had felt earlier returned. They got stronger, and it became harder and harder to breathe. He got up weakly, noting the clock – it was 3:00 a.m. He stumbled to the couch in the living room.

"Something's wrong," he yelled, as loudly as he could. "Fanoly! Casto! Wake up!"

They both came running out at the same time. "¡*Padre*! Pe! What's happening?"

"I think I'm having a heart attack. Call 911."

When the ambulance arrived about fifteen minutes later, *Padre* Sanders was feeling better, sitting up on the couch, drinking a glass of water Casto had brought him. They checked his blood pressure and pulse and asked what had happened. When he told them, the ambulance worker said, "Your vital signs are OK, blood pressure a little high, but not terrible. There is a Haitian woman having a baby not far from here. We need to get her, too."

Padre Sanders sighed. There was only one ambulance in town, and the clinic was closed at this hour. The idea of a woman in labor tore at him.

"I'm OK," he sighed. "Go and get her."

"Are you sure?" The paramedic didn't seem to know what to do.

He nodded. "I'm sure."

He convinced Fanoly and Casto that he was fine and went back into his room to lie down. Shortly after, he heard Fanoly talking on the phone.

"You better come, *hermana*. He's sick but he sent the ambulance away."

Soon, Richard heard the front door open and Sister Octavia's voice talking to Fanoly and Casto. They sounded worried. There was a soft knock on his bedroom door and Octavia entered quietly.

"*¿Padre? Despiértese.* Wake up. *¿Que le pasa?* What's happening to you?"

"*Estoy un poco enfermo,*" he responded weakly. I'm a little sick.

After confirming his symptoms she went into the kitchen and he heard her calling the ambulance again. They would come back as soon as they got the woman having her baby to the hospital in Naples, which would be an hour and a half. Fanoly offered to drive him but *Pe* Sanders insisted he could wait.

He lay on his bed for what seemed like an eternity, praying for strength and for the pains to stop. Finally, he slipped into a deep dreamlike state. When the ambulance arrived, there was no discussion – they started an IV and carried him out on a stretcher. The sun was coming up as they pulled out of the driveway and he looked up, noting the beautiful light against the tops of the tall pines. The clouds looked like brush strokes, laid out in opposing patterns all over the sky. He slipped into unconsciousness, dreaming of Mepkin and the monks chanting in choir.

The kingdom of God is near, yes near to us.

Not long afterwards, Lolo and Esmeralda arrived at the rectory. Sister Octavia met them at the door.

"I'm sorry but the meeting is cancelled," she said, shakily. "*Padre* Sanders is in the hospital. We think he had a heart attack last night."

"*¡O Dios mío!*" said Esmeralda.

They looked around the living room and saw opened IV bags and other evidence of medical assistance. The ambulance had just left.

"*¡Vamos a seguirlo!*" said Esmeralda, "We'll follow him!"

"Don't go," said Sister Octavia, fighting back tears. "He won't even know you're there. He was semi-comatose when they took him. Go and pray. Tell everyone to go to the church and pray."

When Richard woke up he realized he was in the hospital, and the events of the morning came back to him. He vaguely remembered people working on him in the emergency room, but little else after that. He pushed the call bell for the nurse who came in and smiled.

"You're looking better," she said.

"What happened? What's happening?"

"The doctor will be in soon, and will explain it. In the meantime, try to stay calm and rest. Everything's going to be fine."

The doctor arrived about an hour later and looked at the tests and chart notes from the admitting physician.

"You had a heart attack," he said, without emotion.

Richard, hoping for an outside chance that it was something else, sighed. He should have slowed down, especially after the first attack in Indiana.

"You're lucky you're alive," the doctor continued. "You should have called the ambulance yesterday when you had those first symptoms. But what really hurt you was the delay after the attack you had early this morning. The ambulance should have brought you here immediately."

Richard thought of the Haitian baby and was sure he had made the right choice.

The doctor continued. "The delay resulted in significant damage so you're probably going to need surgery." They were calling in a cardiologist from Miami who would hopefully be in Naples in a day or two. "In the meantime, you'll stay here and rest. Oh, and you have visitors. We usually don't allow people in this early, but we're going to let them in to see you because they are so worried. They can only stay for a minute."

Yolanda came in first. He could tell she had been crying. "Oh, Dick! Sister Octavia called and I came right away. What happened?"

He smiled weakly and shrugged his shoulders. "I guess it finally caught up with me." He held her hand reassuringly. "I'm sorry I made you drive all the way over from Miami. *No te preocupes.*" Don't worry.

Sisters Octavia and Eileen came in next. Their communication was also brief, because he told them to go back to Immokalee.

"You two are going to be in charge until I get back."

"What should we tell the people?"

"Tell them I had a minor heart problem and would appreciate their prayers. No need for you to worry, either."

When they protested, he reassured them, weakly. "Go. I'm fine. Our people need you there."

Late that afternoon his brother arrived. "How did you hear?" asked Richard, surprised but pleased to see him.

"Yolanda called, and I flew right down," said Jim. "How are you?"

"Weak and it's kind of hard to breathe if I try to move much."

"Is it serious?"

Richard shook his head, not wanting to believe it himself. "Just too much stress. My blood pressure is pretty high."

He could tell by Jim's face that he flashed back to their father's death. He immediately reassured his brother. "Really, it's not that bad. I just have to rest a while."

Jim looked relieved. "Mom's not feeling well or she would have come herself."

"What?"

"She's been tired lately. She's not sure if it's part of aging or something is wrong. She's been losing a little weight, too. She has a doctor's appointment in a few days."

"How's Gail dealing with it?"

"He's got some problems of his own, so Mom's friends are keeping an eye on her. You better call, though. Otherwise she'll worry."

Jim left the next morning and Richard was glad he had convinced his brother that he was fine. Jim had enough on his mind with his work and family, and their mother.

Padre Sanders stayed a full week in Naples Hospital where he read the Bible, worked on plans for the parish and talked with the many people who came to see him. The specialist came to examine him and decided he would need tests that could only be done in Miami.

"You're in serious shape here, Father," he said. "You need to get these tests as soon as possible."

Richard did not like his manner any more than that of the first doctor. He was brusque and hurried, and seemed to just want to get out of there. The doctor left to make a call and came back to say the tests were scheduled for January 23rd at Mercy Hospital. When the doctor left, he prayed to get back to health and to his people. He was staring out the window at a beautiful live oak tree and a redbird that sat on one of its branches when he heard someone come in.

"Barbara," he said, smiling weakly.

She sat down in the chair next to his bed. They did not speak for a few minutes. She had grown used to his love for silences.

"How do you feel?"

"Tired," he smiled again without moving. Then he asked about an educational session she was working on, for an upcoming meeting about the County Master Plan.

"Are the people ready?"

She sighed, thinking of the job he had left her. Ten Hispanic and Haitian leaders in the church were going to present the plan and argue its points. They were intelligent but had limited education, and they had to present pages of scholarly information.

"Don't worry, we're fine," she lied. "It's all under control."

"Of course I'm not worried. You're in charge."

During visiting hours people were in his room constantly. The nurses suggested that they restrict his visitors, but he would not hear of it.

The bishop even came. Richard looked up at him in surprise and could see his concern. He told the bishop what the doctor had said, and they talked about what would happen next. Richard got distracted again by the bird outside the window.

"Father Sanders, you need to start thinking about slowing down in general. Maybe some other kind of work that would be less stressful. Maybe another parish."

Richard's head snapped back toward the bishop, his eyes open wide.

"Away from Immokalee?"

The bishop nodded but Richard shook his head strongly. "Please don't take me away from there, no matter what happens," he pleaded, remembering being torn from other people he loved. "I'm going to be fine. Don't take me from my people." He felt so stressed just hearing this suggestion that his blood pressure went up and he could feel his heart racing again.

"No, no, don't worry about that," said the bishop, noting the reaction. "We'll do everything we can to keep you there. Just focus on getting well. But you need to do whatever that doctor tells you to do. This could be serious."

Back in Immokalee, the grotto was filled with more candles than anyone had ever seen, and people stood and knelt there day and night, praying. Cristina and Cande and their children often came at night when the glow of the candles softly illuminated Our Lady of Guadalupe. Little Lupita told her mother it was probably as beautiful as when Our Lady appeared to Juan Diego.

"*Sí, mijita,*" said Cristina sadly, gently running her hand over her daughter's hair. Yes, my little one. "It's probably very much like that."

A few days later, Yolanda took the day off and drove over to get him, to bring him to Mercy Hospital for the tests. He was nervous, and happy that his old friend would be there; she was such a source of strength for him. They arrived early and as they sat together in the waiting room, a man came in, in a wheelchair pushed by his wife. The woman talked with Richard and Yolanda as they waited together, but the man stared ahead at nothing and did not speak. His right shoulder sagged and the arm hung limply, his hand resting awkwardly in his lap.

"His whole right side is paralyzed and he can't talk," explained the woman.

"I'm sorry," Yolanda said, looking directly into the man's eyes that seemed to brighten for a moment. Then she turned to the wife. "How did that happen?"

"He had a stroke fourteen years ago."

"Fourteen years! Did he have rehabilitation therapy?"

"Yes," nodded the woman, sadly. "It allowed him to reach this point, but he never regained the ability to speak or walk. We're just here for some tests to see if there has been any improvement that we can't see."

When the nurse called their name, the couple said goodbye and good luck to Richard and Yolanda.

Father Sanders looked pensive. "You know, Yoli, that's one thing I don't think I could stand. I've asked God over and over to please not let that happen to me. Can you imagine what it would be like, to be awake and aware, but not able to move or speak?"

"*Sí*, Dick, *entiendo*. I understand. I will pray about that, too."

Yolanda stayed in the waiting room while they did the tests but Richard asked that she be brought in to hear the results. The specialist looked serious, and told them that Father Sanders would need a bypass operation.

"What!" Richard had not expected this.

"You have serious blockage in your arteries. There is other no way to treat it."

"What are the risks of that operation?"

"Not bad, for what it can do. There is always the possibility that you will not come through it, of course, and there will be a long recovery period."

Richard was again annoyed with the lack of compassion. The man sounded like a technician who forgot his patients were human beings.

"Not come through it?"

"The chance of a stroke is always a possibility, and it's more likely for you than for others because of your family history." Then he added, almost as an afterthought, "But there's a good chance you'll get through it without any problems."

Richard thought again of being unable to care for himself, dependent on others. That could never happen. He shook his head.

"That's too much of a risk," he told the doctor, adopting the same cold, objective tone. "What about pills, or diet, or exercise? There has to be an alternative."

"Waiting would be risky but we could try putting you on medication and a restricted diet. I doubt it will help, though. Your arteries are badly clogged."

"I'm feeling a lot better from just resting. Can we delay it a little while and see if it improves?"

"Your life, your choice," said the doctor, shrugging his shoulders. "Get back in here in a couple of weeks so we can evaluate any changes, but I doubt we'll see any."

Richard could tell Yolanda was as irritated as he was at the doctor's impersonal attitude, but steered her away from protesting. He was just pleased that he had some time. He wanted a chance to try and heal by himself. The phrases, "surgical risk of stroke" and "long recovery period" were two that would cause him to wait as long as possible. He would stay in Miami, however, close to the hospital in case something happened, take medication, and rest.

"Maybe I could rest in Immokalee."

Yolanda insisted that he not do that – too many things there would distract him.

"You'd be working," she said. "Anyway, you should be close by, like the doctor said. Too bad we don't live closer or you could stay with us. The other problem is that Ron and I are both working during the day and there would be nobody around if you had a problem."

Richard shook his head and smiled. "No, my dear friend, you have far too much going on to have another person to take care of. Mike Murphy said I can stay at his new rectory, not far from Miami. When the date gets closer, I can stay at the Haitian Catholic Center. It's closer to the hospital so it will be easy to get there for tests."

Yolanda took him to Father Murphy's rectory in a Miami suburb and said goodbye. Sister Eileen came over the next day and Richard got quickly down to business.

"You and Octavia are going to be in charge, Eileen, because it looks like I'm going to be out for a while. They're talking surgery maybe in a month or so, but I'm going to try to avoid it. I just have to rest. I can't do much now. I can hardly breathe and am too weak to even walk very far. You need to go back and not worry about me. You have the effects of the freeze to deal with. A lot of people are going to need help and they're in your care."

Eileen frowned, but of course he was right. "They're saying there might not be a crop to harvest until April, and there are about two thousand more workers than usual in Immokalee, because this freeze affected the whole state."

He sighed, wishing he could be there to help her. "Don't worry about me. I'm in good hands, and you'll be fine without me. You and Octavia can run everything."

"We can't say Mass. We're going to need a priest."

"Ask the diocese to send someone, at least on weekends. Father Darbouze will come for the Haitians as often as he can."

She hated to bother him but had another question. "What about during the week? It's important to some of the sisters."

"Maybe you can get one of the priests I mentioned to stay over for Monday and come out on Friday. Also, check with the diocese. Maybe they can get someone to come and stay. But the priests are only to say Mass and administer sacraments; no administrative decisions. I want you and Octavia to run the parish."

Over the next three weeks, Yolanda visited often and Sister Octavia came every couple of days to fill him in on what was happening. The sisters had decided to tell the people in Immokalee that they were not to visit at this time, but Octavia brought many cards and letters from them. One Saturday, Eileen came with Octavia. She had taken his words to heart and stayed in Immokalee, but insisted on visiting once in a while. She said nothing as she took in the sight of him lying weakly against pillows on the couch and he gazed back at her. After a moment, Octavia broke the silence.

"They are praying for you every day and every night at the grotto, *Padre*. Sometimes as many as one hundred people, together. I've never seen so many candles there before! We keep the church open now too, and people come day and night to pray. It's beautiful to see how much they love you."

He smiled. "Please tell them their prayers are working and I'm feeling better. Are you getting priests to cover the Masses?"

"The diocese sent a list of priests to call."

"The biggest problem we have," said Octavia, "is that people keep going into your office, your room, and taking things. I finally told Cristina to lock the door."

The *Padre* became agitated, something Octavia had rarely seen. "Don't lock the door! People are more important than things! Tell Cristina the people should feel free to use my room and anything in it, including my bed and bathroom. And my things. Those are not my things; they belong to everyone."

He turned to Eileen who had not yet spoken. "How is your work going?"

She knew better than to try to sugarcoat the truth. "It's not good, but we're managing. The people are managing. The freeze...."

Richard nodded his head. She didn't need to go further. He could envision the line. Eileen shook her head.

"But we have some good news, too," she said, noting the depressing effect her mood was having on Richard. "We interviewed twenty-five women who are receiving welfare but would prefer to work. With the help of that special program I told you about, three of them are now ready to go to the Naples Vo-Tech School. They will learn skills and get steady jobs."

He shook his head and smiled. "That is indeed good news, Eileen. Let us pray for more like it."

CHAPTER THIRTY-EIGHT – THY WILL BE DONE – 1985

In late February, Richard moved to the Haitian Catholic Center and received his Lenten ashes at the Church of *Notre-Dame D'Haiti* in Little Haiti. It took all the energy he had just to walk over there, but still he prayed that the medication would help and that surgery could be avoided. He thought about his people in Immokalee and wondered who was blessing their foreheads with ashes in the Sign of the Cross. This Lent would be perhaps the most difficult of his life. He longed for the days at Mepkin when food restrictions seemed significant. Being away from his people, even for this short time, was the greatest sacrifice he could make.

Two weeks later, Yolanda drove him to Mercy Hospital again. They did more tests and the doctor shook his head as he gave them the news. Richard's mood sank as he listened.

"There's no improvement. You are definitely going to need surgery, probably a quadruple bypass. I should have insisted we do it right away, but you seemed so determined to avoid it that I thought it might be possible. I scheduled you for next Wednesday."

"So soon!"

"It'll be fine. The operation has been done before, many times, successfully."

He hesitated then, however, and Richard asked why.

"Well, I mentioned there's a potential of a stroke, particularly with your personal and family medical history. I need you to be aware of that."

"But, there must be some way to help prevent it."

"We'll do everything we can," said the doctor, not so reassuringly. "You need to rest and try not to worry. That's the best thing you can do to help avoid any problems."

Over the next week he tried to focus positively and spent a lot of time reading the Bible. It reassured him. He grew increasingly nervous, though, more every day. He called his brother. He had told Jim earlier there was a possibility of surgery, but back then he was hoping to avoid it.

"Jim, I'm going in for a heart bypass operation next Wednesday. I just wanted to let you know." He tried to sound confident. "They do a lot of them these days so I'm not worried about it."

Jim blew out a long breath. "I'll tell Mom and we'll fly down."

"No, that's not necessary. I don't want her to worry. Actually, I'd prefer that you don't tell her. Like I said, it's no big deal."

The next day Sister Eileen came to visit. Richard was sitting in a recliner in the living room and she sat on a chair next to him. "So are you making out OK without me?"

"We're fine but we miss you, of course. Are you nervous?"

He adjusted the pillow behind his back. "A little. They think I might need a quadruple bypass and it's possible the operation could lead to a stroke."

Eileen looked up quickly and frowned. "Didn't your father have a stroke?"

"Yes, but not from heart surgery. And my mom had one, too, but she recovered completely. It'll probably be fine."

"You're very brave," said Eileen, smiling.

Then he lost his cavalier attitude. "I'm not afraid to die, Eileen, but living, paralyzed from a stroke, scares me more than anything. If I wake up dependent, paralyzed, worse yet, brain dead, pray that I die."

Eileen smiled gently and took his hand. "I'll pray that you don't have a stroke at all and that you come through with flying colors and come back to us soon. I won't mention your concerns to the people, but know that they are praying for you constantly."

"*Sí, hermana*. It's comforting."

The day before the surgery, Yolanda took him to the hospital and they put him in a private room. He felt more apprehensive every moment. Just after noon, Sisters Octavia and Aida came in and Richard suggested that Yolanda take a break and get some lunch. After she left, he talked to the sisters about something he didn't want to put Yolanda through.

"*Hermanas*, in case something happens tomorrow, I want to plan my funeral."

Aida responded, "I'd rather plan the Mass that we will celebrate when the operation is a success and you get back to Immokalee."

"OK, let's do that. It's easier. Either way, it's a celebration, right?"

They nodded and Octavia took out a pen and paper.

"We'll have it outside, of course, with lots of flowers," he said.

Octavia smiled. "*Sí, Padre*, lots of flowers. The yellow rose bushes I planted last month across from the grotto have buds. Maybe they'll be blooming."

"Oh, I hope so," he smiled. "The Mass should be in three languages, of course, four with the Guatemalans singing?"

Aida nodded. "What are your favorite songs?"

"Anything the choir sings is my favorite, *hermana*, but happy things, I think. How about *Vienen Con Alegría*, Come with Joy?"

Octavia interjected. "I like that one too."

"Then how about *Whatsoever You Do*?" She sang it softly, "'Whatsoever you do, to the least of my brothers, that you do unto me.'"

The *Padre* nodded and looked out the window for a moment. "Oh, and *I Am the Bread of Life*. That's perfect."

Aida thought but did not add, "...for a funeral."

"Then let's finish with my favorite, *Somos un Pueblo que Camina*. That way everyone will feel like one people as they, um... as we leave to continue our work. What do you think?"

The sisters nodded. Noting his weak body and gray countenance, they realized that they might indeed be planning his funeral.

Then Octavia had a suggestion. "What about a picture of you in the little booklet with the Mass?"

"*¿Sí?* Don't you think that's too egotistical?"

Octavia said, "No, not at all. They would love to have a picture."

"Find something where I look really happy, so they know how much I love them and how happy they have made me."

She smiled. "I know – the one from your birthday last year at Cande and Cristina's where you're opening Lupita's present."

"Yes," he smiled. "I like that picture too. That was one of my favorite birthdays."

"*Muchos más vienen*," she smiled. Many more are coming.

He smiled thoughtfully. "What's the date?"

"March 12th."

"You know, it's almost four years to the day that I first came to Immokalee."

"Then that's good luck for the operation too," said Aida. She looked at her watch. "We'd better get back. I have choir practice this evening."

"*Ay, hermanas, me siento tan solo.* I feel so alone. Octavia, do you have to go?"

Sister Aida smiled at his fears and nodded to Octavia. Aida would handle things in Immokalee so Octavia could stay.

He started to laugh. "Oh, thank you! You don't know how much I appreciate that!"

"OK, *Padre*, now rest," said Octavia. "I'll check in with Yolanda and be back soon."

Later that day, Octavia and Yolanda left for a while and he fell into a kind of half sleep. As he lay there, a sense of doom darkened his thoughts.

He called his brother again. "Jim, I'm scared."

"I thought you weren't worried."

"There's something weird happening. It's almost like I'm having a premonition that things are not going to come out well. I don't know what it is, but I'm thinking this might be more serious than I originally thought. Can you and Mom come down after all?"

"Yes, absolutely. I'll break it to her gently and we'll be there tomorrow when you wake up."

The next morning before the sun was up, the night nurses came, shaved his chest and pre-medicated him for the operation. When Yolanda and Sister Barbara arrived he was already beginning to feel groggy from the pre-surgery medication.

"How did you sleep?"

He smiled, looking peaceful. "I read the Bible and prayed for my fears to be relieved, and they have been. I slept well, with peaceful dreams. Now I say, 'God, I give you thanks, I am prepared for whatever you want, and I offer my life for Immokalee.'"

Yolanda interjected, "Well, if it's all the same to you, we'd like to have you continue your life in the Immokalee."

She was right, of course. Richard smiled and started to tell them what was on his mind. He was still working.

"Octavia, keep on with the plans for the *Tercero Encuentro* in Atlanta." He paused for a moment, remembering the *Segundo Encuentro*, walking arm and arm with Yolanda and thousands of others. The experience had cemented his destiny. "That conference is important. We have to keep inspiring the people in their work and their self-confidence. And make sure you get that questionnaire done. I know it's a lot of work, going to the houses, compiling the results, but it's really important."

"*Sí, Padre,* we'll take care of it."

Richard was pleased with how happy they looked. It gave him confidence that the operation would go well. Just then the nurse came in to tell him the phone was ringing off the hook with calls for him.

"I can't let them through, of course, but wanted you to know. We've also got a lot of cards for you to open, after the operation."

He was not scheduled to go into surgery until 8:00, so he suggested his friends get some breakfast. "Just because they won't let me eat, doesn't mean you shouldn't. Besides, I would like to rest a little. The drugs are taking effect."

He lay back down and fell into a peaceful sleep.

"Dick." He heard Yolanda's sweet voice and felt her gently shake his shoulder. "The priest is here with the Eucharist."

Why hadn't she gone for breakfast?

"I wasn't hungry," she said, "So I decided to stay with you."

He heard an unfamiliar voice say, "The body of Christ." The priest was trying to place the Host on Richard's tongue but he was so groggy that he could not open his mouth wide enough for it.

Then he heard Yolanda's voice again. "I'll share it with him." She broke off a small piece of the Host, placed it on his tongue and put the rest in her own mouth. Together, for the last time, they shared the Body and Blood of Jesus Christ.

He closed his eyes and lay back peacefully for a moment, but then opened them to look again at Yolanda. Things were coming to him that he had forgotten to tell anyone. He was falling asleep quickly and suddenly this was important.

"If something happens, I want them to give all my things to the poor, OK? And I want a plain wooden casket. And I want to be buried in Immokalee."

"You'll have to write that last part down, Dick. They won't believe me. And I think your mother would want you buried with the rest of the family, wouldn't she? But, you're not gonna die, anyway. You're gonna be fine."

He propped himself up shakily on his left elbow, took a pen and paper from the table and wrote one sentence, hoping he could still write legibly.

"I want to be buried in Immokalee," and he signed it "Rev. Richard Sanders." Then he fell back down into his pillow and slept.

The next thing he was conscious of was Father Mike Murphy in the room with them. Richard smiled up at him but then realized that his friend was saying the Anointing of the Sick, that used to be called Last Rites.

"Through this holy anointing, may the Lord in His love and mercy help you with the grace of the Holy Spirit."

Richard had said those words himself, many times. He felt Mike making the Sign of the Cross gently on his eyes, ears, nostrils, mouth and the backs of his hands. "May the Lord who frees you from sin save you and raise you up." Then he heard Mike's voice break up and realized his friend was crying. He reached over and patted his hand weakly.

"Don't worry, Michael. It's going to be OK."

He heard the voices of his other friends as he felt himself being moved from the bed to a gurney. Octavia had returned, and she and Yolanda walked with him down the hall into the elevator and up to the operating waiting room.

Richard woke long enough to experience a moment of panic.

"*¡No me dejen, no me dejen!*" Don't leave me!

Yolanda put her hand over his and said gently, "We can't go in there; they won't let us. But we will be right here when you come out. Don't be afraid. Everything is going to be fine."

He thought of Jesus' prayer in the garden of Gethsemani and felt calmer. "Father, if this cup cannot pass away unless I drink it, thy will be done."

The operation lasted several hours and it was mid-afternoon before the doctor came out to see them. He was smiling. "The operation was a complete success!"

Sister Octavia made the Sign of the Cross, smiling through misty eyes as she thanked God for this beautiful news.

"He's in intensive care. You can see him but he is not conscious. He'll probably be out most of the day. I wouldn't even bother to come back tonight. If he wakes up at all he's going to be groggy."

They went in and saw him lying there peacefully, breathing comfortably, then left to get some rest. The next morning, Sister Barbara arrived early and found Yolanda in the waiting room.

"Were you here all night?"

Yolanda shook her head. "No. They called this morning. I'm waiting for the doctor now. I think it's bad news."

They prayed together and soon Sister Octavia joined them and they went to Richard's bedside. He was still unconscious but was aware that he could not move. Surprised that he was not distressed at being paralyzed, he heard the monks at Mepkin.

Lose your life and you may welcome Christ
Give up all to Christ, that you may see the Father

After a few minutes, he heard the doctor's voice. "I have bad news."

Yolanda turned quickly. "But you said yesterday that it went well."

"It did, but there was a side effect, one that I was afraid of – stroke. His left side is paralyzed."

The sisters immediately left the room, Barbara to call John Witchger and Octavia talked to Eileen. "Let the people know he had a stroke and will need their prayers, strong prayers. Tell everyone you can to get to the church and pray!" Yolanda, in the meantime, called Joan Sanders and told her the bad news. Joan said Jim was already on his way.

Later that afternoon, Maria and Ruben Marquez arrived and stood at his bedside with an idea. "He can come and stay with us. We'll take care of him."

Hearing their kind offer, with all his strength Richard tried to open his eyes slightly and convey a look that said, "No!" Not dependent, he thought. Not paralyzed. Not like this. But he could not move.

Sister Aida and Sister Jane arrived not long after. Aida tried to wake him, taking his hand in hers. "*Padre*, do you hear me. I am Sister Aida. Do you hear my voice? *Padre*, if you hear my voice press my hand."

"He did it!" exclaimed Aida, turning to the others excitedly. "He pressed my hand!"

The doctor looked at her sadly and said nothing, shaking his head.

"The only thing that can help him now are your prayers."

Later that morning, Jim Sanders arrived. He sat with Octavia, Barbara, Jane and Yolanda until the doctor came out. "It's bad," the doctor said heavily. "It turns out Father Sanders had more blood clots, and one went to his brain and caused a second stroke. His brain function is completely destroyed. He won't regain consciousness."

"But what about therapy and rehabilitation?" said Yolanda, in shock. "Sometimes people have strokes and get over it with a lot of work?"

The doctor shook his head. "We have a neurologist scheduled to come tomorrow to check his brain activity, but I don't expect him to find anything."

Jim frowned. "What will happen then?"

"I recommend that you take him off life-support. By law, we'll have to leave him on it for twenty-four hours after the neurologist makes his evaluation, but I don't see any reason to continue it beyond that."

The group went in together to Richard's bedside but he was completely non-responsive. Yolanda stayed with him while the others went to the cafeteria.

"How much younger are you than Richard?" Barbara asked Jim, as they sat, drinking coffee.

"I'm older," said Jim, surprised by the question. "Eight years older."

Octavia felt a twinge of guilt, comparing their appearances. "Did we do that to him?"

"Maybe," smiled Jim. "But if you did, it was worth it. He was happier in Immokalee than he'd ever been before."

Octavia decided she should get back. It was Saturday and they had Masses to prepare for. Before she left, she stopped into the *Padre's* room to say a tearful goodbye to her beloved priest.

The next morning, Sunday morning, Yolanda, Barbara and Jane arrived at the hospital at the same time and found Jim sitting there. They talked in the waiting area before they went in.

"This is the last day," said Jim. "The neurologist will be here in a few hours to confirm, but the doctor has already assured me there is too much damage for him to ever recover."

"Do you think there is any chance?" Yolanda was still in disbelief. "What about a miracle? The prayers Dick said and the migrants' prayers saved me from cancer, I'm sure of it. Maybe that could happen here."

Jim shook his head. "I doubt we get to see too many miracles in one lifetime. Dick coming back from this much damage would almost be as big as Lazarus rising from the dead."

Soon the neurologist came out and approached Jim. He sat down and shook his head.

"I'm sorry, but we have confirmed that Father Sanders is in a state commonly called, 'brain dead.' Only the machines are keeping him alive."

He showed a copy of the brain scan to Jim, who nodded seriously. Shortly after, the cardiologist came. He, too, addressed his comments to Jim. "As we discussed, the most compassionate thing to do now, for everyone concerned, is to remove life-support."

"You said we have to wait twenty-four hours."

The doctor nodded and Jim knew what to do. "I'll call the bishop. I think he has to give the order."

When Bishop Nevins arrived at Mercy Hospital on Monday, he talked with Jim, Yolanda, Barbara and Jane. They went in together to say goodbye, and then the bishop asked them to leave.

"It's time to let him go."

As they all stood with tears in their eyes, Yolanda bent and kissed her dear friend's forehead, and the others said goodbye in their own ways. Then they went and waited.

When the bishop came back out he said softly, "Our beloved brother is in heaven now."

Chapter Thirty-Nine –
¿No Estoy Yo Aquí Que Soy Tu Madre?

He was aware now only of a nearness to God that he had never felt before. He was lightheaded. He thought of Yolanda and the calling that sent her to him.

"It felt as if I had been lifted up out of my body. I felt the greenness of the blades of grass, the wetness of dew."

It was like that, yet different, the most beautiful peace he had ever known. Then he saw the white doors opening – the doors Corina saw when she died for a short time. No wonder she had not been able to describe it. He started to move toward the doors in complete bliss, gliding rather than walking, and then saw a vision, not a human figure, yet one he recognized. He felt afraid for a moment, but then she spoke.

"Do not be afraid of anything. *¿No estoy yo aquí que soy tú Madre?*" Am I not here, who is your mother?

A feeling of pure joy filled his spirit and a million questions overwhelmed him. She nodded before he even got the first one out.

"Yes, my Son has been with you all your life, in many people who have crossed your path."

"He was in my brother Jim, who inspired me to enter religious life with his own vocation, wasn't He?"

He sensed a nod.

"And at the Abbey, in Brother Boniface making corn bread when I was so depressed?"

The vision made no sound but Richard could feel her smiling. The importance of small actions. What went between them no longer sounded like words.

"In the Abbot of Mepkin and Father Robinson who helped me make my way out into the world? And my sister-in-law Joan, with her wisdom and deep faith?"

Again, he felt her say "yes" without actually hearing it.

"And Yolanda's calling, the voice that said, 'Help my migrants, help my people.'" He paused for a moment, remembering. "Yolanda was thinking of going to Texas. Thank God Father Hanley sent her that ad."

"Yes, thank God."

He smiled back.

They walked a little further. "Adán Hernandez?"

"Of course. Adán helped you get to know the migrants and told you about Immokalee."

He looked at the vision directly now, not seeing but sensing. "I know He was in Corina."

She smiled. "Corina was praying for you to come before you even considered leaving the Abbey."

Richard thought forward, or was it back, to Immokalee again. Things became dreamlike and he looked ahead at the white doors that were becoming clearer.

"What about Fanoly, so dedicated to the Church and the Haitian people?"

"Definitely Fanoly," was the unspoken response.

"Sister Eileen, so sweet and strong..."

The vision nodded.

"Others?" he asked. "Ida Singletary? Stanford Williams? Sister Ellen? We could go on forever."

"We have forever," she seemed to smile. "And yes, there were many others. At one time or another, He was in all of them, as He was in you."

He was feeling happier than he had ever felt in his life, ecstatic, in a way, yet immensely peaceful. But then he grew sad as he heard the distant sound of crying and the bells of Our Lady of Guadalupe Church. Suddenly he realized that, in spite of the beauty here, he did not want to be torn from his people again.

"What about the migrants, the immigrants? How can I leave them?"

"*No te preocupes,*" she smiled. Don't worry. "We have a lot of them here."

"What about what Corina said about *Voluntad de Dios* – the will of God? 'If we help people for so many years but God still needs us here, we will stay here.'"

The vision seemed to be fading.

"Wait!" he cried out. "If I were truly helping people, why am I here, so young? Why didn't you leave me there?"

"We did leave you there, in a way."

He felt a different hand on his shoulder, gently guiding him through the white doors.

"Come Brother. I'll explain as we go."

CHAPTER FORTY –
MASS OF THE RESURRECTION – 1985

Sister Octavia awoke before dawn on Monday morning, drove over to the church and found it filled with people who had held a prayer vigil all night, led by Sister Aida. Outside, the candles at the grotto cast an ethereal shadow over the statue of Our Lady of Guadalupe as the people knelt there, praying the rosary.

Father Murphy said the early Mass, grateful for the support of the Guadalupana Sisters. He was still in shock at the news coming from the hospital.

As the congregation began to recite the Lord's Prayer, the church darkened as thunder rolled and lightning flashed outside the windows. The power went out, leaving them without lights or fans for ten minutes. Intensified in their faith, they continued to pray.

One of the volunteers came to tell Sister Eileen there was a call from Miami. After a few minutes, Eileen returned to the church that was still full. She approached the altar, genuflected slowly and then went to the podium.

"*Padre* Sanders was taken off life support," she announced weakly, then paused. "He died a few minutes ago."

A shudder went through the church as the people gasped. Then there was nothing but the sound of weeping. Casto walked quietly to the back and turned on the switch that started the church bell tolling.

That afternoon Betty arrived at the Miami Airport. Jim met her and his face gave her the tragic news that she was too late to say goodbye. She was initially in shock, shaking her head and telling Jim she needed to get her bag, but on the way to the hospital she sobbed, as Jim told her the details.

When they got to the waiting room, Yolanda and Sister Barbara greeted Richard's mother and expressed their sympathy. Betty went in to spend a few last minutes with her youngest son and then came out and said, stoically, "We should bury him in the family plot in Peru."

Yolanda had expected this. "He said he wanted to be buried in Immokalee."

Betty frowned and shook her head. "No, there's no family in Immokalee. Why would he be buried there? He should come home."

Yolanda showed her the note. "He told me before the operation. I said, 'Well Dick you'll have to write that down; they'll never believe me.' So he did. It's what he wanted."

Betty hesitated, looked at Jim, and then nodded her agreement.

Yolanda offered to call Kolski Funeral Home in Miami to do the embalming and Betty and Jim gratefully accepted her help. Most of Yolanda's family had been buried through Kolski and she knew the people there. She came back a few minutes later.

"He's not too busy, and can get it done by tomorrow morning if he – I mean the body – is ready soon."

The nurse nodded that they could come for Father Sanders any time. Sister Barbara called Eileen and asked her to contact John Brister to make arrangements with Lake Trafford cemetery. When Eileen hung up the phone, she talked to the staff and together they came up with another idea.

She called John Brister. "Could *Padre* Sanders be buried next to the church, across from the grotto of Our Lady of Guadalupe?"

John was as saddened as they all were about Father Sanders' death and loved the idea.

"I'll call the Jacksonville Health Department, and Sister, you call the Diocese. It'll require a petition and some paperwork, but I'm pretty sure we can get it approved."

When the embalming was done, John would drive over and pick up the *Padre's* body. They would have the viewing on Tuesday afternoon, the wake Tuesday evening, and the funeral on Wednesday. Jim went to a phone booth to call his wife. Joan and the two girls would fly down the next day. Yolanda offered to take care of the details, including the selection of the coffin. "I know what he wanted. A plain wooden box, like a poor person."

Betty frowned at the idea of a pauper's casket for her son, but Jim convinced her.

"Mom, it's what he would have wanted. It's what most of his people will be buried in."

There was no reason for any of them to stay at the hospital anymore. After signing required forms, Betty and Jim drove back to Immokalee with

Sister Barbara. Betty asked to sit in the back seat so she could rest, and Jim continued to share memories of how he and Dick grew up.

By the time they got to Immokalee it was early evening, already dark, and cold. Another late cold snap had chilled the whole state and the forecast predicted it would drop into the thirties overnight.

"We've never been here," said Jim, looking around as they drove past packinghouses, poor streets and men in tee-shirts shivering in front of fires burning in metal barrels.

As they turned down 9th Street, they noted dozens of cars parked at the church and the lights on inside. Stunned and saddened people milled around the grounds. The grotto was surrounded by people in prayer, many on their knees.

Sister Barbara parked as close as she could get the church. As they walked in the front doors, Betty was surprised to see the small church her son had talked about in his letters. She had not envisioned anything this poor. Inside were about thirty Haitians. Betty frowned and Jim realized that his mother had had little, if any, contact with people of color or poor people.

When they saw the "*blancs*," white people, the Haitians realized it must be *Pe* Sanders' family and came to the back of the church to greet them. One after another they stepped up, crying and embracing Betty and Jim, telling them what *Pe* Sanders had meant to them. Neither Jim nor Betty understood much of what they said, but they did understand the tremendous outpouring of grief, love and respect for their beloved pastor's family.

Afterwards they walked over to the soup kitchen where the Hispanic community was holding choir practice for the funeral. Betty again hesitated, noting their dark skin and poor clothing, but, without a word of introduction, they came up one by one to her and to Jim, expressing their love and sorrow.

Later, when they arrived at the motel, all the sisters were there to welcome and comfort them. Betty was overwhelmed by the love they showed.

The next day at noon, Jim drove to the airport to pick up his wife Joan and their two daughters. Betty rode with him. When they returned, Jim had to park near the road because the parking lot was full. *Padre* Sanders' family walked slowly into the church.

Crying as they worked, the Haitians had cut out paper dolls to illustrate the story of the Good Shepherd and were hanging the happy images on the wall over the spot where *Pe* Sanders would be laid out. Sister Octavia was there, too, arranging flowers. Many more people were in the soup kitchen preparing food for the reception after the funeral.

Not long after, John Brister arrived in the hearse and placed the casket with Father Sanders' body on the trolley, parallel to the altar in front of the painting of Our Lady of Guadalupe. Casto went to turn the church bells on again to announce the viewing as John opened the top half of the coffin. The *Padre* still looked ashen, John thought. They should have put more color on his face. He would ask Mary to add some.

At Yolanda's request, Kolski's had dressed the *Padre* in his favorite chasuble, the one with a large oval image of Our Lady of Guadalupe on its breast. Sister Octavia carefully folded his colorful Mexican stole over the mid-section of the coffin and placed his chalice next to it.

Betty, still in shock, walked slowly toward the coffin, leaning on Jim. She stood quietly, silent tears streaming down her face, and then wiped her eyes and bent and kissed her son's forehead. Then she moved with Jim to sit the front pew.

She watched gratefully as people came in a constant stream, kneeling in the pews or in front of the body, praying and crying. The church was already full, but, as the day went on, so many came that they spilled out into the church grounds. Many had come directly from the fields and were still in their work clothes.

Later that evening, Father Mike Murphy said the prayers of the wake and led the mourning congregation in a rosary in honor of their beloved *Padre*. Afterwards and throughout the night, Eucharistic Ministers dressed in white robes took turns sitting at both the head and feet of the *Padre's* body. They were not alone; many people stayed in the church. The sound of crying filled the night as the church bells continued to toll.

"What a mournful sound," said Sister Eileen. "I feel as if I will hear it forever, in my bones."

At dawn on Wednesday, March 20, Casto turned off the bell and went to help set up the outside platform and folding chairs. Mourners who had been there all night left to get a few hours of sleep and were replaced by those arriving in the early morning. Grief hung like a dark shadow over the whole town. It was cool and cloudy but soon the temperature would warm. You could never tell what March weather would be like in Southwest Florida.

Sister Octavia covered the front of the platform with flowers as people delivered large bouquets and arrangements – purple flowers in the shape of large crosses, bright yellow mums and delicate white lilies. The outdoor altar area was framed by the roof of Our Lady of Guadalupe Church on the left and the soup kitchen with its massive wooden cross on the right. Directly behind the platform on a tree, over the spot where the coffin would rest for the Mass, they fastened the painting of Our Lady of Guadalupe.

By the time the Funeral Mass of the Resurrection started at 11:00 a.m., the seats were filled and people stood behind and on the side of the rows of chairs. The people in the crowd, dressed in everything from suits to work clothes, stretched from the front of the rectory to the religious education building to the soup kitchen to the opposite side of the church and out to 9th Street.

Betty Sanders, wearing her favorite cream-colored suit, sat in the front row with Jim and his wife and daughters. Sister Eileen sat next to them with Yolanda, Ron and their children. Betty, Jim and Joan kept staring around behind them, unable to grasp the number of mourners. There were close to a thousand, Jim estimated. A television camera from the local news station panned the crowd and the altar. Among the people were Corina Hernandez and her family, taking up a full row, as usual. Cande and Christina and their children sat behind Yolanda. Lupita wore a colorful Mexican dress that the *Padre* had loved. Sister Ellen Robertson from Camp St. Mary's and Margaret Shell from Columbia, SC, sat with Santos Ramirez and her family. Lolo and Esmeralda were a little farther back. Miguel Flores stood alone across from the grotto, near the empty grave.

John Brister, Fanoly, Casto and four other men waited inside the church with the coffin, which John had closed and sealed.

John smiled sadly. "This is the first funeral he wasn't late for." Then he looked out the side door at the crowd. "I guarantee you the farmers are having trouble getting labor in the fields today."

The Guadalupana sisters distributed the Mass pamphlets, created the way they had discussed with the *Padre*, with the music he wanted and the picture of him excitedly opening his birthday present. The outside cover was printed in color, white lilies with yellow stamens and green leaves, emblazoned with the word, "ALLELUIA." They also gave out prayer cards with a picture of Our Lady of Guadalupe on the front and a scripture quote from Matthew 25:40 in three languages on the back.

In Loving Memory of Rev. Richard E. Sanders
Born July 29, 1937, Died March 18, 1985

"As long as you did it for one of these least ones, you did it for me."
"Cuando lo hizo para alguno de estos mas pequeños, lo hizo para mi."
"Chak foua nou té fe sa pou younn na pi piti pami frè-m yo, se pou mouin no té fe li."

Octavia noted that the yellow roses across from the grotto were starting to bloom. She thought sadly that she did not know when she planted them that she was preparing his tomb.

The ceremony began with Richard's first funeral song request, *Vienen Con Alegría.* "Come with Joy." It signaled the beginning of the formal procession that was led by uniformed Boy Scouts carrying an American flag. Betty, Jim, Joan and their daughters watched in amazement as priest after priest dressed in white vestments followed the Boy Scouts in procession and filled in the reserved front rows of seats. There had to be forty or fifty of them from different orders, regular and diocesan clergy. There were many religious sisters in the crowd as well, some dressed in street clothes and others in white or black habits.

About thirty altar boys in white robes processed in next with hands folded in prayer, the younger, smaller ones first and then the taller boys. After them came women in white robes, the Eucharistic Ministers who had kept watch over the body the previous evening and all through the night.

The people grew silent as Casto, carrying the *Padre's* chalice, led the pallbearers down the aisle between the hundreds of folding chairs. They lifted the plain casket up the four stairs of the platform and placed it on the trolley, positioned so that if he stood up, *Padre* Sanders would be facing the people. Two priests laid his Mexican stole across the coffin.

More priests followed and went up the platform stairs. Then three bishops processed in, removing their miter hats as they bowed in front of Father Sanders' casket before ascending the steps.

Just as Bishop Nevins approached the altar to start the Mass, two swallow-tailed kites flew in low over the crowd. The "migrant birds" had returned home from their winter in South America in time to pay homage to *Padre* Sanders. Their broad white wings were like those of angels, black tips and tails seeming to honor the people's grief. Altar boy José Dimas thought the birds were the Holy Spirit, as he pictured the *Padre* smiling, "It's OK boys, take your time, relax, and if you make a mistake, don't worry. Just be happy."

Bishop Nevins came to the podium and addressed the people.

"As we gather here, I offer my deepest sympathy to Father's mother, brother and family and to all of you, his brothers and sisters in this beautiful parish of Immokalee, and all of you in the new diocese of Venice. I think in a very special way you can take pride that this priest you are giving to the Lord is one of the finest, and a model for all of us. Although it is with deep sorrow that we part with him, at the same time we part with him with joy, for the beautiful life he lived and inspired all of us to follow his example."

He began the service with prayers in Spanish, then English and then Haitian Creole. After sprinkling holy water three times on the coffin, two priests covered it with a white coffin cloth.

The choir led the people in *Señor ten Piedad*. Lord Have Mercy. Directly behind the platform, Our Lady of Guadalupe seemed to be smiling down at the *Padre's* coffin and out at the mourning people.

When the time came for the first reading, Jim Sanders climbed the stairs to the podium and Joan Sanders put her arm around Betty.

"A reading from the book of the Prophet Isaia 58: 6-9. 'This is the fasting that I wish: releasing those bound unjustly, untying the thongs of the yoke; setting free the oppressed, breaking every yoke; sharing your bread with the hungry, sheltering the oppressed and the homeless; clothing the naked when you see them, and not turning your back on your own."

Jim looked up, still amazed at the number of grieving people, and his voice began to quiver. He knew Dick had done good work, but knew nothing of the depth of the people's love, and how many lives his brother had touched. He finished the reading, hoping to get through it without tears. Fanoly read the second reading in Haitian Creole and led the psalm responsorial, accompanied by Haitian drums.

One of the priests purified the podium with incense and then held the pages of the Gospel to keep them from being blown by the wind.

"A reading from the Gospel according to Matthew 5: 3-13. 'Blessed are the poor in spirit, for the reign of God is theirs. Blessed too are the sorrowing, they shall be consoled....'"

As he read, crying voices could be heard throughout the crowd.

Bishop Nevins gave the homily, beginning in Haitian Creole, calling Richard "*Pe Sanders, te zanmi tout-moun*," Father Sanders was a beloved friend of all people. He then switched to Spanish and finally English.

"No priest could ask for more, if he could say at the end of his life, 'Despite my own frailties, my human frailties and simpleness, I have really tried to ignite the love of Christ in each person whom I served.' So regardless of how long a man, woman or child lives, what really matters is 'How well did I live? ...Did I leave my imprint, my mark, my love in the hearts and the souls of my family members and friends? These are the important and timely questions."

After the homily and the prayer of the faithful, there was a long silence that was finally broken by the sound of drums, as two lines of Haitian women and men approached the altar, swaying back and forth in a slow, mournful Caribbean dance. As they moved, carrying flowers and colorful fruit, they sang the Haitian song *Ofrann*. Betty, Jim, Joan and the girls turned and watched them and it occurred to Jim that they could have been in another country, actually several different countries. When the Haitians reached the front of the platform, one of the bishops came to the bottom of the stairs to receive their gifts and handed them to different priests who carried them up to be added to the others on the platform.

As the priests purified the coffin and then the crowd with incense, Betty leaned to Jim and told him she felt dizzy. It had gotten warm, up toward 80 degrees. Jim, worried about her health in general, looked around for help. Sister Manuela nodded, ran to the rectory and returned with a cold glass of water and an umbrella, which Joan held over her mother-in-law's head to block the sun.

The Kiss of Peace was another long part of the Mass, sung in Spanish as the people hugged and cried. Betty sat in a daze as priests came down from the platform to take her hand. "Peace be with you." Peace be with you. Peace be with you.

As the Eucharist was being prepared, Jim looked up at his brother's coffin and noticed again the image of Our Lady of Guadalupe glowing behind it in the sunlight. The choir sang, "Whatsoever you do, for the least of my brothers, that you do unto me."

The Mass lasted for over two hours, ending when one of the priests made a final sprinkling of holy water on the casket and the bishops donned their mitre hats. Each altar boy picked up a floral arrangement and stepped down the stairs for the final procession as the choir sang the song Richard most loved, particularly for these, his people, *Somos un Pueblo que Camina.* We are a People Moving Forward.

The Boy Scouts led the procession through the aisle to the back of the crowd as the people watched mournfully. The altar boys followed, and then six pallbearers took hold of the coffin and brought it down the stairs. Jim Sanders held the front right handle. Casto, dressed in a grey suit, white shirt and black tie, walked between the altar boys and the coffin, carrying Father Sanders' chalice and a large altar candle.

Leaving the altar with Jim Sanders as right front pallbearer

Then suddenly, the altar boys started to laugh. The priests and people nearby were stunned and the boys' parents pushed through the crowd and whispered, shocked at their behavior. "What are you doing? How can you be laughing?"

"I don't know why," giggled José Dimas as he tried to explain, whispering back. "We know he's dead, but suddenly we feel so joyous!"

"But this is the saddest of days," said another mother. "The funeral of our beloved *Padre.*"

José looked at the other boys who laughed even harder, then shrugged. "We know he's in heaven because he told us that's where we will all be. I guess that's why we're so happy!"

After the procession had gone a short ways, a man tapped Jim Sanders on the shoulder and took his place, and others did the same with the other pallbearers. Jim moved back to walk with his family.

Music from acoustic guitars, accordion, drums, tambourines and saxophone filled the air as a band followed the coffin and led the procession around the church grounds. As they walked, people continued to replace each other as pallbearers, like men cutting in at a dance – everyone wanted to carry him. Soon Yolanda took the front right position and patted the head of the coffin gently, staring at it. She refused to let go as the other five positions continued to change hands.

Yolanda at right front and Casto carrying chalice

The procession continued for over an hour, moving from the church grounds to 9th Street and back, with hundreds of people following along behind, filling the grounds with flowers as they walked. The Haitians sang a song with a tune similar to that of "I'm only going over Jordan." "*Mwen pral lòt bò-a laka-y Papa mwen....*" I'm going there to my Father's home, No more weariness for me, when I cross that river, My Mother will give me her heart, to lay down my head." Then the band played again, mournfully. "*Te vas Angel Mio, dejas mi alma herida y mi corazón sufiendo...* My angel you're departing, you leave my soul wounded and my heart to suffer."

Miguel remained near the gravesite, too saddened to take part in carrying his friend. Also, he felt strange. He was from central Mexico where people were stoic about death.

"I don't want to cry," he said to Octavia when she came near, "but my tears keep coming out. I want to throw myself to the ground, kicking my feet and sobbing!"

"*Entiendo,* Miguel," she said, trying to control her own tears. I understand.

Miguel noted the small live oak tree growing there that would someday shade the *Padre's* grave, and the roses that Sister Octavia had planted that would continue to grow at his feet.

Jim Sanders worried about his mother holding up, but she seemed to gain strength from the love of the people. When they reached the gravesite, Casto presented Betty with her son's silver chalice and the *Padre's* beautiful Mexican stole.

The gravesite had been prepared and the large mound of dirt covered in green plastic, with wooden boards to support the casket for the final prayers. The last group of pallbearers, with John Brister's guidance, placed the casket gently on the supports. Miguel, finally overcome with grief, threw himself over the right side of the coffin. Yolanda did the same on the left side, but stoically, without tears. Just before the bishop said the final prayers, Yolanda looked up and asked to speak.

"Father Sanders told me to tell all of you that he was going to offer any suffering that he would endure for all the dear people of Immokalee, of Naples and all the farm workers throughout America who he has served and all who have been very close to him. He knew he would be in heaven, so he is with us and he does not want us to be sad. My heart is broken but I cannot cry today because I know that he has been looking down, and he loves each and every one of us. One thing that Father established here is that the Church is not just the bishop and the priests. Let us not be afraid of who comes, because we the people are the Church – the Church goes from the bottom up, and we are the ones who have to praise God and follow the example that he has set for us, because he really believed that Jesus came to establish His church among the poor, and that the leadership should come from the poor."

The bishop said the final prayers and then John Brister ended the service. Food was being served at the soup kitchen, and many of them gathered there to share thoughts and memories of their beloved *Padre*.

Betty, exhausted from the long ceremony and her own grief, was anxious to get back to the motel. She went with Jim and Joan to the soup kitchen, intending to stay only for a few minutes, but then she overheard someone talking to one of the sisters.

"How are we going to continue this work? He's not here anymore and we can't do it. Our leader is gone."

The sister shook her head. "You know, really, it's like what he always said to us. He planted the seed. It is up to us to take it forward."

Once she heard that, Betty wanted to hear from the others, and insisted on personally greeting everyone there.

One of the farm workers shook Betty's hand. "If the *Padre* is going to be judged like the Bible said, for helping the poor and all those things, I think he has made it."

Others waited patiently. When it was their turn they came up individually and took her hand or hugged her, saying a few words to explain to the mother of their beloved *Padre* what he meant to them.

"He saw all people as the same, white, black, brown. There has been a lot of activity since he came here. We were together, in all the languages."

"Father Sanders was a great person. I have always wanted to live my life like his. He was always telling us in the Youth Group that we were the future."

"The way he was and the way he looked, even, was like Jesus. He was a quiet man but was very friendly and went out to the people."

"He came to me, talked to me, about how to live with my wife, and love my wife very much. After that you know, I started going to church. Father Sanders opened his heart for everybody."

"He didn't talk much but he listened to the people. He wanted the people to be together in one community."

"Sometimes I think he was Jesus Christ walking, here on earth. Even his look, because his beard and his hair were long, like the picture you see of Jesus."

"He was a very spiritual person. When you were in his presence his whole attention was focused on you, like nobody else was around."

"It is heart wrenching to work with the people of Immokalee," said Sister Eileen, "and I think that Richard felt the pain of his people. In fact, because of his deep contemplative center, he may have felt it even more than most of us. The deeper the connection with God, the deeper the connection with others."

Santos came up, tearfully. "He always encouraged me, and all of us, to do more than working in the fields picking tomatoes or doing labor."

"The last word you would use to describe him would be a 'leader,'" said one of the sisters from the clinic, "but in his own quiet way he moved mountains. He was very holy but very accessible. If Christ came on earth today I think that's who he would be. He didn't buy all that stuff where you have to treat priests special or put them on a pedestal. He said priests are sinners like everybody else. He felt privileged to work among the poor."

"The whole time he was here and in Naples," said Miguel, "he was always talking about 'empowering the people, empowering the people.' A lot of those leaders will stay involved and do a lot of work for the church. They were empowered and they will stay empowered."

More and more people approached to tell her what he meant to them, and Betty seemed to grow stronger from their comments.

"He wanted to give us the power to make decisions. When we met him, he was able to get the best out of us, the best of our abilities. He was able to discover what each of us could and would do for the community."

"He opened our eyes to know that it didn't have to stay this way – that we had to work for others and against injustice. He was quiet, reserved, but when he spoke, I felt like I was in the presence of Jesus. That's all I can explain it as. Because of his look, his serenity, his peacefulness."

"It didn't matter to him if they were poor or uneducated, but he always believed that the people could be strong leaders in the parish and the community. Usually priests look for people who have education, degrees or something, but *Padre* Sanders didn't think that way. He knew that people could develop a leadership ministry in the community if they had the training. He gave the people that pride of being what they were. He had a special passion for poor people."

"We can't see Father Sanders but I know that he sees us," said Fanoly. "I know when I see him in heaven, we're all gonna be angels. I know I'm gonna meet him in heaven."

Cristina came up next. "He never liked anyone to mistreat people. He used to say, 'It's important, whatever job anyone does, but this job, working in the fields, is so hard. They don't get good pay and they don't have any benefits, no anything, no respect at all.' Some people, if they see someone who is dirty from the fields, they don't want to get close to him or they make faces, but for him, the field workers were the most important people."

Little Lupita gave Betty a long hug. "I always reached out towards his cloak, the one he wore to Mass. It blew out around him when he walked, and I would try to walk in it. He walked fast. It made me feel safe because he walked so strong."

As the people began to leave, John Brister summed up many of their thoughts. "He was the finest priest we've ever had here. He loved his people and they returned it, too. The people became his family. He gave, not monetarily, but time, consideration, respect, kindness – he gave them hope. He increased attendance at the church because of his interaction with the people, and they became involved under his leadership. He cared about them and their struggles. It seemed like this *was* his home and they *were* his family."

Tears filled Betty's eyes as she looked lovingly at everyone there. "After today, I understand why my son never wanted to leave Immokalee."

Later, when the church grounds were empty and the grieving people had gone home, workers lowered the casket and filled in the dirt. Later, Juan Ramírez arrived. He stood at the grave alone, gazing up at the pink and lilac evening sky. With a deep sigh, he straightened his shoulders up and back, hiked up his pants, thrust out his chest and chanted, "*La muerte llega, no sabemos cómo, no sabemos cuándo, y nomás los recuerdos llevamos.*" Death comes, we know not how, we know not why, and all we have left are memories.

Then he cried out tearfully into the tall pines,
"*¡Adiós, Adiós, Padre!*"

EPILOGUE – 2008

A Mexican field worker kneels at the grave where the headstone reads:

RICHARD SANDERS
PRIEST
JULY 29, 1937   MARCH 18, 1985

LOVE ONE ANOTHER, AS I HAVE
LOVED YOU   JOHN 13:34

"*¿Por qué estás orando aquí?*" I ask. Why are you praying here?
"*Porque él era un santo,*" he answers, without looking up. He was a saint.
"Did you know him?"
"*No.*"
"Then why are you praying to him?"
"*Era un santo.*"

Father Sanders' grave, 2008

THANKS

Many people have helped me over the past four years, and I credit them for portraying Father Sanders lovingly and as accurately as memories will allow. They deserve credit for this book, but where there are inaccuracies or oversights, I alone assume the blame.

First I wish to thank Father Sanders' brother, Jim Sanders, for an immeasurable amount of help, and Jim's sadly now-deceased wife, Joan, for her insight into Father Sanders' spirit. Lucy Ortiz in Immokalee not only told me stories but found others, helped with research, translations and review. Sister Lorraine Soukup, S.S.N.D., inspired me to write the book in the first place, and set up interviews with key people. Jim Keane was another early encourager. Sister Maureen Kelleher, R.S.H.M., has supported and encouraged me since this work began. Father Ettore Rubin, C.S., pastor of Our Lady of Guadalupe Church in Immokalee, provided a model for Father Sanders' spirituality and helped with interpretations of Vatican II documents. Yolanda Wohl, Father Sanders' long-time friend and companion, spent hours telling stories of South Carolina and Florida, and provided a video of Father Sander's funeral.

For edits of the near-final manuscript, I first and foremost thank my friend and singing partner, Nancy Koerner, author of *Belize Survivor: Darker Side of Paradise*, who painstakingly and creatively edited this book. Other helpful editors/reviewers were Kathleen Hawryluk; Silvia Casabianca, author of *Regaining Body Wisdom: A Multi-dimensional View*; Stuart Wisong, author of *Angel Come Home*, Ryan Hadlock and Grace Ballenger.

People who helped specifically with the Vigils section include Father Sanders' old friends James Wimbiscus, Joe Story who is now-deceased, Art and Pat Trompeter, Adolf "Duke" Micheli who sent me St. Bede Yearbooks, Celeste McClain Reckamp, Ken Piletic, Barbara Meyers and Father Ron

Margherio from St. Bede Academy. The description of Gethsemani was completed thanks to *The Abbey of Gethsemani: Place of Peace and Paradox* by Dianne Aprile.

For Lauds, the abbey years, I thank James Jarzembowski, who entered Mepkin Abbey close to the same time Father Sanders entered and was invaluable in helping me piece together a story of monks who lived together in pre-Vatican II silence. Other past and present monks who helped with the story wished to remain anonymous, but I am most grateful for their help. For additional resources for the Abbey years I used the Mepkin website, www. mepkinabbey.org; many of Thomas Merton's books but primarily *The Seven Storey Mountain*; a beautiful book about Mepkin Abbey called *Trappist: Living in the Land of Desire*, by Michael Downey; a documentary based in Mepkin Abbey called *Trappist*, co-produced by Charlotte Public Television and Paulist Media Works; a CD called *O Listen, My Son*, recorded at Mepkin Abbey; *Baking with Brother Boniface* from Mepkin Abbey; *Voices of Silence: Lives of the Trappists Today* by Frank Bianco; *Temptations* by Paul Wilkes; *The Man Who Got Even with God* by Rev. M. Raymond, O.C.S.O. and, of course, *St. Benedict's Rule*.

Marianne Cawley of the South Carolina Room at the Charleston County Public Library provided a brochure about Our Lady of Mepkin dated April 29, 1958, one year after Father Sanders entered there, and an article called "Our Lady of Mepkin" by John A. Chase, published in the "Sandlapper" in December, 1969. They both contained pictures and descriptions that allowed me to describe Mepkin Abbey before remodeling and rebuilding that came later. I pray that I have captured the beauty and peace of Our Lady of Mepkin Abbey and the holy yet mortal men who live there.

For the Second Vatican Council and its resulting changes, especially those related to social justice, I relied heavily on books suggested by Sister Sallie Latkowitz, including *Justice & Peace: A Christian Primer* by J. Milburn Thompson and *Catholic Social Teaching: Our Best Kept Secret* by Henriot, DeBerri and Schultheis. The Vatican website (www.vatican.va) was used for original texts of Vatican-issued documents.

The Union Heights chapters were written with the help of Ida Singletary Taylor, Stanford Williams, Sister Colleen Waterman, Yvette Hill Richardson and Barbara Roehm. Chris Dodd from Catholic Extension magazine sent an article called "Project Cabrini: Love...Faith...and Hope" by Bruce Cook from March, 1966, that told the story of "Echo House." Charleston Diocese archivist Brian Fahey sent copies of many articles, including one with a photograph of Father Sanders kneeling on a protest line just before being arrested.

For the chapter set in Columbia, Bill Lundy helped with memories, dates and a copy of Terry Lundy's Communion Mass. I also thank John Chapiesky, Marge McCallom, Father Jimmy Carter, Father Mike Burton and Father Peter Clarke. Margaret Shull, who died before I started this research, created a photo and article album about Father Sanders' death for Betty Sanders who is also now deceased, and Jim Sanders gave it to me.

The story of Camp St. Mary's was made possible partially by a Master's Thesis by Rebecca Ann Lee-Grigg, Ph.D., called *Belles of St. Mary's: A rural alternative school for teenage mothers*, because Sister Ellen died before I started this book. I also thank her sister, Mary Ann Robertson, who sent a copy of Sister Ellen's unfinished biography; a Carolina Morning News article, "Remembering Sister Ellen" by Frank Morris, June 16, 2002 and an article from The Island Packet, Saturday, May 18, 2002, "Sister Ellen: She changed the Low Country, one struggling life at a time." Mary Ann also reviewed my attempt to capture the spirit of her sister. Others who helped include Susan Carter Barnwell and Cathy Coder. The image of Anyika's home and mother came from a photograph by Diane Arbus.

Adán Hernandez from Immokalee told me stories of Father Sanders in South Carolina and again, Yolanda Wohl related her memories. Father Frank Hanley, Father Don Abbot and Father Jimmy Carter were also helpful.

For the Naples, Florida years, I thank N. Noble Cook, Ph.D. at Florida International University in Miami for his encouragement to research the story of Corina Hernandez, Victor Uribe, Ph.D. at FIU for allowing me to read books Father Sanders read as part of my independent studies, and Sherry Johnson, Ph.D. at FIU who first identified Father Sanders' activities as Liberation Theology. Miguel Montalvo was extremely helpful in identifying books he and Father Sanders shared and also his memories. Corina Hernandez and several of her children, Martin, Janie, Rita, Maria, Guadalupe, Jesse and Luis Jr. all helped with stories of *Padre* Sanders. Martin Hernandez died unexpectedly not long after I interviewed him, and I miss Martin's presence on the earth. Pat Stockton of the Miami Archdiocese provided information about the Rural Live Bureau and Father John McMahon also shared memories.

For Vespers, the Immokalee years, again I have to mention Lucy Ortiz and Father Ettore Rubin. John and Mary Brister provided extremely useful information and impressions of Father Sanders and of funerals. Many others helped the Immokalee section, including Pedro Jove, Adán Hernandez, Rosa Hernandez, Fanoly Dervil, Santos Aponte, Cristina Vazquez, Lupita Vazquez, Candelario Vazquez, Jr., Guadalupana Sisters Octavia Ortega and Aida Sansor, Cynthia Garcia, Maria Marquez, Olivia Urbina. Sister Eileen Eppig, S.S.N.D. helped greatly with her memories plus left us copies of her beautiful monthly letters to donors. Lolo and Esmeralda Duarte told stories and provided an audio tape copy of Father Sanders' last Christmas Eve Mass, *Misa de Gallo,* that Patty and Jorge Jontza Anez translated. Others who helped include Sisters Barbara Pfarr, S.S.N.D., Sister Jane Burke, S.S.N.D. and Sister Marie McFadden, S.S.N.D.; Rob Williams, Lynne Peterson, John Witchger, Maria Teresa Gaston, Sister Jane Scanlan, S.S.N.D., Bishop Thomas Wenski, Eduwiges Alvarez, Talí Ortiz, Maggie Garza, Eduardo Galvan, Joseph Dunois, Father Dick Notter and previous altar boys Jose Dimas, Neftali Ortiz and Frankey Ligas. Jeanne Hickey from the Venice Diocese provided the press release related to his death.

Others who helped with Immokalee are Father Isaia Birollo, C.S., who took Father Sanders' place six months after he died; Father Jean Woady Louis, Nora Marquez, Joanne McPeek, Roette Belgarde, Jayson Cede, Nathale Alcime, Evelyne Dorcely, Wendie Aris, Marvin François, Multar Dorval, Phil Levering and Sister Genevieve Murphy, R.S.H.M. Terry Rey, Ph.D. helped with the interpretation of Our Lady of Perpetual Help and I also relied on his book, *Our Lady of Class Struggle.*

For Compline, the final months, I thank the above-named people plus Ron Wohl, Ronaldo Carneiro, M.D., Kathleen Galatro, M.D. and Millie Cary.

Many reviewers helped with drafts over the four years in which I pieced the story together. They include my mother, Mary Thissen, Sister Maureen Kelleher, R.S.H.M., Father Fred Conoscenti, Sister Judy Dohner, H.M., John Miller and my nephews Charles Pike and Eugene Pickett.

Last, but never least, I thank my husband, Barry Kotek, for his encouragement, for sitting through eternal drafts read aloud and silently, and for adding his male perspective to my interpretations of Father Sanders.

Printed in the United States
139845LV00004B/2/P